STORM SHADOW

K.S. Paulsen

GAEA PRESS

2016 Gaea Press Paperback Edition

Printed in the United States of America
Published in the United States by Gaea Press
www.kspaulsen.com

ISBN 978-0-9973585-0-6

For Savvy—*my light in the darkness.*

With endless thanks to Mariel, Miriam, and
many friends who inspired and helped me
bring this work to its beautiful fruition.
I couldn't have done it without you!

STORM SHADOW

STORM SHADOW—

a rare, natural phenomenon in which an enormous storm casts a large, ominous shadow across a clear sky.

PROLOGUE

"Come on, damn you!" Buck Dugan shoved his hand deep into the fleece-lined pocket of his arctic parka to retrieve his highly-prized, though rarely-used, satellite phone from its concealed position. His one big purchase, in celebration of his dream job—Lead Biologist aboard a 230-foot fisheries research ship operating on the Bering Sea—offered both hope and exasperation in his moment of greatest need. His career, maybe even his life, was on the brink of implosion, his dream of making a difference, about to vanish into sea spray, and he couldn't get a single bar of reception!

Moving quickly from bow to stern, Buck stole another quick glance at the sat phone, and tried simultaneously to hold it high enough to intercept signal, yet shield it from the view of potential witnesses.

"Just need a couple bars, Mama Gaia," he whispered to the only eternal, impartial witness he'd ever been willing to acknowledge—a force neither benevolent, nor malevolent, which presided over the waxing and waning of life, experiencing all.

Like a dying lover, Buck coaxed the object of his affection for one last kiss, "Help me get through and I'll make it worth your while."

The ship lifted on a swell of churning, frostbitten sea and two bars magically appeared on the touch screen. His heart lodged in his throat, grateful for such a timely response, even as his sarcastic nature slipped into gear. The air temperature was a balmy thirty-eight degrees

Fahrenheit, and rising, but the sea was about as placid as a shiver of sharks—*an excellent day to risk life and limb for a bunch of whales!*

"No sweat," he said aloud to calm his own nerves, "this is exactly why you became a biologist."

Palms damp, nerves jittery—but not from the cold—Buck's fingers moved quickly over the key pad. Within seconds, his Bluetooth earpiece came to life, the loud ring assaulting his recently injured ear.

He secured the phone high on the nearest rigging, to maximize the signal, then began disentangling the buoy line he was about to drop into the arctic water. He'd been trapped on this Trojan seahorse for weeks, performing his duties under false pretenses, all the while formulating and dismissing multiple fallible plans; if they suspected him of noncompliance, or whistle-blowing, he'd be fish bait.

After four seemingly interminable rings, the voice of his former college heartthrob came through loud and clear.

"Well hello there, stranger! I was just thinking about you. How's the—"

"Kait, listen; I don't have much time."

"What's wrong, Buck?" Her voice changed instantly from happy-to-hear-from-you friend, to alert problem solver. Not for the first time, he cursed himself for having been too busy, and too shortsighted, to grab hold of the best woman he had ever known.

"Someone bought the count! This ship is a phantom; the whole study is a fabrication. You've got to warn people, collect *real* data to contradict what they present to the IWC at the next legislative session. They're padding the numbers to get the kill-ban removed on Blues."

Static crackled in his ears, mixing with Kait's voice as he struggled to hear her. "I'm losing you, Kait! Did you hear me?"

"I heard—" silence, then static, "—you sure? —are you?"

The hairs on Buck's neck stood on end, signaling that someone was near. He stopped working the buoy line and gazed at Mother Nature's finest canvas. Before him, the horizon rolled-on in an endless expanse of slate-blue sea, juxtaposed by the first luminous rays of dawn breaking through low cumulous clouds. It would be a beautiful August day on the Bering—sunny and warm, he predicted with feigned optimism—a rare occurrence, and the only chance he'd had to raise the proverbial red flag for the rest of the world.

Static turned to prolonged silence in his earpiece.

Bad time for a dropped call.

"Ty chyo blya?" came a deep, rusty voice. "*What ze fuck you do?"*

Buck had grown accustomed to the saw-tooth rantings of the ship's captain, a 6-foot, 6-inch Russian behemoth, who'd spent more of his life at sea than on land, and had the weathered skin and scars to prove it. His hostility, if not his words, were unmistakable.

"Just untangling this buoy, Cap."

Captain Vladokov glowered and moved closer, edging Buck against the steel rail of the ship. His piercing blue eyes spoke volumes as he pulled the wool cap from Buck's head and glared at the Bluetooth resting on his ear.

With a tilt of his head, the captain's eyes locked first on the sat-phone clipped above their heads, then on Buck with a small shake of his head. "I told zem you ver boy scout," he said in disgust.

"Too late, Vladokov. The cavalry has been warned."

Buck felt his feet leave the deck as Vladokov shoved him effortlessly over the rail. He didn't resist his fate—he'd always known he would die young. Violence always took the peaceful warriors who were brave enough to show humanity another option.

Death was a heavy price to pay for trying to do good and protect others, but he'd accomplished much in his life, and experienced everything that mattered.

No regrets.

For just a moment, Buck felt himself suspended mid-air, his life flashing before his eyes—Kait laughing, his mother crying, friends rejoicing after triumphant rallies, protests, and demonstrations, incredible places he'd seen with his own eyes and experienced with his own senses, beauty and madness he'd witnessed firsthand, the birth of a baby blue whale, and the slaughter of hundreds of dolphins and whales—then icy water stabbed at every inch of his body, engulfing him.

His lungs heaved in shock as he sank to the murky depths of Davy Jones' tomb. He embraced the pain, knowing that when it ceased, so too would his amazing life. He would freeze to death before the ship came back to retrieve his body, and he was certain they wouldn't grant him even that small honor.

He only hoped Kait had understood his call.

ONE

"Dude, we are seriously screwed!" A scruffy young man buzzed anxiously around an open hatch on the main deck of an aging oceanographic research boat.

"Stow it, Frankie. Hand me the retainer wrench."

Frankie watched a grease-covered hand reach through the air from behind an engine larger than the Mini Cooper Roadster he'd been drooling over for the past month. Checking his watch for the tenth time in as many minutes, he slapped the wrench into the disembodied hand. "We're already two hours late! If you don't get this tub running, we'll miss the first drop. He'll skin us alive and throw us to the sharks!"

And I won't get my hands on that car.

"He's not going to kill us, Frankie. He needs us." Determination shaped the voice from below, and maybe a touch of arrogance.

"You're wrong, Doc. He don't need nobody. Flunkies are a dime a dozen in his world. You think he needs us, 'cause we need him, but that just ain't the way it is."

"We're not flunkies, and I've had enough of your dire predictions and paranoia." A pair of swamp-green eyes looked up from the engine, stressed to the edge and ready to strangle Frankie if he didn't zip his lips. Those same green eyes looked past Frankie's carrot-top head at a glistening blur of white rounding the far end of the private pier. "What in blue blazes is he doing *here*? Is he a raving lunatic?"

Frankie looked up, his face transforming from worried anticipation to instant immobilizing fear. “Shit! Oh, shit! We’re dead!”

“Game face, Frankie. Now! Guide them to dock behind the *Triton*. Stall them there while I get rid of the security guard. We’ve got to get them out of here before anyone sees them and starts asking questions.”

The two parted ways, their nerves strained to the breaking point. One sent the aging security guard on a fool’s errand, while the other rushed to appease the Devil.

To the casual observer, the Devil was a suave Latino businessman with black, silver-flecked hair, whose lean body and sharp edges were masterfully disguised by his custom-tailored, white sport suit and loafers. Those unfortunate enough to know him were painfully aware that his deceptively refined appearance hid the criminal, often dastardly tactics he used to sculpt his world.

His hulking bodyguard, devoid of empathy or any other form of basic human decency, stood like a sentry at the gates of Hell. Black sunglasses obscured his dark, square face, and his long, black hair greased into a short tail was knotted with a black leather tie. A black suit and an even blacker AK-47 completed his ensemble, the ominous weapon balanced in his blocky hands as if permanently attached.

The Devil and his minion stood stoically on the deck of the sleek 85-foot ocean yacht as Frankie approached. His stomach lurched as he stepped aboard, ready to beg forgiveness and buy some time.

Without waiting for an explanation, the Devil spoke in a soft, fluid mixture of Spanish and English, making his displeasure clear. “Frankie, you disappoint me.”

Soulless eyes looked to the bodyguard for only a moment; instantly, the butt of the AK-47 slammed into Frankie’s gut and the wafer-thin punk doubled over in pain.

Returning from the security booth, Doc saw the exchange and hurried to intervene. "It's not his fault," he said coolly as he too stepped aboard the yacht. "The engine on my rig blew. We've been trying to fix it."

"You think to violate our agreement?"

"No, just explaining the delay. It couldn't be helped."

Colder than the cosmos, the Devil stepped closer, eye to eye. "She is not the only rig at your disposal, Doctor Russell. Take another."

"That's not possible on such short notice..." His words died on the breeze as a long switchblade appeared at his throat. Beads of sweat formed at his temples and his heart began to race.

"Are you so weak, so insignificant that you cannot take any rig you want?" The Devil's voice cut through the air with contempt, "Maybe you are the wrong man for the job."

Stuffing down his ego's need for retaliation, Doctor Russell carefully responded with his customary authority. "The other research vessels are at sea—we have numerous projects underway at all times. Only the *Neptune II* is under my exclusive command. I can have her repaired and underway within a day or two."

"And ruin my reputation for delivering on time?" The Devil pressed harder with his knife, drawing a thin line of blood. "I don't think you understand the nature of our arrangement. I say jump, you jump—even off a 100-foot cliff." His eyes drifted to the *Triton*. "You have places to go, people to meet. Pull some strings."

Swallowing back the angry bile bubbling up his throat, the doctor made one last attempt at reason. "Switching to another vessel would draw unwanted attention. The *Triton* came in last night and she'll be going right back out on Monday. They're working on a top priority project. If I take her, there will be too many questions."

"No more excuses," said the Devil with gallows conviction.

From behind him, the bodyguard slammed the rifle into Doctor Russell's kidney, blasting pain through every cell in his body. The fifty-something baby-boomer fell to his knees as the cold barrel of the AK-47 pressed against his cheek, threatening certain death if he didn't think of an immediate solution. The situation was quickly escalating far beyond anything he'd bargained for when he'd first crossed that shadowy line between need and greed, right and wrong.

Deals with the Devil always come at a much higher cost than expected.

He and Frankie had passed the point of no return. They had no choice but to keep navigating the treacherous waters around them. The alternatives were death or exposure—neither one tolerable to a man who, until recently, had played by society's rules and elevated himself through education, sacrifice, and the sweat of his own brow. If he was exposed, the consequences would be staggering. He would lose everything he'd worked so hard to achieve and be forced to endure a painfully bleak future. Death, on the other hand, would preclude a future entirely—the epic fail to end all epic fails.

Hindsight renders the genius a fool.

The bodyguard's finger twitched hungrily on the trigger and the doctor ceded to his fate. "All right, all right! Give me one hour to cover our tracks and smooth the way. We'll meet you at the rendezvous location in two."

TWO

Kaitlyn O'Donnell drove north toward La Jolla, California, heading to her office on Saturday morning after only a few hours of restless sleep. Weekends were too short these days; she needed every minute to prepare for another two weeks at sea. Taking a deep breath, she massaged her neck with one hand while steering with the other.

Four weeks down, six to go, she thought wearily, *then we can all take a nice long breather.*

Reviewing a mental list of everything she had to accomplish in the next 24-hours, Kait marveled at the fact that things were going so smoothly. Thanks to that fateful call from Buck—*Was it really only ten weeks ago?*—and the charitable cooperation of key members of the Board of Directors at Scotts Institute of Marine Research (SIMR), four reputable research teams were well on their way to derailing what could be the biggest ecological scam since the Gulf Oil Spill. Some days she still couldn't believe she'd been able to pull everything together on such short notice, or that she'd even had to.

Was there no end to the greed of humanity?

As it turned out, endangered blue whale populations in the Pacific and Atlantic Oceans were in serious jeopardy thanks to a deceptive team of "experts" bought and paid for by unidentified members of the whaling industry. Those "experts" had spent the entire summer orchestrating false population counts in the whales' sub-polar summer feeding grounds, allegedly padding the numbers in an attempt to get the species delisted under the Endangered Species Act and removed from the worldwide hunting ban regulated by the International Whaling Commission (IWC).

The consortium of eighty-eight countries was constantly challenged to balance the conservation of whales against the demands of an obsolescing industry as well as the cultural and economic preservation of subsistence-whale-hunting tribes.

Everything the fake research team had done thus far *looked* perfectly scientific and above-board—Kait couldn't prove anything without a willing eyewitness and a lot of evidence. Unfortunately Buck had dropped completely off the grid after his mysterious call, laying the burden of collecting irrefutable proof squarely in her lap.

After a week of failed attempts to track him down, Kait had shocked everyone, including herself, and used several long-overdue vacation days to fly to Alaska and find him. She'd needed confirmation that the situation was really as dire as he'd indicated before sounding the drums of war. This was *not* her first political rodeo, but if she didn't handle it just right, it could certainly be her last.

Her meeting with Captain Vladokov at the edge of an old-growth pine forest, on the rickety planks of an isolated fishing wharf—weathered by at least fifty treacherous years of harsh winters and prolonged summer days—had left her deeply depressed and raging mad. The hard-hearted mercenary claimed that Buck had fallen overboard when nobody was looking. His body had never been found, despite several supposed attempts to do so, and she had been dismissed with a barely-veiled threat she would never forget: *"Best not ask too many qvestions, Missy. People 'round here don't like strangers. Bad things can happen."*

Kait shivered from the memory. Every time she closed her eyes, she saw Buck drowning, frozen and alone, in the Bering Sea. A tear slid down her cheek. Nobody deserved to die like that, certainly not the idealistic humanitarian she'd secretly swooned over in college. He'd introduced her to the exciting world of activism, and taught her that some fights were too important to watch from the sidelines.

By calling to warn her, without having an escape plan if he got caught, Buck had thrown down the gauntlet; by accepting his challenge, and picking up the battle where he'd left off, she'd made herself susceptible to the same horrible fate. Part of her had wanted to pretend that nothing had really happened, to go on about her life as if she'd never answered his call, never gone to Alaska, but the guilt and depression would have been more than she could bear. Indeed, there'd been no real question; if she had chosen to do nothing, her life would have become meaningless, and Buck's death would have been for nothing.

This was beyond a doubt the greatest challenge she'd ever accepted. At its inception, she'd had no idea how to unveil and debunk a conspiracy, especially one with such global implications. She'd wisely kept her mouth shut until she was safely home in San Diego, then carefully planned her strategy and begun quietly recruiting anyone and everyone who would listen. Growing bolder with each success, she'd eventually hounded the SIMR Board of Directors into cooperation and called in every IOU she could remember, and a few she'd made up. She'd bribed, blackmailed, cajoled, and even resorted to a little harmless pilfering from other projects, but even with her small army of scientists, supporters, and gear, she would still need a slew of miracles to win this fight. Mother Theresa she was not.

The loud ring of her cell phone jolted Kait back to the present. Everyone had their assigned tasks for the weekend—*they* should *know exactly what to do.*

"O'Donnell, here."

"Kait, glad I caught you."

"Hi William," she said with relief. "I'm on my way to the office. What's up?"

"Bad news, Kait. I just got a call from the President of the Board. Apparently some high profile research team requisitioned the *Triton* for the next ten days. He said it was approved a long time ago, but the paperwork got lost in the shuffle. They're putting out to sea today."

"What? They can't take our ship! We only have six weeks left to wrap things up and submit our report to the Commission! The Board gave us priority access to the *Triton* until then."

"Yes they did, but this can't be avoided." William heaved a sigh. "Look, I'm pressed for time. Reach out to the

Poseidon in the Philippines and the *Proteus* down near Peru. Ask them each to put a crew member on whale watch duty while the *Triton* is unavailable. I'm heading north to the *Oceanus Research Platform*. I'll ask them for help too."

"William, this is insane!" Kait's heart raced as she imagined her project sinking faster than the *Titanic* to a deep, watery grave. "Everyone's been working themselves to the bone for this; we're the only ones in a position to contradict the false numbers. You know the Maui team's engine blew up two days ago; without the *Triton* in place next week, we'll have a giant gap in our data! A few reports from vessels in random locations won't fill those gaps in a meaningful way."

"I am perfectly aware of the problem, Kait, but there is nothing I can do about it. The President was adamant. Give your crew a well-earned break. Get the Maui team back on the water ASAP. It's only ten days; you'll have several weeks left to collect additional data when you get the *Triton* back."

"William, we already missed two weeks at the beginning of the migration. We can't afford to lose another week at the height of the season!"

"We have no choice, Kait. Do what you can with the existing data, keep the remaining crews on the water, and sit-tight until they bring the *Triton* back. Whatever you do, don't rock the boat! Need to run—my ride is here."

Kait tossed her cell phone onto the passenger seat and slapped her palms against the steering wheel. Inhaling several deep breaths, she tried to quell the storm brewing in her mind, but a feverish fury began to sweep through her.

That's it? No discussion or recourse?

The Board gives the Triton to another team and we're just supposed to hand it over without a sneeze?

Never mind that her suddenly spineless, jellyfish-of-a-boss had just agreed to quash the most important project of her career. To heck with getting an accurate population estimate on an *endangered species*; the commissioners can bloody well wait until next year for a complete set of data. So what if the whaling industry gets their way in the meantime and drives the Blues closer to extinction!

Kait's body thrummed with anxiety as she flipped a U-turn and headed south. There was no time to go to the office now—she had to get to the wharf and unload her team's data and equipment before the usurpers took over her ship!

She wasn't just fighting an anonymous group of conspirators anymore; now she was being undermined by her own employers. With both of the Pacific teams scuttled for a week or more, her estimate of the North Pacific blue whale population would be less than sterling. Solid data from two long-term studies in the Atlantic would help protect the Atlantic populations, but would be insufficient to counter the falsified numbers for the Pacific populations; she'd be laughed out of the IWC proceedings or ignored completely.

Not acceptable!

The overall findings from all four teams had to be impeccable to prevent this coup. That meant all four teams needed to collect at least another month of solid data just to get their foot in the door and postpone an IWC decision. After that was accomplished, a more complete count of the populations could be conducted by other scientists. A ten day gap in an already truncated count, would leave them dead in the water.

I need more time!

Today, like most days at the SIMR wharf, was as quiet as a graveyard; all but the *Triton* and the *Neptune II* spent the majority of the year in international waters with multiple projects under way. Kait pulled into her usual parking spot, under the only shade tree, and ruminated over William's not so subtle warning. *"Whatever you do, don't rock the boat!"* There was an implied "or else" in that statement.

Or else, what?

After five years working together, William had to know she wouldn't let the *Triton* go without a fight. Under normal circumstances she was a reasonable person—a reliable and dedicated employee, according to her latest performance review—but there was nothing normal about the current situation. This project, and the difficulties entangling it, were pushing every one of her "hot" buttons. She couldn't sit tight and do nothing!

Despite the occasional disagreement, Kait had always been able to work things out with William; he was her mentor, a trusted advisor and friend. He'd been instrumental in helping her get this project up and running—had invested a great deal of his own extremely limited time to help her devise a plan and get through all the red tape—and not once had she felt compelled to contradict his orders.

Until now.

Emerging from her car, Kait stared at William's old pickup. There were too many unknowns to process, too many negative ramifications if she allowed this obstacle to block her, but she couldn't think of a viable solution in such a short timeline. Her thoughts whirled like a hurricane, swamping the calm center that usually sustained her.

Maybe she should defy William's orders and take the ship and her crew out on the water without Captain Hallor and his operations crew. What could they do to stop her?

Send the Coast Guard to escort us back.

Prevent me from getting my Captain's License.

No, absconding wouldn't solve anything. If SIMR was willing to permit such a colossal catastrophe, she might very well lose her job, maybe even destroy her career and the solid reputation she'd worked so hard to build. Not to mention that her actions could jeopardize the jobs and careers of her crew.

She could tell them what was happening, give them the choice to stay or go. Or, she could keep quiet and take the blame for her defiance, alone. If her crew didn't know there was trouble, they might not get the axe.

I can't lead a mutiny. There has to be another way.

Nothing came to her frazzled mind. She hadn't asked Buck to drop this atomic bomb in her lap, but he had. When she'd asked SIMR to get involved, she hadn't expected them to entrust the task to her, but they had, despite her protests that she didn't have what it would take to get the job done. Now, after everything had been resolved and the teams were up and running, they were pulling the rug out from under her, practically pushing the button on the atomic bomb. She couldn't ignore this new obstacle, and if she couldn't find a way around it, she'd have to find a way to push through it.

That's why Buck had passed the baton to her in the first place; he'd known she would fight, had known she wouldn't back down, no matter the personal cost, when it came to defending the innocent. The threat was real and Buck had given his life to stop it. He was counting on her to rise to the challenge, and she was doing her best not to let him down.

"Skirt or pants, you're the toughest, smartest person I know, KO. You'll always be the knock-out that delivers the knockout blow!" His parting words when they'd said goodbye after college had shocked her to the core. They weren't true, but the sentiment had been incredibly sweet. She wasn't so tough or special, just tenacious—perhaps to a fault.

Over the years, Kait had learned time and again, that when she wanted something, it was up to her to make it happen. Nobody was going to do it for her and nobody was going to make things easy; *Nobody* was a cold-hearted son-of-a-sea-slug. She no longer questioned the lows to which people could sink and no longer apologized for reaching for what she wanted. Buck had been a way-shower in her life, a shining point of light that inspired others to integrity and right-action. He had kicked butt when it was needed, but in a gentle and loving way. He had taught her and others, not by pontification, but by demonstration, in every aspect of his life.

Poor Buck. Each time she imagined him sinking into a frozen abyss, her stomach clenched with an overwhelming sense of doom. She couldn't let him down. She had to fight for justice, for the whales, and for Buck, even if it meant losing her job!

Biting back on the urge to scream at the world, she headed for the pier. "It's just one more roadblock," she said aloud as she walked. "I'll never concede victory to a bunch of lying butchers who'd wipe out every species on the planet to pad their own coffers!"

Focusing on the most immediate problem, Kait began calculating possibilities and forming a new plan. The crew had left most of their personal belongings, and all of the most important equipment and samples, aboard the *Triton* during their weekend respite. She had to get ready to abandon ship and call the crew back for emergency salvage duty.

Jogging down a sidewalk edged by ice plant, she stopped to call her first mate and put the crew on alert. When Bowie didn't answer, she called the second mate, who answered after only one ring.

"Randy, it's Kait."

"Hey there, boss lady. You're supposed to be sleeping-in this fine morning."

"No time—the project is in big trouble. I don't have time to explain, but I need you to call Bowie and the rest of the crew and get them down here to the pier, ASAP. We need to make sure all data has been transferred from the ship to the lab; unload all the equipment and samples; start tracking down an alternate vessel, maybe several."

"What's happening?"

"Another research team is commandeering our rig; the Board put us on mandatory shore leave for ten days! That's all I know right now. I'm going to try to put a stop to this, but if I can't, we'll need a backup plan."

Kait stopped in her tracks. "What the…?"

As the private pier came into view, she saw a large unfamiliar yacht docked directly behind the *Triton*. The *Neptune II* sat at the far end of the pier on the opposite side; it was docked more often than not lately, but she was still surprised to see it there. Red flags of warning waved in her mind as she hurried toward the security gate. "Randy, I'll have to call you back. Round up everyone as fast as you can and get down here. I've gotta go—there's a strange yacht at the dock."

"Kait, don't—" Randy hollered into the already silent phone.

Kait reached the abandoned security booth and buzzed herself through the gate with her badge. Barney, the long-time guardsman she'd befriended, was nowhere to be seen. With any luck he was already investigating the trespassing vessel. If he wasn't, she would have to take matters into her own hands.

Don't I have enough problems on my plate today?

What if the people aboard this vessel are responsible for said problems?

Then they're about to get an earful from one very unhappy biologist!

Kait walked brazenly out onto the pier, her hackles rising to a whole new level. The yacht wouldn't belong to the scientists from the invading research crew; scientists didn't make enough money for such luxuries. Maybe it was someone from the Board; only a big SIMR muckety-muck would dare to dock alongside the private pier, and if that was the case...well, she just might salvage this day after all!

Mighty fine ship, she thought in a brief moment of conniving admiration. The *Spanish Maiden* was a real beauty with sleek lines and curves: undoubtedly fast in the water, and easy to handle without need for a licensed captain, or an operations crew. She'd be a nice substitute for the *Triton* if push came to shove, one that Kait could handle on her own with only her small team.

Yeah, and if wishes were fishes they'd all swim away.

As she passed the *Triton* and neared the *Spanish Maiden*, a vortex of butterflies began swirling in her stomach. Her mother's disapproving voice echoed unwanted through her mind, *"There you go again, sticking your neck out where it doesn't belong. One of these days you'll find out it's not worth the effort."*

Just as quickly, her brother's voice washed it out. *"Don't let her jinx you, Kit-Cat. Today is* not *that day."*

A moment of dread gave her pause; in the two days since the Maui team had informed her of their engine blowout, her worst fear had been the possibility of sabotage. She had kept her fear to herself, not wanting to spook the crew. What if she caught someone vandalizing her ship? What if they ruined all the equipment, or worse, destroyed the data her team had worked so hard to collect?

Don't get swept away by paranoia just yet.

Kait took a deep breath to calm her nerves. The loss of the *Triton* and the Maui team's engine blowup could be mere coincidence—both of the Atlantic teams were still on track at last report—but a nagging thought at the back of her mind refused to quiet. It might be wise to check out her own ship before hailing the unauthorized yacht.

Kait doubled back and quietly boarded the main deck of the *Triton*. First, she took the stairs up to the helm room on the second level and checked the control panel; the ship's computer, radio, navigation system, and GPS systems looked fine—no sign of tampering. Next, she descended to the first level and inspected the wet lab and equipment lockers; everything was in place, exactly as the crew had left it last night. The blood and tissue samples waiting to be catalogued still sat in orderly rows, by date, in the refrigerator—she'd have to speak with James about the samples; he looked to be about a week behind schedule with his analyses.

Below the main deck, the dry lab looked ship-shape. She made a quick sweep through the crew's quarters in the hold, and was only mildly relieved to find that everything was locked up tight with nothing out of place.

Just because you didn't find trouble, doesn't mean it's not there. She'd have to investigate the intruding yacht to know for sure, but Kait felt herself growing more reluctant.

Where the heck is Barney?

Stepping off the *Triton*, she walked farther down the pier to the *Spanish Maiden*. A salty breeze lifted her hair, whipping it across her eyes. "Ahoy the yacht!"

Silence stilled the air around her as she waited for a reply. There had to be someone around keeping an eye on things. It was inconceivable that a trespasser would dock illegally and then just abandon such a primo vessel. Of course, if it was a board member, then they probably had a key to the security gate and had no doubt gone up to the warehouse facilities.

Pulling out her cell phone, Kait decided to call Barney and request his assistance. After three rings she heard the distinct ringtone he'd programmed into his phone for her number: "Hot Blooded" by Foreigner. He loved to tease her about how she made him feel like a young high school stud again instead of a sixty-something bag of bones. The song was muffled, but sounded like it was coming from somewhere nearby—*he must be aboard the yacht.*

When Barney didn't answer her call, she started to worry in earnest. He could be having trouble with his diabetes again, like when she'd found him passed out on the floor of his security booth a few months ago.

Kait boarded the rear platform of the interloping yacht, not at all sure that it was the wisest course of action. As she climbed the stairs to the main deck, the engine purred to life, a low rumble vibrating the air. She hesitated, looking back at the dock, then crossed to a sliding glass door that hung open, and called inside the luxurious salon. "Hello! Barney? Can anyone hear me?"

The yacht swayed mildly and issued a chorus of quiet creaks and moans as it absorbed rolling tidal swells. Hearing a distant thump, Kait stepped inside the plush cabin. She could see all the way forward, past a velvet sitting area and an elegant galley amidships to the polished navigation bridge. The luminous salon was empty but a flash of movement reflected by a window caught her eye and she called out again. "Barney, is that you?"

Again there was no answer. Her nerves tingled with alarm and she felt the distinct urge to run. As she turned to make good on that urge, she was instantly stopped by a large man blocking the sliding door. She looked up slowly and swallowed the fear that clogged her throat.

"Hello there. I'm sorry to intrude," Kait said casually as she tried to calm her nerves. "Are you the owner of this yacht?"

A large, black-haired, muscle-bound thug stood before her, his feet spread in a wide stance, his ring-studded hands crossed casually in front of him. When he didn't respond, she knew she was in trouble. This was no muckety-muck; he looked more like a wrestler-cum-Mexican Mafioso.

Stiffening her spine and standing as tall as she could, Kait called on every ounce of authority she could muster, despite the lurching in her stomach. "I'm from the Institute and unless you have some official business here, you'll have to move your vessel." Softening her tone slightly, she added an explanation, "You're docked illegally, trespassing on private property, but if you leave now, I won't report the violation."

Sensing movement behind her, she turned just slightly to see that another man, thinner, and of a more average build, stood behind her blocking the path through the salon. He looked sleeker, his hair smooth and wet with gel, and he wore three gold chains draped around his neck. Neither of the men looked like they were in any mood to talk, much less cooperate.

Holy mackerel! Not good!

When Kait turned back toward the man blocking her exit, a large rifle had materialized in his hands, pointing directly at her chest. With the rifle he motioned for her to go down a set of stairs to the lower deck of the yacht.

Good criminy! Keep it together and get out of here!

Trapped between the two men, her skin crawled with anxiety as she turned to comply. She had to act fast, remembering somewhere deep in the recesses of her mind that nine times out of ten, going along with any attacker was tantamount to embracing a horrifying death. They moved in closer, forcing her toward the stairs.

With speed she didn't know she possessed, Kait whirled around and knocked the man's arm and gun away from her; it swung into the other man's face and struck him. There was no way to get past them so she ran down the steep steps into a dark corridor. She opened the only door on the left hoping to distract them, and then ran down the short hallway to the right. It was a dead end with three small doors. She opened the door closest to the stairs and slipped inside, quietly closing it as they came around the corner.

Kate found herself in a tiny bathroom—the portal too small to climb through—no way out except back the way she had just come.

Leaning against the door, she willed the men to pass her by. The confined space held nothing she could use as a weapon—dumb luck was her only hope now.

When heavy footsteps approached, she held her breath. A nearby door creaked as it opened and her heart nearly stopped. Seconds felt like an eternity as she held perfectly still, waiting for them to move forward to the last door; when they did, she nearly fainted with relief. On shaky legs, she opened the door and made a dash for the stairs and the deck beyond. She had never wanted anything as fervently as she wanted, right now, to be off this yacht.

Kait could smell her freedom on the salty breeze, see it as she reached the top of the stairs. Her feet carried her swiftly, the men pounding up the steps right behind her. She sailed through the doorway into the bright sunlight and rounded a corner heading for the starboard bow, then toppled to her hands and knees. Scrambling to her feet again, she spared a quick glance back to see what she had tripped on—*a body!*

A blood-curdling scream ripped through Kait's lips. Her heart thumped hard then skipped a beat. In the next second, as she turned to run, her head seemed to explode with pain. Everything around her swirled into bright colors as her feet and arms went heavy. She was falling ever so slowly, like a feather, midair. Bright colors faded to black.

THREE

Kait regained consciousness slowly, the enveloping darkness weighing on her senses like a death pall. Starved of oxygen, she tried to inhale slowly, deeply, but each attempt brought in mouthfuls of dust, coating her throat and choking her lungs. Something scratchy and musty covered her face, making a full breath impossible.

Calling out for assistance, a sickly moan was the only sound that escaped her lips. Trying to erect herself, her body resisted all movement. Her legs were heavy, her back stiff, arms numb, except the fingertips which prickled with returning sensation. If she couldn't move or make noise, nobody would know she needed help.

Don't panic.

Focusing outside of her urgent need for air, Kait took stock of her perilous state, desperate and determined to understand what was happening. Heat and moisture crawled on her skin. The residue of something bitter puckered her mouth. Her torso and face pulsed and throbbed where they pressed heavily against a hard surface that swayed with the customary rocking of a ship at sea. That, at least, was familiar.

With startling clarity, the image of a man flashed in her mind: Latin, slick black hair, gold chains—he'd trapped her on a boat. Sensation began to swamp her as the numbness of unnatural sleep finally wore off. Cramps in her arms and legs began to scream for release. Her head throbbed and her lungs burned. She wanted, no *needed,* to rub the pain away and get her blood pumping to carry more oxygen to her tissues, but she couldn't. Writhing like a fish out of water, struggling for one decent breath, she finally realized that her hands were bound behind her back.

Panic clawed deeper—she could do nothing to help herself!

Another flash of memory invaded: a hand covering her mouth with a moist rag, a sickening smell—bitter like the taste in her mouth. First, she'd been hit over the head—that's why her head felt like it was splitting in two—then, when she'd started to wake up, she'd been drugged.

How long was I out?

Distant voices began to trickle through the ringing in her ears. She tried again to call for help but only managed a choked whisper. She needed more air, needed her hands free. Lying there silently, unmoving, she tried to think—listened for clues—willed the nightmare to end. After a time, the voices became clearer, more distinct—*closer.*

When claw-like hands suddenly yanked her from the darkness, her mind and body snapped to attention. On her feet now—braced against something hard—barely able to hold her balance, Kait teetered on the brink of hysteria. Harsh hands tore a sack from her head, nearly knocking her down in the process.

Moist, salty air flooded her mouth and lungs and she inhaled several great gulps, greedily, trying to take in more than her lungs could hold. Squinting against a bright light, which swayed back and forth in the surrounding darkness, her vision blurred. Tears of fright and pain streamed down her face as the man before her waved something long and glittery in front of her face—*a knife!*

She flinched away from it, fearing its sting. Then another set of hands pulled at her, turning her forcefully. In the space of a moment, her hands were free, cut-ropes dangling from each wrist.

Is this a rescue?

When her eyes focused on the man before her, Kait knew he was no friend; his vile intentions were spelled out clearly across his ugly face. He was big and burley, covered with stubble and grime. He grabbed her arms, squeezing them like putty, and threw her down on the fiberglass deck of a fishing boat. She landed hard, flat on her back, the precious air knocked from her lungs once more. Then a squeezing pressure seized her chest as her captor straddled her with his legs, crushing her under his weight.

"We gonna have a little fiesta with our pretty señorita, now she's awake."

A horrible stench surrounded the man above her—the sweat of several days mixed with the bitter smells of alcohol and tobacco. As he bent over her, she screamed and squirmed to avoid him. His toxic breath made her swoon with nausea and his evil eyes told her, without words, that she was doomed.

Her heart raced like a trapped animal, her screams rising to a crescendo as his knees pressed deeply into her flesh. When he released the full force of his weight, his ears no longer able to withstand her high-pitched screams, a small thread of hope dangled in her mind: *you'll live through this—you have to!*

Still pinning her torso under his weight, the stinking hulk once again leaned down, taking her face in his callused hands. "C'mon, little fish. Gimme a kiss."

Kait kicked her feet wildly and writhed like an eel, her feeble attempts to escape failing miserably. Chills raced up and down her spine as he continued to taunt and torment her. When she spit in his face, he laughed wickedly and slammed his hand across her cheek, knocking her senseless for a moment. He grabbed her hair then and pulled her face to his.

"Hey, Chaco!" came a whiny voice from somewhere very near. "Save some for me."

The brute turned arrogantly toward his subordinate, "No problema, mi amigo! *No problem, my friend.* You can have what's left when I'm through!"

No longer paralyzed by pain, Kait's mind raced through the self-defense moves she'd learned several years ago. She'd sparred with classmates of all sizes and abilities, even taken a healthy blow to her midsection from the instructor's overzealous assistant. There had to be something she could do to free herself. But the few moves she could remember all required the use of her hands and feet. This man was so huge, that it seemed impossible to get him off her.

Focus, darn it! It's now or never. Live or die!

When her captor leaned down again, Kait bit-down on his nose like a wild animal and held on with all her might. Roaring like a barbarian, he grabbed her head and tried to pull away. The salty taste of his sweat and blood made her gag but she bit down even harder until he knocked her loose and reeled away from her. His weight shifted, freeing both of her arms; once free, she reached up and clawed at his eyes, then swung her hand toward his throat with a hard karate chop. He fell backward, grasping his neck with both hands, struggling to breathe.

This was her one chance—*move!*

Rising to her hands and knees, Kait back-kicked her assailant in the face as hard as she could, then scrambled forward. The other man lunged for her, but missed by some miracle, and slammed to the deck behind her. Staggering, half-crawling toward the bow, she looked around frantically. The darkness of night enveloped the boat; the ocean was her only escape, the full moon her only guide through the black water. With all the speed and energy she could muster, Kait climbed over the railing and dove away from the death trap.

A loud blast registered in her ears as she hit the water in a wild belly flop that stole her breath. Then a sharp sting slashed across her temple, just above her left eye. Her scream lodged in her throat as water filled her mouth. Stunned, she felt herself sink like lead in the water.

FOUR

Michael Storm lay restless in bed, sweating from the exertion of his overactive dreams and the ceaseless humidity of tropical Mexico. The frolicking birds of the jungle had concluded their chatter until dawn, succumbing to their natural circadian rhythms hours ago. He would shave years off his own life if it meant he could do the same, but in four miserable years he'd conquered neither his nightmares nor his insomnia.

True, the frequency and clarity of his unwanted visions were decreasing slowly, by degrees—he couldn't argue with that part of his brother's insistence that time healed all wounds—but equally true was the fact that the darker side of life always found new ways to trounce him. Tonight, it was the far-off clap of thunder echoing through the warm night air. The thunder always brought his demons back. With practiced, if not genuine optimism, he extended the deadline for his small but essential mission: get a solid night of sleep when the rainy season ends.

Clinging to the numbing effects of sleep, he closed his eyes tightly for a few more minutes, tossing and turning with agitation. Frustration crept in, entangling his thoughts like the vines that forever assaulted the perimeter walls of his villa. Resistance was futile—even now, at two in the morning, he felt more refreshed than he should—he was growing too accustomed to operating on only three hours of sleep.

To hell with this!

Giving up, he slid from his plush, oversized bed and threw on some cool cotton shorts, a gray muscle shirt and running shoes. A rigorous run through the night air was the best way to combat his wakefulness.

Fully awake now, Michael headed to the balcony and down the outside staircase. As he crossed the lawn of his sweeping clifftop estate, he was cooled by a subtle breeze carrying the sweet scent of night-blooming jasmine. Setting a fast but steady pace through the lush vegetation, he headed for his private oasis. At a fork in the path, his legs carried him automatically down the worn trail to the right, bypassing the overgrown trail into the depths of the jungle. The momentum of his body propelled him with increasing speed down the cliff-side trail until he reached the bottom. Half-mile in three minutes, ten seconds; he'd just beaten his personal record by five seconds.

His mind much clearer now, Michael remembered the sound that had awakened him. *Thunder?* The tropics had a propensity for giving birth to sudden, brief but torrential storms from June to October—even a hurricane on rare occasions. This was mid-October, the end of the rainy season, so the frequency and severity of storms should be decreasing. The most recent monsoon had swept through the area more than a week ago, dropping nearly two inches of rain in two hours. The resulting flash floods had been horrendous, killing five people and countless livestock, and damaging structures in several small towns along its path. Tonight, there wasn't a cloud in the sky, and the dry winter season was only weeks away.

What was it then?

Recalling the sound more clearly, now that all pistons were firing, he realized it had been more akin to the echo of gunfire.

Couldn't be, he reasoned, *there are no banditos or drug lords hiding in the crags of* my *jungle.* The cities were their preferred destinations in the modern millennium.

Except for the growers and cookers, he countered, searching for another explanation. Few people these days were willing to trade the convenience of city life for the anonymity of the rural wilds. Furthermore, the only people who had ever inhabited this particular stretch of land, other than himself, had abandoned it long ago: tribal natives, pirates of forgotten lore, and maybe a few ghosts.

I'd know if someone was invading my territory.

Gazing at the peaceful night scape, Michael dismissed the idea of gunfire as a remnant of his recurring nightmares. In the distance, the halo of light over Hotel Careyes, the nearest modern facility for miles, was still shining dimly at the edge of the ocean. A blanket of stars twinkled in the black velvet sky above, the full moon basking in their glow. Michael's studious eyes wandered across the horizon, catching on the running lights of a fishing boat shrunken by distance. Within seconds it disappeared behind the black cliffs that jutted into the ocean less than a mile down the beach.

Abandoning the cliffs, his gaze reconnected with the shoreline on which he now stood. He'd memorized every inch of the scene during his nightly visits to the sea; it was the one place where he could still feel life humming in the air, trying to penetrate his defenses. He smiled, feeling just a touch of the inner peace that commonly eluded his grasp. Through the darkness, the water reflected the moon's glow, casting golden peaks on the waves, spreading pale light over the sandy beach. How many times had he and Maria walked along this cove together, hand-in-hand, teasing, playing, caressing?

Not nearly enough.

Standing in the shallows, staring hard into the bright full moon he could almost see her smiling back at him in the shadows that blotted its surface. "This was the first place we made love, *mi amor*. I miss you."

In the answering silence, he dove into the beckoning ocean to wash the sweat from his body and cool off. The soothing water plunged around him, rocking his body as waves broke and surged past him to the shore. Relaxing his muscles, his mind drifted, lost in a bittersweet memory.

Maria's arms wrapped languorously around his shoulders, holding him, her breasts soft against his back. Her fingers caressed the length of his arms, her lips whispering sweet promises in his ear.

Memory merged with nightmare when she called out to him in a strangled voice, *"Help me!"*

Michael's nerves pricked with apprehension. She sounded so real, so close! He fought the irresistible pull of his own fantasy as it blurred and morphed into an entirely new nightmare, but he had to follow through. Turning to embrace her, to save her—crash!

A wall of salt water blasted his face as a large wave swept him off his feet and dragged him under. Smooth flesh mingled with his, clawing at his legs and back as he tumbled beneath the crushing water. The strange creature tangled with him as he tried to push away from it, but failed. Then, he could feel it beneath him, still under the water as he rose to his feet in the shallow surf, coughing, gasping for air.

Kait didn't know how long she'd been floating in the ocean—had no idea how far from shore she might be. She'd been drifting in and out of a daze, trying to keep from drowning for what felt like an eternity. Now suddenly, the tide smashed her against an island of jagged rocks, pounding her mercilessly. Her numb fingers searched for something to grasp but failed to gain purchase as the current dragged her around the craggy rocks and carried her away again.

A silhouette of land rising from the ocean gave her a brief moment of hope, but it seemed terribly distant. Continuing to drift, she gathered what strength she could from deep within her soul. She could swim the distance with ease if her body didn't hurt so much—if she wasn't so completely exhausted and cold.

With each small surge of confidence and energy, Kait swam. The breaststroke kept her going when she could no longer lift her arms from the water. Floating gave her time to rebuild her resolve and renew her energy when she would otherwise drown. But she was losing it now, no longer able to rally her reserves, unable to muster the strength for one last attempt. She could no longer feel her arms, couldn't swim another stroke. The shore was closer, but not nearly close enough.

The crash of waves tickled her ears—would they drag her into another jagged outcrop? She didn't have the strength left to resist their battering force. Each rolling wave that swelled beneath her carried her closer to shore until at last the swells turned into curling white peaks. The next wave carried her faster and farther, but she could no longer hold her head out of the water. Struggling for one more breath, she began to sink. Suddenly, a figure emerged from the darkness, directly in her path. A wave lifted her, and with her last gasp for air she cried out, "Help me."

The wave crashed over her, throwing her headlong into the man before her. She clawed and grabbed at him, trying desperately to catch hold as they both tumbled under the water. Her lungs were on fire, bursting with the need for air when she hit bottom. Water infiltrated her throat and lungs and she finally succumbed.

Michael's eyes and nose burned from the salt water he'd just inhaled. Rubbing his eyes, he forced them open and focused on the shadowy figure floating beneath him in the shallow surf. *Christ Almighty!* He reached into the water and grabbed the drowned woman, hoisting her out of the water and onto shore. Her skin was cold and pale in the moonlight—chilled to the bone. Her pulse was faint, her heart beating with arrhythmic cadence. Wiping her long brown hair from her face, Michael made sure her mouth was empty and jutted her jaw forward to check her breathing. Chilling stillness enveloped her like an ominous cloud as he bent over her listening, watching, waiting for the smallest breath.

Nothing!

He ignored the apprehension filling his veins and shifted instantly into autopilot, pinching her nose closed as he began mouth-to-mouth resuscitation.

This can't be happening!

It was nothing like the nightmares that had plied his subconscious nightly for the past four years, but the salt burning his eyes felt real enough, as did the lifeless body of the woman beneath him—he didn't dare stop. Once, twice, three times he pressed his lips to hers, breathing life back into her with a fervor he'd long forgotten. Within seconds water gushed from her lungs and her body gasped for air.

Supporting her neck, he quickly turned her on her side to keep her airway clear.

"That's right lady…breathe."

Michael hovered over her, his muscles twitching with keen awareness; she was still unconscious but her heartbeat grew stronger with each rasping breath. Realization struck him like lightning. Not only was she real, but she was alive—he hadn't failed!

Startled by the accomplishment, Michael regained his focus, cutting off any trace of emotion or memory—anything that made him weak—and began surveying her body for injuries. Only then did he notice the narrow gash along her hairline.

"Damn it!" He tore off his shirt to blot her wound.

The cover of darkness robbed him of any significant details, making it impossible to discern the nature of her injury. Head injuries were tricky and highly unpredictable; he would need to address it immediately. Pressing softly on the wound, he sensed the pain rushing through her body, radiating from her like shock waves after an earthquake. When he began to lift her, she moaned from some distant realm of pain. He paused, not wanting to hurt her, but determination assailed him—no matter what he found when he took her to the villa, he wouldn't let her die!

Not this time.

Michael's old office faced the rugged peaks of the Sierra Madre on the eastern side of the proud old Spanish villa he called home. He could carry her there and utilize whatever supplies remained, but he'd long ago closed the doors to the medical clinic he'd built next door, and rejected everything it entailed. As far as he knew those doors remained locked, and he had no desire to breech them.

Instead he climbed the massive, curving steps to the balcony overlooking the beach and entered a glass-paneled door to his own bedroom. Tearing back the tangled sheets, he laid the woman down.

With the glow of a bedside lamp and his energy buzzing from adrenaline, he once again scanned the woman's body for injuries. The size and shape of the gash on her forehead was suddenly a little too familiar. The echo of gunfire reverberated through his thoughts confirming that a bullet had most likely torn her flesh. Around her wrists were the severed remains of a rope that had once bound her arms. Horrified by the sight, he immediately worked to remove them.

The ominous revelation led to a slew of questions. Who had held this woman captive, and why? How had she ended up in the ocean? He'd heard the report of a single gunshot at least twenty minutes before he'd found her. Had her attackers chased her into the water? If so, were they still out there skulking through the underbrush on *his* land? And what were they doing out here in the middle of nowhere?

The scenario didn't make sense; he was forgetting something—*aha!* Triumphantly he latched onto his brief sighting of a boat rounding the cliffs in the moonlight. She hadn't plunged into the ocean from the shore to escape her captors; she had fled the boat seeking land! Michael stared at the woman with amazement, quickly estimating that she must have had to swim a half-mile, maybe more, to reach shore—it was a miracle she had survived in her condition. Fortune or fate had kept her alive through her obvious ordeal and he would do his part to keep her that way.

Gently checking the rest of her body for severe injuries, he palpated her abdomen and chest for signs of internal bleeding, checked her limbs for broken or dislocated bones. Fortunately, there were no other signs of major trauma beyond the fact that she remained unconscious.

The chilling stillness of her lungs when he'd first assessed her on the beach clamored in his brain, blending with the haunting memory of cold, wet skin under his touch. The circumstances were vastly different this time, but his actions had been nearly the same. For one victim, the pallor and chill of death had become permanent, but color was quickly returning to this woman's cheeks, the blue of her lips fading to a healthy pink. This...*woman*—he rejected the labels victim and patient equally, not wanting to revisit the untenable history associated with either word—had a fighting chance if he could just get a grip on his unwelcome emotions and stop tripping down memory lane.

Shaking himself out of a momentary trance, Michael began to strip away the woman's sopping wet T-shirt and jeans; he had to warm her. The anxiety that had seized him when he'd pulled her from the surf had somehow been replaced by fortitude, maybe even a little exhilaration—he'd never expected to feel either emotion again.

She appeared to be out of immediate danger, so he covered her with warm blankets and sat down on the edge of the bed. He had time now for a much more thorough inspection of the numerous, less severe wounds scattered across her slender, athletic frame. Her hands were covered with small abrasions, each wrist encircled with rope burns and bruises. The left side of her face was slightly swollen and red, indicating a newer injury, and she had a massive purplish bump on the back of her head that was possibly days old.

Looking deeper, he studied her battered body, his mind conjuring images of how she might have obtained each injury. A soul-deep rage built with each imagined terror until his composure nearly cracked under a tide of sensations. His fingers itched to wring the neck of any man who would visit such harm on a woman. He harbored no tolerance for monsters who would abuse those they should protect.

When he finished his assessment, Michael stared hard at the phone on his nightstand, undecided on his next course of action. Did he dare call Ian and ask for help from the TEAM? Did her circumstances warrant such extreme measures? Would they help without demanding their pound of flesh in return?

Not a chance. That made it an easy, if not obvious decision. He picked up the phone to call his former partner. Doctor Anton de la Vega was a much safer bet, an honorable man and an excellent physician. After several rings Michael grew impatient.

"Hola," answered a deep, groggy voice.

"Anton, I have an emergency here at the villa. A woman has been injured—washed up on my beach with a gunshot wound."

"Muerta?" he asked with instant recognition as he emerged quickly from the fog of sleep.

"No, she isn't dead, just unconscious. The bullet grazed her temple. She may have a concussion." Michael gave his friend a quick but thorough rundown of the woman's injuries. "I'd like you to come take a look at her, maybe bring a few supplies. I'm sure whatever we had at the clinic expired long ago."

"Are you serious?" he asked with disbelief. "You don't expect me to bring everything down there right now…it takes at least two hours to drive there, plus loading and unloading the equipment. It would be much better to bring her here, to the *emergencia* in Puerto Vallarta."

"No, Anton. I don't want to move her. I don't believe her wounds are severe, but she may still be in danger and I need a second opinion. She'll have a lot of aches and pains, but right now what she needs most are some meds and a safe place to rest."

Michael paused, unsure if his friend would acquiesce. He'd always managed to keep Anton out of TEAM business, by unanimous agreement, but he'd been unable to protect him from the hellfire that had rained down from nowhere and ruined his life four years ago. He hated asking for help again, but the alternative was even less tenable.

"I know it's a lot to ask. Our friendship has placed you in impossible situations too many times. I just need you to make sure I haven't missed anything. After that I'll take care of everything and leave you out of it. If she is in danger, anyone looking for her will check the hospitals. I can't take that chance until I know what happened to her."

Michael waited as silence strained the line.

Anton struggled with the ethics of the situation but loyalty prevailed. "Nothing has changed, my friend. I find that now, more than ever, I cannot refuse you. You are a crazy *gringo*, a magnet for trouble, but I love you like a brother. I'll fly the Cessna to the Careyes Hotel and rent a car—it should only take about an hour that way. Keep doing what you can for her. I'll be there as soon as possible with supplies."

The line went silent and relief trickled through Michael, but he couldn't pinpoint just one reason why—there were too many reasons to count.

Shifting focus, Michael barreled through the villa and across the courtyard to the once thriving medical clinic he'd established with Ian, Anton, and five other physicians to help rural people who needed medical care but couldn't afford it and had limited or no access. Consuela had kept some basic medical supplies on hand hoping he would change his mind someday and return to medicine, that much he knew, but to his surprise he found the clinic in almost perfect order: clean, dust-free, well-stocked with non-perishable basics, no cobwebs. He made a mental note to thank her the next time he saw her.

Passing through the empty waiting area, memories of the first time he'd seen his beautiful, emerald-eyed Maria engulfed him. She'd walked into the clinic, escorting her mother, and had immediately coaxed a smile from an ill child resting uncomfortably in its mother's arms. He'd made excuses to linger near reception and watch her. She'd sat down between her mother and a wise old crone—who'd conceded to her first-ever visit to an actual physician at the ripe age of seventy-six—to discuss the use of local herbs for sleeplessness. She'd captured his heart from the first moment he'd looked into her gentle soul.

He'd been young and naïve back then—*"full of piss and vinegar,"* as his granddad used to say—raring to save the world, or at least one small corner of it. When he'd seen the poverty and illness in Mexico during a deep-sea fishing trip with his family, he'd seen an opportunity to make a real contribution to humanity.

It had been a fool-hearted venture—he knew that now—but he'd convinced his brother Ian to make regular trips with him to offer free medical services in the numerous villages seated far from the fringes of Puerto Vallarta and Acapulco.

What had started out as two brothers setting up a mobile clinic in a beat-up old van once a month, had quickly escalated into twice, and even four times a month until they'd built a team of eight doctors committed to the humanitarian project. The mobile unit had grown into a fleet of four vans that carried supplies and volunteers far and wide. Then, on one fateful trip, the brothers had run into a "unique opportunity" as Ian had called it, to be "on call" and respond to emergencies for a private tactical rescue team. Save lives and increase funding—what could go wrong?

With new funds available, Michael had purchased and renovated an abandoned villa near Chamela Bay, established a full-time clinic headquarters on the premises, and tossed away his posh position in San Diego to become a permanent resident. He hadn't known it, but fate had been working against him back then. If he'd seen even a flicker of what was coming, he'd have made some vastly different choices.

Entering his private office—now a dormant reminder of that bygone life—Michael quietly gathered the materials and tools he would need to treat the woman lying upstairs in his bed. From the outside, he gave the appearance of a detached man, calm and collected, a man who knew what to do in any given situation, or had the wherewithal to figure it out quickly and take action. Fate had squashed that man like a bug for his arrogance. On the inside, his soul was smoldering, his mind and heart alight with chaotic energy and ideas. He was on the verge of something unthinkable, had been for several months, but refused to voice it or acknowledge it in any way.

Supplies in hand, he quashed the memories and the chaos, and returned to the villa. The death of his last gunshot patient had ended his life in countless ways; knowing what he did now, he didn't want that life back. He sat down beside his newest gunshot patient, and the ember started to smolder again, finally taking recognizable form. Hope glimmered in the depths of his soul, made him wonder if this was his one chance at redemption. If he truly saved this woman's life, would that finally begin his penance for past mistakes?

Did saving one life expiate the loss of others?

For a moment, the woman stirred, crunching her face in pain, moaning as the pain overtook her and she lost consciousness again.

She's one hell of a fighter, he thought, grateful for her strength and tenacity. Michael set to work cleaning and stitching the worst of her wounds, like an artist restoring a damaged masterpiece. Occasionally he spared a brief glance out the window, wondering if the sun had forgotten to rise or if time had ceased to exist.

FIVE

Michael's bedroom was sparsely decorated with dark oak flooring, a mahogany dresser, a set of matching nightstands and a four-poster bed. The green velvet drapes allowed only minimal light to peek through the cracks between their gaping swags, casting a hazy pallor over the room. He had fallen asleep, his chest resting on the bed, head tucked against his folded arms. The approach of a car made the gravel on the driveway below crackle and grind, and he jumped at the sound, unsure how long he had dozed.

Noting the time, he was surprised it had taken Anton so long to arrive. It was already 0530 hours—more than three hours since Michael had rescued the woman. The front door squealed as it opened, then slammed shut.

"Dónde estás?" yelled Anton.

"Upstairs!" Michael shouted from the doorway, revived by the arrival of his friend. "In my bedroom."

Mammoth-like steps echoed up the staircase and along the hallway. At last, Anton entered the room, a portly man with dark-brown eyes and hair, and a gray, neatly-trimmed beard. Though he was shorter than Michael, he was vividly self-confident and imposing.

"How is the patient?" Anton asked slightly out of breath but trying hard not to show it. "What are her vitals?"

"Blood pressure stable at 115 over 65, pulse 60 beats per minute." Michael watched as Anton began inserting an IV line. "How are Adele and the kids? It's been a long time."

"She'll be mad as a hornet when she realizes I came and saw you without her. She wonders when you will stop acting like a hermit crab."

Michael ignored the rebuke. "She'll get over it. She doesn't have it in her to hold a grudge." Rising from his chair to shake off the fog surrounding his brain, Michael continued, "Besides, you'll sweet talk her like you always do and she'll understand the circumstances. After all, emergencies are the business of doctors."

"You were always the sweet talker, amigo, not I." Taking a closer look at their patient, Anton gasped, "Jesus, Mary, and Joseph! She's beautiful, no? Even with her injuries. Just the sort of patient you need, I think, to get you back in the action." At the risk of ruffling Michael's feathers, he continued his teasing while assessing her injuries. "Maybe she'll give you some inspiration…put some spark back in your life, eh old man?" A devilish twinkle lit Anton's eyes.

"Don't start with me, *old man!* You've got at least fifteen years on me…and I don't need any sparks in my life. I've got more than I can handle with all those boat renovations sitting downstairs waiting for my attention."

The serious get-down-to-business tone in their voices had swiftly mutated into the good-humored banter of old friends happy to see one another, which pleased Anton beyond words. He filled a syringe with antibiotic, cast a smug smile at Michael, and then proceeded to sterilize a small patch of skin on the woman's hip.

"None of her wounds are deep, but it wouldn't hurt to give her a tetanus booster since we don't know where she's been, or what she's been exposed to." Anton rummaged through his black satchel and pulled out a vial of liquid. "She'll be up and about in no time."

Anton paused for a moment and became slightly more serious. "I have to say, old friend, it's great to see you back in action. I knew someday you'd return to medicine—it's in your blood." He inspected the wounds that Michael had tended, delighted by the perfection with which they had been treated. "She may have a concussion from that bump on her head, but it doesn't look like she suffered any other internal damage."

Michael nodded his agreement, his eyes riveted to the darkening bruise on her face. "She's been through hell."

Anton observed Michael with great interest, trying to read his innermost thoughts. No matter how calm Michael appeared on the outside, he had no doubt his soft-hearted friend was chaffing on the inside, worrying about the decisions he'd made and torturing himself for past failings. "Relax Storm, take a few deep breaths and cool your heels. By the look of things, she'll be fine in a matter of days."

Snapping out of his trance, Michael placed his hand on Anton's shoulder and spoke with a note of pride. "That scar on her forehead shouldn't be too bad."

"No kidding, in a couple of months she won't even know it was there! I always said you could have gone into cosmetic surgery."

Anton disappeared into the walk-in closet and returned with one of Michael's long-sleeved, button-down shirts, "Put this on her while I make some coffee then we'll talk about what to do next."

Instead, Michael prepared the adjoining room and tucked a warm blanket around the woman, then lifted her from the damp sheets. Removing her limp body from his bed was an easy task. Dressing her in his own shirt was another matter entirely—one he intended to avoid.

Several minutes passed with Michael keeping a steady watch over his patient, hoping she'd wake up and enlighten his troubled mind with whatever incredible story she had to tell. It probably wouldn't hold a candle to the wild scenarios he'd been imagining all night. Whatever her story, Michael knew he was already hooked—snared by his own maddening addiction to preserving life. He would do anything in his power to help her, regardless of the fact that he knew nothing about her.

Anton finally returned with coffee and a smile for his good friend. "This'll perk you up."

Michael took the steaming mug, but set it down on the nightstand without hazarding even a sip of the potent black concoction. Anton's inability to make a decent cup of coffee was legendary, and had not improved with time.

Anton noticed, but let it pass without a care. "I brought a stretcher. I don't think I could fly the plane and hold her head up in the seat," Anton joked, "unless you'd like to come with me to Puerto Vallarta."

Michael's tension returned instantly—strangled him with some intangible need deep within. Already, he felt constrained by an invisible connection to this woman, as if they shared a common thread that, if pulled, would unravel them both. She tugged at his heart with that thread, but he couldn't begin to explain such vague feelings to Anton; he couldn't even explain it to himself.

Michael quickly refused Anton's suggestion. "She'll stay here for now. I have plenty of room and no one will disturb her," he announced firmly. "We have no idea who shot her or if they're still out there somewhere looking for her."

"Exactly," Anton balked. "You have no idea who this woman is, where she came from, who shot her, or why. She could be involved with militia or drug runners, anything!"

"Or she could be an innocent! A woman who through no fault of her own has been beaten to a pulp and nearly killed!" Michael fought to control his temper and the timbre of his voice. "I pulled her out of a watery grave just in the nick of time, Anton, and I have no intention of letting whoever did this, finish the job!"

Anton could see that the woman and her injuries were dredging up a slew of heavy emotions for Michael, but he offered one last attempt at reason. "She should be taken to a proper medical facility and the authorities notified. You've already saved her life. If you keep her here, Michael...if she is not an "innocent" as you say, or even if she is, you don't know who might be hunting her. You could suffer the same ill fate as your beloved Maria."

Michael glared at Anton in silent warning. He didn't owe him any further explanations. Helping this woman was a chance to reclaim an ounce of peace in his life, to repay a debt that had been hanging over him for four endless years. It was a chance to restore life where once he had failed.

"I said I would take care of her, and I meant it. You're involvement ends here," Michael said finally, tamping down on the hot-natured temper that had emerged only after the injustice of life had reared its ugly head and torn him apart. He'd never been quick to anger before that day, and part of him had been out of balance ever since. "She washed up on my beach, she's in my care, and from here on out, I am taking full responsibility for her!"

Anton realized any further argument was futile. "Ah...maybe you're right," he said lightly, shrugging his shoulders and throwing up his hands in defeat. "She has obviously gotten under your skin. Who knows, maybe you can help each other. Only promise me one thing. Promise, dear friend, that you will call Ian if there is *any* trouble."

Michael flushed with displeasure, but held it in check. He would not hold his friend's honest and well-justified concerns against him. "I'd rather keep Ian and the TEAM out of this, if possible. Here," Michael handed Anton the shirt, "why don't *you* put it on her? I need to wash up." Michael disappeared down the hall thankful that he'd extracted himself from both the task and the argument.

Anton conceded to his friend's request, working quickly, but taking great care in dressing the woman. Then, hearing Michael returning, he decided to try again for the camaraderie they had shared so easily only moments ago. "I noticed your latest project when I drove up. I'll bet that broken-down old boat against my speed machine—they won't even bother to look for her, whoever they are."

"You may be right. She was pretty far gone when I found her. I don't expect anyone will come snooping around, but if they do, I'll be ready," Michael said speaking mostly to himself. Then bumping Anton with his shoulder as he stopped alongside him, he added, "It isn't a broken-down old boat, she's a rare thing of beauty—an antique worthy of complete restoration!"

"Si, si," Anton agreed, "whatever you say, but I prefer power and speed over vintage and valor any day!" Together they stripped the soiled bedding and carried the mattress outside to dry in the sunlight, then examined the woman one last time. Anton looked at his watch and sighed. "I must get back. Don't you have a hug for your long lost amigo?"

Michael smiled; Anton was every bit the softy his wife claimed him to be, so long as he wasn't riled. And he never held a grudge. "I'm sorry it's been so long since my last call." Michael walked into Anton's open arms and the men gave each other a fierce squeeze. "Thanks for your help. She'll heal much faster thanks to you."

"And you will sleep better," Anton winked. "There are pain pills on the table there. She's in the most capable hands I know—other than my own of course. You just be careful she doesn't end up biting the hand that saved her!" Anton gave Michael another smile as he left the room.

Alone with his mystery woman for the duration, Michael dragged a recliner in from the study and placed it near the bed where she lie sleeping, then opened the door to the balcony and sat down beside her. The fresh morning air was heavy with moisture, a cool sixty-five degrees Fahrenheit, and warming quickly. His patient shivered involuntarily with feverish chills, and Michael was starting to feel several aftereffects from the adrenaline rush caused by the day's events. He needed sleep more than ever but couldn't risk taking sleeping pills under the circumstances. Instead, he built a fire in the stone-faced hearth that spanned nearly one full wall.

With the room aglow in an orange haze that warmed and dried the air, his mind went to work again, trying to figure out the puzzle. She'd been through a major ordeal but he was certain that she would live to tell about it. Who she was and where she had come from were less certain, but he would be here when she awoke to reassure her that she was safe. Holding her hand, he stared at her battered but tranquil face, amazed at the unexpected turn of events and his intense reaction. He then set the puzzle aside and let himself drift to sleep.

After several hours, the afternoon sun pierced the room, brightening the surroundings with a healing energy. The fire had died as the sun rose to take its place. Michael awoke and gazed intently at the woman lying motionless under the deep blue comforter. He could see her features much more clearly in the light of a new day. No longer haunted by visions of his past, he could observe her with a more rational mind and observe things he hadn't noticed before.

Anton had called her beautiful, but that wasn't the right word. She could be descended from any number of European ancestors, but her pale skin and dark, wavy hair gave her an exotic flare not shared by the golden, stereotypically beautiful blondes of the world. She was certainly attractive—slender and curvy in all the right places—but she had a free and wild look to her and seemed more athletic than the society darlings he'd known growing up. She was wholesome and enchanting: no sign of smudged makeup, no trace of jewelry around her fingers, wrists, or neck, no chipped fingernail polish or bleached hair. The more he saw, the more his imagination took flight, filling the gaps in his information with endless possibilities.

Suddenly, her eyelids flickered, her face crunching in agony. "Shh, you're safe," he said in a soothing voice. "Everything is going to be okay. Try to relax."

At the realization that she wasn't alone, the woman jerked herself upright in bed, then faltered under a gush of pain and nausea. Her deepest survival instincts spurred her on and she turned away from him, trying to get up. Michael grabbed her shoulders and pulled her back gently, forcing her to lie down; she was too weak to offer any real resistance.

"Calm down. I'm here to help you," he soothed. "Can you tell me your name?"

She didn't answer, just glared at him with all her wrath like *he* was the enemy. Her body trembled on the edge of hysteria, and Michael backed away slightly to give her a little space. She watched him like prey caught in the crosshairs of an attacker, her eyes filled with fear.

"Who are you? Wh...where am I?" she demanded.

Michael reached to give her a glass of water, not meaning to ignite her defensive instincts. She rolled away from him with a speed and strength he didn't expect, then teetered at the opposite edge of the bed. He dropped the glass and dashed to the other side but she fell to the ground before he could reach her, her feet unable to withstand any weight. She hit the ground with a thud.

Apprehension pumped hard and fast through his body, like jet fuel through twin engines—*you're screwing this up, royally!* Sliding one arm under her knees and the other behind her back, he scooped her up off the floor.

Terrified and half-crazed, she swung her arms wildly and kicked the air like a hellcat, trying to get away from him. Standing up quickly, he released her legs, narrowly avoiding her knee to his jaw, and realigned their bodies, effectively trapping her legs with his, arms locked around her low back, holding most of her weight so she wouldn't collapse again. He didn't want to compound her fear by restraining her completely, but he couldn't afford to let her hurt him either.

In this new position his head and face were still vulnerable. With her concussion, he couldn't toss her over his shoulder. All he could do was wrap himself more tightly around her and tuck his head into the crook of her neck. Her fists continued to fly, pounding the only parts of him she could reach—his back and head—with a fury that far exceeded her strength. He took the blows, waiting out the storm, unsure how to calm her.

"Let me go!" she shrieked at last, striking his back a few more times, exhausting herself.

She was hurting herself more than she was hurting him, but if he released her she would try to run again. He moved to the edge of the bed, still holding her tightly with one arm, and started patting her back softly with the other. Instinctively, he began rocking her like a small child, whispering shh below her ear, over and over until she stopped moving. "I'm not going to hurt you. You're safe here."

She gave it one last attempt, trying to insert her arms between them to push him away or break his hold, but her strength ebbed and she finally collapsed against him—still conscious but utterly spent—unable to continue fighting. He sat down on the bed and lifted her onto his lap—her heart racing, her breathing erratic—her head pitched sideways against his chest. Clutching his arm with both hands, her eyes clenched tightly against her fear and pain, and within seconds she slipped once more into the darkness of sleep.

Her sudden awakening had caught Michael seriously off guard and the terror in her eyes had set his imagination racing. Maybe she was the wife of a wealthy businessman and she'd been kidnapped by gorillas in order to win a ransom. Maybe she'd been abducted by a human-trafficking ring, or maybe she was the victim of modern day pirates on the high seas. Whatever her story, he hadn't been prepared for her agility after pulling her from death's clutches, nor her desperate attempts to escape. Remorse struck him in the aftermath—*what a jackass!*

He would not, *could not* fail her like that again.

The feel of her body, warm and alive, lent small comfort as he held her a few moments longer, taking her pulse, checking for fever, and confirming that she was truly unconsciousness, not just waiting for a more opportune moment to escape. An eternity had passed since he'd held anything more than an etheric memory so close—he'd thought the rest of eternity would pass without ever having to hold a flesh and blood woman again. Eternity was apparently a much shorter span of time than expected.

Unbidden, Maria's last moments flashed through every cell in his body. Her lifeblood had seeped into his clothes and the red clay soil beneath her as easily as her spirit had slipped free of its mortal shell and drifted away on a butterfly breeze. There'd been so many words unspoken, so many emotions glimmering in her bright, knowing eyes as the light dimmed. Like a candle lit in an open doorway, she'd been extinguished before she'd even really had the chance to burn.

Michael quickly laid the woman back in bed and released her, the sheer power and clarity of the memory lashing him to the bone.

It's different this time, he asserted, trying to convince both himself and the Universe. This woman's injuries weren't fatal. She's strong enough to fight.

Maria was strong too, his conscience corrected. Time and place had been against her.

True—and this woman found me here, *in the middle of nowhere, at just the right moment.*

Despite his rational protests, Michael's subconscious continued to draw small similarities in circumstance, reminding him of details he'd finally managed to lock away. The past was resurrecting and reenacting itself through this woman's rescue, forcing him to do everything over again, giving him a chance to analyze and repair his mistakes, but the story now had a completely different ending.

"You didn't make any mistakes," his brother had insisted time and again.

A new set of rules was in force and they emphasized a key point Michael had never been able to accept; he'd done everything he could have, *should* have done to save Maria. It wasn't his fault she had died. He'd done everything humanly possible to save her. On a logical level he knew that, but Maria, unlike this stranger, simply hadn't had the will to survive.

Why?

Michael left the room seeking refuge from the plague of emotions resurfacing after years of repression, but he couldn't stop them from taking root. After Maria's death, he'd ceased caring about anything. He'd cast away everything that had been part of his life in a futile attempt to save some small corner of his heart. His career as a doctor, his family and friends, his commitment to the TEAM—he'd abandoned them all. He'd cared too much before and that had brought him nothing but misery.

Now, with this woman lying helplessly in his home, relying on him to make her well again, it seemed that everything he'd thrown away was suddenly galloping back. It was up to him to take hold of the chalice and run with it, or throw it away again, and any chance for life with it.

SIX

Kait felt peaceful and rested when she stretched and yawned, trying to open her eyes several hours later. The sun was setting and a warm fire crackled, sending shadows dancing through the room. Silky sheets rustled against her skin as she came fully awake, oblivious to the fact that her world was not right. As she glanced around the room, her focus wavering in and out, she was soothed by the vibrant shades of royal blue and aquamarine, and several lovely ocean scenes hanging on the walls. Though she felt rather strange, kind of woozy and light, she began to feel right at home, as she always had at the edge of the deep blue sea.

Emerging from a concussive haze, her eyes finally began to steady as she surveyed the comforting room, taking note of the smaller details painstakingly placed here and there to complete the ocean motif. A giant conch sat atop an ornate chest inlaid with small coiled shells, abalone, and mother of pearl. A perfectly preserved nautilus claimed the center of a wide mantle of weathered driftwood with all its natural curves and knots. The velveteen drapes cascaded toward the floor like a waterfall, and the grainy warmth of the wooden floor reminded her of a well-seasoned ship's deck.

Heaven, she mused, completely oblivious to her momentary amnesia and her recent brush with death. For the first time in longer than she could remember, she felt completely at ease—not a care in the world, as if nothing was hanging over her demanding her constant attention and effort. No stress of deadlines, no mother troubles, no bills to pay—no insurmountable problems. This must be what it felt like to finally take a real vacation, and heaven knows how badly she needed one.

Just as she began to settle into the moment, accepting the beautiful surroundings as a perfectly natural and wonderful place to be, she began to feel a subtle, foreboding sense of danger prickling the back of her neck.

This is not reality.

Bits and pieces of memory flashed through her mind bringing confusion and a hint of worry. Slowly she became aware of the tingling sensation in her hands and a steadily increasing, needle-like pain in her left temple.

If this is a vacation, why does my body hurt?

Kait looked down at her hands with shock and a growing sense of dread. They were each bound firmly with layers of gauze, reminding her of two white stumps, her fingertips poking out the only evidence that they were still intact.

Vacation or nightmare?

Discordant alarm began its insidious ascent from the pit of her stomach, up her spine, increasing as it wove its way to the top of her head where a pulsating pain competed with a constant pressure, like a hat that was much too tight. With her bare fingertips, she felt her head and realized it too was wrapped with bandages, but that didn't make any sense.

What in the name of Poseidon is going on?

In a flash of memory, the shattering sound of gunfire ricocheted through her mind and Kait remembered diving off a fishing boat, felt her head hitting the water like a wall of ice. Seeing the steely pistol grasped loosely in a large, brutish hand, she relived the sharp sting that slashed across her forehead and gasped aloud, "I've been shot?"

Like a volcano inside her skull, the pressure built until it was nearly impossible to think or remember any further details. Lifting the sheet, she inspected her legs, bent her knees and wiggled her toes to make sure everything worked properly. They were free and relatively unscathed. Next she felt her abdomen and chest, trying desperately to hold back the panic that threatened to consumer her. Nothing hurt terribly except her head, and she could find no life threatening injuries, so maybe she hadn't been shot after all.

Maybe this is just a crazy bad dream—a rare occurrence for her unless she was sick, because she worked herself to the bone each day to ensure that she would sleep like the dead. She didn't want to dream; she had no control over what would come, good or bad.

Okay, time to wake up—she was probably sleeping in some awkward position that had cut off her circulation and made her hands fall asleep. She needed to move and shake them out, get the blood flowing again, maybe drink some water to quench her parched throat.

Struggling against her own weight and lethargy, she tried to sit up and shift her legs to the side of the large bed. She could do nothing more than roll to her side with a deep moan. Vivid images of a man hovering over her, holding her down, flooded her mind with new waves of fear and adrenaline. Her eyes snapped open, her defensive instincts kicking in as she pushed herself up and searched for the dark stranger who'd grabbed her.

Who is he?

More importantly, where is he?

Observing that she was still in the tranquil ocean room, she reined-in the panic. She was still dreaming. He was only a figment of her fevered imagination, and soon Lilly or Nick would come to check on her and wake her up to take some medicine. Everything was going to be okay. She closed her eyes within her dream and waited.

After countless, immeasurable moments, Kait made another attempt to wake herself up and get out of bed, but she made precious little progress, her head as heavy as a bowling ball. Her brain drifted off on a tangent as she lifted the blankets again to look at herself.

What am I wearing—a man's dress shirt?

The dream was becoming more and more bizarre. Fighting to control the erratic and disquieting rhythm of her own heartbeat, Kait swore that no matter how unsettling it was to awaken from one nightmare and find herself in another, plagued with bandages and scattered, violent memories, she would not give in to panic.

Squirming uncomfortably, she felt like she was caught in a bad episode of *The Twilight Zone*, an unwitting character in a macabre, twisted world where reality had been sucked into a big black hole in outer space. As the minutes ticked by at a blistering crawl, she began to doubt whether Lilly or Nick would come and wake her. Clearly, she was on her own here, utterly lost and confused, unable to wake herself for reasons unknown.

Maybe she wasn't sick but had actually gotten hurt somehow and was drugged-out on painkillers in a hospital—*just like the time I was hit by a car*. That would certainly explain her pain and inability to rouse herself or make sense of anything. The room around her was too pleasant to be a hospital room, but it certainly wasn't a safe refuge where she could let her guard down and relax.

Focus—observe—devise a plan.

Yes, that's what Lilly would do.

As Kait scrutinized the severity of her wounds, fear crept into every fiber of her body until she trembled with an urgent need to escape.

From what?

Dream or reality, she knew only two things: the danger was not over and she had only herself on which to rely.

First, get out of this room.

Mustering her flagging strength, Kait crept out of bed feeling woozy again, like she would float right up to the ceiling. A gentle tug at her wrist brought her attention to the IV line taped to her wrist. "Oh jeez," she moaned, swallowing the bile bubbling up her throat at the sight. She'd never held the slightest affinity for needles. Sure, she could inject animals and even other people with any needle great or small, but just point it in her direction and all bets were off. To make matters worse, she was practically infamous for her ability to pass out at the sight of her own blood. She wouldn't get very far tethered to an IV, and she'd get nowhere fast if she let the blasted thing get the best of her.

It's simply mind over matter—if she could control her squeamish mind, a little bit of discomfort wouldn't matter. She couldn't afford to waste what might turn out to be her only chance at escape.

Using her free hand to hold the line steady, Kait peeled away the tape with her teeth. Hesitating only a moment, she squeezed her eyes shut and pulled the tube away from her wrist with a strangled yelp, then pressed where the IV had been. If blood came gushing out, she'd be toast. Determined to tough it out, Kait plastered the tape back over the area to maintain pressure against the blood flow, and prayed she hadn't caused herself any additional damage.

What's a small bruised vein compared to death?

Stop being melodramatic! You're only dreaming!

A new sense of confidence crept through Kait's mind. If she could remove an IV from her own arm, she could do just about anything—*right?* Her energy and self-assurance growing, Kait made another brief survey of the room, this time looking for something to defend herself with if the need arose, but found nothing. A brief sense of déjà vu came and went as her thoughts returned to the towering man who'd stood over her at this very spot. His first words had sounded kind and reassuring, but she'd seen clouds of darkness in his stormy eyes. She didn't dare trust him if he came back. She couldn't trust *anyone* in this topsy-turvy nightmare.

Kait stumbled across the room to the balcony doors and strained to push them open. The lock held tight at first, and not for the first time she cursed the bandages binding her hands. If she had ever mastered controlling her dreams, instead of suppressing them, she could just blink the bandages away and make the door open on a breeze, but that was just wishful thinking. Nothing was ever easy in a nightmare.

At last the bolt yielded and the doors swung open with an almost deafening squeal that made her heart leap.

Did the sound betray me?

A quick glance back revealed that she was still alone.

Almost free!

Stepping out onto the balcony, Kait was assaulted by the sight of an endless expanse of lush, green jungle. Miles and miles of treetops surrounded her, right up to the edge of the courtyard below, along with a high rock wall that seemed to enclose every square inch of the compound. Her heart sank and she moaned with rapidly increasing fatigue.

Where in the world am I?

At last recollection she'd gone to the wharf to do something important. She was confident that home and work were both located in sunny, semi-arid San Diego, and equally sure that not one stretch of California coast looked even remotely like a South American jungle.

How much evidence do you need? It's a dream!

The dense jungle looked ominous, almost threatening, silently urging her to turn back to the relative safety of the villa. She had no idea what creatures lurked in that thick, tree-canopied darkness. There would be snakes of course, maybe some monkeys—those she could handle—but there might also be big cats. Nothing small and cuddly like her precious little housecat, Sheba; whatever lurked out there in the shadows would be large and toothy, several pounds heavier than her, and have paws bigger than her own hands. She'd be no match for a hungry panther, and as much as she loved cats, she was pretty darn sure she didn't want to meet one face to face in her current condition—*not even in a dream!*

A thriving desire to survive kept Kait moving: better to take her chances outside than to stay here and wait for her captor's return. She wobbled across the balcony and peered into the room next door. It too looked dark and unfriendly, just like the jungle…just like her captor.

Kait drifted down the stairs and onto the grass. It felt prickly and wet under her feet sending threads of sensation shivering up her legs and spine. *This is too real—you're not dreaming.* Staring down at her bare legs and feet, unsure where to go or what to do, her mind tangled in a numbing fog.

You're in real danger! Head for the wall!

Kait moved faster now, desperate to escape the dream and wake up. At the base of the wall, she stopped and craned her head skyward at the impossible barrier. "What was I thinking?" she wailed aloud. There was no way she could scale a 12-foot rock wall and traipse off into the jungle looking for help. "I need…" her mind flagged, tired of swimming through the turbulent haze surrounding it. "I need…a car!"

A bitter laugh bubbled up her throat, the hysteria of strangled nerves on the verge of a mental breakdown. Yes, a car was a far better plan of escape. Whoever lived in this mansion must have one sitting around somewhere. Never mind that she'd need keys to start the car; she would cross that bridge when—*if*—she got there.

Michael had quietly looked in on his mystery woman every thirty minutes after leaving her room, half afraid he'd imagined the entire scenario. This time when he entered the room, her bed was empty, the IV abandoned and dripping on the floor, the balcony doors hanging open. Shocked into action, he burst through the doors and saw her stumbling haphazardly across the lawn. She was heading toward the garage, probably hoping to make an escape. She looked so helpless and lost that he wondered if she even remembered what had happened to her.

Feigning calm, Michael called to her across the distance, "Miss! Stay where you are, I'm coming down." She stumbled then broke into a staggered run without looking back. "Be careful," he yelled, his feet moving like lightning, "you'll hurt yourself. Don't run!"

Within seconds he was down the stairs, running after her, gaining fast. He should have kept quiet and snuck up on her, but he hadn't wanted to frighten her again. Her movements were fractured with indecision, or confusion, her pace slowing with each futile step. Her energy was burning out—a fantastic fireball reduced to glowing embers. She was overexerting herself in this ridiculous attempt to flee, and he had failed her yet again.

She should never have gotten this far!

He was almost upon her when she veered off the grass onto a paved path near the garden shed. She was falling again and he couldn't catch her, but in a flash she was up, her arms swinging something long and narrow in a wide arc as she turned and struck him. Michael fell to the ground, stunned by the instant pounding in his head. Through the ringing in his skull, he growled at the wildcat who'd just flattened him with a shovel. "Christ, woman…I'm trying to help you!"

Clearly not comprehending the situation, she swung at him again, missing his jaw by mere inches, then turned again to escape. She'd nearly knocked him out with that first blow—had caught him by complete surprise—if her second swing had found its mark, he'd be out cold right now.

Indignation colored Michael's cheeks. By all rights, this injured waif should be no match for his size and strength, yet she had eluded his grasp and knocked him on his rear. His patience was suddenly wearing very thin. In one fluid motion he got back on his feet, ready to pounce on her like a lion on a gazelle. There would be no further struggle; she was outsized, outwitted, outmatched in every way, and it was up to him to demonstrate that fact.

"Stop running!" he roared.

She turned to face him then, agony ravaging her body, defeat weighing heavily on her shoulders. Even worse were the fresh waves of fear that washed over her as he approached. Whatever she'd been through before he'd found her, he had been the one to put that look in her eyes right now, and it stung like a snake bite. Frustrated to his core, Michael gentled his voice and demeanor. "I'm sorry. I don't mean to frighten you. *Please*—just let me help you," he implored, drawing nearer.

"You're failing miserably, Mic! Step up your game before it's too late." Ian's imagined assessment of the situation cut through Michael's mind as clearly as if his brother was standing beside him watching the debacle unfold instead of going about his day almost two thousand miles and a lifetime away.

Her expression was a mask of disbelief and distrust as she began to hyperventilate. Within a few more steps Michael arrived in front of her again. She raised her face, her eyes glazed—unseeing—and her arms reached out as she stumbled into his chest. Michael caught her quickly and wrapped his arms protectively around her, pulling her close.

Her bandaged hands pushed against his shoulders, automatically renewing their struggle. "I...can't...breathe," she wheezed, tears streaming down her flushed cheeks.

"Bend over. It'll make breathing easier. Take slow, deep breaths." He held her firmly against his side, one arm coiled around her narrow waist in case her legs gave out, the other propped under her forehead, taking the weight of her head off her neck and shoulders. Quickly regaining control over his temper, Michael waited for her breathing to regulate, then plucked her up into his arms, without further resistance, and trudged back toward the house.

It was obvious now, after witnessing firsthand her amazing stamina and will to survive, how she'd managed to evade death. She was a veritable wellspring of courage, the true depths of her character hidden and unfathomable while she'd slept.

For all her obvious strengths, her sudden appearance in his life only gave further testament to his own failings. As her caretaker and guardian, he should have anticipated her every move, should have stayed beside her every minute and prevented this whole damned fiasco. Instead, he'd been off-center, plagued with emotions from the moment he'd laid eyes on her lifeless body in the water. His judgment had been impaired and he'd allowed himself to wallow in the misery of his past, second guessing himself and castigating with indecision. While he'd been sorting out his emotions, he'd left his patient exposed and vulnerable.

No more!

Time to focus, not on the past, but on the present, and the needs of this woman. He'd been a damned good doctor once upon a time, capable of far greater finesse than he had demonstrated in the past few hours. From this moment on, he would prove it.

SEVEN

No longer able to fight or flee, Kait finally felt the crush of defeat—if her captor carried her right up to the gates of Hell, she wouldn't be able to stop him. She'd spent nearly every ounce of energy she had vying for escape, and what little was left had vanished under the cloud of his thundering voice and her lack of oxygen. Despite the warnings still echoing through her brain, she'd succumbed to the mental and physical exhaustion that swathed her like a coat of lead.

It's useless to keep fighting—she knew it was true, but struggled to accept it—*he had you beat from the word go.*

Caught once again in the vice-like grip of a stranger, she tried to quash her fear with logic and internalize her pain so he wouldn't know how vulnerable she felt, but she couldn't even manage to silence her whimpers and moans. She was literally at the bottom of the barrel, dredging for the last precious drops of energy and courage she needed to get through whatever came next.

She craved rest and refuge, her body too weak, her emotions too frayed to keep up with the outlandish demands, but she refused to accept defeat. Instead, she withdrew into passive resistance, reclaiming what little power she could by staging her own silent rebellion. Whatever this man wanted from her, she would simply refuse to capitulate, no matter what nightmares he threatened her with!

"You'll be all right," the stranger murmured near her ear. "I hope you'll forgive me for yelling at you back there."

Yelling at me? Was that his greatest misdeed?

How about taking her captive against her will, terrorizing her, and making her body ache to the bone? His paltry apology meant nothing, but she didn't have the energy to tell him so, and there might be repercussions if she did. After all, he was the one in control—at least for the moment.

As he laid her back in bed, the stranger flashed his most apologetic, nonthreatening look. It was almost funny considering the circumstances. Since when did predators apologize to their prey?

"My name is Michael Storm. You're at my home near Chamela Bay."

This can't be real.

Kait refused to look at him, in part because her head was splitting, but also because she refused to fall for his "mister nice guy" charade. The man was holding her captive against her will and might be planning to do any number of unspeakable things to her. At the very least, he was a kidnapper and a tyrant. Did he really think she would just yield to his soothing voice and coaxing words like some naïve child?

"Do you understand what I'm saying?" He asked in a slightly more insistent tone. When she didn't answer, he continued. "I found you on the beach last night, half-drowned and bleeding."

Again, Kait heard the echo of the nearly fatal shot—so loud, so close that she flinched. She remembered struggling to stay afloat in the black ocean, the cutting rocks and battering surf that had nearly torn her apart—*don't give in; none of this is real!*

It sure feels real…

If it's real, then you're toast!

Kait kept her mouth shut and closed her eyes to free herself from the sight of him.

He's trying to quiet you so you won't run again.

He can't hurt you if you wake up!

"This is my home. I treated your wounds—don't worry, I'm a doctor—you'll be fine in a matter of days if you'll just rest a while and stop hurting yourself."

Stop hurting myself?

Kait opened her eyes and stared at him, amazed at his audacity. She hadn't done *anything* to hurt herself. Every infernal pain in her body had been inflicted by a series of bastards who'd wanted to hurt or control her.

The eyes staring back at her were deep, dark pools of concern and...something else. He was being very cautious, for lack of a better word, and though he was invading her personal space, she could feel a reticence and distance emanating from him. He had the look of someone who'd seen much more than he'd ever wanted to see, and lived to regret it. Those eyes, and the hidden messages they contained, left her wondering for the first time if this stranger might have actually saved her as he was indicating. Unsure of the situation, her defiance began to wane.

"Were you on vacation? Perhaps visiting Puerto Vallarta?" he continued with stubborn persistence.

"Puerto Vallarta?" she gasped unintentionally, shocked by his words. "You mean this really is Mexico? That's impos—" Kait's voice died in her throat. How could she be in Mexico? Wasn't she in San Diego just yesterday?

Michael's voice broke through the thickening haze, "Do you remember what happened?" He stared at her steadily, analyzing her as though she was a great mystery to be solved.

"Today is Sunday," Kait said to reassure herself, though she was no longer sure of anything. She looked at Michael for confirmation and watched his eyes squint ever so slightly.

"No," he replied, setting his hand over hers, "it's Tuesday."

Tuesday! She yanked her hand from his, scalded by the information as much as his touch. "It can't be!" Her crew had come ashore for the weekend on Friday night, and she'd gone back to the wharf on Saturday morning. If today was Tuesday, she'd lost three whole days and nights! That certainly explained how she could have ended up so far from home, but it didn't do diddly-squat for the gaps in her memory, or the time she'd lost.

Because it's only a crazy dream! Get that through your thick flipping skull!

In the next instant, fragments of memory whirled into her mind in a torrent, the images coming too fast, too incomplete to make sense: a fishing boat, scratchy, musty cloth that had nearly choked her, a filth-ridden man holding her down, trying to rape her. The barrage was more than Kait could withstand and she closed her eyes tightly, struggling to regain control.

More images came: a yacht, a man with gold chains, a big, scary-looking rifle—the synapses in her brain must be misfiring, playing tricks on her. This man and the rest of the nefarious characters in this story were nothing more than a figment of her imagination, conjured up in the worst nightmare she'd ever had. She was at home in bed, safe and sound right where she should be, with Sheba snuggled close by her side.

It's all some terrible hallucination.

The wheels of her mind kept spinning, processing the images she'd seen, trying to analyze the dream. One of her mother's most frequent criticisms, insidiously disguised as genuine parental concern and voiced at every opportunity, zipped through her mind: *"She's nothing if not analytical. Why she'd analyze a bucket of popcorn if I let her."*

Kait's head pounded with the effort to make sense of the senseless. San Diego was right on the border of Mexico, a stone's throw from Tijuana, but she'd never had any great urge to visit, much less take a vacation there. She had no idea how far Puerto Vallarta was from San Diego, or how long it would take to get there by boat, but she was certainly going to find out. And she'd been working on something of great importance. She was short on time—up against an impossible deadline.

The whales! She was supposed to be collecting data to present to the whaling commission—she wouldn't just up and take a blasted vacation! That more than anything else proved this was all just a horrifying dream, but it didn't explain the pain in her head and hands, or why her body ached like she'd been struck by a semi. Even the simple task of breathing was proving difficult right now.

"How long have I been unconscious?" she asked warily. "How did I get here?"

"I found you early this morning, before dawn. You've been asleep all day."

Okay, that clarified the past few hours, but told her nothing about the supposedly missing days. Kait didn't have a clue what was real and what wasn't, but her instincts were screaming that something was irrevocably wrong in her world. Vital information was missing from her memory banks.

The *Spanish Maiden* flashed in her head again bringing splinters of pain that reverberated like a pinball inside her skull. She tried to wade through it, expel it on each stifled breath, but the waves of thunder kept rolling in on her, drowning out any thoughts that might clarify the situation. She couldn't think anymore; it would be far better to rest a while, rebuild her strength and retreat to the peaceful quiet of sleep. Kait closed her eyes hoping the man in front of her would dissolve back into her subconscious.

"Are you all right?"

She barely registered Michael's question as she tried to settle into a quiet place deep inside. "Leave me alone."

"I can't do that. You've been injured and I need to ask you some questions."

"You're not real. Go away," Kait huffed. In her mind's eye she could see his facial expression: soft, alluring, passive. He was probably feeling sorry for her.

"Tell me your name and then I'll go away."

No, not sorry. Patronizing was a better word.

Growing angry with her disobedient dream Kait sat up slowly and stared at him again, projecting as much authority as she could muster. He was sitting on the bed right beside her, a veritable tower, but he leaned back ever so slightly to accommodate her.

"I need to sleep, and you're giving me a headache."

A fresh wave of pain assaulted her senses, lending further doubt to the dream theory. Kait lifted both hands to forcefully push Michael back, but after one tentative touch she pulled back. He was crowding her, asserting authority he had no right to possess and invading her space. For a figment of her imagination, he seemed very solid and real. She could smell his masculine scent, could almost feel the pulsating energy surrounding him.

She dropped her hands back in her lap. "This is a dream," Kait asserted weakly on the verge of tears.

Michael hesitated, then placed his hand gently on her leg and gave a slight squeeze. The heat emanating from it seemed to spread several inches in each direction and his touch sent every nerve in her body into overload. The last strands of resistance slipped away as she finally accepted the truth—*he's real!*

Those last moments of struggle in the frothing ocean came storming back to her with startling clarity. Her will to keep swimming had been shredded and this man had been her final glimmer of hope. The shadowy silhouette of a man standing in the surf, just before she'd crashed into him, flashed through her mind and suddenly she was certain that Michael had been the one to pull her from the hands of death.

At last, the dam broke and the floodgates released a torrent of emotions, wracking her body with violent shivers as tears streamed down her cheeks. "I don't know what happened! I don't know how I got here! I've lost—" Kait buried her face in her hands, trying to hide her break-down, but she couldn't stop the release if she built a hundred dams across the river of pain, fear, and confusion she'd been trying to hold back. "I've lost days!"

Michael wrapped his arms around her and pulled her into his lap, rocking her gently to sooth the turmoil. This time she went willingly—she didn't give a fig about anything else right now, she just needed a lifeline—wrapping her arms around him, she held on tight while the tears flowed free.

After several minutes, the sobs were replaced by hiccups. Kait felt completely drained, but slightly bolstered, like she might actually survive whatever insanity had taken over her life.

The rocking stopped and she realized she was sitting in Michael's lap as he reached to pull a blanket around her shoulders. She had soaked the front of his shirt with her tears—her face was probably swollen and red—but that wasn't the worst of it. Incredibly, she had wailed like a banshee, lowered her guard so completely and bared her soul in front of a total stranger!

Under normal circumstances she would be completely mortified at her colossal loss of self-control and display of weakness. In this instance, however, she wasn't sure she could really hold herself to the usual standard. Her life had gone so far beyond normal that she wasn't sure if normal still existed.

Give yourself a break. It's not every day you get kidnapped and nearly killed! Kait took a deep breath and resigned herself to the path before her as she slid off his lap, and wiped her eyes.

"I'm sorry," she whispered, lifting her face to look at him. She could only hold his gaze for a moment; her emotions were still rushing like meteors along already frazzled nerves. "I'm very...disoriented, and...confused."

"Yes, you must be exhausted," he added with a note of sympathy. "I'm sorry you've been through such an ordeal. I know you're in pain, but if you'll try to relax a little, I think you might feel some relief. I don't want to make things worse, but I would like to know who you are."

"Kait," she replied reticently. "Kaitlyn O'Donnell."

Hallelujah!

Michael offered her only a small smile, afraid to express the full measure of his gratitude at finally making some sort of progress. Now that he had her name he could begin an official search to find out more about his mysterious damsel in distress. He wanted to know what had happened to her and who might be after her, where she was from and how she'd gotten into this predicament in the first place.

He'd finally managed to crack her defenses—though only slightly—and would need to keep finding ways to earn her trust and cooperation until the walls were torn down completely. But first, he needed to check her wounds and assess the severity of her concussion while she was awake and cooperating.

One hurdle at a time.

"That's a pretty name. Do you mind if I have a look at your bandages, Kait?"

She hesitated only for a moment then held out her hands for inspection. Her response didn't demonstrate a new level of gratitude or acceptance—more like compliance—but it was a hell of a lot better than outright defiance. If he had any hope of winning her over, it seemed necessary to begin by rebuilding her self-confidence.

"You sure seem to know your way around a shovel, Kait. Are you a gardener?" Michael rubbed his head and unleashed a teasing smile, noting the tiny twinkle of pride that glittered in her bright blue eyes. He thought she almost smiled back, but instead she raised her walls again; she didn't trust him any farther than she could throw him. She was just playing along, doing whatever she thought necessary to ensure her own survival. Her crystal eyes conveyed a rebellious and independent nature; it would take nothing less than a miracle to win her over. "I didn't know gardening was a form of self-defense."

Kait relaxed into the pillows behind her and closed her eyes, shutting him out as he began removing the dirt-stained bandages from her hands.

Michael observed her while he worked, captivated by the long brown tresses flowing freely around her shoulders—the locks of a nature goddess, though thoroughly mussed. Her muscles were taut with veiled anxiety, ready to react at the first sign of trouble, and her face reflected a calm that was only a pretense.

Beads of perspiration dripped down her temples, the only remaining evidence that she had tried to escape. The lady was tough, stronger than she appeared. It was growing quickly evident that she didn't back-down easily from a problem, and didn't wilt at the idea of defending herself from danger—two things that had surprised him. Despite her injuries, she moved gracefully and fast—not the rough and tumble moves of a tomboy, or the dainty, fragile moves of a debutant, but the elegant poise and assurance of a cat.

Unconscious, she'd looked fragile and weak, like a helpless kitten. Her feminine exterior had fooled him at first, but he realized now, that it was absurd to compare her to something so simple or tame—she was far more complex and wild. Whoever she was at her core, kitten or full-blown wildcat, Michael knew that helping her would be anything but easy.

She's tough, but no match for a Storm.

EIGHT

Lillian Zamora—a 5-foot, 3-inch whirlwind with jet-black, corkscrew hair and a chip on her shoulder the size of Texas—stomped through the abnormally quiet police station and slammed a stack of manila files down on Holden "Hold" Bryson's desk. "Still sitting on your ass, I see! How the hell do you ever expect to find a lead on this den of thieves if you never hit the streets?"

Bryson held up a finger to shush her while he finished his call, then quickly grabbed a pen and jotted down several lines of indecipherable chicken scratch. When he hung up, he lifted the glamour-puss face that had melted many a female felon to her knees, then frowned and tugged at his chin. "Ever heard that little saying that you can catch more flies with honey than you can with a swatter, Zamora?"

Lillian snorted at his butchered phrase, and pushed the stack in front of him. "Detailed lists of everything taken from every house within a ten mile radius, from March 'til now; statements from each homeowner about the comings and goings of all yard-workers, meter-readers, delivery people, etc. for a month prior to each hit—as requested. Additional files about all gang activities and arrests during the same time period. Can I get you anything else, your highness?"

"Yeah, but we both know Hell will freeze over before you start acting like a lady. Your sweet little roommate on the other hand, didn't you say she works over there at Scott's Aquarium or something?"

Lilly bristled at his jibe but refrained from splitting his lip with her fist, distracted by the sudden change in topic. "Not the aquarium, the *research institute*...she's a marine biologist. But I understand how a big, dumb jock like you could get mixed up. Why do you ask?"

"Well, someone just called to report a dead body in the water down at the harbor. Said they weren't sure, but they think it's the SIMR security guard that went missing."

"Missing? What are you talking about, and why is this the first I'm hearing about it?" Lilly went on instant alert at the mention of Kait's place of employment, the hairs on her neck pricking to attention.

"Old guy named Barney was reported missing from his post at the marine research facility in Point Loma on Saturday. They had to call in a temp to guard the pier. Guard house was left unattended at least half the day. Several people used their badges to buzz through. Kelley and I checked it out and found no signs of foul play, plus the old guy's house was empty—no sign of forced entry and nothing obviously missing. Kelley is on his way to where the floater was found to check it out. We've been trying to track down everyone that buzzed themselves through."

Bryson rose from his desk, grabbed his jacket to conceal the black 1911 handgun holstered under his arm, and started heading for the door. "Guess I'll get off my 'royal ass' and go meet him."

Lilly grabbed his arm and stopped him. "Wait a minute! Kait's research ship comes and goes from that pier. She was probably down there on Saturday morning, and I haven't seen or heard from her since! Why in the name of everything holy didn't you tell me there was trouble?"

Bryson went back to his desk and pulled a file from his drawer. "What did you say your roommate's name is?"

Lilly snatched the file from his hands and quickly scanned the list of people who had accessed the pier and the times they had gone in and out. "Kaitlyn O'Donnell; she buzzed in at 0835 hours. It doesn't say when she buzzed out. Where's the rest of the list?"

"O'Donnell's your roommate? We've been trying to reach her for a couple days now. No answer at her office or her cell." Bryson's frown deepened as his usually good-humored attitude grew deadly serious. "Course we haven't been able to reach half the people on that list, and we don't know who else might have gone through the gates while the guard was still at his station; his log for the day is missing."

Lilly scanned the list of names again, her stomach churning with nerves. Things hadn't been going well with Kait's project; she'd been stressed to the max, running herself ragged trying to meet her deadline. Lilly had been feeling agitated for several days, unable to pinpoint the problem, until now. Kait wouldn't just take off for another stint on the water without checking in, yet she had done just that. She hadn't left a note or even restocked Sheba's food supply.

Something's wrong.

Lilly looked up from the file at Bryson's questioning stare. She set her mind and gave him her most menacing glare to avoid an argument. "I'm coming with you!"

NINE

Kait felt comfortable and relaxed the next time she awoke, still under the spell of the pain medication Michael had given her. The bandages on her hands had been replaced and the room was quiet and dark. She glanced around, expecting to find Michael hovering near, but her mysterious rescuer was gone. She was alone, and not at all sure that she wanted to remain that way.

The darkness of night shrouded the room with a heavy, ominous weight as she lie in bed trying to comfort herself and steady her nerves. She was alive and safe. She had escaped her captors, relatively unharmed, and would soon be on her way home. Michael was somewhere nearby, so she wasn't actually alone, but she'd never felt more alone in her life. He'd offered her rest and refuge, help getting through the disaster that had nearly torn her apart both literally and figuratively. He was a complete stranger and a totally unknown quantity, but for the first time, she actually considered letting him help. Given her circumstances, she wasn't sure she had any other choice.

Lying in the giant bed with all her fears and demons, Kait closed her eyes and began to push everything out of her mind. Meditation was a tried and true method of silencing her monsters, if only for a little while. Within seconds, the familiar void settled around her, the quiet rhythm of her own breathing the only sign of life marching onward. She took comfort in the void, settled into its nothingness like a cozy cocoon from which she would emerge stronger, more balanced, and somehow a little brighter than when she had gone in.

At least that's how it was supposed to work, and had in the past. This time was catastrophically different.

Taking on a life and a power all its own, this void began to seep through the darkness, spreading its tendrils far beyond the borders of her mind and body, beyond the edges of the giant bed. This void was contaminated by a new level of fear that yawned and stretched, engulfing the room and everything in it, like an oil slick shrouding a stretch of ocean in death. Paralyzed by its power, she watched it expand in her mind until it swallowed the mansion, the cliff and jungle around the mansion, all of Mexico. Heart racing with distress, Kait watched the swath of darkness mushroom and spread until it blanketed the darkened half of Earth, cloaked in its own nightly shadow. The void stopped, finally, at the edge of that darkness and pulsated, as if assessing its ability to invade the light.

Chills raced through her body as a long-suppressed childhood fear surfaced and took shape. In the blink of an eye, everyone in the world disappeared, leaving her utterly alone, the last person alive on the planet. The first time she'd felt this way, her father had come home from a work trip unexpectedly, argued with her mother, and her mother's friend Charles, then left home without a backward glance. She'd felt the warmth and comfort of his love leave her life that day, like a soul departs the body that once housed it. He'd returned only once, frowned at her hope-filled pleas to take her with him, then taken her brother Nick instead, and abandoned her to her fate. She'd never seen, nor heard from her father again, and when Nick had returned several months later, without their father, he had never been mentioned again.

Why her current circumstances would trigger those particular feelings again was a mystery, but Kait did her best to shake it off and reverse the process of shutting everything out. As she opened her senses again to the dark world around her, the floorboards began to creek, one-by-one, walls moaned, wind billowed, and somewhere in the distance birds screamed. The noises grew louder, came closer, filling her ears with a cacophony of chaos, until she thought she would lose her mind. She'd opened-up too much and couldn't shut it down again.

Opening her eyes, Kait found that the cover of night had transformed the world into a discomfiting, hostile imitation of the daylight realm. She'd never liked darkness—it was too easy to succumb to one's innate flaws during that nightly transition from wakeful avoidance to deep unconscious sleep—but she'd learned to cope. Now, recalling the chilling events that had nearly killed her and the frightening man dripping with gold chains and hatred who'd been responsible for those events, the darkness reduced her to a quaking child with much more tangible fears. If she survived this ordeal, she would never again dismiss Lilly's fervent warnings about the evil in the world. She had seen it face to face and would be forever haunted by it.

Turning her attention to the darkest corner of the room, a hazy glow of red and white horizontal stripes seemed to fade in and out of sight. Her imagination took over and Kait could almost see the outline of a tall, bulky form standing there watching her, rocking back-and-forth from heel to toe. *Red and white stripes*—the shadows conjured fresh images of the stinking man that had tried to rape her on the fishing boat. He'd been wearing a shirt with red and white stripes.

Is he standing there in the corner?

No, you're safe in Michael's villa. He couldn't possibly find you here.

You're losing it. Take deep breaths: in–out, in–out.

It wasn't working. Instead of calming her nerves she felt ready to hyperventilate again and was nearly overcome with the urge to run and hide.

What if he does find me?

Kait's pulse quickened and her mouth went dry. Michael could already be lying dead somewhere as one of her attackers slithered toward her, searching his home, eager to finish the job they had started. Kait bolted upright, ignoring the ensuing pain that stabbed at her temple. Creeping quietly out of bed, she headed toward the door, carefully avoiding the dark corner where she'd seen stripes. It was probably only a product of her concussion, but on the off chance that she was wrong, she didn't want to take a closer look. Let him kill her from behind, if that was her fate, but she couldn’t handle another face-to-face encounter right now.

At the doorway, the floorboards shifted and creaked underfoot, sending a wave of chills across her skin and up her spine. She steadied herself and opened the door anyway. The gossamer rays of moonlight streaming past the edges of the drapes disappeared completely beyond the doorway, into a yawning cavern of formless black space. She had no idea of her location within Michael’s home, or his location for that matter. She was on the second floor, but if there was a hallway or stairs in front of her she couldn’t see them. Unsure which direction to go, her eyes searched the darkness for any other glimmer of light.

Shaken by the violent images rocketing through her mind, Kait stepped even further away from reality. She needed to find Michael, fast, but she couldn't call out for help; her attackers would hear. They were definitely here in the house somewhere; she could feel them creeping closer. What if they had already caught her rescuer? He could be hurt, or dying.

Run! Get out while you still can, urged a semi-hysterical inner voice. But she couldn't just abandon the man who had saved her life. She needed to find him and warn him. Another creak sounded in the floorboards, too close for comfort, sending her heart into overdrive. She couldn't contain the scream that burst from her lungs. "Michael!"

Instantly, a door next to her whooshed open and Michael appeared in a flood of light. The wild look in his eyes said he was ready to slay even the greatest of demons—*her demons.*

"What’s wrong?" he asked, looking around anxiously for signs of trouble.

"I heard a noise! I...I was afraid those horrible men had killed you."

Michael hurried through the doorway into her room and turned on the light, checking everywhere for signs of an invader. Finding nothing, he came back into the hallway and checked the other rooms nearby, leaving every light aglow to show her that all was well. As the bright lights cleared both the shadows in her mind and the space around her, Kait fought for control of her frenzied thoughts and emotions. There was no danger here, only the wild imaginings of a woman on the edge. "I'm sorry…guess I'm a little paranoid at the moment."

"Don't be." He stopped in front of her. "There's nobody else here, just you and I, but it never hurts to make sure." He leaned closer, appraising her.

"Don't be what?" Kait asked, her brows crunching together in confusion.

"Don't be sorry. You have every right to be afraid after what you've been through."

Kait's thoughts chased each other round and round, her head pounding with the effort to regain control. "I need a clone, and my phothes. I mean a phone, and my clothes. I need to call home and let them know I'm okay. Not my clothes, I mean I need to call my family..."

No, can't call Nick—don't know where he is at the moment. Can't call mom either—she's on a cruise in the Riviera with her latest boy toy. That was probably for the best. It was common knowledge within their tiny, highly dysfunctional family unit that Margaret O'Donnell had a knack for making even the best days lose their luster. Kait didn't really want to find out what her mother could do to the worst days.

"My boss…," *no, that's no good either.* "Um, Lilly! Yes, I should call and tell Lilly I'm coming home soon, so she won't worry."

Unconscious of her actions, Kait lifted her hands to massage her temples. She felt wholly incapable of controlling her brain at the moment. Her imagination was running rampant, words were popping out of her mouth unfiltered, lacking the capacity to make any sense. Michael did not look pleased.

"Your boss is Lilly?"

"No, my roommate is Lilly. My boss is William."

Was it her imagination or was he moving closer, stalking her like a predator? His eyes flashed with concern and Kait realized she wasn't making sense again. She had to stop blabbering like an idiot and start over fresh.

She spoke slowly this time, enunciating every word as clearly as she could. "What I mean to say is that I feel much better. Thank you for saving my life, but I really should be going. I have some terribly important business to attend."

Kait tugged the bottom of her shirt, wishing it would extend past her thighs. She felt incredibly vulnerable standing there in nothing but *his* shirt, her body injured and weak, her memories riddled with unexplained gaps. More than anything, she wished she was safe at home with Lilly and Sheba, getting ready for another day of work at the job she loved. Her simple, comfortable life had been obliterated in one fateful instant, and she was very much afraid it would never be simple or comfortable again.

Michael stared at Kaitlyn, assessing the situation. If her concussion was getting worse he would need to get her to a hospital right away; she was rambling, her words confused, but he didn't miss her meaning. She wanted to go home. Her pupils were evenly dilated—that was a good sign—but she looked much too fragile and pale to be out of bed. He knew almost nothing about her situation yet: where she lived, what had happened to her, who might be after her. He couldn't just let her leave. She was in need of assistance and as far as he was concerned, he was the only one capable of providing it.

He placed his hands gently on her shoulders and started to guide her back to bed. "You aren't going anywhere in your condition."

"Stop!" Kait tried to pull away from him. "What are you doing? I said I want a telephone. I want to go home! You can't keep me here."

Michael released her immediately but remained close, in case she passed out or decided to bolt again. Patiently, he reminded her, just in case she had forgotten, "Kaitlyn, I'm trying to help you. You've suffered a concussion and you aren't thinking clearly yet. I know you're frightened, but you are in no condition to care for yourself right now."

"Nonsense, I am perfectly capable of caring for myself. I just need a taxi or a bus," Kait paused, straining to remember something important. "Oh yeah, I guess if I'm truly in Mexico, then what I really need is an airplane, but I don't suppose you'd have one of those handy."

Please say no. I can't bear to fly in a plane again for at least ten years!

Kait began massaging her temples, trying to alleviate the pounding in her head. "I need to get to the police."

Alarm sounded in Michael's thoughts. Many of the local police were just as corrupt as the criminals they hunted; he'd have no way to protect her if she went to the police for assistance. To compound matters, Kaitlyn's behavior was far too erratic and unpredictable to leave her to her own devices. She'd just end up in more trouble than she was in already.

"I don't think you want to do that just yet. Why don't we sit down and talk. I promise to do whatever I can to help you, but you need to rest right now. Trust me; you *don't* want to go to the police."

"Trust you? For all I know you're one of the bastards who kidnapped and shot me! You could be a drug lord, an axe murderer, or maybe you work for those lying SOBs that started this whole mess!"

Her verbal eruption ended abruptly as she stared at him, warily, as if waiting for him to pounce. The onslaught of information set his mind spinning and a storm of rage began to churn in his gut. "You were kidnapped?"

She hesitated a moment, "Yes."

Progress at last. Maybe her concussion was improving, instead of getting worse. She was retaining post-trauma memories and regaining some pre-trauma memories.

"By whom and why?" he prodded, hoping she wouldn't clam-up again. Already she looked troubled. She couldn't seem to choose between chattering about nonsense, or choking-up and saying nothing at all.

When she finally spoke, she was so quiet that Michael could hardly hear her. "I don't know."

"You don't know who, or you don't know why?"

"Take your pick."

"You must remember *something*—have some idea who did this."

Kaitlyn's face burned with a deep flush as her confusion turned to embarrassment, then to anger.

"I have no idea who they were; they were complete strangers. I'd never seen either one of them before. Besides that, they attacked me from behind, and it's none of your business anyhow. Where are my clothes?"

None of my business? Stubborn pride reared its ugly head and Michael's determination solidified into something harder than any rock or mineral.

"They were ruined—torn to shreds on the rocks—but you won't need them. You aren't in any condition to leave. Doctor's orders." That said, he swept her into his arms again and carried her back to bed.

Setting her down gently on top of the covers, Michael blocked her escape, planting his fists firmly in the sheets on each side of her waist, pinning her between him and the bed.

Kaitlyn held her head high in defiance. "You have no right to keep me here. I will not be bullied by you or any other man. Let me up.

Michael stared resolutely into her cool blue eyes—a sea of churning ice. "Why did the men who kidnapped you, shoot you?"

Kaitlyn's eyes focused in more sharply on him as her ire magnified. "How should I know? I was too busy trying to get away from them!"

Incredible! After everything Kaitlyn had been through, she wouldn't be cowed! Despite her wounds, fear, and confusion, she was ready to fight—*probably 'til her dying breath*—no matter the odds against her, no matter the foe.

Time was of the essence and Michael was getting tired of stumbling around in the dark, waiting for her to trust him. He needed *all* the facts, and he needed them now! If she was still in danger, he was the only one here to keep her from further harm. "What did they want from you? Did they talk to you?"

Kaitlyn pushed at him weakly, her injured hands too delicate to exert much force, but he wasn't about to budge. Her icy gaze flashed with vulnerability and an unexpected plea; she needed to feel safe, to reclaim the power that had been taken from her so violently. From the moment he'd fished her out of the ocean, he'd been doing his damnedest to deliver on both of those basic needs, but she'd given very little indication that he was succeeding.

She sat there, motionless, waiting for him to back down, but instinct told him to wait her out. Another moment passed and her silent plea transformed into a softer, wondering expression. *Not fear. Not anger. Was it hope?* Maybe he was finally getting through to her. Her unspoken question encouraged him to push a little harder and break through that tough façade. He needed to know much more than she was willing to share, needed her to know that he wasn't her foe—that he wouldn't lift a finger against her. She could trust him with her life, if only she would open herself up to assistance. "You *can* trust me, Kaitlyn. You're not alone."

Her eyes grew watery with tears and her lips began to quiver as she tried to hold back. Her wall was about to crack again—not what he was aiming for—he needed her strong, but compliant. Unsure if he should keep pushing or leave her in peace, he decided to give her space to bolster herself. He didn't want to frighten her any more than he already had.

As he started to rise from the bed, she stopped him with a touch of her hand. "Don't leave—" she breathed, lowering her eyes.

Michael touched her chin and lifted her gaze to meet his. "Don't ever be ashamed of needing help, Kaitlyn O'Donnell. You're the strongest, bravest woman I've ever met."

Her tears fell then in earnest, and when she wrapped her arms around him and pressed her face into the crook of his neck, he couldn't have been more surprised. He wrapped his arms around her too and stroked her back softly as she shook with the effort of trying to contain all the emotions that threatened to break free.

After several minutes, absolute silence filled the room. Michael sat there holding her, lending whatever comfort and strength he could against her troubles. Time slipped to a standstill with her clinging to him like a life raft. He could have been holding her for a moment or an eternity—it didn't really matter, because he'd tasted her pain, shared her grief. Suddenly, his world tilted, as if entering another dimension. To his great surprise, and almost immediate shame, he imagined himself, just for a moment, falling effortlessly into her endless blue depths, and settling there.

He was in dangerous territory, inexplicably drawn to Kaitlyn by some invisible force he could neither explain nor understand. He'd only just met her, knew nothing about her, and already he wanted to prove himself to her, to show her that he could protect and care for her better than anyone else. He had no idea what she was involved in, yet he was ready to go toe-to-toe with whatever cretin had harmed her, and stop whoever dared to try again. And he didn't care what he might lose in the process.

"He's finally gone 'round the bend," his dad would say if he was here watching the scene unfold. His wild, irrepressible brother, Ian, on the other hand, would probably say, *"Welcome back to the land of the living."*

He should follow Anton's advice and send her to a hospital—*that's what any intelligent, self-respecting recluse would do*—but if anyone had ever needed to be rescued, it was Kaitlyn O'Donnell. Guilty, or innocent, the waves of distress and pain rolling off her told him the simple truth; she was in more trouble than she could handle.

Michael tamped down on the inexplicable urge to let himself fall, and sought refuge in more practical matters. No matter what demons or fires she stirred inside him, he couldn't let her leave; she was better off under *his* care, safe from the men who'd nearly killed her. He couldn't abandon her to make his own path easier. She needed a port in the storm, and the fates had literally dropped her in his lap.

Kaitlyn finally released him and swiped at her tear-streaked face. When she looked at him again, her eyes conveyed a new sense of calm he hadn't seen in her before, but deciphering the secrets hidden within her glassy blue depths was impossible. Raw emotion flashed then disappeared quickly behind a wall of self-protective armor.

Michael stood and moved to the foot of the bed, giving her time to steady her nerves—he'd pushed her hard enough for the moment—and was only half surprised that she didn't bolt for the door again. Instead she sat quietly assessing him, like a chess player, unreadable.

"Are you all right, Kaitlyn?"

Kait didn't know what to think of the perplexing, salient man standing in the dusky glow of the fire in the hearth. She should have put a stop to his brazen intrusion when he'd set her on the bed and pushed his way into her space—should have demanded that he take her to the police and then sent him away—but she'd desperately needed to feel safe. Michael's steadying warmth and soothing hands had melted the icy pangs of fear and doubt that had frozen her to the bone in the black ocean and gripped her ever since. She wasn't alone in her turmoil anymore; she was alive because he had pulled her from the ocean before it could claim her.

During their brief connection, Kait's fears and anguish had miraculously disappeared, vaporized under his reassuring touch. Time had ceased for those few luxurious moments while she allowed herself to drift in Michael's gentle currents, but then she'd realized she was in danger of drowning again, on a very different level. He was breaking down her defenses, as surely as the ceaseless waves of the ocean smoothed jagged cliffs and rocks into fine tapestries and sculptures.

She could no longer ignore the indomitable will of the man staring her down. Her hero was virile and strong, a force to be reckoned with when provoked, but Kait had learned time and again not to count on anyone but herself. Now was certainly no exception—she'd never felt more weak, frightened, or alone in her life—but that didn't mean she could just give up and let someone else take over. She had to be strong, fight her way through whatever trouble came next, and maintain her independence.

Why is he so determined to help me?

Her pessimistic side remained reluctant to place her full trust in Michael, her mother's bitter words still ringing in her ears as clearly as the day her father had walked away. *"Men always leave, Kaitlyn. Best you learn that lesson now, and protect your heart from their selfish nature."*

She had indeed learned that lesson, but the softness of Michael's touch, the soothing in his voice, and his infinite patience were a direct contradiction to her experience, a balm to her deeply frayed nerves. Twice in the past 24-hours, she'd succumbed to the overwhelming urge to seek shelter in the safety of this man's arms and the security of his protection—an urge she'd never felt before or believed possible. While lost in his embrace she hadn't had to think about shadows in corners, murderers hunting her in the dark, or jungles filled with predators.

Now, her skin all but simmered under his silent scrutiny, begging him to hold her close again and set her world right. But he was still a stranger, and she was still afraid. *Good criminy, I am definitely losing my mind!* She had no business seeking refuge in a stranger's arms, especially since she knew absolutely nothing about him. He could be spinning a web of lies, lulling her into a false sense of security.

To what end?

He could be in league with her kidnappers! Even as she feared the worst, her instincts told her it wasn't true. From the moment Michael had found her, he'd done nothing but help her, even after she'd attacked him. Yet, Lilly was forever recounting horrible stories, cases about children and women who'd been deceived by a smooth-talking man only to find their lives forever ruined. Almost all of them eventually said the same thing, *"He seemed so nice at first."* It was a mistake Kait hoped never to make, but she had precious few facts with which to reconstruct the gaps in her memory, and knew even less about her supposed benefactor. Could she really trust her own instincts when they had failed her so completely in the first place?

Michael was still watching her, waiting for an answer. If she was honest or cooperative he would stay and ask her more questions—frightening questions that she didn't know the answers to, and didn't know if she *should* share even if she did know the answers. What she needed right now, more than anything else, was time and space to regain her equilibrium. Unsure of any other way to achieve it, Kait finally responded to Michael's concerned question with a challenge. "Is this your usual MO? Save a woman's life then take over like you own her?"

Kait had tried for aloof—she'd wanted to make him mad enough to leave her alone, but not so angry that he would retaliate. If she'd succeeded, she couldn't tell. His face was a mask of indifference. The man who moments earlier had melted her resistance with a heart-felt hug, might just as well have ice flowing through his veins. He didn't smile, didn't grimace, and didn't move; she wasn't even sure he was breathing. He just stared at her silently, mercilessly. She had no idea what he was thinking or what to do next.

At last, Michael rose and headed for the door. In a hardened voice he replied, "My mistake. I thought you needed reassurance." With that he left the room.

TEN

The *Triton* reached its northernmost rendezvous coordinates just before dusk on Tuesday. A heavy bank of fog crept across the water while the two-man crew performed their usual tasks and waited for the small boat that would inevitably come. They sat twenty-four nautical miles off Point Saint George—the last hospitable stretch of land along the rugged "Lost Coast" of northern California, and the last place from which a boat could be launched safely into unpredictable, often hostile waters. Pablo's instructions had them loitering precociously in the home territory of the Coast Guard patrol boat, USCGC *Dorado*.

"Switch to running lights only, Frankie. We don't want to draw any unwanted attention." Dr. Russell finished inspecting the three-meter, satellite-monitored data buoy and stepped back aboard the *Triton*.

Frankie nodded and ran to the helm to cut the restricted-maneuverability warning lights they used when holding a position in the water. His eyes did a quick search though the darkening haze for any sign of another boat; the ocean was unusually quiet tonight. He returned quickly, his nerves clanging. "They should be here anytime, Doc."

"Keep a sharp eye out," Russell warned as he packed up his tool kit. "I'll check the radar. Take the lantern to the bow and wait for my signal."

Both men had worked themselves to the point of exhaustion conducting all the requisite SIMR activities while they travelled 700 nautical miles up the coast, zigzagging in and out of US territorial waters. It was the same route they'd been running for years in the *Neptune II*—they should've been able to do it blindfolded—but the *Triton* was too large for a two-man crew. Everything took longer, was more difficult, and came with greater risk to the men and the ship. Thankfully the *Triton* was also a lot faster in the water; they'd made all the usual stops to collect water samples, inspect weather and tsunami buoys, and record other scientific observations along their route, then hauled-ass between stops to stay on schedule.

Dr. Russell updated the ship's log with precise details about their regular work activities, carefully covering the tracks of their upcoming rendezvous and three previous meetings at Point Conception, Point Sur, and Point Arena. He'd quickly abandoned the lie about a miscommunication with a visiting research crew, because ultimately there was no manufacturable evidence to prove they existed. Instead, he'd been forced to contact the ship's usual captain, Captain Hallor, and insist on commandeering the vessel temporarily for his own needs, due to the failure of the *Neptune II's* engine.

Hallor had protested vehemently, threatening numerous repercussions, but Russell had calmly reminded him of several onerous misdeeds he'd witnessed over the years, which would come to light if he failed to cooperate. Having already taken command of the ship, Russell had worried for days that the U.S. Coast Guard would show up to arrest him for hijacking the *Triton;* he'd had no other options and there'd been no turning back once it had been accomplished. Days later, nothing had happened; Hallor had capitulated, and despite a nearly catastrophic start, this trip was running much smoother than their inaugural run the previous month.

The lies were coming too easily; he was adapting to this nefarious lifestyle much too quickly and couldn't help but wonder how many times he would have to risk everything to get out from under Pablo's thumb.

The handheld radio squawked from its holster on Russell's belt and Frankie's voice came through. "I can't see anything in this soup, Doc."

Russell adjusted the signal until a small blip appeared on the starboard side of the radar screen. He watched it for a moment to make sure it wasn't clutter then determined its distance and bearing. "There's a vessel about eight miles out, headed our direction. Wait until they're close enough to identify. If it's them, flash green to guide them in, then go below and prep the cargo for transfer. Don't bring anything topside until you hear the all clear."

"You got it, Doc."

Glancing down to determine their speed, a second much larger blip appeared on the opposite side of the radar screen. A moment later the ship's radio sounded from the console—they were being hailed by the USCGC *Dorado*.

"Holy hell!" *So much for Hallor's cooperation!* Russell gripped the handheld radio. "Frankie! Flash red, starboard, three-and-three! Coasties approaching port side, eleven miles out!" Praying that their unique emergency code would warn off the small boat in time, he picked up the receiver and responded to the Coast Guard's hail.

"This is S-I-M-R *Triton*. Captain Russell here, over."

"Captain Russell of the S-I-M-R *Neptune II*? Over."

"Affirmative." Keeping his voice much calmer than he felt, Russell told them just enough to allay any suspicions. "We lost our engine on the *Neptune II* and had to make the run this month with an alternate vessel. I alerted the harbor master of the change, over."

During a brief pause, Russell watched the smaller blip on the starboard side of the radar screen veer north and increase speed away from their location. Frankie materialized by his side with the lantern in hand and a feral, frightened look in his eyes. "What do we do, Doc?"

"Keep it together. We have every right to be here, and that was a recreational boater who had no business on the ocean in this fog. Start the engine and get us moving, slow and easy, due north."

Frankie nodded and set to work as the Coast Guard came back on the line. "The harbor master concurs with your report. Your running lights indicate that you are underway, but your vessel hasn't moved. Is your boat under command, Captain Russell?"

"Affirmative. We're under command and getting under way. There was a slight delay with the buoy check, but we're moving on."

A familiar and friendly voice came on the line.

"Captain Callahan, here. How's the Big Blue treatin' ya this trip, ya old sea dog?"

Russell released a deep breath and motioned for Frankie to pick up the pace. If Hallor had sent them, Callahan would be all business, bark, and bite, despite their years of camaraderie. Callahan was waxing nostalgic, probably nipping the flask, but they weren't in the clear just yet—if his old buddy asked to come aboard for a visit, he would need a reasonable excuse to refuse.

"You know me and the Blue, Callahan. We're like a pair of lusty lovers—can't get enough of each other."

Laughter came through the line. "You in some kind of hurry, Russell? Thought we might share a bit o' the hair o' the dog—swap some stories."

"We've got a tight schedule to keep. Gotta make the last buoy inspection tonight then head out to open water—the usual drill. The *Triton* is due back in port on Sunday for her regular crew."

The *Dorado* changed course, veering south as she picked up speed in the opposite direction of the other boat. "Understood. I'll catch you next time, Russell—just got a distress call about a possible collision twenty miles south."

"Go get 'em, Callahan! Over and out."

Frankie sagged in his seat, deflated by the release of too much tension. "Doc, you got more luck than a cat with nine lives! I swear you handle this shit a hellofalot better 'n me!"

Russell smacked Frankie on the back. "We'll get through this, kid. Just find me that damned boat!"

ELEVEN

Morning came too early for Michael. He'd been awake most of the night watching over Kaitlyn, remembering all too well the last time he'd left her alone. Fortunately, she had fallen asleep quickly after their test of wills. She'd lashed out at him for pushing her too hard, and he'd backed down, but the battle was far from over.

He still had no real answers about his mystery woman, other than her name and a very vague account of having been abducted. She'd been genuinely shocked and distressed to find out she was in Mexico and had lost time, but she hadn't volunteered anything else about her situation. He knew precious little about Kaitlyn, and more importantly, he had no idea whether trouble was hot on her heels. He had to assume the worst.

The sound of the front door closing, followed by rapid footsteps traveling toward the kitchen, jolted him from his thoughts. He jumped up and slid silently out of the room without waking Kaitlyn, then ran downstairs to intercept Consuela.

Consuela Conchita Alejandra Maria Castañeda had been Michael's faithful housekeeper, cook, and confidant for several years. She was a good-natured woman of fifty-something years, with dark, slightly aging skin, and long, gray-and-brown hair which she always kept braided and pinned into a bun.

From the first moment she'd met Michael, she'd treated him like a son. She'd happily kept his world in order, content in her old-fashioned belief that it was women's duty to take care of their men folk. More recently, she'd done her best to keep him from falling too far into the abyss, despite her own woes. Her husband had been killed years ago, her eldest son had long since moved on to create his own life, and her only daughter had died.

How does she keep going? The only answer he could ever settle upon, was Consuela's continued devotion to her younger son, Andres, and to himself.

Michael entered the kitchen behind Consuela and offered her the respectful endearment that made her smile every time she came to check on him, though today he was even more out of sorts than usual, "Good morning, *mi viejita.*"

"My God!" she gasped. "What happened to your head, *mi hijo*? Sit down and let me look at it!"

"It's nothing, really, Consuela. I'm fine, but I have a favor to ask of you. Please sit with me in the den."

As they walked to the den and sat side by side, Michael could see the concern on her weathered face. She knew something was dreadfully wrong; there was no fooling this wily woman who'd seen more than her fair share of problems.

"You look so troubled, mi hijo. Whatever it is can't be that bad. Tell me," she said patiently.

"We have a situation here at the villa and I don't want you to get involved. I don't think you should come back for a while."

"Michael, it can't be that bad. You know you can tell me anything."

Against his better judgment, Michael told her the quick version of his extraordinary tale about the injured woman upstairs. "I think it would be best if you visit your sister in Venezuela. I'll buy a pair of round-trip tickets for you and Andres."

"Oh, Michael, *no es necesario.* I can stay here and help her."

"No, Consuela, it's not safe here for any of us. I'm going to take her away. The villa is too close to where I found her. If the people who hurt her decide to come back, they won't have to search very hard. There aren't many homes in the area; it's only a matter of time before they look here. I don't want you to stay at your home either. It would be too easy for them to connect you to Villa del Sol. Do you understand?"

"Si, Michael. If you insist then I will take Andres and go to Venezuela, but first I want to meet our guest." No longer able to contain her excitement, Consuela sprang out of her seat and quickly headed upstairs to take a peek at Kaitlyn.

Michael stopped her on the stairs. "Are you upset?" he asked carefully.

"Oh no! Not at all, mi hijo. I want to meet your new woman, make her feel comfortable and welcome. I know how *rígido* you can appear sometimes, and it's been ages since we had a pretty *señorita* around to liven up the place!"

"Consuela, she isn't *my* woman. I'm just helping her through this dilemma."

"Of course Michael, whatever you say."

Michael was relieved that Consuela was taking everything so well, though deep down he'd known she would accept Kaitlyn. She was a loyal woman, especially to the dearly departed, and Maria had been her pride and joy.

"I should probably go in first and announce you. She isn't ready to trust anyone and I don't want to frighten her." He would wait to see how Kaitlyn responded before deciding if he could risk leaving the two of them here together while he went to town for supplies.

Michael entered the room and found Kaitlyn asleep in the middle of rumpled sheets. When he turned to leave, she called out to him.

"Michael? Is that you?"

"Yes," he answered approaching the side of her bed. "Do you mind if I have a look at your stitches? I need to check for signs of infection."

"Go ahead," she said still half asleep. "Do you think I could borrow some clothes? Something a little more *comfortable,* like sweats?"

Sweats? Michael could just imagine her wearing a set of his old Stanford sweats. She'd be swamped in them from head to toe, but maybe that was the effect she was looking for. Removing the bandages from her hands, he tried to ease her worries. "These are healing very quickly. I think we'll let them get some air for a while and maybe give them a good soak in some warm water."

Next he removed the bandage around her head and took a close look at the small row of stitches just below her hairline. "Looks pretty good—no sign of infection."

He placed his hand gently across her forehead to check for fever, ignoring the fact that his own temperature spiked just from being in such close proximity. Instantly reprimanding himself, he turned away from her and headed to his room through the adjoining door.

"I think I've got sweats in here somewhere," he hollered back. Returning in less than a minute, he set a small pile of cardinal-red clothes at the foot of the bed. "These should keep you cozy until I find something more suitable."

Kaitlyn lifted her head off the pillow in alarm. "You're not leaving me..."

"Don't worry, you won't be alone. A very dear friend of mine has agreed to stay with you—just for a little while. As soon as I'm back, she'll be on her way again."

Kaitlyn's eyes grew wide and she opened her mouth to protest, but Michael cut her off. "Ah-ah-ah, Consuela! Come in here, please." He looked back at Kaitlyn with a silent plea that she trust him. "Everything will be fine, you'll see."

Consuela walked quietly into the room and went straight to Kaitlyn's side without hesitation. Smiling brightly, she extended her greatest charms. "Good morning, señorita. How are you feeling?" She paused only a moment to give Kaitlyn a chance to respond, then rushed on trying to comfort her. "I'm so glad to have you here with us. If there is anything you need, please don't hesitate to ask."

Michael touched Kaitlyn's hand in a feather-light caress, trying to quell the mixed emotions brewing in her eyes. She didn't move, but goose bumps broke out across her skin. She wasn't ready to accept anyone else poking at her defenses, but she wasn't ready to bolt either. She was finally beginning to trust him despite herself.

This was exactly the opportunity he needed—a chance to do some investigating without leaving her alone. She hadn't given him much to go on, but he was determined to find out who was after her and why. The fact that she had escaped her captors by diving off of a fishing boat near his home wasn't his only clue, but he needed a lot more information in order to form a solid plan. He was certain she was holding back important facts, either because she couldn't remember, or because she wasn't ready. In either case, time was the crucial factor.

"I'll leave the two of you to get acquainted, and I promise I won't be gone long."

Heading for the door, he turned back to address Consuela. "Is there anything we need for the house?"

"Oh, yes. I was hoping you would go to the market today," she answered, pulling a list of groceries and household cleaners from her apron pocket. She gave it to him, pecked him on the cheek and patted his shoulder, "Everything will be just fine. You'll see, mi hijo. Don't brood so much."

"Just let her rest while I am gone, Consuela. Perhaps tempt her with some of your delicious food."

He watched Kaitlyn turn away from them, pretending to be unaffected by the change in circumstances. She was far too unpredictable and frightened to be left alone for very long, and she might easily outmatch Consuela if she decided to flee. To both of them he gently warned, "Stay inside, away from the windows, and keep the doors locked."

Michael made his escape and sped down the long narrow driveway in his green jaguar, eager to find whatever information he could in town and get back to the house before there was any trouble.

Kait wasn't at all comfortable with the sudden turn of events as she watched Consuela disappear into the bathroom looking for something.

"You look like you need to cool off," Consuela said, as she emerged with a wash basin and hand towel. "Let me help you."

"No, that's not necessary," Kait squawked, trying to pull the covers higher.

Consuela pulled the blankets back all the way to Kait's knees. "My God, what are you wearing?" she asked, shocked to find Kait wearing one of Michael's shirts and nothing else.

Kait blushed and reached to retrieve the covers. "I...Michael said my clothes were ruined. He set some other clothes at the foot of the bed for me."

Consuela inspected the garments only for a moment and sighed. "These will not do. We can't have a pretty señorita like you hiding in these baggy things! I know just the place to find some suitable clothes."

Consuela smiled and left the room, calling back to Kait, "*Un momento, mi bonita.* I'll be right back."

Kait had no idea where the woman was going, or what tricks she might have up her sleeve, but she took advantage of her moment alone. "I think I'll just take a shower instead," she mumbled to herself as she eyed the old-fashioned wash basin with disdain. While she still had the chance, Kait rolled out of bed, grabbed the red sweats and stumbled into the bathroom, locking the door behind her. Her legs felt like lead stilts, stiff and sore from so much bed rest.

Safe inside the small room, Kait turned to take stock of her resources. Instead of the typical modern shower she'd hoped for, an old-fashioned claw-footed bathtub sat in one corner, a soft flowing curtain pulled to one side.

Well, that's not so bad. A hot bath might be just what she needed to relieve her sore muscles, and Michael had said she should soak her hands. She hadn't really intended to take a shower or bath just yet, but she had no intention of being bathed by a complete stranger.

Taking great care not to hurt her hands, Kait gingerly turned the faucet to the right temperature and began filling the bathtub.

Consuela returned with a brown bag cradled in her hands and squealed at the empty room. "Aye, bonita!" She tried to open the bathroom door. "Let me in! You'll wear yourself out."

"I'm fine, Consuela. I really don't need help. I can bathe and dress myself, but thank you for your kindness."

"Oh no, señorita, I will take care of everything. You must lie back in bed and rest!" Consuela rapped on the door. "Please, bonita. Michael said you must rest. He'll be terribly upset."

"Don't you worry, Consuela, I'll handle Michael when he returns. I'm already feeling much better than I did yesterday and I think a bath is exactly what I need right now."

Silence reigned on the other side of the bathroom door, but Kait was sure the woman was still standing there in a quandary, trying to figure out what to do about the situation. When the tub was full, Kait stepped in and melted into the hot water, unable to contain the sigh of relief as the heat immediately began to work its way into her tense muscles. "I promise you I'm okay. This feels wonderful, and I will be sure to let you know when I'm finished."

Consuela conceded reluctantly. "I'll stay close by—in case you need help."

"That won't be necessary. Thank you."

After another long pause, a deflated voice answered, "All right, I'll just go make breakfast then. I've brought down a wonderful dress from the attic for you. I made it for my daughter many years ago."

Kait listened for any further movement on the other side of the door. After several minutes of silence she felt relieved and a little guilty. The woman had sounded so despondent, trying to figure out what to do about her errant charge, and genuinely worried about Kait's health. It was silly to have to hide from her in this bathroom, but for now it seemed to be the only option.

Michael returned several hours later, laden with supplies for the house and packages for Kait. He'd also purchased other essential commodities like gasoline, food and water for the journey, and extra bullets in case they needed protection. Kait had already been shot once and he had no intention of getting caught without plenty of ammunition.

His investigation had been a wash: no missing Americans, male or female, no new fishing boats in the harbor, and no banditos snooping around asking questions. In fact, Chamela had been unusually quiet with only a few tourists milling around at the *mercado* haggling over their purchases. The only news he'd garnered from the trip, was that a fully-fledged hurricane was spiraling up the coast, a rarity in the western Pacific compared to the frequent smaller storms of the rainy season. Hurricane Heidi was purportedly the last and biggest hurrah of the season, and was expected to pack quite a punch.

At least getting out of the house had cleared his head and given him time to form a plan. He would take Kaitlyn to Puerto Vallarta and leave her with Anton while he continue his investigation. The marina there was large enough to dock a boat the size of the one he'd seen, and it was a much more happening place: more tourists, more police, more drug runners and criminals, and hopefully more information. From there, he would take Kaitlyn back to the U.S., where he could safely hand her over to authorities for protection if she was still in danger. No need to call Ian, no need to get sucked back into something he couldn't abide.

Everything seemed calm and quiet when he deposited some bags on the table in the kitchen, but he could see that Consuela was badly out of sorts. She didn't say a word to him when he handed her the cleaning supplies, only nodded and sighed. Things had obviously not gone well in his absence.

"What happened?" he asked, preparing for the worst.

"Aye, Michael. She wouldn't stay in bed like you told me, and she wouldn't let me bathe her. She locked herself in the bathroom. I tried to get her to come out, but she wouldn't listen. I made her some breakfast and found her some clothes, but she wouldn't get back in bed after her bath. She insisted on resting in the study.

"It's all right, Consuela. Kaitlyn has been through a lot. I'm sure it was nothing personal. She didn't listen to me at first, either." He leaned over and gave her a comforting hug. "Thank you for watching over her. You've been a big help. And by the way, you've taken wonderful care of the clinic. I had no idea you'd kept it intact."

Consuela's distraught face broke into a small smile. "Si, Michael. I knew you would want it again." She winked at him and gave him a quick hug. "*Bueno.* I'm going home now to get Andres. You take good care of that señorita and be very careful. I have a bad feeling in my leg."

"A taxi will pick you up at eight in the morning, and your tickets will be waiting at the airport. Here's some spending money. I don't know how long I'll be gone." Michael walked her out and gave her a long hug goodbye. If it was the last time he saw her, he wanted her to know he cared.

After Consuela drove away, Michael headed upstairs to find Kaitlyn. Her room was empty, but it didn't faze him this time. She was probably in the study where Consuela had left her, resting. He moved quietly in case she was asleep.

Far across the room, wide glass-paneled doors hung open, sheer ivory drapes flapping in the breeze. The study was empty too and Michael's heart jolted with apprehension as he abandoned stealth mode and raced toward the balcony to find her. Stopping short, he was only slightly relieved to see her leaning against the railing, lost in thought. She hadn't tried to escape again, but the west-facing balcony was exposed to the ocean, vulnerable. Anyone searching the coastline below would see her immediately. They'd know she was alive.

Michael quickly scanned the horizon for anyone or anything that shouldn't be there. When he was satisfied that nobody was stalking her, he turned his attention back to Kaitlyn and watched her for a moment—*a siren of the sea.* He was afraid she would vanish like mist if he moved or even blinked.

She looked radiant and relaxed gazing out over the water, even swathed in his baggy red sweats. Sunlight glistened in her hair, highlighting strands of gold and bronze. Her face glowed with new confidence and what he hoped was the desire to open up, to believe that he wanted only to rescue her from her tormentors. She was still bruised and fragile, but she was recovering quickly.

The view of the azure-colored ocean and crystalline surf was magnificent. Kait gazed at the water imagining colorful fish and sea life beckoning from the shallows. It was calming to her nerves at first, but the rocks and waves quickly awakened disquieting flashes of memory. The *Spanish Maiden* materialized from the recesses of her mind, docked directly behind the *Triton* on the end of the SIMR pier.

Who would so boldly invade a private wharf and abduct a biologist? It's not like SIMR was a top-secret research facility—*we're just a bunch of fish huggers and science geeks!* Whoever the culprit, they hadn't been the least bit worried about being caught.

Kait's heart fluttered with remembered fear as she tried to recall the hazy details. Hostile faces flashed through her mind one-by-one. She was sure the men at the SIMR pier had not been the same ones on the fishing boat; that meant she'd been attacked by at least four different men. She couldn't recall much of what they'd said—they'd spoken mostly Spanish, and she only knew enough to recognize a word here or there.

What were they doing there?

The men on the yacht had fit the perfect stereotype of Mexican mafia—especially the one with gold chains draped around his neck—but they could just as easily have been arms dealers, actors, or human traffickers. Without a doubt, they were *not* scientists there to steal her vessel out from under her.

Like the rush of a waterfall, memories came flooding back: Buck's suspicious death, the fake population count, the trouble she'd had orchestrating a real one, and the rapidly approaching deadline. She remembered losing the *Triton*, and all the extra work she would have to do to salvage the project. She remembered week after week spending every waking hour coordinating the efforts of four different teams across seven different time zones to make sure there was enough data being collected, and that it would meet the exacting standards of the IWC's scientific panel. She hadn't gotten more than four hours of quality sleep per night for at least six weeks!

Of all the ways she had imagined her anonymous opponents could interfere with her work, sending Latino thugs to kidnap and kill her would never have crossed her mind—it seemed way too risky and over the top—but since they had done exactly that, the onus was now on her to step-up even more, and do something about it. Nobody ever said that crime made sense—crimes of passion, crimes based on lack, even crimes for the sake of revenge she could understand on some basic human level—but environmental crimes that impacted everyone on the planet made the least sense of all in her mind.

Why go to such lengths to bring back hunting on an endangered species when there were so many alternative options available?

Despite the total lack of evidence, Kait was now even more convinced that Buck had been murdered for revealing his employer's devious plan. If she was right, then his death and her abduction proved just how far the whaling industry was willing to go to put blues back on the menu. Eliminating a pesky biologist and anyone else that dared to stand in their way was apparently nothing to these bastards! She had to warn her crew before anyone else disappeared, and alert the proper authorities as soon as possible.

Lilly's words echoed in her mind from the night she had shared her suspicions about Buck's death: *"You have no evidence, Kait. Without evidence they could sue you for slander."* She'd wanted to expose their villainy to everyone, make them pay for extinguishing such a bright light; she'd been on the verge of telling anyone who would listen.

Kait couldn't let them get away with murder, and now kidnapping, but she still had no evidence to back her claims and there were too many unanswered questions cluttering her mind. Why would the whaling conspirators take the risk of hiring thugs to kidnap her when they could have simply staged another "accident" and killed her?

Maybe they didn't.

Maybe I got in the way of their real task.

If so, then what was their real task? And how in the world was she going to find another vessel and get the population count back on track when she was stranded in Mexico? Kait didn't have answers for any of her questions and felt tendrils of stress seep back into her bones despite the serene view before her.

Fixing her eyes on a gull swooping overhead, a warm sensation spread through her. She turned abruptly and bumped into a solid wall of man—*Michael.* Her hands rose automatically to catch herself, but he caught and held her gently in his arms.

Waves of heat and musk rolled off him, assaulting her senses. The rigid muscles of his chest flexed under her fingertips, and for a moment she felt almost safe, no longer afraid of him. It would be so easy to dump all her problems in Michael's willing lap and let him take care of everything. She could huddle in his comforting embrace and forget what was happening—let go of everything she had to do—but that wasn't her style. When Kait had a problem, she grappled with it head-on, fought her own battles and won her own victories.

This time you're on the losing end.

What could she do? She was only one person, yet her project had the potential to impact countless others: people, marine ecosystems in the Atlantic and Pacific, an entire species, and the numerous other species involved in its food web. If she didn't get home and get back to business, the losses would be inconceivable and catastrophic—not to mention that she personally stood to lose everything that mattered in her life.

"What's wrong, Kaitlyn?"

His deep voice cut straight through her resolve. She looked up at him silently, knowing she couldn't hide the torment and worry she was feeling.

"Whatever trouble you're in, you can tell me. I promise I'll do my best to help you."

Lowering her eyes, she resisted the urge to lean against him. There were probably a hundred things she should be doing right now to set things right, but she had no idea where to begin. All she wanted to do was run home and hide like a coward, but she couldn't even manage that; she had no identification, no money or clothes, and no transportation.

Michael would probably give her anything she asked for within reason. *Hasn't he already done enough?* Then again, he might try to stop her.

Even if she had the proper identification, she could easily be detained at the border—Americans were often delayed until greedy palms were greased, sometimes for several days—it was the main reason she'd always avoided Tijuana.

When friends had wanted to party at the nightclubs, she'd stayed home. When Buck had made one of his numerous trips across the border to buy medication for his dad at a discount, she'd waited by the phone. Just about anything could happen to people south of the border and Kait had heard one too many horror stories from Lilly to ever take the chance. Now, here she was in the worst place she could imagine, already down by three flipping days, and likely to lose even more! She had to do something drastic, and fast, but she didn't know what.

Ask him to take you home.

Kait hated the thought of drawing Michael further into her nightmare, but she couldn't find an acceptable alternative. Without a passport, she was sure to be stopped at the border and she had nothing to offer as a bribe. If corruption truly ran rampant through the ranks of the Mexican police, she might end up in a dilapidated jail cell on trumped up charges for weeks or even months. Her life would take on a whole new level of misery.

She had to be practical—what if he knew a simple way to get her across the border without being waylaid?

If he offered her a way home, she would have to accept it, but she wouldn't ask for more than that. She was grateful for his help, even glad he was here with her right now, but with such treacherous games afoot she couldn't risk his life to save her own. "I'm all right," she answered finally, "just tired and a bit achy."

"We should go inside."

Kait took a steadying breath and followed him into the house. He looked relieved and disappointed at the same time—cooperation wasn't enough. He wanted much more from her than that, but she couldn't bring herself to give it yet and felt a slight pang of guilt.

Why is it so hard to trust him?

Her only answer came in the form of another question.

Why is he so keen to get involved?

She was a total stranger, dangerous and burdensome, yet he refused to leave her to her own defenses. His patience seemed unwavering while he waited for her to accept his help, but he had no idea just how much trouble she was in. If their roles were reversed, she'd probably be running the other way, letting the authorities do their job and help him. Then again, if their roles were reversed, she wouldn't feel so threatened and out of her element. She might be a lot more willing to stick her neck out for a stranger if she felt safe in her own territory.

Down on the sandy beach, where Michael had pulled Kait out of the water, a small motor boat sat beached on the shore. A single set of footprints followed the steep path into the jungle surrounding the seaside villa. Stealthy feet crept quietly through the underbrush, abandoning the path just twenty-five yards away from the perimeter wall. The intruder knew the chance of finding his target inside was slim to none, but he crept closer to observe the occupants of the villa, just in case. If she was still alive, he would find her, or pay heavy consequences.

TWELVE

Safely inside, away from the danger and disquiet of the outside world, Michael led Kaitlyn to the bag of clothes he'd left on the forest green sofa. "I'm glad you're feeling a little better."

"Much better, thank you."

Kaitlyn veered away from him and averted her eyes, trying once again to conceal any sign of vulnerability or apprehension, but her movements and posture betrayed her. She was still weak, still wary of him and her surroundings. He couldn't really fault her for it—she needed time to stabilize.

Anyone would after such trauma.

In a perfect world he would give her all the time she needed, chip away slowly at her defenses and protect her until she trusted him enough to open up and tell him everything. Leaving Kaitlyn alone with Consuela before she'd been ready to accept such an intrusion had been risky but necessary. Thus far, she'd been unable or unwilling to give him the information he needed to ensure her safety. The longer he waited for answers, the more uncertain the situation would become; a little distance from her, and time to clear his head had been a good thing. At least now he had a plan.

For all the good it'll do!

In his absence she'd bolstered her walls and gained distance from him as well. The trip had been more costly than expected, and the result more fruitless. At least nothing terrible had happened—*thank heaven for small favors.*

As if she'd read his mind, Kaitlyn spoke with reluctance. "I'm sorry to have caused you so much trouble, and I'm sorry for upsetting your friend. You've both been very kind, but…I needed some time…alone."

Her head dropped a notch and Michael felt compelled to ease her discomfort. "She'll be fine," he assured her, "just a slightly bruised ego. She had only the best of intentions. Don't worry, I sent her home with a bonus and a paid vacation."

Kaitlyn looked up with wide-eyed amazement, unsure if he was joking or chastising her. When their eyes met, she quickly disguised her surprise with indifference.

"Actually," he continued, "she's quite used to dealing with stubborn personalities," he said, mocking himself to lighten the mood. "She's had to deal with me on a regular basis for several years. You may not know it yet, but I can be quite an ogre when my hackles are up. I doubt your evasion had any lasting effects."

Michael's humor didn't make a dent in Kaitlyn's tough façade, so he changed the subject. "Why don't you take a look in the bag? I wasn't sure what you'd want so I got a little of everything."

How long since I bought clothes for a woman?

When Maria was alive he hadn't needed to; she'd taken charge of all shopping, gift-buying, decorating and such, except when the gift was for her. The memory of his last gift to Maria pierced his heart—one of countless, painfully exquisite memories he'd tucked away to be savored sometime far in the future, when they wouldn't cut him so sharply. This was far too soon to remember their last Valentine's Day together, her standing before him in the pink silk negligée with black lace trim he'd ordered from Paris, or the incredible evening that had followed, but that didn't stop it from rushing forward and taking center stage in his mind.

He'd meant to give her the bags and leave, to give her some privacy while exploring the contents. Before he could do so, Kait reached into the bag. *Too late*—he watched her hands move unerringly to the tissue-wrapped bundle of cotton bras and panties he'd had to buy to replace the ones he'd destroyed when he'd cut them off her body to assess her wounds. Her cheeks flushed when she realized what she was holding.

Irrational anger bubbled up—anger at himself for thinking about anyone other than Maria, anger at Kait for invading his life, anger at the whole untenable situation. He slammed the heart-rending Valentine memory back down into the icy crags of his soul.

Backing away, he explained apologetically, "I'm didn't mean to invade your privacy. I knew you'd need the basics to get through the next few days, and I wasn't sure when another opportunity would arise. I'll give you some time and space to make sure everything's all right. The other bag contains a few less *personal* essentials: toothbrush, hair-brush, things to hold your hair, shampoo—the whole bit. I'll be back in a while with a suitcase and some lunch."

"Are we going somewhere?" she asked in alarm.

"Well," he snapped, unable to hide his vexation, "based on the total lack of information I've been granted so far, I think that would be the wisest option.

Michael headed for the door, his mind in a state of increasing chaos. Frustration, worry, and anticipation all tugged at him, each vying for his undivided attention. He paused two feet from the door and turned back, surprised to find Kaitlyn trailing right behind him.

"Don't go out on the balcony again," he said sternly. "We wouldn't want anyone to come looking for trouble."

"Thank you," she responded sincerely, despite his reproach. "You've done so much. I hope I can find a way to repay you someday."

Before his eyes, her vibrant, grateful gaze dissolved into something much more complex and subtle, and she quickly retreated to the couch. She was an intriguing puzzle—one he felt inexplicably compelled to piece together and understand—but he needed to focus on preparations in order to get ahead of the situation.

After Michael had gone, Kait settled back on the couch to devise a plan and rebuild her defenses for the next encounter. She was determined to find a way home without bringing more trouble to his door. This man who had once frightened her with his very existence, was now capsizing her reserve—tempting her to accept his generosity.

Would it really be so awful to let him help?

Yes! You could get him killed for his kindness!

Not acceptable.

Okay, then where to begin?

She'd noticed a television in the corner, practically hidden among all the books and magazines. Perhaps she'd get lucky and find a news channel. Maybe the folks back home were already searching for her, flooding the airwaves with news of her untimely disappearance and offering rewards for any information that would lead to her safe return.

Kait turned on the TV and was instantly bombarded by a loud, obnoxious commercial. She turned the volume down then searched for other channels. To her dismay there appeared to be only one clear channel, and of course it was in Spanish. Hadn't the man ever heard of cable? She waited for the commercials to end, and a cheesy American soap opera came on, dubbed over in Spanish. She could try to translate the show to distract herself, but her Spanish was pretty rusty, and the show really wasn't worth the effort.

Abandoning the television and any hope for news, she walked across the room to a large picture window wishing she could venture outside and feel the breeze. Now more than ever she needed a diversion to take her mind off the seemingly insurmountable odds stacking up in front of her. Even if the police were offering rewards for information about her, there would be no takers. There hadn't been any witnesses, no clues left behind to point them south to Mexico—*assuming that anyone even knows I'm missing.*

Kait sorted through the possibilities in her mind. If she could find Nick, he could probably use his news connections to help her get home in one piece. He was a world-wise, street-smart freelance writer who'd spent years travelling to all the most dangerous places around the globe doing exposés and human interest pieces. If he knew she was in trouble, he'd be there for her in an instant—had been for as long as she could remember, since they hadn't had much in the way of reliable parenting—but he was on assignment somewhere covering his next big story. These days they were lucky to talk to each other once every couple of months. He'd be clueless about her disappearance, and she didn't know how to reach him without her cell phone.

Mom definitely won't notice that I'm missing—they rarely spoke to each other, and Margaret was usually too busy denying that she was even a mother to notice when Kait needed help. She was pretty useless in an emergency anyway. Her idea of a life-or-death challenge was figuring out how to wring every last drop of attention and money she could out of a wealthy man. When that failed, she could always track down her beloved son in whichever glamorous part of the world he was working, and guilt him into taking care of her until she found her next target.

Kait massaged her temples as her stress increased. She didn't think there were two more opposite women in the world than she and her mother.

The most likely person to know Kait was missing, was her best friend and roommate, Lilly. She was a sure bet in an emergency, but she was used to Kait being away for days and weeks at a time, especially now with everything that was going on at work. Lilly may not have realized that things had gone drastically wrong since their last conversation, but once Kait managed to get home, Lilly would know exactly what to do. She was always her ace in the hole.

William should know she was missing by now, but he had probably celebrated when she'd given up the *Triton* without a fight. If that was the case, then she was doomed. Thank gods she'd called Randy to let him know something was up. Surely when he and the crew arrived at the pier they'd discovered her disappearance and contacted the authorities. With any luck, they were searching for her at this very moment.

What if Randy hasn't put it together yet?

Something was seriously out of whack in her life if she could be kidnapped and killed without anyone taking notice. Where was her guardian angel when she needed one?

A name sounded in the back of her mind, barely a whisper. *Michael is with you.* A chill raced up her spine and she turned to see who was there. The room was empty—completely still except for the pounding of her heart. As she looked around, a ghostly void settled over her. A hollow place deep inside yawned and stretched toward the surface. Standing on an invisible precipice, she held it in and battened it down, wavering in the midst of a daunting challenge she would never have chosen.

Trust was not something she could give lightly—especially not after the hard lessons of her youth—yet here she was considering it. There would be a certain sense of peace in yielding to this man. Perhaps it was her recent proximity to death, or Michael's calming influence, but Kait wanted to reach for that peace. She sank onto the couch and closed her eyes, one-by-one releasing all her pent up worries and fears as she slipped into an almost hypnotic trance.

She could *let go and trust him; he'd earned that much.*

Kait sat there and just breathed for a while, trying to get comfortable with the idea. Several minutes passed without her feeling the need to launch herself into a dark corner and hide, but an annoying buzz invaded her ears. Opening her eyes and sitting upright, she looked to see what was wrong with the television. A news flash appeared to be breaking in on the soap. She watched curiously, straining to pick out even one word of Spanish that she might remember from her classes so long ago. They were speaking too fast.

The first part of the broadcast showed a torrential hurricane pounding a seaside village. Small ramshackle houses were being leveled by wind and surf, and a few terrified people were being washed into the sea while others tried in vain to throw them a line. Kait sat riveted to the scene, hoping it was some place far away as she recalled her own harrowing battle with the ocean. It made her stomach queasy, but her heartbeat remained steady and calm.

Trust.

Another breaking story flashed onto the screen. Police photos displayed two men, but she couldn't understand what was being said about them. She rose to her feet, about to turn away when another photo caught her eye. She turned back to the television, stricken with horror. "Oh my Godss! That's him!" she breathed, choking on her fright. The next images sent her mind reeling. Her legs collapsed beneath her as she watched the camera pan across a gruesome scene. Lost in the moment, she didn't even feel herself falling, or register the fact that Michael had caught her.

"Kaitlyn, Kait...what's wrong?" Michael forced her to look away from the bloody massacre on television, turning her toward him to divert her attention.

She fought her way back toward the screen to see the rest of the broadcast and whispered in a strange, almost shattered voice, "What are they saying?"

Within moments the news flash ended and the station returned to its regular programming. Kaitlyn turned back to Michael with wide, glassy eyes, teetering on the edge of hysteria. "What did they say?"

Michael sat her down on the sofa and knelt on one knee in front of her to keep her steady. He could tell by her reaction that these men were somehow involved in what had happened to her, but he needed to know how. "Three men were...executed at sea. Their boat was found drifting on the open ocean by local fishermen who towed the boat to shore. A fourth man washed up on the beach last night near Manzanillo." He didn't tell her that was only fifty miles south.

Kaitlyn's body trembled in his grasp and Michael worried that she would overtax her nervous system with the rush of adrenaline. Her pulse had skyrocketed; her blood pressure was probably going through the roof. He had to calm her down. "Kaitlyn, look at me. Forget what you just saw on TV and focus on me. You've got to relax or you're going to burn out."

"How can I?" she cried. "I just saw the man who tried to...he almost—"

"Shh, it's okay. You don't have to say it." Michael did his best to soothe her.

"I almost didn't recognize him, but I'm sure...I know it was him! He looked so different in that mug shot, but I'll never forget his face." Tears began to well in her eyes until at last they broke free and raced down her cheeks in a deluge of sobs. She buried her face in her hands, "I don't remember the others, but I know he wasn't alone."

"Kaitlyn, he can't hurt you anymore."

"Is he...was he one of the ones...executed?"

"Yes, he's dead."

"All that blood—" Kaitlyn sniffed, trying to stop sobbing. "Who would do such a thing?"

"Don't worry about that right now. All you need to do is get better. Tomorrow we'll take a trip together to a place that's safe, where no one can find you, but I need you to work with me as a team. Do you think you can do that?"

"No." She sniffed, her head popping up in defiance. "I have to get home and go to the police."

That was not what he wanted to hear, but Michael kept his cool and tried to keep her talking. "Where is your home, Kaitlyn?"

She looked at him, the tears still streaming down her flushed face. "San Diego."

"Really?" Michael sighed in deep relief. Lady Luck had just smiled upon both of them, or perhaps it was fate. "That's exactly where I want to take you."

Kaitlyn gave him a doubtful look. "What else did they say?" she demanded, now that she was regaining her equilibrium. "Who were they? What were they doing on that boat?"

Michael was reluctant to answer her questions. He didn't know if the answers would help her or frighten her even more. Less than 48-hours ago Kaitlyn had been brutally attacked. Now the culprit was dead, along with three other dubious souls. The broadcaster had announced that two of the dead men were former members of a Colombian drug cartel which had recently merged with an up-and-coming Mexican cartel operated by none other than Pablo "El Diablo" Castañeda.

That small tidbit of information had hit him like a ton of bricks, but he'd managed to contain his instinctive reaction. Thank Heaven he'd sent Consuela away. She didn't need to hear that her oldest son, one of the most ornery, cruel-hearted men he'd ever had the displeasure of knowing, was now the leader of a major drug cartel.

Was Pablo involved in Kaitlyn's kidnapping?

Michael realized that her possible connection to Pablo didn't bode well for her situation. He knew first-hand how easily a good person could get sucked into the dangerous world of drug dealers and dictators, but he couldn't imagine that she had willingly chosen that particular path. Her sheer terror and numerous wounds were ample evidence to the contrary, but he'd been wrong about people before.

If she had somehow gotten tangled in Pablo's snare, Michael would do everything in his power to free her. For now, it seemed that justice had prevailed. One or more of Kaitlyn's attackers had been treated to a dose of their own medicine and would never again unleash their nefarious nature on another soul. As comforting as that knowledge was, Michael couldn't help but ponder the ramifications of another encounter with Pablo.

THIRTEEN

Kaitlyn sat quiet as a statue and just as still, barely even breathing. Tears had given way to silent shock, and Michael tried to maintain a gentle tone despite his growing sense of urgency. "Kaitlyn, I need you to tell me whatever you know. Did you recognize any of the other men in the pictures? Were there others involved that they didn't show on the television?"

She processed his question, shocked by the answer that came. "There was another man. I didn't see him. He could have been one of the men in the pictures and I wouldn't know. But the men on the yacht were very different from the men on the second boat."

"A yacht; are you sure? Why don't you start from the beginning? Try to remember the sequence of events and any names or faces you can think of. We need to figure out why you were kidnapped in the first place."

Kaitlyn thought back to that morning at the pier, wracked her brain searching for helpful details, for where to begin and what to tell him. "I don't know of a single reason why anyone would want to kidnap me. I'm not rich or famous. I'm just a biologist at SIMR. I spend weeks at a time out on the ocean conducting research. The rest of my time is spent recording data, running statistics on a computer, or conducting tests in the lab. It's all very benign. I go down to the pier on a regular basis and it's a private, protected area—research vessels and employees only."

Michael was immediately intrigued to learn something about Kaitlyn's personal life. He would never have guessed that she was a biologist—she didn't fit the stereotype in his head—but he could tell she was intelligent, fit, and well educated. To make a career out of studying animals in the ocean, he decided, she had to be inordinately brave and extremely independent.

"Is that where you encountered the yacht? At this private pier?"

"Yes." Kaitlyn continued with her story, hoping it would help her to organize everything in her own mind. When she left out key information it was only an attempt to preserve his health and safety. Once she got home to San Diego, she would send him on his way and hope she hadn't put him in too much jeopardy by accepting his help.

"I've been working on a very important project and the whole thing is at risk right now because someone usurped my research vessel. When I went to the *Triton*, I saw the yacht and...I b-boarded it looking for the owner. The next thing I knew, I tripped over something and...ended up here."

"What did you trip over?"

Pain skittered across her face and he knew she didn't want to remember.

"A body...a man," she answered in a haunted tone, "but I didn't see his face. They must have killed him just before I—"

"Wait, they killed someone? Who? Did you see it happen?"

"No...he didn't move when I...I tried to run, but—"

"Do you remember any names, any other faces?" Michael cut her off, hoping to avoid another breakdown. He needed to keep her talking.

"I'd remember the man with the gold chains, but I'm not sure about the other one. He was a big guy with muscles. I didn't get a very good look at his face."

A shiver raced up Kaitlyn's spine and a faint look of accusation crossed her face. "That's all I remember. I don't know why I'm still alive when so many others are dead, but I want to put this nightmare to an end and get back to my life. If you know something that will help me...I've got to get home. Nobody even knows where I am. I need to tell the police, and I've got to get an accurate count of the blue whales and make population projections by the end of November!"

"Wait a minute. Are you saying you're more concerned about your research project than you are about the fact that you were almost killed?"

"No, it's just that...well, I have no idea how to deal with everything that has happened. I can't let that divert me from what's really important. I'm not talking about one little, insignificant individual here, Michael. The survival of an entire species could depend on *my* crew getting the evidence we need to refute some totally bogus data and the people behind it."

Michael couldn't believe what he was hearing. Either she'd gone temporarily insane from the stress, or she was totally naïve. Either way, she was losing her grasp on reality. Here she was in imminent danger from a notorious drug lord—it had to be Pablo on the yacht wearing the gold chains—and all she could think about was her damned research!

"Kaitlyn, the men that were butchered on that boat last night were drug runners. They're probably dead because they let you escape, and if their leader finds out you're alive, he'll send more thugs to finish the job. He is one hell of a nasty bastard. What I need to know is why a Mexican drug lord would be interested in you, and why his yacht was docked at your research facility."

"That can't be right. You're making some huge assumptions. Why would the whaling industry hire drug smugglers to wreck my research?"

Michael positioned himself squarely in front of her like a roadblock, desperate to make her understand. "They wouldn't. The men who attacked you weren't after your project. They couldn't care less about a bunch of whales."

"Well, they weren't after me!" she exclaimed in self-defense. "I don't know anything about drug smuggling!"

Michael softened his tone, "I know it's frightening, but we can't ignore the possibility that *you* were the target. You can't just waltz back into your life and pick up where you left off—not until we know what's really going on." He took her hands in his. "Try to think objectively. Is there anyone who would want to hurt you? Did someone close to you get involved with the wrong people or maybe try their luck at a new side business? There's no way your run-in with the yacht was a coincidence. Whatever the case, we have to assume that you pose a greater risk to them now than before because you've seen them. They'll stop at nothing to eliminate that risk, Kaitlyn."

Kait knew he was only trying to help, but damn if he wasn't scaring the wits out of her in the process. If his assumptions were correct, then her problems had tipped the scales so far off balance that she didn't stand a chance on her own. She couldn't think of anyone who would want to hurt her, except someone trying to scuttle her research and help the whalers win over the commission.

As for someone at SIMR being in league with drug smugglers, the idea was preposterous—*though it would be an ingenious cover.* Research vessels were always getting clearance to enter territorial waters, the exclusive economic zones adjacent to coastal countries. They often danced back and forth across the invisible borders between jurisdictions and the lawless high seas for weeks at a time with little to no supervision. Occasionally they'd encounter a Coast Guard cutter on patrol, deep-sea fishermen, and massive cargo ships, but for the most part the ocean was a vast expanse of wild, open territory. Ships in international waters were governed by the laws of their own country, or by universal jurisdiction in cases of certain criminal acts, but there was precious little enforcement per square mile.

People could get away with murder or anything else that sparked their interest.

Before long, Kait found herself cataloging the people at work, trying to eliminate suspects. Most of her coworkers seemed squeaky clean. They wouldn't disturb the sanctity of their workplace with murder, and they wouldn't jeopardize their careers and livelihoods to smuggle drugs up the coast. They were scientists and academics—a law abiding crowd if ever there was one. Some were rebels and most were adventurers, but she couldn't think of a single person that would be so malicious.

How can I be sure?

How does one go about making such a judgment?

Would it be someone with a lower education and income? Someone who looked a little rough around the edges? Or maybe it would be someone smooth as silk that no one would ever suspect. Kait didn't think there was a single person on the planet without some character flaw or social indictment against them. The rich were often more corrupt than the poor, the educated more vicious than the uneducated, and the beautiful more sinister than the average Joe.

She could rely on instinct, that little voice that says, *"Stay away from that guy, he's a user,"* or *"Head for the hills, here comes the energy vampire."* Kait liked the people she worked with, got along well with just about everyone, but there were nearly 300 employees all together, plus the Board, and maybe fifty volunteers to consider. That didn't even include the endless stream of external research crews that came and went throughout the year. She was really only familiar with a small fraction of the potential suspects, so without getting to know everyone, instinct would get her nowhere.

Logic and scientific observation might send the hunt in the right direction, but she would have to be much cleverer than she'd been so far. Of course, that meant she would need to get back as soon as possible and begin an investigation, but how would she observe potential suspects without being seen herself? The minute someone recognized her, the game would be over and she would become a target again. Not to mention that she still had to get the project back on track.

Clearly this was not a problem she could solve on her own. She would have to involve the police. Maybe they could send someone in undercover to infiltrate the smuggling ring, but that would take time. Time was not something Kait had in her possession. By the time the police ever figured out who was behind her abduction, her research would be down the toilet, her job gone the way of the dodo, and her life such as it was at the moment, a pile of rubble requiring complete renovation.

Getting a little more creative, Kait considered the possibility of hiring a private detective to help her roust any budding criminals from the tightly woven network at SIMR.

With a little bit of Irish luck—*make that a lot*—she might get the information she needed by enlisting help from a few close friends like William and Randy. They would certainly be willing to help, but then they too would be in jeopardy. She couldn't place her friends in danger to save her own neck.

Just when Kait found herself back at square one, alone and unequipped to solve her rapidly mounting problems, Michael interrupted her thoughts.

"Do you understand what I'm trying to tell you?"

He looked genuinely concerned for her, but somehow much surer of himself, and her chances for a positive outcome than she felt at the moment. "It's all becoming just a little too clear for my peace of mind," she sighed. "I'd much rather rescue my project. At least I'd have some idea where to begin."

Kait's mind wandered for a moment, weaving back and forth through time before settling once again on her fateful morning reconnaissance. "Oh my gods!"

"What?" Michael asked hesitantly, as if waiting for her to drop another bombshell.

"I called Barney to ask for help. I heard his cell phone ring and thought..." Kait rubbed her eyes as she tried to remember what she had seen when she fell. "What if that was Barney? What if they killed him?" Tears began to pool in her eyes again despite her best attempts not to cry.

Michael sat down next to her on the sofa and held both of her hands in his. "Don't jump to conclusions. You have no way of knowing it was him or if he's even dead. He might have been knocked out like you were, or...if he was on the yacht, then he might be the one conspiring against you. Maybe he was simply paid off. Why don't you tell me exactly how things happened?"

Kaitlyn's face transformed from worry to indignation. "Barney wouldn't conspire against me, and he wouldn't let himself be bought off!"

"How can you be sure? How well do you know him?"

"He's my friend, and a retired military policeman! I...I saved his life not so long ago."

Michael prayed for the strength and patience to listen to the rest of her story without breaking something. He hated to make her relive the frightening memories, but he needed more clues to figure out what was really going on.

Kaitlyn closed her eyes and concentrated. "I remember thinking that I'd better check things out on the *Triton* first. I didn't find anything out of place, and I was worried about Barney so I boarded the yacht."

As Michael listened to her trek back through the events that led to her abduction, his anger continued to build. She'd been completely careless with her own safety, just like Maria, and had almost paid for her lapse in judgment with her life. The more he heard, the more inclined he felt to ring her beautiful, perfect neck, but he held his temper in check. If she had gone for help instead of taking matters into her own hands, she might have avoided the whole frightening experience.

And I never would have met her.

Focusing on her words, instead of his anger, he realized her voice had taken on a haunted, almost misty tone. "I knew the moment I looked in his eyes. The man with gold chains was the harbinger of my death." Her eyes met Michael's then, conveying without words the fear she'd felt at that moment. "I really don't know why I'm still alive."

That was the last straw. He couldn't stand to watch her relive the fear for another moment. She'd been incredibly brave, tremendously naïve, and unbelievably lucky. She hadn't had a clue she was in such danger, and she'd taken no precautions to protect herself. It was pure providence that she had made it off that fishing boat alive and washed up on his beach at just the right moment. If it had been even a few minutes later, he might have been too late.

Infuriated, Michael wondered for the first time if there was a man in Kaitlyn's life, someone who should have been watching out for her, protecting her from the evils of the world. Maria had been innocent and trusting too, and despite Michael's best attempts to protect her, her naivety had gotten her killed. He couldn't forgive himself for his failure, and he damn sure wouldn't forgive anyone that had failed Kaitlyn so badly.

Michael hugged her tightly against him, whispering in her ear. "It's all right. Don't think about it anymore; just rest." He wished he could have been there for her, done something to prevent her personal nightmare, but all he could do now was offer comfort and some measure of safety while she picked up the pieces of her life.

Kaitlyn accepted his embrace for a few peaceful moments, but before long she looked up into his eyes with renewed determination. "Did the newscaster say anything else about those men?"

Michael wasn't sure how much to tell her, but based on her story he was pretty certain Pablo was the man she'd called the harbinger of her death. The less Kaitlyn knew about Pablo, the better she would sleep. He was the ring leader—they'd said as much on the news—and only someone as crazy as Pablo would think that he could murder two people at a renowned research facility in the States and get away with it.

Of course there was a small chance that Pablo had nothing to do with Kaitlyn's abduction, but it was a long shot. Blatant disregard for the law was Pablo's strong suit and docking at a private wharf while he conducted his illegal business was just his style. "Those men were from a local cartel with many hidden connections, and we're sitting smack in the middle of their territory." He watched the muscles in her body contract with tension. "We're sitting ducks out here in the middle of nowhere. We'll have to leave first thing in the morning."

"I think the man with gold chains was in charge."

"What makes you think that?"

"Instinct I guess. There was something different about him, something much more sinister, more…calculating than the others."

Yep, that was Pablo—diabolical to the core—the Devil incarnate as his nickname suggested. How such a man could have been related to Consuela was beyond comprehension.

Michael quietly absorbed all that he had learned. Kaitlyn wasn't in league with drug dealers, but she was definitely in over her head. And though she was trying to be tough and stay calm about her predicament, she was exhausted and emotionally drained. She was still holding back, resisting the urge to lean on a friendly shoulder and let down her guard, but at least she was finally talking.

Kaitlyn was a smart and independent woman, of that he had no doubt. She was used to being in control of her own life and her world. While some women might have been brutally murdered or drowned in the ocean, Kaitlyn had taken risks and fought for her survival. Now that she was safe, she was struggling with the role of the wounded female, slowed by her injuries and agitated by her feelings of helplessness.

Even after all she'd revealed, he knew there was more; he didn't need to hear the words to know she'd been terrorized on both of the boats—it was written clearly in her expressive face and every cut and bruise on her body. Her survival instincts had kept her alive and Michael would do whatever it took to keep her that way.

Unfortunately, Kaitlyn was still operating under the mistaken notion that she had to handle everything on her own. Despite his continuing efforts, she was already withdrawing again, gearing up to tell him that she didn't need or want his help. Her stubborn independence was sure to drive him crazy in the coming days, but there was no way he would leave her to her own defenses. Whether Kaitlyn new it or not, she had gained a very tenacious ally.

"We need to come up with a plan," Michael suggested, trying to get things rolling. "I don't think we should go to the Mexican police. They will only give us trouble. I know a place in San Diego where we can lay low for a while, but we have to get you out of Mexico undetected. We'll have to assume these guys are watching the airports and buses on the off chance that you survived. The fact that you don't have a passport makes it even more difficult. We don't have many options."

"Then how do I get out?"

Michael didn't have a definite answer for her, but he had a couple of ideas tumbling around in his head, and a lot of questions. "Do you trust me?"

"Yes," she answered cautiously, "but, I don't want you to get involved. You might get hurt."

There it was, just as he'd predicted. "It's too late for that kind of nonsense, Kaitlyn. In case you haven't noticed, I've been involved since the moment I found you."

Michael fought to curb his frustration. "I trust you, and you trust me. That's a good start, but we still have no idea who else can be trusted. It's obvious that you are out of your depth, and I do not intend to let you traipse off on your own and get killed."

Kaitlyn huffed in indignation. "I may have stumbled into deep water, but I assure you I can handle myself!"

"Anybody could be involved in this, including the authorities. I won't let you step back into the line of fire alone and blind to the possibilities. If you think I'm just going to send you home to California and hope that the police do their part to protect you, you'd better think again. I'm in this till the final count."

Michael leaned closer, drawn like a magnet toward Kaitlyn. He wanted her trust more than he'd wanted anything in a very long time. He needed to make her see just how much danger she was in, so she would stay with him and cooperate, but he was loath to frighten her any more than he already had. He wanted to pull her close and comfort her until she gave in to reason, but that was dangerous territory too. Instead, his hand came to rest on her knee and slid unconsciously toward her thigh, applying gentle pressure against the soft warmth of her body.

Her breathing grew rapid and shallow; her eyes dilated as she held perfectly still like a deer in the headlights of an oncoming car. The air between them vibrated with intensity and Michael suddenly realized how tempted he was to steal a kiss from those perfect pink lips.

Unfathomable, and totally inappropriate!

After all that he'd been through with Maria, romance was the last thing he would ever pursue, and kissing Kaitlyn when she was still so frightened and unsure of him, was a sure-fire way to make her run the other way.

Gathering his self-control, Michael rose to his feet and headed for the door. "I'll bring you a suitcase. Get some rest and pack your things. We'll just have to drive to California."

FOURTEEN

Kait sat in a stupor long after her intense moment with Michael, wondering what in the world had happened. His words and actions had been visceral and powerful, a demand that she lower her protective shields and allow him complete access to her life. With more than words, he'd conveyed that his was more than a simple desire to assist a stranger in need; he was committed to rescuing her from perils too numerous to name, and wanted nothing in return, except her trust and cooperation.

For one brief, heart-pounding moment, she'd seriously thought he would either shake her or kiss her senseless in order to get his way, but the greater shock to her system had been her total desire to capitulate in either case.

What about Randy?

Her conscience reminded her that just two weeks ago, during their previous shore leave, she and Randy had gone for a run together along the boardwalk. Feeling playful and relaxed for the first time in months, she'd snagged his ever-present baseball cap from his head and searched it, teasing him about hiding something. He'd chased and caught her with much greater ease than she'd thought possible—*the man moved like a stealth jet*—and when she'd tried to withhold the cap, he'd wrapped his long arms around her and deftly snatched it back.

With the cap settled back on his head, he'd bent down and reprimanded her, *"Careful where you poke your nose, Kait. It's liable to get bit one day."* He'd looked her in the eye sternly for several seconds, issuing a silent and much more serious warning, then kissed the tip of her nose and released her.

Remembering the look on his face, Kait swore he'd surprised himself as much as he'd surprised her, but the seed had been planted, sprouting whole new ideas about what to do with a handsome, aspiring biologist.

Wishing she had a bucket of cold water handy, Kait doused herself with reality. Hers was a sinking ship and she had no desire to take Michael or Randy down with her. Randy was a wildcard: a good guy playing at being bad, or a bad guy playing at being good—she wasn't sure yet. If he ever managed to figure out what to do with his life, he'd be an amazing boyfriend. And Michael, her stoic hero, was perhaps the one *good* thing that had come from all of this treachery. Despite her best efforts to keep him at a distance, he'd melted her resolve and won the battle before it had even really begun. And then he'd simply turned and walked away!

Darn the man! He actually made her want *his help.*

Maybe she was crazy—or a bit weaker than she was willing to admit—but the prospect of evading murderous drug runners and making an illegal dash across the border seemed far less daunting with him by her side. Her rescuer was stubborn, commanding, outright irritating in some respects, but for some inexplicable reason he was determined to protect her and see that she made it home safely. After only one day in his presence, she knew he was an honorable man.

That's why he's getting to you so quickly.

Michael was also the most intriguing man she'd ever observed. He was generous, but not because he wanted something in return. He was protective in ways she'd never experienced, yet treated her as a smart and capable equal, despite the fact that she was a complete and unexpected nuisance in his life. Equally appealing was the prospect that he might treat *all* women with such respect and compassion, rather than as indentured servants or temporary amusements. His obvious admiration for his house-keeper was one such example.

Did his positive traits outweigh the negative traits? He'd practically beaten his fists like Tarzan, proclaiming that she *needed* him and couldn't possibly survive without him when she'd tried to refuse his help. Whether it was true or not, was immaterial. She usually chaffed at such behavior, and yet somehow, in this instance, she found it forgivable, if not a little endearing.

"One day, Kaitlyn, you'll find that circumstances have a way of mitigating life's little irritations." Her mother's once mystifying statement floated through her mind, and she finally understood their meaning.

Replaying his words in her mind, Kait realized he'd won her over the moment he'd said he trusted her, which was amazing considering how little he actually knew about her. What man in his right mind would knowingly take in a stranger being hunted by drug runners? It didn't make sense, but for some reason it felt right, like he really was her guardian angel. She hadn't expected him to take such offense at being offered a way out of a losing proposition, and she certainly hadn't expected him to plunge himself headlong into her problems, but since he had, she felt obligated to do everything in her power to ease the burden he'd accepted on her behalf.

Stepping out onto a balcony overlooking the grassy yard and jungle, Kait watched as Michael tinkered with the Bronco in his garage. Once or twice, she heard him cursing the vehicle for its apparent lack of cooperation, and that made her smile for the first time in days. She wasn't the only uncooperative challenge he had to contend with.

Time drifted by excruciatingly slow, and Kait moved back inside to rest and wait. With each passing hour she grew more impatient to pitch in and help with preparations, excited to get on the road and get home, and anxious about the unknown dangers that awaited them along the way. No longer content to sit and watch from a distance, she realized that she needed to *do* something, *anything* to take her mind off the fear that loomed just behind her, waiting to drag her down again. Michael had spun a thread of hope in her heart, and she had to cling to that hope and move forward. If she kept looking back at where she'd already been, the danger was liable to catch her again, and swallow her whole.

Unable to withstand another moment of endless waiting, Kait went downstairs and found the kitchen. The telephone was a temptation—she could call Lilly and let her know she was coming home, but then again she'd have to explain everything that had happened to her in the past few days and that could trigger a whole chain of events she wasn't ready for—*best to stay below the radar a bit longer.*

Searching the cabinets and refrigerator, she found food for their trip, made four huge sandwiches and placed them in the refrigerator along with some freshly washed fruit and carrots. She had no idea how long it would take to drive to California, so she located a can opener and some canned food, just in case, and left them in a bag on the counter for Michael to load.

Briefly, Kait thought about going outside to see if she could help with anything else, but fatigue and light-headedness washed over her. She needed to lie down before she fell down.

Slowly, she backtracked her way through the house, noting the eclectic combination of rustic Mexican furnishings alongside more modern selections. She stopped at a console table filled with framed pictures of people that must be Michael's family and friends; she could see the resemblance to some, but not all of them. When she found the stairs that led back to her room, she wavered; they seemed much too steep to conquer at the moment.

Small beads of perspiration broke out on her skin. She wasn't sure she could make it to the top without passing out.

Jeez, what a wimp!

Taking a deep breath she started upward, determined to make it. She wasn't a wimp—she'd simply overexerted herself. After a seeming eternity of heavy panting and frequent stops to brace herself against calamitous vertigo, she made it to the top, stumbled to her room, dizzy with the effort, and climbed into bed. She fell asleep as soon as her head hit the pillow.

The remainder of the day drifted by at a snail's pace. Michael changed the oil in his refurbished—*soon to be classic*—Ford Bronco, deciding it was a much safer bet than the Jaguar for their journey. Anxious to hit the road, and looking for excuses to keep busy, he checked the tires, brakes and radiator, then prepared everything they would need for the two and one-half day drive to San Diego. When the Bronco was ready, he cleaned the handgun his brother had given him for his thirtieth birthday; in Ian's words it was *"a little extra insurance for those dark, lonely roads* he was so fond of wandering." With any luck, they wouldn't need it, but he couldn't afford to take any chances.

Michael kept cool and calm, purposely maintaining a casual attitude for Kaitlyn's benefit. He didn't relish the idea of driving north through already dangerous territory, with the possibility of more trouble on their heels, but he wasn't going to voice his concerns unless it became absolutely necessary. He'd seen Kaitlyn watching him several times and she seemed to be regaining some equilibrium; he wanted that trend to continue.

The highways of Mexico were nothing like the Interstate freeways in the States. Paved segments were pocked with ruts and potholes, and unpaved stretches could tear the bottom out of any car. The Bronco would perform well enough, but the worst part of the journey wouldn't be the rough roads. Far more dangerous were the vast stretches of isolation and the banditos that waited for unsuspecting travelers. They'd grown much more brazen and treacherous in their attacks, especially on wealthy, American tourists. The banditos would want only one thing—money—and he was reasonably confident about buying his way past their checkpoints.

Michael had dealt with a few banditos in his day, and though they were always risky, he thought he could handle them. He couldn't say the same for Kaitlyn. It was much riskier with a beautiful woman to protect. Some of the banditos might not be satisfied with mere money if they saw her—he would have to rig a place for her to hide.

For the umpteenth time, Michael wondered if he should call Ian and get some help from the TEAM. Pablo was no simple matter to contend with, but if the devil thought Kaitlyn was dead, he wouldn't be looking for her. Dealing with the TEAM however, made Michael's blood run cold. They had a way of "helping out" that was both final and exacting—no witnesses, no evidence, no fear of retaliation. The mere idea of getting involved with them again elevated his blood pressure.

For now, Michael decided to continue on his present course and do what he could for Kaitlyn under his own power and authority. When he had completed every chore possible, loaded everything except what they would need during the night and the bags of food he'd found in the kitchen, he returned upstairs to check on Kaitlyn.

He found her sound asleep.

Settling into the recliner beside her bed, Michael watched her sleep for a few minutes before his own eyes drifted shut. The sun dipped into the ocean, leaving vibrant hues of lavender and rose splashed across the sky, but neither of them was awake to observe the splendor.

FIFTEEN

Kait awoke early the next morning to the glaring red glow of the alarm clock beside the bed and darkness outside—0500 hours. Michael was sound asleep in the recliner, the vague outline of his body sprawled uncomfortably in his overstuffed chair. He was probably exhausted from watching over her so diligently the past two nights, but she was suddenly wide awake.

Kait crept quietly out of bed and peeked through the glass doors at the soft pink glow lighting the edges of gray clouds in the East. The sun's rays stretched across the land in luminous tendrils. *Red sky at night, sailor's delight. Red sky in morning, sailor take warning.* She'd always loved that phrase, but today it sent shivers up her spine.

Trying not to disturb Michael, Kait crossed the hall, opened the doors, and looked to the west at black clouds hanging heavy over the ocean. A serious storm was brewing out there—a tangible equivalent of the stormy thoughts shadowing her mind. Stepping outside into the thick haze blanketing the coast, she was energized by the dramatic scene. She remembered Michael's warning about going outside, but surely it was safe to explore the grounds a little at this mystical predawn hour—even the jungle denizens were still asleep!

Venturing across the balcony and down the stairs, she wandered across the manicured lawn to the cliff-edge. Rooting her bare feet on solid ground always had a strangely restorative effect when she'd been at sea too long, or felt off-kilter. Today, her inner mermaid definitely needed legs on which to rely—her fins were feeling just a bit frayed.

Scanning the shoreline of the pristine cove below, Kait noticed a small motorized dingy beached in the sand. *Was it there yesterday?* Straining to remember her view from the balcony, a resounding no came to mind, making her heart skip a beat. She took a deep breath and tried to convince herself that it was just her overwrought nerves making her jump at nothing, but the menacing eyes of an unknown stalker seemed to bore into her.

Get back inside—back to Michael!

Goose bumps rolled through her, raising the hair on her arms and neck. The stairs were suddenly too far away and impossibly tall. She didn't know who was out there, but she knew he was watching her, creeping closer. Kait began to run, her heart bursting with fright when a shadow materialized just thirty feet away and ran straight toward her.

Through the darkness the balcony loomed overhead. Kait wondered briefly how she could have been so foolish as to leave the safety of Michael's home. Atop the balcony another shadowed figure emerged from the mansion and raced down the steps to intercept her; the shadow behind her was gaining too fast. Veering right, she ran around the side of the mansion, then behind the garage, and dove to the ground under a patch of thick vegetation. Footsteps moved past her, then stopped just a few feet away. Her assailant was practically standing on top of her; she held her breath and made herself as still as a statue.

Michael sat up with a jolt when he realized Kaitlyn was no longer in the room. She was in trouble; he could feel it in his bones, sense it in the air.

She wouldn't venture outside alone, would she?

The door standing open in the study confirmed his fear, a solid lump of dread clogging his throat. As he stepped out onto the balcony, a small figure approached the stairs and then dashed around the corner, out of sight. Another figure gave chase close behind. Without hesitation he ran down the stairs into the darkness, picked up a shovel leaning against the house, and gave chase. It wasn't much of a weapon, but it was better than nothing—like an idiot, he'd already stashed his gun in the Bronco.

Moving quietly, he snuck up behind a thin figure standing on the path, scanning the grounds in search of his prey. Michael crept closer and gave him one good whack over the head with the shovel. The man dropped silently to the ground and Michael stepped over him, edging up against the wall of the garage to look for others lurking nearby. Peering around a corner, the shovel raised and ready, he didn't see Kaitlyn or hear any signs of struggle. He took another step, scanning the shadows and openings in the dawning light, then froze when the hammer of a gun cocked behind his head. A deep menacing voice broke the silence.

"Hands in the air—don't turn around or I'll kill you."

Michael reluctantly complied with each command, dropping the shovel at his feet.

"Now, call the woman. Tell her to come out."

Anger flooded Michael's veins when he recognized the voice. Pablo *was* involved in this debacle—he should never have doubted it. The man had been a troublemaker since the day he was born and his presence at the estate this morning was no coincidence. He'd come for Kaitlyn. Waiting for his chance, Michael weighed the risk of trying to overpower Pablo without getting shot. He wouldn't call Kaitlyn out of hiding, and he couldn't make a move with the gun at his head. He'd be of no use to her dead.

Stalemate.

A small rustling to the left caught their attention and both men turned expecting to see Kaitlyn running for cover. Instead, she swung an old rusty rake at Pablo, cracking him in the shoulder. The gun fired as Michael ducked and the bullet whizzed into the wall of the garage.

Pablo grimaced in pain, but recovered quickly and advanced on her, pointing the gun in her face. Kaitlyn froze with sudden recognition, but Michael sprang into action sending several swift blows into Pablo's kidneys. When

Pablo turned to defend himself, Kaitlyn took another swing with the rake and knocked the gun from his hand. Moving fast, Michael locked his arm in a choke-hold around Pablo's throat.

Pablo struggled for freedom, "You can't save her...pendejo. *Bastard.* She's...dead."

Squeezing harder, Michael's blood boiled with the need for vindication. Pablo gasped as he continued to struggle, "Maybe...she'll give...our regards...to Maria."

"Get the truck!" Michael yelled to Kaitlyn.

"Where are the keys?"

"Pocket..."

Reluctantly, Kaitlyn moved closer and snatched the keys, as several pairs of feet thumped along the gravel drive, moving in fast from the periphery.

Shifting his weight, Pablo rammed his elbow into Michael's gut then flipped him head over heels. Michael hit the ground hard and scrambled to get up, but Pablo kicked his ribs with brutal accuracy and turned to find his gun in the overgrown brush. In a flash, Michael grabbed Pablo's boot and brought him to the ground with a hard twist. They wrestled, each trying to pin the other, then both men leaped to their feet, circling like great cats getting ready for the final pounce.

Pablo's thugs arrived and surrounded them, moving toward Michael with menace in their faces and violence in their bones. Pablo's eyes burned with fire and brimstone, "Alto ahí, hermanos." *Stop there, brothers.* "Él es mío." *He is mine.*

Michael and Pablo locked eyes, their long awaited standoff finally at hand. For unspoken reasons, neither had been willing to rush their rivalry—an eternity in the making—to its inevitable conclusion.

No matter who won the battle, they would both lose. If Michael defeated Pablo, his men would never let him walk away free with Kaitlyn; if Pablo won, Michael would be dead and Kaitlyn would be at the mercy of a merciless butcher. Michael squared himself with his fate, determined to win if only for Kaitlyn's sake.

Seconds later, the Bronco crashed through the closed garage door, sending splintered chunks of wood flying through the air. Clods of dirt and gravel flew in every direction, as the 4X4 accelerated straight toward them. Michael reacted quickly, diving out of the way just as the front of the Bronco plowed into two of Pablo's men and Pablo himself.

Screams rent the air as their bodies flew several feet, and the Bronco screeched to a halt.

Michael ran to the driver's door and yanked it open, pushing a wild-eyed Kaitlyn across the bench seat as he hopped in and took over. Two men gave chase while three others rushed to their leader. Steering around the bodies, he pressed the gas pedal to the floor and peeled down the driveway without looking back.

Several miles down the road Michael released a sigh of relief—he couldn't believe they had escaped. Pablo had brought a small army to storm the villa and take Kaitlyn, but he hadn't thought to leave men posted at the highway. He'd underestimated Michael and Kaitlyn both, and paid a steep price for the blunder.

Why is he interested in Kaitlyn?

How did he know where to find her?

Whatever the answers, Pablo was now utterly aware of Michael's involvement and taking it very personally.

Remembering the sickening sound of the Bronco plowing into Pablo and his men, Michael turned to check on Kaitlyn. She was staring out the window, her arms wrapped tightly around her midsection, her back turned slightly toward him. She was hiding again—trying to be strong and hold back the tears. He cursed under his breath and stretched his hand across the seat to rest on her knee. "Kaitlyn, are you all right?"

She shrugged her shoulders and kept silent.

"Look at me, Kaitlyn. We're going to be okay. Do you hear me?"

Turning to face him, she responded in a fractured, incredulous voice, "I killed them!"

A single tear slid down her pale face and Michael saw the distraught expression in her watery eyes. "We don't know that. You probably just knocked them out. The truck wasn't moving fast enough to kill anyone." *Too bad*—he'd feel a lot safer if Pablo and a couple of his mercenaries really were dead but that wasn't what she needed to hear right now.

Michael wiped away the tear on her chin then broke loose with a smile. "You did great, Kaitlyn. You saved both of our lives!" He patted the space next to him on the bench seat, "Come over here and get some rest." To his surprise she snuggled up next to him without hesitation, finally accepting his warmth and encouragement. He curled his free arm around her shoulders and pulled her close.

After several minutes of silence, she finally began to relax. "Maybe I just knocked them out." There was surprise and lightness in her voice. In the midst of a nearly hopeless battle, they had made a pretty good team, and he knew she finally trusted him when she closed her eyes and settled in for the long drive.

Lush green jungle crowded the narrow two-lane road that ascended in sharp curves and steep inclines, running high into the rugged Sierra Madre. Their speed fluctuated between 30- and 60-mph, stretching time to its limits as they drove toward safety. It took more than an hour to reach the highway's summit, about 1,500 feet above sea level, and then they began the long, slow descent back toward the coast. Once they hit town they would continue north toward San Blas, pick up Highway 15 and be well on their way to California.

Eager to reach Puerto Vallarta and hide among the crowds, Michael zoomed past the occasional jalopy, slowing just enough to make the curves, then hotfooting it on each straightaway. There were few road signs, and no mile markers, but he'd traveled highway 200 often. Many of the sparse dirt roads branching off this stretch of highway eventually led to a secluded beach or cove. They were already in the vicinity of Yelapa, so they only had another thirty miles to go.

As the Bronco rounded the next blind curve, a slow-moving tour bus materialized in front of them, as if out of thin air. The Bronco nearly kissed the rear bumper of the green and white bus, but Michael hit the brakes, waited for his chance, then sped around it, leaving it far behind. Fast asleep against his side, Kaitlyn didn't even flinch from the sharp movements. She was recovering quickly from her wounds, but still quite weak and easily overtaxed by any physical exertion. She was in no condition for this kind of trip, but he could think of no alternative.

Worry continued to nag him, and pushed him to drive faster, to reach safety before something else happened.

Focused on the road ahead, Michael caught only a flash of chrome and black steel in the rearview mirror seconds before a full-size Chevy pickup rear-ended them. As the jolt threw Kaitlyn forward, Michael tried to hold her back and shield her from the dash.

Ripped abruptly from her sleep, Kaitlyn screamed as they swerved across the road, just missing a large boulder on the opposite shoulder, then corrected back into the middle of the highway. The black demon barreled toward them again, then pulled up along the passenger side and began edging them off the road.

"Look out!" Kaitlyn screamed again as the truck rammed against her door. She struggled to fasten her seatbelt as the truck swerved side-to-side.

The windows were tinted jet-black to obscure the driver from view, but Michael recognized the vehicle. There was only one like it in the surrounding area, and it had belonged to Pablo's right-hand-man and bodyguard, the muscle-bound thug that had probably been with him on the yacht when they had abducted Kaitlyn.

Red fire strokes painted on the sides of the truck seemed to fan and grow larger as both vehicles increased speed. Michael floored the gas pedal, but the Chevy matched their pace and rammed them again from the side, locking fender with fender as it pushed them closer to the edge of the road. Using the weight of the Bronco, Michael pushed back in the opposite direction as they rounded another curve in the road. He prayed there were no other cars on the road ahead of them.

Coming safely out of the curve, the dark driver-side window of the Chevy began to roll down in slow motion. The black barrel of a handgun emerged and fired at Kaitlyn; the bullet drilled a hole in the glass and the seat between her and Michael, shattering the tempered glass into a crackled sheet of tiny square blocks. Their view was obscured, but the safety glass held and her lap remained glass-free.

Desperate to remove Kaitlyn from the line of fire, Michael stomped on the brakes, tearing the locked fenders apart with an angry squeal of twisting metal. The Chevy over-corrected, then swerved across their path out of control. There was nowhere to go and barely enough time to react. Michael turned the steering wheel hard, trying to avoid a head-on collision, and both trucks ramped off the side of the road. They landed hard, bouncing several times on the oversized off-road tires as they careened down the side of the hill.

Still moving, both vehicles accelerated downward, side by side, toward a sheer drop-off. Michael's stomach perched in his chest, and as he pumped the brakes and they continued to plummet through brush and over rocks, the Bronco bounced wildly, tossing them around in the seat. Kaitlyn crossed her arms over her head and closed her eyes as they neared the edge. She didn't want to see the outcome if he couldn't stop in time, and he didn't blame her.

In a last ditch effort to avoid the inevitable, Michael turned the steering wheel hard left, toward a wall of vegetation to avoid plunging over the cliff to certain death. He pumped even harder on the brakes hoping they wouldn't lock and they finally began to slow down. When the Bronco crashed into a large boulder and flipped on its side, their world spun out of control. A lone tree, tall and sturdy at the edge of the cliff, finally stopped the Bronco's tumbling motion.

Kait returned to consciousness hanging upside-down in the cab of the Bronco, her seat belt threatening to cut off the circulation in her legs. She reached to push against the ceiling and alleviate some of the pressure, but felt Michael's body instead. He was sprawled face-down, motionless beneath her. Outside she could hear the angry hissing and spitting of the engine and other parts of the wrecked Bronco. Smoke billowed around them, invading the cab, robbing them of breathable air. "Michael! Wake up," she pleaded in a ragged voice. "We need to get out!"

Forcing herself not to think about the men who might be traversing the hill at this very moment to finish them off, she worked to remove her seatbelt.

"Michael, can you hear me? I'm stuck." Kait felt along his body, trying to nudge him awake. She petted his head and felt the sensation of warm, sticky blood on her hand. "Oh my gods! Michael! Please wake up! Don't leave me here like this!"

Panic began to set in as blood rushed to Kait's head, pounding in her ears, making her head throb. She reached for the release on her seat belt again and struggled to free herself, but it wouldn't budge. When she noticed the Swiss Army knife in Michael's back pocket, she stretched to reach it and began frantically sawing at the lap belt that held her. Within seconds, she fell on top of him, landing with a thud.

As Michael regained consciousness, he tried to move but stopped when Kaitlyn moaned. Her legs were draped across his back, her head and body heavy on his legs. Smoke filled the air, choking him as he struggled to breath.

The Bronco's on fire!

Pushing himself onto his hands and knees, Kaitlyn rolled off to the side with a low grunt. He grabbed her arms and pulled her to a sitting position in the cab of the truck, surprised when her eyes popped open and stared straight at him in a daze. "We have to get out, right now! You first." Michael kicked the driver-side window out and pushed her to crawl through. He looked back for just a moment and grabbed his backpack, then followed her out.

Free of the flaming, smoking inferno, Michael pulled Kaitlyn to her feet and held her tightly against his side as they ran for cover. Just ten feet clear of the Bronco, the gasoline blew—they had barely made it out. The explosion echoed through the jungle, up the steep slopes, and down the winding canyons, sending every creature in the vicinity in search of refuge.

SIXTEEN

Michael lay face-down on the ground beside Kaitlyn, stunned from the impact of the explosion. His mouth tasted of grass, dirt, and blood, and his throat was raw and scratchy from inhaling too much smoke. The rest of his body was blissfully numb—no pain—it was either a very good sign or a very bad one.

After several moments of silence, he heard Kaitlyn moan and felt her strain to sit up. Then she tugged at him, trying to turn him over onto his back. Lending her some assistance, he gritted his teeth against a sudden stabbing pain in his chest as he rolled over. With her goal accomplished, she collapsed over him from the exertion. After only a few seconds she stirred again, trying to lift herself off him; when her elbow dug into his ribs, he couldn't contain the pain. Gasping aloud, he quickly moved her elbow aside, wrapped his arms around her waist and pulled her back down on top of him.

"Be still." His voice was gravely when he spoke.

For what seemed like an eternity, she simply laid there on top of him, running her fingers gently through his hair.

Kait gazed at Michael's smoke-streaked face with gratitude, amazement, and worry, wondering how badly he was hurt. Before the explosion, she'd thought for a few hair-raising moments that he was dead, that somehow her guardian angel had managed once again to save her life, but had lost his own in the process. It had been too frightening to consider.

His eyes were closed, his face stoic while he rested, though his lips pressed tightly together to prevent any stray noises from escaping. A thin stream of blood had trickled down the side of his face from a small cut just below his hairline; it was already clotting. Remembering the blood on her hand from his scalp, she tenderly probed the rest of his head looking for additional wounds or swelling. His soft brown hair slid effortlessly through her fingers everywhere except for the small patch that was matted with blood and dirt. Gently, she searched there as well, to make sure it was not concealing another gash.

Only slightly relieved, Kait took a deep breath and tried once again to get up. He was in pain—she knew that by the way he'd moved her elbow so quickly. Her weight on his body couldn't be helping matters, and her position made it impossible to see if he had any other injuries.

"Michael, you're injured, let me up."

"Not a chance." Her soothing caresses felt like a dream, and he wasn't ready to wake up. For now, he wanted to hold her and lie here without a care.

"I need to make sure you're okay." She pressed lightly against the small cut on his head.

"I'm fine; just resting. Can't have you floating off to heaven without me."

When his head finally stopped spinning, Michael opened his eyes to do a little inspection of his own. Kaitlyn looked okay, just a few new scratches on her chin and cheeks. The bandage on her forehead was about to fall off, but she didn't seem any worse for the wear.

Staring at her worried face, he realized she looked better than okay; she looked great! Her seatbelt had saved her from any further damage. Too bad he couldn't say the same for himself. The numbness from the blast was finally wearing off and his head now throbbed, distracting him from the stabbing sensation in his chest. Slowly he flexed different muscles, testing his limbs, neck and back. Everything felt and moved as it should—their accident could have been much worse.

"Are you sure you're okay?" Kaitlyn asked skeptically.

"As long as you're here and in one piece, I'm all right, but what happened to the black truck?" Still holding her close he lifted his head to scan the area. He could see the ruined Bronco, burning and twisted into a useless heap, but the black truck was nowhere to be seen.

Kaitlyn lifted her gaze as well, her eyes sweeping the area. "I don't see it." She looked at him again, a silent question burning in her eyes.

"Must have gone to meet his maker."

That's one bastard who won't harm her again.

Behind her the sky had turned into a darkening blue mist. Hurricane Heidi, which had ravaged Acapulco, was fast approaching and they needed to get moving.

Michael relinquished his firm hold on Kaitlyn's waist and gently wiped at the mixture of dirt and blood crusting at the corner of her mouth. His hand stroked her tangled hair, the softness as excruciating and exquisite as a bounty of food placed before a man dying of starvation. In this moment—surrounded by primitive jungle, billowing clouds, and untold danger—he wanted nothing more than to pull her tender lips to his and quench the hunger that had been building mercilessly since the night he had breathed life back into her quiescent lungs. He had to taste her again, now that she was vibrant and alive—*just once*—to reassure himself that this wasn't a dream; only then could he get up and seek shelter.

Before he could make good on the fool-hearty decision, Kaitlyn grabbed her opportunity and carefully sat up, doing her best not to jab his sore ribs. She cleared her throat as she rose to her feet and looked around. "I think you're right. I don't see any sign of the other truck."

She looked down at her soiled clothes and began brushing herself off. Michael forced himself to get up and get back to business.

She was wise to run. You're a fool to think you can kiss her once and be done with it.

Movement through the underbrush was slow at best. Sharp pain assaulted Michael's ribs with every step, but a cracked rib or two was nothing more than a nuisance at this point; the blow to his head was of greater concern. Fortunately, the resulting headache was already subsiding and he could feel no sign of concussion. He couldn't say the same for Kaitlyn. She'd hardly received a scratch thanks to her seat belt, but Michael worried that all the jolting and bouncing had aggravated her condition. They'd only been walking for fifteen minutes and already she was stumbling over branches and rocks, falling behind. Wishing he could stop and do a more thorough examination, Michael knew he had to keep her moving—they couldn't afford to stop and rest with the hurricane rolling in.

Keeping a close eye on her, Michael assessed the tender cut on his own forehead and tried to lighten the mood. "I wonder if they sell matching his and hers bandages at the local pharmacy."

Kaitlyn scowled at him. "Don't joke, Michael. You—*we* could have been killed."

"That's true, but we weren't. Let's not question our good fortune, okay?" His mouth curved in a fake grin as he took her hand and urged her forward. "Don't worry, Kaitlyn. We'll get out of this mess, together."

His forced smile had almost spread to Kaitlyn when her thoughts shifted back to sobering darkness. "Do you know where we're going? I don't see the road anymore."

"Never fear, I know exactly where we are. I've driven these roads for years, but I think it's best if we keep out of sight. We don't need any more adventures today."

El Diablo was too damned close to winning this round, and when he discovered that his brother in crime had gone over the cliff, there would be hell to pay. If he found Kaitlyn, she'd be the one to pay. Erring on the side of caution, Michael hoped that staying away from the main highway would prevent Pablo's men from tracking them down to retaliate for the hit-and-run at his villa, but he wasn't a betting man. Pablo had countless people at his disposal, and they would scour the roads endlessly to find Kaitlyn before she slipped away again.

As they tromped through the tall, thick underbrush, Michael began to brood over the situation. Their encounter with the black fireball had rattled his sense of control, leaving them at a far greater disadvantage than before—outnumbered, outgunned, and now, outpaced. They'd lost nearly everything in the crash: transportation, food, water, clothes, and worst of all, his medical kit. The fire had claimed everything but the backpack.

At least I had the brains to grab that. His emergency go-bag would see them through.

Time passed quietly and progress was slow until a loud engine whined on the invisible road above them, pulling Michael from his doom and gloom. "Get down!"

He pulled Kaitlyn to the ground, quickly ducking below the vegetation of the forest floor. The engine grew louder, more menacing, until finally a tour bus appeared, passed quickly by, and left them in its silent wake. Too late Michael remembered passing the green and white behemoth. If they'd been closer to the road they could have flagged it down and caught a ride.

Hell and damnation. So much for playing it safe!

At the first off-road vehicle trail they encountered, Michael and Kaitlyn turned toward the coast, glad to travel on a secluded, albeit rugged dirt road for a while. Walking would be much easier here, and safer than the main highway. They'd make much better time, and eventually with a little luck, they'd end up close to the sleepy beach village of Yelapa, where they could rest and recuperate for the night.

The trail was lonely and quiet, rarely used. At best guess they were within three to five miles of the village. At the end of the trail, they would have to traverse the steep, thickly vegetated slopes to find the footpath frequented by tourists visiting the 150-foot waterfall above the village. Once they found it, their journey would be easy, only another twenty minutes or so to the beach. Finding the path to the village however, would be like searching for a flea on a dog's back: arduous, yet not impossible. There were no easy access routes to Yelapa—nobody to offer assistance if they got lost in the jungle. The only real way in and out of the backwoods village was to cross the Bay of Banderas by boat; Yelapa was an ideal place to hide out for a day or two.

Kait was exhausted, disheartened, and completely miserable. It seemed like they'd been walking forever down this rutted road. Her hands itched like crazy from the dirt and grass that had infiltrated what remained of her sodden bandages. She had a fresh new battalion of aches and pains to replace the ones that had begun to heal. The linen outfit Michael had bought her was nearly in shreds, and her feet and sandals were caked in the powdery red clay of the road. Michael had fared better in his jeans and running shoes, reminding her that the next time he went shopping for her, she'd tell him to forget the flimsy, feminine beach wear and buy something practical.

As she walked, Kait tried to quiet her mind, but failed miserably. Her thoughts circled round and round, revisiting each harrowing experience, asking questions for which she had no answers, and wondering about the man in front of her. He was an enigma, a man with great heart and great strength, yet haunted by darkness, and shrouded in mystery. He volunteered nothing about himself but insisted on knowing every detail about her. Fiery currents burned just below his kind, gentle surface, hinting at something wild and dangerous contained within, struggling to get out. She could see him fighting an emotional tug of war with himself: one minute joking and making light of their situation, and the next minute brooding and angry. He was complicated and perplexing, but she was grateful to have him on her side.

Focusing more on her aching muscles and less on the intriguing companion who'd nearly kissed her after their crash—she'd seen the lusty, almost reverent glint in his eyes—Kait realized she was perilously close to the end of her rope. She was in desperate need of rest but they were already moving too slow; they couldn't stop. Michael had slowed his pace repeatedly to match hers, and had stopped to wait for her whenever she fell too far behind. He was handling the rugged terrain with far greater finesse than she, his long legs carrying him farther in one stride than two of her own. It was embarrassing to feel so weak and worn out, but she simply had nothing left.

Just keep moving—one foot after the other.

Thunder rolled overhead as the late morning clouds gave way to the leading edge of Hurricane Heidi. Rain-heavy air settled over the hillside, the sky growing more ominous with every step. In another five minutes, they'd be drenched from head to toe. Michael stopped mid-stride, turning to talk to Kaitlyn. She walked straight into him and he had to catch and hold her until she regained her footing. Gently he tilted her face to his. "How many fingers am I holding up?"

Kaitlyn stared at him for several seconds, then at his hand. "I'm tired, not delirious."

"Humor me, please." She looked as pale as a ghost, like she would pass out at any moment. He masked his concern with stern determination.

Kaitlyn huffed before she answered, "Three. And I feel fine. I'm just tired."

"Follow my finger with your eyes. No, don't move your head, just your eyes." He moved his index finger slowly back and forth in front of her face. She tried to follow his instructions, but her impulses were off, her reactions slow.

Michael turned around and squatted down, motioning for her to climb on his back. "I'll carry you for a while. You need to rest," he suggested.

"Don't be ridiculous, I can walk. I'm not an invalid!"

"Kaitlyn, don't argue with me. It'll be a lot worse when it starts raining. We need to push harder and faster to beat the flash floods. This is your last opportunity to rest. Hop on."

Taking the path of passive resistance she walked past him, "Let's just sit and rest for a while on this nice log." She plopped herself down and faked a smile as she motioned for him to join her.

Michael didn't reply. What could he possibly say to gain her cooperation?

As he slumped against a tree, about to give in and let her rest, Kaitlyn shrieked and jumped up off the log. "Get it off me!" she squealed, trying to shake loose of the giant tarantula hanging from her pants.

Michael moved quickly, swiping it off her with his bare hand, and she immediately climbed into his arms, scrambling to get as far off the ground as possible, while desperately scanning the jungle floor to see where the spider had gone. Just then, a gust of wind blasted them, followed by the downpour he had predicted. Kaitlyn shivered in his arms and reluctantly made eye contact, begging him to tell her this was all some horrible nightmare. He didn't.

"I give up." She lowered herself from Michael's arms, took the backpack and slung it around her shoulders, then climbed up on his back.

Once she'd wrapped her arms firmly around his neck, he slid his hands up her thighs, grabbing hold and pushing her higher on his hips, then slid his hands behind her knees and held her firmly in place as he began walking. Briefly, he wondered how something as simple as his hands sliding along her thighs could feel so damned good, then he laughed at himself, blaming it on sheer fatigue and the satin water drops drenching them.

When they finally reached the end of the road, Michael surveyed the steep drop-off. The hillside below was thick with vegetation, but this looked like as good a place as any to start blazing a trail to Yelapa. Setting Kaitlyn down, Michael felt so light that he almost floated over the edge of the ravine without her. He caught his balance as the rain pelted them, no longer a sheer curtain of soft rain, but a frenzy of heavy drops falling in sheets that made it difficult to see or hear anything. Michael turned to face Kaitlyn, shouting so she could hear him. "The ravine will start flooding soon! We need to cut down the side of this hill and find the trail to the falls. Do you think you can manage?"

Kaitlyn squinted through the rain trailing down her face, then nodded and motioned for him to lead the way. Michael reclaimed the backpack and pulled out a bottle of water and a rope. While she took a drink, he tied one end of the rope around her waist and the other around himself, leaving ten feet of play between them. He couldn't take the chance that she would fall down the steep slope and break her lovely, troublesome neck. When he was done, he took a swig of the water and strapped on the backpack. "Let's go."

After an hour of wandering down the hillside, slipping on the muddy slopes and saturated vegetation, they found the footpath and discovered that they were already well below the falls. The river thundered in their ears, flowing fast with the added runoff, jumping the banks in several places. Within minutes, Michael and Kaitlyn emerged from the jungle onto a sandy beach, just 30-feet from the roiling ocean. Small thatched huts known as palapas lined the beach in the distance, and beyond them stood the small village and one of only two hotels. Struggling along the narrow strip of unprotected beach, they clung to each other against the 60-mph wind gusts.

With a hurricane pounding the coast, all the tourists and villagers had been evacuated; the village and homes were deserted. Michael thought about taking shelter in one of the huts farthest from the water, but decided the hotel would provide more resources. The Polynesian-style waterfront village had only a few modern conveniences, and almost no way of coping with natural disasters: no roads or cars, no telephones, and no electricity after 2300 hours.

When Kaitlyn and Michael burst through the doors of the Nuevo Lagunita Hotel, the only solid looking structure around, the wide eyes of the owner greeted them.

"We need shelter and food, señor," Michael said with easy authority.

The man ran a quick glance over them, eyeing Kaitlyn as she slid behind Michael. "Storm coming! Boat gone! You rent palapa, one hundred American dollars. Maybe boat come back tomorrow."

Michael's exhaustion was quickly replaced with anger. "No palapa—the wind is too strong. We need a room here in the hotel; one hundred for the room, extra blankets and towels, food and water."

A small woman emerged from the doorway behind the shopkeeper and argued with her husband. Michael knew the wife had won the battle when the man threw his hands in the air and left the room.

"My apologies *señor y señora*. My husband thought you would bring trouble to our hotel, but I can see that you need rest." She handed Michael an empty bag, "Take what you need from the store, and I will lead you to your room. I pray the storm will pass in the night and leave our village in one piece."

Kaitlyn sank onto a rustic wooden bench, her back against the wall, and sleep claimed her within seconds. Michael untied the rope from their waists, filled the bag with a few essentials, then gave it back to the woman to carry, and scooped up Kaitlyn from the bench. He followed the woman upstairs, Kaitlyn fast asleep in his arms.

"It is the best room we have, señor." She eyed Kaitlyn, limp on the bed where Michael placed her. "I hope she will feel better soon."

"Si señora, she is only tired. Thank you very much for your hospitality." He placed two hundred dollars in her hand as he kissed it and folded her fingers over it, "For your trouble."

The woman smiled and closed the door leaving Michael and Kaitlyn alone for the night. Michael set immediately to the task of cleaning Kaitlyn's muddy feet and removing their sopping wet clothes. He wrapped her in a warm blanket from the full-size bed, wrapped himself in another, and laid down beside her, snuggling close to share his warmth. Within seconds he too fell asleep. The afternoon drifted on without them and crept into nightfall while they slept.

SEVENTEEN

Torrential winds billowed and howled outside, rattling the windows and bending the trees. The walls of the hotel creaked under duress, fighting to stand their ground against the battering gusts of rain, surf spray, and wind. Kait awoke amidst the dark and the din, tucked safely in a cocoon of softness, a heavy weight draped around her protectively. She couldn't see Michael in the dark of the night, but she could feel him beside her—warm and solid—a comforting juxtaposition to the raging elements outside.

Her senses instantly heightened by the powerful stimuli all around her, a cascade of hormones beset her body as she lay there motionless. His face was nestled in her hair, his breath tickling her ear with its steady rhythm. Her pulse and breathing quickened even as she tried to deny the cause. She was under siege in every sense of the word—the frothing hurricane overpowering her from the outside, Michael's mass, breath, and heat oppressing and tantalizing her all at once from the inside.

It's only the storm—nothing to get worked-up about!

Feeling suddenly trapped and overheated, Kait needed to move her sore, overtaxed body, stretch her limbs, and cool off. Conserving every move, she tried to extract herself from the bed without disturbing his much-needed sleep. It was impossible; she was wrapped tightly in a blanket and his embrace, and completely naked underneath.

Flushing with embarrassment, she was suddenly glad for the darkness.

Good criminy! He's already seen everything.

She gasped when a deep voice rumbled low in her ear. "Good evening, Kaitlyn."

Kait halted her movement. His deep, sexy voice made her bones quiver subtly as an age-old battle broke out between her analytical mind and her hopeful heart. "Sorry, to wake you," she whispered.

Wrong time, wrong place, wrong man!

Michael lifted his head, clicked on a flashlight and stood it upright like a lantern on the bedside table, then started to pull her even closer—*if that was even possible*—but stopped the instant his eyes connected with hers.

After a long pause, he relaxed his grip.

When Michael looked away, Kait was more than happy to accept his retreat, but she hadn't missed the brief, unguarded look in his eyes, nor the dark warning that had followed: *here be dragons best left alone.*

Unwilling to analyze the sudden temptation to stay there and explore the warm tendrils of awareness seeping through her body, Kait focused her attention on much more tangible and practical needs.

Survival mode, remember?

As if on cue, her stomach growled its confirmation of her most pressing need.

"Time to get up." Michael pulled one arm out from under her neck and propped himself up on his elbow, then shifted his other arm and leg to free her from their weight. "You must be starving. I grabbed a bag of chips and some canned tuna and beans. They didn't have much to choose from. I'm afraid we'll have to rough it for now."

Kait sat up quickly, seizing her chance to escape from temptation, and slung her legs over the side of the bed, clutching her head and her blanket as her world went spinning.

His eyes flashed with layers of awareness, "Whoa there, take it easy."

"I'm okay," she stared down at her feet, heart racing at the thought that he might be able to read her with more ease than he could read the Sunday morning paper. "I'm just a little...dizzy."

He nodded, the corner of his mouth creasing in a repentant frown, “Too much bouncing around this morning.” Michael slid off the bed and knelt in front of her, shining the flashlight above her head to avoid blinding her as he appraised her. “How do you feel?”

Holy buckets! Confused, afraid, excited, wary—totally off balance. His question was loaded with enough dynamite to sink the Queen Mary and he didn’t even know it!

“I’m hungry enough to eat a whole plate of sushi if that’s all there was," she said reaching for safety, sanity, and a dash of humor to cut the tension.

"What?” The crease lifted somewhere between a sly grin and a wry smirk. “Am I to understand that a marine biologist is opposed to sushi?"

"Hey, I study fish; that doesn't mean I have to eat them raw." He nodded, but didn’t respond further. Instead, the narrow beam of light flashed across the room in search of the bag of food and the mattress shifted under her as he used it to stand up. He wrapped the blanket around his waist and tucked one end in like a beach towel, locking it into place. His sculpted abdominal muscles flexed as he moved, drawing attention to places much too intimate to be contemplated at the moment.

Suddenly Kait realized that he was just as *vulnerable* beneath his blanket as she was beneath hers. Michael approached her with the bag and sat down beside her on the bed again. An unwanted shiver of attraction raced up her spine. *This is so* not *what I need right now!*

"You don't happen to have any clean clothes in there do you?" she asked hopefully, trying to divert her attention to more appropriate matters.

He opened the bag as the semi-permanent frown returned to his face. "As a matter of fact, no. I wasn't thinking that far in advance when I did our shopping." Opening a can of tuna, he handed it to her. "You need some protein to rebuild your strength." Next, he pulled two bottles of water out of the bag, and removed the cap from one. "Try to make this last a while. There were only a couple of bottles left down there."

Kait took a few gulps then recapped her bottle to conserve the remaining fluid. "You'd think after being soaked to the bone I wouldn't be so thirsty, but I want the water more than the food!" She laughed nervously, eyeing the tuna as she debated her ability to eat gracefully without a utensil.

Heck with that. I'm too hungry to care. Without further hesitation she pinched up the tuna between two fingers and plopped the bite in her mouth. "Mmm," a pleasure-filled moan slipped from her throat as her taste buds sprang to life and savored the morsels.

Feeling instantly self-conscious, she swallowed the bite and offered Michael the can. He stared at her for a long moment and another shiver raced through her at the hungry gleam in his eyes. He looked much more interested in devouring her than the food, but he held up a second can of tuna indicating that they didn't have to share, then stood the flashlight on its end to illuminate their small part of the room, and began eating.

Relieved that he was reading her "stay away" signals, and feeling suddenly quite ravenous, Kait focused all her attention on the food in her hand. Nothing had ever tasted so good in her life and she wondered if it was the result of their prolonged fasting, or because of her recent brushes with death. In either case, she was oblivious to the small murmurs and groans of satisfaction emanating from her until Michael interrupted her reverie by shoving a bag of chips at her. She flushed with embarrassment again when she realized he was doing his best to ignore her litany of noises. As quietly as possible she licked the last bits of tuna from her fingertips. "I guess I was a little hungrier than I thought."

Michael hopped up and began pacing back and forth anxiously, his can of tuna hardly touched. Kait ate several handfuls of salty corn chips and drank nearly half of her water trying to ignore his much too obvious presence.

With her stomach quite satisfied for the moment, a different type of hunger surfaced throughout her body: a craving for more of the man who radiated masculine energy, an intense yearning to be safe and secure by his side again, to while the night away in the comfort of his arms, clothing optional and problems of the world be damned.

Good criminy, I am definitely losing my mind!

Maybe she was in the midst of discovering a new illness—damsel in distress syndrome. There was no denying that Michael was the McDreamy in her personal episode of Grey's Anatomy: gentle, intelligent, handsome, and stunningly virile at the moment—everything she'd ever wanted in a man. But hadn't she just a week ago decided to take Lilly's advice and explore certain possibilities with Randy, otherwise dubbed McSteamy?

Holy mackerel—it's just hormones!

That was probably true, but this veritable sea god had managed to save her life twice—no, three times—over the course of several days, and not once had he abandoned her or complained. In fact, he'd shocked her right down to her shoes when he'd held her tightly after their wreck this morning and stroked her hair as if she was the most beautiful woman he'd ever seen!

Leave it alone. It was just the heat of the moment.

Kait was nothing if not a practical, down-to-earth, career-minded woman. She had problems to fix, evil-doers to evade, a semi-reliable, yet incredibly hunky deckhand waiting for her at home. She was nowhere near ready to explore the possibility of a romantic tryst, or anything else, with Michael—*in memory, fantasy, or otherwise.* Better to ignore the sudden and unwanted desire he was igniting with his tantalizing gestures before it shredded what little was left of her sense of control.

Time to figure out our next move.

With sudden boldness, Kait rose from the bed and stepped in front of Michael, blocking his path as he paced. He started to swerve around her but she blocked him again, stepping squarely into his path. He was off somewhere else, lost in thought and completely unaware of her. "So what's the plan? When do we get out of here?"

Michael stopped in his tracks, unaware at first of the nature of the obstacle in his path. He'd been so deep in thought, concentrating so hard on not yielding to his lower instincts, that he'd nearly plowed right over her. When he'd tried to step aside, she had followed, then she'd lifted her hand to his naked chest, her eyes wide with concern.

He stared down at her with momentary disbelief then came to his senses and mentally knocked himself back to the present. Hurricane Heidi was still raging outside, Pablo's thugs were still out there hunting Kaitlyn, and he was still her only line of defense. She didn't need the added trouble of unwanted advances from a hopelessly hollowed-out failure with nothing real to give.

Their eyes met in the twilight, all other sounds smothered by the swirling wind pummeling the hotel and the thrashing trees nearby. Again he saw something he hadn't seen in her before—determination. She was recovering her equilibrium far faster than he had imagined.

Kaitlyn lowered her fingers and gently traced the edge of several dark bruises around his sternum. He'd been hiding them from her, not wanting her to know he was injured. Her determination faded as defeat reared its ugly head again and her hands fell limp at her sides. "Do they hurt terribly?"

"Not much. Nothing you need to worry about."

"I'm sorry you've been hurt...almost killed...because of me." She looked up at him, searching his face for a truth that had so far eluded her. "Why are you doing this, Michael?"

"Doing what?"

"Don't be obtuse. You know exactly what I mean."

He lowered his guarded gaze to hers. "If not me, then who?" he asked cryptically.

Before she could respond, a palm tree punctured the darkened window a few feet away, flinging shattered glass toward them. Wind swirled rampantly through the room tugging at their blankets. Rain poured through the jagged hole soaking the bed they'd been sleeping on.

Michael swept Kaitlyn off her feet, tossing her over his shoulder, grabbed the backpack, the bag of supplies and the flashlight, and tromped out the door into the pitch-black hallway. "Are you all right? Did the glass cut you?" He asked urgently.

He set her down carefully in the hallway and Kaitlyn inspected herself quickly in the glow of the flashlight. "I'm fine. What about you? Your feet?"

"My feet are fine." He shined the light up and down the corridor looking for the next closest room, then pushed his way through the door on the opposite wall. Moving quickly to inspect the room, Michael tripped on his blanket, then stubbed his toes when he caught himself. He cursed a blue streak as he pulled her in behind him and fumbled with the bags and the flashlight. Their new quarters were much smaller: two small beds and a nightstand.

Snagging the light from him, Kait surveyed Michael, looking for cuts or any other wounds he might be hiding from her. "Sit down and show me your feet. You shouldn't have carried me through the glass!"

"I told you I'm fine, Kaitlyn. Just a little...damp."

She planted one hand on her hip and shined the light directly on his chest, standing her ground directly in front of him. "I'll be the judge of that. And in case you've gotten overly comfortable with the idea that I'll just blindly go along with whatever you say, let me share a little secret. I am as stubborn as they come, and I know how to get what I want."

"Of that I have no doubt, Kaitlyn. And since you brought it up, let me enlighten *you* about a little something. I don't have all the details, but it's not hard to guess that it's that stubborn willfulness that got you into this mess in the first place. You had no business traipsing onto a stranger's yacht, private pier or not. You had no business wandering outside at my villa *alone* after I warned you not to. And you have no business keeping secrets from me, the one person you can count as an ally."

A chill pricked her skin as her spine stood to attention. She'd never seen Michael so riled—granted they hadn't known each other very long—but she didn't like it one bit. She wasn't about to back down from his challenge.

"*Who's* keeping secrets?" she punctuated her question with a gentle tap of her finger against his bruised sternum. "Secrets that could jeopardize your safety and mine while we make an illegal run for the border!

"As I recall, I've answered all of your questions and cooperated fully with your every request. You on the other hand, have shared almost nothing about yourself and seem to think that it's perfectly acceptable to hide your injuries and who knows what else from me. Lying by omission, is still lying, Michael."

She knew she'd plucked the right string when he squinted ever so slightly, cocked one eyebrow and shifted his weight slightly closer, subconsciously trying to exert his will and hold his temper. "I haven't lied to you about a single thing, Kaitlyn, though I'm not sure *you* can say the same."

Without giving her time to respond to his subtle accusation, he sat down on the edge of a bed and lifted first one foot, then the other, to show her that he was unscathed. "Satisfied?"

She hid her surprise over his acquiescence, and backed off from his accusation that she hadn't been completely truthful with him, because he was absolutely right. "Not by a long shot."

A knock at the door made Kaitlyn jump in surprise, and stopped her from saying more. Michael rose to his feet and stepped toward the door, automatically putting himself between her and the intruder, instantly on alert. He motioned for her to hunker down behind the farthest bed before he opened the door, and to their mutual relief, found the owner of the hotel waiting with a bag of water, food, and clothes, no doubt sent by his wife.

Michael accepted the bag with thanks, told him about the broken window in the other room and offered to help board it up after the danger had passed. When he closed the door again, he stood there a moment before turning to face her again, his anger in check, apologies on the tip of his tongue.

Kait carefully masked her own harried emotions—she didn't dare try to pick up where they had left off—unsure which of them would explode first if they continued to argue. She couldn't afford to alienate her one and only ally, and she really didn't want to fight. He didn't deserve the trouble he had inherited when he'd saved her life—nor did he deserve her misplaced anger—and she was a grown woman who could ignore a little elemental heat here and there by staying out of his embrace, out of his bed, and away from his lips.

"I think we should both get some sleep," she announced with finality.

EIGHTEEN

Friday brought with it the eye of Hurricane Heidi, one of the largest eastern Pacific cyclones on record, and by Saturday morning, the storm had spiraled up the coast to Baja and headed out to sea, where it began to dissipate. Michael assessed the damage from the hurricane as he walked along the beach looking for Kaitlyn. She'd gone to the other hotel in search of more bottled water and had apparently discovered the same thing he'd just been told—there was none left.

The small village was a disaster. Debris and destruction stretched along nearly every inch of the shore. Thatched roofs, windows, and doors were broken or missing on most of the palapas, and several of the tiny huts had been swept away completely. The hotels had weathered the hurricane surprisingly well, aside from a few shattered windows and torn up rooftops. His villa was likely in far better shape thanks to the countless renovations he'd done to bring it to code. Overall, the greatest damage from the storm had been to the fragile connection he'd been trying to forge with Kaitlyn.

Scanning the beach, he found her sitting in the shade of a palm tree, staring at the ocean. "You'll be glad to know the ferry is on its way from Puerto Vallarta," he said as he approached. "The locals are returning with supplies to repair their village."

"Well it's about time!" Kaitlyn nodded and started to get up. "All this sitting around is killing me, and my project!"

Michael offered his hand to pull her up, but she ignored it, and slipped smoothly past him. In the 30-plus hours since their quarrel, she'd become increasingly agitated, distant, and uncooperative. She'd spent nearly every waking moment wracking her brain with questions she couldn't answer, and inventing clever, discrete ways to avoid spending too much time together in confined quarters. Despite her displeasure, he hadn't let her out of his sight.

"Kaitlyn, you know the danger isn't over."

She stopped in her tracks and turned to face him. "What are you trying to say, Michael?"

"Now that the hurricane has passed, they'll be looking for you again. They haven't forgotten about us, and we're heading right into the heart of their territory."

"I can't let that stop me. I have to get back to San Diego as fast as possible! I've already been away for a solid week. I have to call my team, check on them...*warn* them about the danger. I should have called them days ago; anything could be happening."

Moving toward her, Michael stopped himself from reaching out to her again. Kaitlyn bristled and stepped back, then headed toward the hotel.

Obviously, their brief contretemps had quickly become the least of her worries. While he'd been resisting increasing and unacceptable urges, she'd become entirely immune to the electricity humming between them. He wanted to break through her resistance, tear down her walls, and convince her to trust him. Against his own better judgment, he wanted to hold her, touch her, and kiss her more than ever—despite the innumerable reasons why he should not. Instead, he struggled to give her the appearance of space, while still protecting her, and to remain detached, focused on the goal of keeping her safe. It wasn't easy given her rebellious attitude, and it wouldn't get any easier once they left the relative safety of Yelapa. It didn't matter; he was fully committed to the cause.

An hour later, the boat from Puerto Vallarta announced its arrival with a series of blasts from its horn. Kait was relieved to be moving on, but worried beyond measure. If anyone had been hurt in her absence, she'd never be able to forgive herself for not making contact sooner. She'd foolishly overlooked her only opportunity to use a phone, and been kicking herself for the blunder ever since. Compounding matters, her team had likely been unable to collect data while she'd been MIA, and they'd likely miss several more days before she could do anything about it.

With any luck, Randy and the rest of the crew had taken matters into their own hands during her absence. If they had found a way to get back on the water, there would be much less for her to worry about when she returned, but the odds were woefully stacked against them. Even if she managed to get home tomorrow, the *Triton* wouldn't be returned for another two days. Busting their buckets to get back on the water for those two days would be downright unreasonable given their lack of resources or a viable plan. And that didn't even address the issue of safety. If there was still a price on her head when she returned, then her presence would place everyone and everything they were trying to accomplish in jeopardy.

So what's the solution?

I have no freaking idea.

Kait stared across the bay, waiting for the small launch that would carry her to the much larger ferry. The local dock had been destroyed by the storm, and the ferry could not enter the shallows without hitting bottom. There was probably a good metaphor for her life in there somewhere, but she was tired of thinking. Her time in paradise was nearly over and she'd accomplished nothing.

Making a 360-degree turn, she did her best to memorize the scene before she departed—*never to return.* Her eyes landed first on the boarded-up window of the room she had shared with Michael during their first night in Yelapa. Her stomach clenched; the natural beauty of this place and the lusty, romantic vibration it cast over visitors hadn't been *completely* lost on her. She was, after all, a flesh and blood woman with complex feelings and desires—

which were no doubt being magnified and twisted by the stress of her situation.

Turning her back on the unpleasant reminder, her eyes caught next on Michael's solid figure jogging up the beach toward her like a gladiator ready for battle. Their days in Yelapa had been some of the most vexing of her life. When she hadn't been watching obsessively for strangers or jumping at shadows on walls, she'd been trying to avoid her overly attractive, far too imperious companion—nothing had worked.

Since their flight from his villa, Michael had tried to control her every move, *"for her own safety,"* and vexed her with his maddening stoicism. This morning he'd finally relented and given her a modicum of much-needed space out of his immediate reach—*none too soon!* Between her own fears and his constant scrutiny, her nerves were strained to the max. She was on the verge of a meltdown and anxious to get home.

Kait accepted the hand of a teenage Yelapan boy in the inflatable launch, even as Michael placed his hands on her waist and lifted her over the wide, port-side tube, setting her down in the boat. A spark of awareness shot through her body and Kait took refuge in the irony of the situation. Most people came to paradise to find romance and adventure; she on the other hand had experienced far too much adventure for one lifetime, and was running as fast as she could *away* from the possibility of romance.

The nearly empty ferry crossed the Bay of Banderas, taking Kait and Michael to Puerto Vallarta after delivering a full load of Yelapans and supplies to their ransacked village. To Kait's momentary delight, a pod of nearly four hundred bottlenose dolphins escorted the boat, racing its keel and riding its wake. Blissfully, she watched them play, enjoying the view from the upper deck of the 50-foot ferry. She was glad to be part of something beautiful again, back on the water where she was most at home, and at least for the moment, to be reminded that not everything in the world had gone to Hades.

The ferry followed the natural curve of the bay, passing a site where the ocean had used its natural artistry to carve an arch out of the enormous abutment called Los Arcos. She committed to memory the brief magic of her ride aboard the *Reina Delfín*, which Michael had translated to mean dolphin queen. Maybe someday she would come back for a real vacation, if she ever got past the stark fear that shot through her nerves at the mere thought of Mexico.

Within an hour, the *Reina Delfín* passed the pier designated for cruise ships and docked at a much shorter pier in closer proximity to the primary complex. She was surprised by the size of the marina and the large number of boats; there had to be more than one hundred recreational sailboats, motor boats, and yachts, ranging in length from twenty to sixty feet. It displayed a side of Mexico she'd never considered.

Kait and Michael waited for the crew to set up the gangway and carefully scanned the area for any signs of trouble before disembarking. Far above them, the sun was trying to break through thin clouds and Kait began to feel a glimmer of new hope. She didn't know which gave her more comfort these days, the fluid motion of water, or the solid support of land beneath her feet. The slight sway of the floating dock reminded her of home as soon as she stepped off the ramp. She felt almost normal here, more sure of herself and of Michael than she had in Yelapa.

As she walked the long arm of the dock behind Michael and a few men from the ferry crew, a shadow materialized, reaching from behind her to close around her throat. She didn't have time to scream or think as she watched a silver blade come at her from the left. She moved automatically, swiftly blocking the knife with her arm and ramming her other elbow backward into her assailant's stomach. Adrenaline rushed through her body as she turned to face her attacker. She didn't recognize him.

Yet another man that wants me dead!

Cursing her as a slippery fish, the man lunged with his knife, just missing her as Michael pulled her out of the way.

Momentum carried the man forward and Michael stepped quickly to the side then rammed his fist into the man's jaw as he came back around. Michael was clearly bigger, stronger too, but he would soon be outnumbered—Kait spotted another man running their direction as the crew of the *Reina Delfín* slipped out of sight.

"Stay behind me!" Michael commanded as he crouched like a wrestler and plowed headlong into her assailant. Both men fell to the deck, a heap of flying fists and feet as they fought for control of the knife. Kait watched in horror as the other man drew closer.

Desperate to help, she searched the dock for anything she could use to stop the second man. Her eyes landed on the sailboat moored beside her: the mainsheet was cleated tightly to lock the boom in place, the sail folded neatly and tied. She went straight to the mainsheet and released it, then held the boom steady so it wouldn't swing out until she was ready. When the second man reached Michael and drew a gun from his belt, Kait pushed the boom—it swung out fast and hard, hitting the second man in the face. The gun dropped from his hand to the deck and the man collapsed a moment later.

He didn't get back up.

The first man reached for the pistol just a few feet away but Michael grabbed him from behind, hauled him backward and tossed him to the deck. When he tried to regain his feet, Michael delivered a knock-out blow.

In the distance, three more men ran onto the dock; they didn't look friendly. "Michael! We have to get out of here!" She pointed in their direction.

He picked up the handgun and the knife, looked at the incapacitated would-be attacker, and took Kait's hand with an arched brow as she stepped off the sailboat. "Come on!"

Michael grimaced as they started to run—his ribs hurting from the tussle—and Kait stopped him and took the backpack, strapping it on to keep her hands free. He didn't have time to argue. The men were approaching fast, blocking their exit.

Turning the opposite direction, they ran to the end of a short, solitary dock. They were only 70-feet from shore, but otherwise trapped.

"Can you swim?" Kait asked urgently.

"Do I live at the edge of the ocean?"

Kate did a double take, quickly analyzing his face and words, surprised by his sarcasm. "Then swim for it!"

With practiced precision, she dove into the water, spared a moment to make sure Michael followed, then swam as fast as she could to gain distance from the dock. Bullets rent the air all around them, slicing through the water, zinging past her like darting fish. The backpack weighed her down, creating more drag than she was used to, but she dove underwater and kept swimming, praying they would both survive this new onslaught.

When she came up for air the bullets had stopped, but Michael was nowhere to be seen. *Oh, gods—no!* If he'd been shot, he would drown!

Kait searched the water frantically as the men ran back the way they had come. They would try to intercept her on the beach; she didn't have much time.

"Michael!" She dove under water again hoping to find him before it was too late. Holding her breath, she swiveled full-circle like a periscope and saw no sign of him. Swimming back toward the dock, she searched desperately until her lungs were on fire from the lack of oxygen, then kicked toward the surface.

The moment Michael's feet touched bottom, he stood up and looked for Kaitlyn in the surf. A small wave tugged at his legs, reminding him of their first encounter at his private cove; icy chills raced up his spine. She was nowhere in sight and his heart nearly stopped. "Kaitlyn!"

Damn it! She'd been right beside him when they dove into the water, and he'd struggled to keep up with her, his ribs protesting with every move. When she'd gone under water to escape the gunfire he'd lost sight of her, but he hadn't dared stop. She was a damned good swimmer—faster than him on his worst day, and maybe even fast enough to give him a challenge on one of his best.

Standing in the shallows he scanned the water, searching for any splash or movement. He was about to backtrack when her head popped out of the water just 30-feet away. She saw him and adjusted course quickly, swimming straight toward him. A small swell lifted her, pushing her even faster into the shallow surf leftover from the storm. Michael waded out and grabbed her arm, pulling her the last few feet to shore.

Down the shore, the men leapt from the dock to the sand, and hit the ground running. "Run, Kaitlyn!" Michael pushed her toward the road, then drew his pistol and fired a volley of shots, aiming to maim, but not kill. He clipped two men in the leg, but missed the third, who dove for cover and returned fire as Michael ran to catch up with Kaitlyn.

He was right behind her now, gaining fast in the harder sand as they ran up the vegetated beach to the coastal road. In the wake of the storm, traffic was sparse, but still moving fast. Searching for their best chance, Michael spotted a taxi driver who had stopped alongside the road and emerged from his car to watch the commotion on the beach. "There! Head for that taxi."

When the driver saw Michael and Kait running his direction, he raced back to his car and started the engine. Michael dashed in front of the taxi and aimed his gun at the driver to prevent him from leaving without them. "We need a ride, señor!"

The driver immediately raised his hands in surrender and they hopped into the back seat.

"Downtown, pronto!"

Michael and Kait ducked low and sprawled in the backseat as the taxi wove through the shadows of the strip hotels. Equally exhausted from their narrow escape, they each took a few minutes to catch their breath. Kait kept watch through the rear window, making sure they were not being followed, and Michael laid his head against the headrest, gun-in-hand, ready to prod the driver if needed.

The scenery changed as they moved across town. Instead of tall coastal resorts built for tourists, the east side of town was built for living: a flurry of markets, banks, apartments, and businesses—most of them built from brick and concrete. The stark contrast was remarkable, a classic case of the old world clashing and eventually blending with the new. Wrestling internally to control the pain, Michael finally opened his eyes and looked at Kait.

"We need another taxi. I don't want this guy to know where we're going."

"Okay—just rest." Sitting forward, she spoke to the driver, "*Alto aquí, señor.*"

He was only too eager to stop and let them out.

Michael grimaced. "I didn't think you knew Spanish."

"Only a little."

Dripping wet and haggard beyond words, the two stepped out into the bustling city. Amidst all the hurricane damage and cleanup activities already under way, their sopping clothes and disheveled appearances fit right in. Michael looked stiff and pale—unwell. Kait looked alert and unsettled.

Doing her best to appear nonchalant, Kait hailed another taxi and they both climbed into the first one that stopped. Unsure where to go, she told the new driver to take them deeper into the city. Michael needed time to rest and she needed time to think.

"Are you okay?" she asked finally, still exhausted from their hard-won escape. Michael had no new visible injuries, but his stiff silence indicated that he was hurting even worse than before. He'd taken several hard blows to his already bruised ribs during the fight on the dock. When she'd asked about the bruises in Yelapa, he'd insisted nothing was broken. Since then he'd been quick to hide any discomfort he might be feeling when she was around. Feeling sorry, she reached to touch his ribs but stopped short of her mark.

"I'm fine, Kaitlyn. It's you I worry about. What the hell happened back there?"

"What do you mean?" she asked warily. He sounded like he was ready to tan her hide.

"How did you end up so far behind me?"

"I couldn't find you and I got scared. I thought you might have been shot. Then I saw you at the shore and—"

"Kaitlyn, those men almost caught you. You've got to be smarter than that. You can't stop to worry about me in a crisis; I can take care of myself. You've got to take care of yourself, first and foremost, if you want to get through this alive."

Kait stared at him, dumbfounded by his vehement, self-sacrificing command. "I'm sorry—" she started to apologize, then thought better of it and stiffened her resolve against his unexpected machismo. "—I knew you were hurt and I wanted to help."

"Well next time, no matter what happens to me, you keep moving. You don't stop for anything or anyone. That little ambush means that Pablo is alive, and we walked right into his God-damned trap. He must have guessed we'd make it to Yelapa and come to Puerto Vallarta as soon as the hurricane passed. All he had to do was position his men and tell them to sit tight and wait for the ferry to make its run."

In their brief time together, Kait hadn't heard Michael sound so desperate or violent, as if he'd suddenly realized for the first time that he was about to lose everything that mattered in his life.

From the beginning he'd been determined to save her and battle her unseen foe, heedless of the risks to himself. Hiding within the safe little cocoon he'd created, she'd almost believed that he really was a guardian angel sent to rescue her from an impossible situation, but stone-cold reality was setting in, and even *he* could finally see the truth. Her entire world had tumbled into a state of chaos so far beyond repair that no matter how hard he fought for her, they could both lose. If one went down, the other was bound to be dragged down too.

Michael was clearly upset, reacting in the heat of the moment to yet another close call. But the problem wasn't his blazing temper—she could handle a few tense words. The real problem was something far more terrifying and hard to accept; he was wounded, suffering visibly from an injury he would not disclose. Protecting her was taking a heavy toll on him, physically and emotionally, yet he was unwilling to relent. Somehow, they'd come to an impasse—unable to communicate with each other and unable to work together as a team.

Interrupting her thoughts, Michael asked in a much gentler tone, "How are your hands?"

Kait looked down at the much smaller scrapes that remained from the night she'd escaped her kidnappers. They'd been scoured clean by their quick dip in the ocean, and seemed to be healing rather quickly. "They'll be as good as new in a few more days."

Reaching over, he took her hands to inspect them for himself and brushed his thumbs along a few faint scars that had already healed.

Kait pondered the contrast, remembering all the times throughout her life that she had compared her own hands against those of a man: her father, Nick, William, and Randy. Men's hands were amazing—she always noticed them because they were usually so much larger than hers, so strong and capable. Michael's hands had the added benefit of being gentle and extremely precise—probably a result of his work as a doctor.

I'm strong and capable too, said her wounded inner child from somewhere deep within. *I don't need a man to protect me.*

Yes, you do, said the grown woman who had patched herself together and bolstered her wounds by building a life she could be proud of. *You can't survive this alone.*

In the midst of all the chaos and turmoil, Kait was growing much too accustomed to Michael's powerful presence and reassuring ways. His domineering manner was uncomfortable at times, but perhaps her circumstances warranted it; he seemed far more prepared to handle danger than she was. The volatile conditions that had thrown them together made their relationship tenuous at best, but did that really matter?

Despite the fact that he was driving her crazy in multiple ways, she was becoming more reliant upon his assistance with each passing day, more reluctant to rely solely on her own instincts and abilities. And if he could get her through this mess alive, didn't the ends justify the means?

What if we're suddenly forced to part ways?

Kait shuddered and tried to cast the ominous thought aside. She didn't want to go it alone, but she couldn't bear Michael suffering on her behalf either. "Where shall we go?" she asked in a hushed tone, watching him struggle to conceal his discomfort.

Michael leaned forward and gave the taxi driver a more specific location, speaking perfect Spanish as if it was his native tongue, then leaned back in the seat without looking at her, and closed his eyes again.

Unsure how far they were from their destination, Kait sat back and watched the scenery blur as they sped past. Shortly after they crossed a narrow, one-way bridge over the Río Cuale, she began to see street merchants with burros carrying wares. The taxi slowed and turned down several cobblestone streets lined with white villas and red-tile roofs. She stared out the window, mesmerized by the changing scenery.

"Alto aquí," Michael said suddenly, startling her.

Shifting his body, he pulled money, soaking wet, from his billfold and paid the driver.

Stepping out of the taxi, Kait stared at the aging façade of the whitewashed villa in front of her. The ground was littered with once brilliant bougainvillea flowers and a large pond and waterfall was clogged with debris. The flagstone walk was lined with broken terra cotta pots once brimming over with splashes of purple, white, and pink flowers, and the unbroken branches of a giant jacaranda tree shaded the arched entrance like an elegant sentry keeping watch. Kait hadn't paid much attention to the details of Michael's home while she was there—hadn't had time before their abrupt departure—but this villa surely rivaled its size and beauty.

When Michael joined her on the walkway, his features and demeanor were instantly transformed. Standing tall, his face hardened against his mystery pain, casting it aside as if it no longer existed. He escorted her up the walkway, stopped in front of the massive carved door and rang the bell.

As the door opened, Kait realized she had no idea whose home this was or why they had come to this particular place. She was surprised when a manicured, formally suited butler appeared in the doorway and ushered them in without a word.

"Michael! I wasn't expecting you to grace us with a visit so soon, but I'm very glad you've come." A large man materialized in front of a winding staircase and threw his arms around Michael in an enthusiastic hug, realizing too late that Michael was soaked from head to toe. He pulled away quickly and patted him vigorously on the back, noting that Michael flinched from the jolt.

"I see you brought our patient. She looks quite well. I knew you hadn't lost your touch."

Anton took Kait's hand in his and kissed it. "Forgive me, señorita. I am Anton de la Vega. I brought Michael some supplies he needed to assist you. May I say that you are even more enchanting, now that you are well again?"

Kait blushed, unsure how to respond. "Thank you, señor, especially for helping me. It appears I owe both of you my life."

"Michael is the true hero; I merely watched."

Michael captured her hand in his and gave it a gentle squeeze. "Anton is a former partner of mine. An excellent physician and one of my most trusted friends."

"Then he can help—"

Michael stopped her with a subtle shake of his head. "And here is his beautiful wife, Adele."

Adele stepped forward cautiously, aware that something was amiss, and Anton stared at Kait expectantly, waiting for her to finish. She could tell by his expression that he knew much more than she'd expected about the situation.

"He's hurt. We were in a car wreck and—"

"It's nothing, Anton. I'm fine. A little worse for the wear at the moment, but we're both as well as can be expected. I hate to intrude on you like this, but we need a quiet place to stay tonight."

Adele stepped in immediately, perfectly in tune with her husband. "Of course, Michael. You and your lovely guest are welcome to stay as long as you wish. We've missed you."

"Yes," Anton agreed. "You need not ask. We are happy to assist you both. But first let's have a look at this war wound of yours. Adele..."

As if on cue, Adele slipped her arm around Kait and led her gently away from the men. "Don't worry. Anton will fix him, good as new. Are *you* well? Perhaps you would do well with a warm bath, a meal, and some rest?"

She turned to her maid as they departed. "Alma, prepare some clothes and two hot baths in the west wing."

NINETEEN

Michael followed Anton through the house, dreading the impending argument. Anton knew the score between Michael and Pablo—had witnessed several of their altercations in the years since Michael had married Maria—but he was unsure how his friend would react to the escalating situation. Maria's trouble-making brother had brought danger to the family and the clinic on several occasions and Michael had tried hard to protect them all from Pablo's increasing criminal proclivity.

Until Michael joined the family, Pablo had been the lone patriarch, ruling over the women and his younger brother in the wake of his father's death. He'd immediately resented the intrusion of another man onto his turf, especially a white American doctor, and he'd railed against Michael's attempts to keep him on the straight and narrow. After several blow-outs they had both decided to steer clear of each other, out of mutual love for Maria. If they hadn't, one or both of them would have ended up dead long ago. Instead, Maria had been the one to die and they'd both suffered a terrible loss; each held the other responsible.

From the moment Michael had discovered Pablo's involvement in Kaitlyn's abduction, he'd been pondering what to do; she would never be free to stop running, to live her life out of the shadows until Pablo was in prison or dead. He and Pablo hated each other with a passion, and Pablo would be only too happy to use Kaitlyn as a way to seek revenge for Maria. The fact that she had already managed to escape him twice, and had actually hit him with the Bronco, only made it that much worse. He wouldn't just kill her—he would make her pay dearly for wounding his pride and reputation. Michael couldn't let that happen.

Still reeling from the debacle at the marina, he cursed himself for having let down his guard. If Kaitlyn had been harmed again, it would have been his fault entirely! He'd been distracted in Yelapa by the storm, by Kait's rapidly improving health and aloof behavior, and by the subsequent game of cat and mouse they'd begun to play as a result. He'd lost sight of how much danger they still faced from Pablo once they emerged from their safe little haven. He had even dared to hope that Pablo really was dead and their troubles were nearly over. Now all he could think of were Pablo's threatening words and menacing eyes just before Kait had run him down. *"Maybe she'll give our regards to Maria."*

Pablo was alive—Michael could feel it in his hardened heart—and no matter what had originally compelled him to go after Kaitlyn, it was now a personal vendetta. Blood-for-blood revenge was his first order of business and he would stop at nothing until he had her in his grasp.

Entering Anton's office, Michael felt like a bomb about to explode. Anton was his best friend and peer; he had always been a voice of reason and wisdom in the early years of their medical practice, but was practically immoveable once he set his opinion.

"Well, let's have a look at your injury. That's a nice gash on your forehead. I take it you had neither the time nor the materials to stitch it properly." Anton shook his head as a disapproving parent would.

"We were caught in that hurricane and I was more concerned with watching for signs of concussion than with visual effects. It's no big deal."

"Of course, you're the picture of health. That's why you flinched when I hugged you. Take off your shirt."

Michael did so reluctantly, revealing large black and blue bruises all around his sternum and a few smaller ones along the right side of his rib cage. There was more swelling now than there had been after the wreck.

"Looks like you took quite a beating. You didn't have your seatbelt on. And these latest welts are not from a car wreck."

"Before you say another word, let me just cut to the chase; I had a run-in with Pablo."

Anton sat down on the edge of his desk, barely fazed by the information, and listened intently as Michael explained the gory details.

"I'd heard about Pablo's new line of work on the news. I couldn't help but wonder if there was some sort of connection. You say you have not yet determined how this woman got involved with him in the first place? It can only be drugs."

"Her name is Kaitlyn, and she's not just some woman. She's a top marine biologist at SIMR, who's inadvertently gotten tangled up in Pablo's miserable excuse for a life. There is absolutely no way she's involved in drug running. You don't know her, Anton—"

"Neither do you, my friend."

"Anton—damn it—will you just listen!" Michael took a deep breath and quelled the frenzy in his heart and mind. He had to convince Anton that Kait was innocent, had to solicit his help on her behalf. "Pablo knows I'm helping Kaitlyn. Because of my involvement she is now in far more danger than she ever was before. He wants to punish me for what happened to Maria. I know him. I know what he's thinking. He doesn't just want to kill her anymore—he wants to make her suffer because he knows that is the surest way to exact his revenge upon me. I can't let him do that, and neither can you."

Anton frowned at the situation as he began wrapping Michael's ribs. "I assume you have some idea what to do next? Where to go? If you're right about Pablo, there is nowhere you can take her to keep her safe. Perhaps if she was in protective custody with the FBI..."

"That's a possibility, but I'd have to get her back to the States first and I can only think of one way to do it."

Kait stretched and yawned, awaking from a long, refreshing nap in a feather-soft bed. A hot aromatherapy bath with lavender and roses, followed by a relaxing manicure and pedicure had worked wonders for her spirit and her nerves. For the moment, all the world was peaceful and calm; she found herself wishing she could stay in bed for a century, like Sleeping Beauty, and sleep her troubles away. Hiding in this small corner of the world would be sorely tempting if she wasn't sitting smack in the middle of a drug runner's playground.

When Kait finally opened her eyes, she was startled to find Michael once again watching over her. Her relaxed vibe vanished instantly—it was disconcerting to always wake up and find the man in your dreams staring at you in the real world. Lately, Michael seemed to be sticking his nose into just about *all* of her dreams.

"How did you get in here? I thought I'd locked the door."

"We have adjoining rooms, of course, not that anything as simple as a locked door would've kept me out. I tried knocking several times and when you didn't answer, I figured I'd better check on you. You were in a pretty deep sleep. Feel any better?"

Kait eyed him suspiciously, noting his change in demeanor. Through his opened, button-down shirt, she could see tight binding around his ribs. "Surprisingly, I feel almost normal. What about you?"

"Just a few bruises. Nothing to be concerned about. Are you hungry? Lunch is waiting."

Kait stared at him waiting for the truth. When he didn't volunteer any further details she started prying. "Anton checked your head and ribs? You don't have a concussion? No broken bones?"

"No concussion, as I told you in Yelapa. Two ribs may be fractured or just very deeply bruised. I'm counting on the latter." He lifted an eyebrow at her.

"What? You're the only one allowed to ask questions?"

"I didn't say that."

"Humph. Lucky for you! While we have a moment of peace, let's get one thing straight." Kait rose from the bed and planted herself right in front of his chair.

Bending down eye to eye, she placed a finger softly on the binding around his ribs, directly over his sternum. "I am *not* a coward and I do *not* abandon people in a crisis. If you think for one second that I'm selfish enough to save my own hide at your expense, or anyone else's, you had better think again. That is not the way I operate."

Michael didn't react—just met her stare with his own unblinking gaze. He was as cool as a sea cucumber.

"So I've noticed."

Kait stared defiantly into his dark brown eyes for a couple more seconds then decided the room was getting a little too hot. Turning away with a shrug of her shoulders, she walked casually to the open window overlooking a beautiful garden. "It's kind of late for lunch. I hope you weren't waiting for me all this time."

"You needed the sleep and I was devising a plan."

Kait waited expectantly for him to explain.

Hoping to spend a few peaceful moments with her, Michael led her outside to a gazebo in the jungle-like back yard. "I had a talk with Anton. He's going to loan us his airplane. We'll depart from a small airport outside the city, and land at a private airport in Del Mar. You'll travel as his wide, Adele, using a disguise to make you look just like her passport photo. Once we're there, we'll meet Anton's nephew to pick up a car and drive to La Jolla. It'll be safe there and you can make contact with your roommate."

Kait's face grew slightly pale as he spoke, and when she frowned, a cloud of doom dissolved their brief moment of concord.

"Is there something wrong?"

"You and Anton should have included me in this little planning session of yours. Maybe I had something else in mind."

Her agitation was evident, had been ever since the cab ride when he'd blown up at her. Whatever she was thinking couldn't be good, but he took the bait. "Like what?"

Bowing her head, she was quiet for a moment, but when she looked up again she was far from complacent. “For starters, I don’t like putting Anton and his wife at risk by using their plane and her passport. For another I am not waiting until tomorrow to call my roommate, my family, and my team. I need to know they are all safe before I come home with the Devil on my heels.”

“Nobody will know it’s you, Kaitlyn. You’ll be in disguise. Adele and Anton make this trip several times a year to their home in Encinitas. I used to go with them from time to time, so it won’t draw unusual attention; they’ll be perfectly safe. As for phone calls, it would be better to wait until we are safely across the border before you contact anyone and let them know you’re alive and—”

“Why?” Kait cut him off, impatiently throwing her hands in the air. “Pablo already knows I’m alive; he’s the only one we really have to worry about.”

“Not true,” Michael replied, patiently. “Pablo has eyes and ears everywhere. We don’t know how extensive his resources are, but I guarantee he has police on both sides of the border in his pocket. They can trace a call instantly.”

Her temper flaring, Kait started pacing the small space of the gazebo. “All the more reason to warn the people I care about. I’ve left them hanging for more than a week, Michael. I should have warned them of the danger days ago. If Pablo is so desperate to hunt me down, what will stop him from using them as bait? They need to know what’s going on so they can take measures to protect themselves. If anything happens to any of them, it will be *my* fault!”

Michael couldn’t argue with her logic—Pablo wouldn’t hesitate to use anyone and everyone she cared about to take her down—but he also knew he shouldn’t let her make the calls. They could lose whatever element of surprise they had. He was convinced that someone close to her was involved with Pablo and directly to blame for everything that had happened to her as a result. “Kaitlyn, we don’t know who’s working with Pablo. We don’t know how you got dragged into all this.”

Fire and ice crackled in her eyes as she came to a stop in front of him and made herself as menacing as possible, cutting him off again. “There is no way that Lilly or Nick, or anyone on my crew is involved with Pablo! You know as well as I do that they are all in just as much danger as I am!"

"Not true." Michael kept his hands loose at his sides. He wanted to reach out and shake some sense into her, but he'd learned the hard way to keep his hands off her when she was riled. "They will be in far greater danger if he finds out how much you care about them."

Her eyes widened, the pupils dilating to large black pools of fear. "Don't you *dare* try to scare me into compliance! I let you talk me out of calling before we left your villa because I thought I would be home by now. I had no idea how much worse things would get, but I sure-as-heck know it now. Telling them they are in danger is the first step to keeping them safe so they can finally take action. I only hope it's not too late!"

She was shaking with adrenaline now and needed to calm down. It was obvious she would not yield on this point no matter how much additional danger it created for her. She cared more about the safety of her loved ones than she did about her own—*all the more reason to protect her*—so he would have to find a way to compromise.

"All right. One phone call—"

"Two, minimum," she planted her fists on her hips in triumph.

"No details," he insisted. "Keep it short and simple. 'You're safe. They are in extreme danger and need to go to the FBI for protection. You'll explain everything else later.' That's it." Michael folded his arms across his chest, warning her that he was immoveable on this point.

"Not quite. I also need to find out if my crew has been able to work in my absence."

"Not a chance, Kaitlyn. Two calls and you need to keep them both as short as possible. We'll buy a disposable cell phone, make the calls from two different locations on the other side of town so we don't give away our location and then we'll toss the cell and drop off the grid again."

She tilted her head, considering his words. "Fine."

"We're in agreement then? One call to warn Lilly, one call to warn someone in your family, and tomorrow we get on that plane and fly to San Diego. You'll let go of your whale project until we know who can be trusted and you are truly safe."

Kait hated the idea of flying all the way home in a tiny plane that could fall out of the sky at the least provocation, but it appeared to be the only viable option. After everything else she had been through, flying seemed far less formidable than it once had, and she felt a lot better knowing she would soon call Lilly and ask her to warn her family. She would use the second call to warn Randy and the crew—just because Michael had twisted her words to fit his wishes didn't mean she was willing to give up on her project!

"Agreed." She glowered, still very displeased.

Michael accepted Kait's much too easy acquiescence, knowing he would have to watch her like a hawk in the coming days. She truly was as stubborn as she had claimed, and he wondered—not for the first time—if there was a problem she hadn't yet revealed. "I know it's been a rough few days, but it'll be easier once we reach the States. We'll go to the FBI and tell them everything that's happened. They'll put you in protective custody until they can neutralize Pablo, and then...you'll have your life back."

Kait knew it was a gross oversimplification of the truth, but she let it slide. "I hope you're right about that."

"Sure, it's standard protocol; you won't have anything to worry about once we're home."

Home. She smiled half-heartedly thinking the word had never sounded quite so appealing. "I hope you're as good at makeup as you are at medicine. I don't know how on Earth you're going to make me look like Adele."

Sunlight spread its warming glow over the waking land as Michael and Kait boarded a small Cessna aircraft the next morning and completed their pre-flight checks. The remainder of their time at Anton's and Adele's sprawling villa had been quiet and uneventful.

Kait had indeed been transformed with the assistance of brown contacts, spray-on tan, temporary dye that made her hair raven-black, a perfectly sculpted bun atop her head, a pair of large, jade-colored sunglasses that covered a third of her face, and an elegant, expensive, if slightly too-tight outfit. The outfit came complete with all the exquisite layers: lace and silk undergarments, stockings and garter belt, a royal-blue sheath dress with matching stiletto heels, a three-quarter length fog coat with a fur collar, gloves to hide the absence of a wedding ring, and a tastefully designed diamond earring and bracelet set that would suit a doctor's wife and sell the part to those who knew Adele at both of the small airports.

As they sped down the runway, a blur of concrete and vegetation on both sides, Michael saw Kait grip her armrests and close her eyes. She was holding her breath. "No worries, Kaitlyn. I've been flying planes since I was sixteen years old. It's a piece of cake."

Kait opened her eyes and stared straight ahead, gulping back her fear, her fingers clenching even harder. "You seem to be a man of…many talents. You save total strangers, hike through rugged jungles, swim faster than most fish, *and* fly airplanes. Is there anything you can't do?"

"I'm sure there must be," he boasted, "but I haven't found it yet. I'm always up for a good challenge." He observed her overly tense muscles, her lips pressed together in grim determination.

Is she afraid to fly or, just plain afraid?

Until he knew more, he said nothing.

All night, and into the morning, Michael had tried to pull Kait out of her worsening funk. She'd pulled some fast-switch tactics and called her crew instead of her out-of-country family, but she had failed to reach either Lilly or Randy. Instead, she'd been forced to leave short, cryptic voicemail messages for both of them, and she was more worried than ever. He'd tried to reassure her that they were both safe—perhaps Lilly was on-duty, and Randy was out on the water counting whales—but nothing had lightened her mood.

Without question, she was relieved to be going home, but she needed more time to process and recover from everything she had been through. He knew she didn't feel safe, and there would be more trouble ahead.

Kait had been evasive in Yelapa, but she was aloof and unreachable now, trying desperately to protect herself by shutting him out and disconnecting from the rest of the world—a trick with which he was well familiar. Michael wondered if she had always been so self-protective, or if it was only the byproduct of her recent, harrowing experiences.

Wishing he could find a way to rebuild their previous connection, he made a mental note to keep his mouth shut and go with the flow if she ever opened up to him again. In the meantime, he tried once again to ease her mind, "We should be in San Diego within a few hours. We're taking a longer route than normal, staying inland; Hurricane Heidi was downgraded to a tropical storm, but she's still churning out at sea, creating a few thunderstorms. The remnants may travel all the way from Baja to southern California, but the most we'll see is a bit of rain."

Kait cast a worried look in Michael's direction. "I should warn you, I get a little airsick. I don't fly anywhere unless I have to."

"Why didn't you tell me you were afraid to fly? There might be some motion sickness pills in the glove box. Take a look."

"Lilly finds it hilarious that I can spend weeks at sea with no problem, but put me in a flying tin can and I...well...you don't want to know."

"Try not to worry. We're skirting the storm to avoid excessive turbulence. There shouldn't be any problems."

The small blue and white Cessna rose higher and higher into the morning sky and the ground features quickly turned into tiny ants and molehills with small dots of color interspersed in a sea of green, then brown. Kait took a double dose of Dramamine pills and fell asleep within 30 minutes, slumped in the passenger seat.

Throughout the flight, radio updates kept Michael informed about the current storm, and forecast one last cyclone for the season developing far out over the western Pacific. If it survived the frigid, deep-water currents, it could affect areas as far north as San Francisco, which was almost unheard of. A tropical storm hadn't made direct landfall in California since 1997, but more than a few hurricane remnants had brought death and destruction to California and other southwestern states over the past century.

The remnant of Hurricane Heidi was an excellent case in point: after pounding Acapulco, Yelapa, and Puerto Vallarta, it was now castigating off the coast of Baja, causing coastal flooding, 25-foot swells, and strong rip currents as far north as Los Angeles. In addition to the fifty-six victims that were dead or missing in Mexico, there were already another six victims sprinkled around the San Diego area. It was extremely rare for a storm like this to swing so far north, but warmer than normal water temperatures were keeping it alive.

The latest report indicated that Del Mar, their destination airport, was socked-in with low-lying clouds. The tide had risen several feet from Chula Vista all the way to San Onofre, necessitating sandbagging in strategic areas of low-lying cities like Ocean Beach and Mission Beach. La Jolla was almost certainly being impacted, but not enough to deviate from the plan. Michael stayed on-route and hoped conditions would improve by the time they landed.

Kait awoke from her mind-numbing sleep praying that they were already on the ground. She opened her eyes, tried to wipe away the last vestiges of fog obscuring her vision, then sat upright and stared out the front window in near panic.

"Almost perfect timing, sleepy head, but you should have waited another ten minutes."

Clouds enclosed them, as thick as pea soup. "Are we landing? You can't see anything! Oh my gods, what are we going to do?"

"Calm down, I don't need to see the ground in order to land. The instrument panel will tell me everything I need to know. Check your seatbelt; we'll touchdown in a few minutes."

The plane bounced and bobbed in a moment of turbulence and Kait closed her eyes and swallowed the scream building in her throat. *He knows what he's doing*—she repeated the words over and over in her mind, clenching her seatbelt with a death grip. When she opened her eyes to peek at their impending doom, the opaque clouds had thinned to a heavy mist and the runway lights glowed within luminous halos. The radio buzzed and a grainy voice sputtered at them. They were clear to land and coming in right on target. A shiver dashed up Kait's spine, then the wheels touched down and she exhaled the breath she'd been holding.

"That wasn't so bad was it?" Michael flashed a winning smile.

"Just get me out of this thing before I ruin the nice leather seats."

True to the plan, Adele's passport got Kaitlyn past security without any questions, and a white Lexus GS350-F Sport awaited them in the secured parking lot of the private air strip. A young man handed Michael the keys, hopped into a waiting Corvette, then disappeared down the road.

TWENTY

Thirty miles off the coast of San Diego the *Triton* pulled up near the starboard bow of the *Spanish Maiden*—they could not tie together without jeopardizing both boats in the rolling swells. It was Sunday morning and Dr. Russell was anxious to get the *Triton* back to SIMR for maintenance and restocking before the rightful crew showed up to reclaim her. He hoped they had found some way to keep their project on track in the *Triton*'s absence, but there was one last task he had to complete before this nightmare would end.

Working with quick precision, Russell and Frankie secured four waterproof cases inside the *Triton*'s inflatable zodiac and lowered it onto the surface of the dark, surging water. Frankie stepped into the raft and turned to face Russell. "He's gonna be major pissed if you don't come with me, Doc."

"It can't be helped; the water is too rough to leave the *Triton* unmanned. Leave the talking to me. Just hand over the cases and get back here as fast as you can. And Frankie, don't step one foot on that yacht."

Frankie's heart sank heavily under the threat of Pablo's wrath, but he started the engine and headed toward the *Spanish Maiden*. Russell straightened his back, standing tall and firm on the deck as Pablo stared across the water with an intense scowl. If he showed any sign of weakness, Pablo would find a way to prolong their arrangement, and that was unacceptable.

Frankie threw a line to one of Pablo's men to hold the zodiac, then began handing them the waterproof cases one-by-one. When he tried to hand them the last case, they did not reach down to take it. Frankie looked back at Russell for instructions, and Russell lifted a megaphone to his mouth, determined to be done with the Devil and his nefarious business. "Señor Castañeda, if your man will take the fourth case, we can conclude our deal before the squall gets worse."

Frankie stretched tall to entice the Latin thug hovering above him to grab the case, but the man ignored him—all eyes were centered on Russell. After a seeming eternity of tense silence, Frankie set the case down and offered up a megaphone to so Russell could hear their reply. Pablo gave a slight nod and one man snatched the megaphone while the other grabbed Frankie and hauled him aboard the yacht. Pablo lifted the megaphone as if in slow motion. "Our *deal* is not over, Dr. Russell. Your obligation to me is over only when *I* say so."

Liquid heat rose through Russell's veins like molten magma. He'd known it was risky to send Frankie over with the money, but he'd had no choice. "I've paid my debt in-full, Castañeda. I agreed to make the run twice and I have no intention of letting you run my life indefinitely."

"Foolish Doctor…it is no longer *your* life." Pablo pulled a deadly handgun from under his coat and aimed it at Frankie's temple while his thug pulled tight on Frankie's arms. "I *own* you and your little mule, and you will do anything and everything I tell you to do."

Frankie turned pale as a ghost while Russell struggled to clamp down on his fear and rage. He could pull his own gun from under his shirt and try to kill Pablo and his men before they shot back, but the odds were not in his favor. They had better weapons, more of them, and they already had Frankie in their grasp. He couldn't involve anyone else in his deadly mistake, and he couldn't make the runs alone; it was a two-man job at least. Even though Frankie had gotten him into this mess, he couldn't let him die for it.

"We'll make another run after the *Neptune II* has been repaired. I can't take the *Triton* again without jeopardizing the whole set-up."

"We will extend our original agreement, but that is no longer your only obligation. One of your female employees has caused many problems. You will find her and bring her to me."

Russell's heart kicked into overdrive. "What...who are you talking about?" Russell did a quick mental catalog of his direct reports, only three of which were female, then flashed a quick glance at Frankie who shrugged, looking just as dumbfounded as Russell felt. "Do you mean someone that works at SIMR?"

"I mean the troublesome cat who runs one of your research crews. The fucking brunette, who ran me over with a truck, killed my second in command, and cost me the lives of several brothers. Right now she is sneaking across the border so that she can run to the fucking DEA and castrate me, you, and this entire operation!"

Even as Russell's mind rejected the information that spewed from Pablo's vile mouth, his instincts told him that the troublesome woman to which Pablo was referring could only be Kaitlyn O'Donnell, the crew-leader of the *Triton*. How in blue blazes had she gotten mixed up in all this, and how could she possibly be responsible for the death of anyone, much less Pablo's scum-sucking, drug-running brothers?

Russell's gut clenched with knowing dread. She had never called him on the satellite phone to demand an explanation or harass him about the loss of the *Triton*. He'd thought it a miracle that she had capitulated without a fight, but now he realized that had never been the case. He should have known better; Kaitlyn O'Donnell had never capitulated to anything for as long as he had known her. Somehow she'd gotten herself in trouble with Pablo, and it was obvious by the vehemence of his words, that Pablo would do much more than kill her if he got ahold of her.

Russell steeled his nerves. "I don't have any females running research crews. You must be mistaken."

Pablo lowered the gun from Frankie's head to his thigh and pulled the trigger. Frankie screamed in pain and sagged against the man holding him as blood soaked his jeans. The man pushed Frankie forward and tossed him over the rail into the cold, churning water. Another man jumped into the zodiac and grabbed the last case, then set the small craft adrift. As the *Spanish Maiden* pulled away from the zodiac and the *Triton*, Pablo lifted the megaphone again. “Bring me the woman!”

Russell kicked off his shoes, stowed his gun, and grabbed a floatation buoy, then dove into the water to rescue Frankie and the zodiac. There was no time to think about finding Kaitlyn and handing her over to the Devil, or returning the *Triton* to her crew so they could salvage their project. There was no time to ponder how he’d gone from the master of his own universe to the lowly minion of a diabolical drug lord. He had to get Frankie out of the water before every shark in the vicinity got a whiff of his blood and came rushing in a frenzy. The Devil was making his escape, and all Hell was ready to break loose!

Forty-five nautical miles away, a well-cared-for, 40-foot, wooden sloop entered the mouth of San Diego Harbor under full sails, splashing its way to the posh marina it called home. Its captain used a satellite phone to check the progress of the hunt while he’d been out on the water taking care of other business that he dare not reveal to his employers.

“Any news?”

A crass voice answered the unceremonious question with an equally informal response. “Couple of flagged names popped up with Homeland Security at the airstrip in Del Mar an hour ago.”

“Elaborate.” He’d had a hunch something was about to break.

“Michael Storm and Adele de la Vega. Per instructions, they were not detained.”

“Anything else?”

“I’m not your secretary; check your fucking voicemail!”

He’d already done so regularly throughout the day. At last report, Lillian Zamora was still searching for her missing roommate, the SIMR security guard had been located and identified, and the *Triton* was still out to sea. There'd been no sign of Kaitlyn O'Donnell for ten days straight, and there was an inordinate amount of tension and activity throughout the border region between Mexico and the United States. If things got any hotter, he just might end up looking for a new source of income!

"Follow up on Storm and the woman with him. Let me know what you find. Keep a tail on Zamora too. I'll check back with you at 1600."

"Follow up on him yourself! I'm not your lapdog."

"Really? Could've fooled me."

The line went dead and the captain began to lower his sails and switch to diesel power. There were too damned many things to do and not half enough hours in which to do them. It was only noon on Sunday and already his day was fucked!

TWENTY ONE

Kait wasn't surprised when Michael pulled the car into the manicured driveway of a beautiful Spanish-style house situated on the famous La Jolla cliffs—she knew he was accustomed to the finer things in life, and shared her affinity for the coast. What did surprise her was the fact that she'd seen this particular house before, driven past it often when she fantasized about which of these incredible mini-mansions she would live in if she ever struck it rich.

The house was dressed in white stucco walls with a blue tile roof, and boasted abundant archways and curves. It was built long and low to maximize views of the ocean, as were most of the oceanfront homes in the area. The landscape, while comprised of native, xerophytic plants, was clean and elegant, but her favorite feature was the stained-glass mural built into the entryway. It showed a pod of whales swimming through an underwater paradise, and conjured feelings of deep familial devotion and sanctuary. Someday she would create a home that evoked those feelings too, if she still had a someday in her future.

As Michael pulled the Lexus into the garage and triggered the automatic door, Kait's attention drifted away from her new, incredibly altered reality. The giant door clattered and settled into place like a giant shield, and she felt the first tentative waves of reassurance wash over her since they'd left Anton's home.

The turbulent flight and the foggy, surreal drive through bumper-to-bumper traffic had strained her nerves unendingly. The once comforting sights and sounds of her hometown now oozed with hidden dangers and fearsome strangers—she'd hunkered down as low in the car seat as possible and scanned every car that came near for any signs of trouble, all the while trying to look and act nonchalant so Michael wouldn't realize how scared she was. The silence between them during the drive had been palpable too; she was certain he had just as many questions as she did, but neither of them was ready to broach the growing list of issues that needed attention.

At least now she was safe on U.S. soil—a simple phone call away from all things familiar—about to enter another beautiful fortress with her very own...bodyguard? White knight? No, more like a bossy, brooding, black knight, but considering everything that had happened in the last ten days, she felt damn lucky to have him and to still be alive. Anything more than that was pure gravy.

When Michael turned off the engine and stared blankly through the windshield, stillness captured the air between them. Kait took a deep, fortifying breath and breeched the silence, "Will we be staying here long?"

Michael blinked, but continued to stare straight ahead. "No. This is only our first refuge. We should be safe here for three, maybe four days."

The tension had been building between them for days and Kait knew things were about to escalate into something far more tangible and inescapable when he turned in his seat, getting ready to share whatever was on his mind. She was nowhere near ready to talk about it, whatever *it* was, so she grabbed the handle and swung open the car door, hopping out of the car with more speed than finesse into the dim light of the cavernous garage.

"Kait, we need to—"

Pretending not to hear him, she closed the car door, cutting him off, and headed for the door into the house. Of course it was locked, and Michael followed close behind her, so within seconds she found herself confined between two very solid, unrelenting objects. She swallowed her nerves and reached for a level of indifference she didn't feel. "Shall we go inside?"

Michael removed her sunglasses and looked down at her, seeing through her perfectly made-up, imposter's face. She had no choice but to look away—anywhere but into those concerned, knowing eyes. She hadn't fooled him one bit.

He knows you're running scared, knows you need him more than he needs you.

Their time together was almost at an end, her future opening wide before her. If she didn't steel herself against the terrible unknowns ahead, she just might crack under the pressure. She needed to get on with her life, get back on task and save the whales and her career, and put El Diablo away in prison where he belonged.

Moving almost imperceptibly closer, Michael hovered mere inches from her for several interminable seconds, then released a heavy sigh and reached past her to open the door. "I need to check out the house. Wait here until I come back." He slipped into stealth mode and disappeared inside, leaving Kait alone in his etheric wake.

A chill crept up her spine at the sudden emptiness of the cold space around her. Pride insisted it had nothing to do with the irrepressible man that so easily dominated every moment they spent together, and she chided herself for trying to avoid the inevitable. Sooner or later he would have his say, and she would listen because they were both reasonable people stuck in a very unreasonable situation.

Purposely shifting her attention to the mundane, Kait looked around speculatively and noticed that the garage was mostly empty except for a few paint cans, light bulbs, and stray pieces of lumber—either someone was an excessive neat-freak, or the house wasn't currently occupied. If it was empty, that would explain why she'd never seen anyone here conducting the business of life when she drove past. No cars in the driveway, no pets bounding around inside or out, and no toys left in the yard by tiny, innocent hands; it was a crying shame.

Kait took several steps toward the car and yelped in surprise when the dim light from the garage door opener winked out, dropping her into total darkness. With the door closed and no windows to welcome the light, she might as well have fallen into a deep-sea abyss; she couldn't see the

Lexus any better than she could see her own hands in front of her searching the inky blackness for something to hold onto.

It's only a few feet in front of you, right where it was when the light went out.

All she had to do was stay calm and keep moving forward, but that was easier said than done when the memory of nearly drowning in the cold, black ocean came rushing back like a tsunami. Bracing her mind against the fear, Kait inched forward until her legs bumped into the Lexus. She fumbled along its perimeter looking for the door handle, then yanked it open with a shaky sigh of relief as the overhead dome-light cast its glow over the sleek leather interior. The light didn't reach more than a few feet into the surrounding darkness, but it was enough to settle her nerves for now. It was completely ridiculous, but she simply couldn't take the dark anymore.

When Michael returned a few minutes later, she was sitting sideways in the driver's seat, her smooth, stocking-clad feet hanging out the door, the stiletto heels in her hands, counting the seconds to keep from going mad.

"What happened?" Michael turned on the garage lights and quickly stepped in front of her, noting how wide her pupils had grown, and how rapidly she was breathing. Seeing her still disguised as Adele was a shock every time he looked at her—she was much darker, both physically and spiritually—a more haunting version of herself. She was still beautiful but somehow irrevocably different with black hair and brown eyes; she couldn't transform back into the blue-eyed mermaid he knew fast enough.

"I'm fine. The light went out and I didn't know where to find the switch."

"I'm sorry. I should have remembered the automatic light was set on the shortest setting. The house has been empty for a while. Everything is set to conserve resources."

"It's okay. I worked it out."

Michael took her hand and guided her into the house. There Kait was surprised to find the interior half-empty, the air stale, and the sparse furniture covered with white sheets. She had always imagined a happy young couple living here with their 2.5 children, a dog, and two cats, but it had been empty.

Who would abandon such a beautiful home?

Walking through the house, Kait felt like an outsider trying to catch a glimpse into someone's life. Briefly, she scanned the formal living room and dining room looking for any personal artifacts that might tell her more about the absentee owner; she found nothing. The table surfaces were empty, the hallways devoid of pictures. Saddened by the stark emptiness of the rooms, Kait realized that the house felt almost like an inanimate expression of the man who had saved her—filled with grand potential, but hollowed out by neglect, and extremely alone. The thought sent her mind wandering down a long and troubling path—one she had been trying to avoid.

Michael hadn't stepped foot in his home town for more than two years; it had been twice as long since he'd walked the halls and rooms of his childhood home. The furniture covers were laden with dust, the blinds and curtains closed tight in every room. The air was stuffy, the cabinets barren—he'd forgotten that little detail—he would have to venture out to get food, a disposable phone, and a few other essentials. Thankfully, he'd kept the electricity and water services operating to maintain the security system and landscaping. It wouldn't take much effort to make her ship-shape again for their stay, and it would be a lot more comfortable than hot-footing it from place to place every night on the run. His clandestine efforts to hide his family home from Pablo would finally pay off.

Watching Kait wander about, pulling pins out of her hair to let it down, stopping here and there to remove linens from the furniture and open windows, Michael realized that the La Jolla house might actually be a refreshing and welcome change from the villa in Mexico. It reflected the happier times of his youth and his bachelor days—the carefree times before he'd met Maria and unwittingly traveled down that ever darkening road.

Maria had been a brilliant light shining amidst a darkness that had eventually swallowed them both. They'd had some beautiful times together, but he'd never guessed the direction his life would take when he'd made his first trips south of the border. Maybe that was the same reason he had never come back—he couldn't feel her presence here, could see no evidence of their brief life together. He'd needed those reminders after she died, so that he wouldn't forget the endearing little details that had brought them together.

Michael snapped to attention when Kait's frustrated murmuring pulled him from his reverie. She had removed her coat and gloves, discarding them in a neat pile on the sofa along with the shoes she had already removed in the garage, and was struggling to open the sliding glass door that led to the vast balcony.

"Blast it! What am I doing wrong?"

She had flipped the lock and tugged on the door several times before he reached up and removed the extra lock above her head. When he did, she glowered at him for a moment, then tugged again and opened the door with visible relief. Except for this tiny outburst, she'd been extremely quiet and blatantly evasive.

What is she thinking about? As much as he wanted to know, he couldn't just force it out of her. Her walls were higher than Mount Everest right now; he had to be patient.

Kait quickly wiped her face and walked outside onto the high wooden deck, her cheeks flushed from...*what?* Had she been more frightened in the garage than she'd revealed? Or was something else bothering her?

Michael followed her to the edge of the deck and noted the surprise on her face when she peered over the railing at the surf fifty feet below. Some visitors looked at the sheer drop with stark terror and immediately ran back inside, but Kait smiled as she leaned against the rail and absorbed the view.

The tide was exceptionally high today, a small strip of sand disappearing and then reemerging each time a wave crashed on the beach. Her muscles began to relax and her breathing slowed, her distress instantly forgotten, if only for the moment. He'd seen that contented look on many a beautiful face over the years—the girls he and Ian had brought home for "study sessions" in high school and college had always swooned over the incredible view, or perhaps the dollar signs attached to it—but it meant much more to see it on Kait's face now.

"Michael, this is incredible! How did you find such a wonderful place to hide out?"

"I didn't. That happy honor goes to my mom. She found it right before I was born and made dad buy it without even getting a peek first. She was afraid someone else would snatch it out from under her."

Kait turned to him, astonished. "You grew up here?"

Her eyes darted around the space, taking everything in, searching for any detail she had missed at first glance. The look on her spray-tanned face was priceless, her kaleidoscopic blue eyes as big as saucers behind brown contact lenses, her mouth hanging agape.

"Pretty lucky, eh?"

"Well, yes! But…it's so…empty and—"

"Cold? I know. I bought it from mom and dad when they decided to pare down and move to Maui. They packed up all their stuff, and Ian and I turned it into a bachelor pad for a while."

"Ian?"

"My older brother. He lives in San Francisco—has a thriving practice there."

The sudden influx of information had Kait completely flummoxed. Her mysterious and elusive guardian not only had a caring mother and father tucked away in Hawaii, but an older brother living in the same state following the same career path!

And I thought he was all alone in the world—ha!
Shows how little I know.

Reading between the lines, Kait realized Michael was sentimental enough to buy his childhood home from his parents, but callous enough to turn it into a bachelor pad—no doubt countless women had been wooed on this deck by the brothers Storm.

"You're shivering, Kaitlyn. We should go inside."

Kait took a step back and glared up at him. "I'm not cold, Michael. I'm mad as a wet cat! I've known you for ten whole days—we've been on the run together, been in several life or death situations, broken I don't know how many laws together, and now that we're about to part ways, you're *finally* ready to tell me something about your personal life? That is so...so...maddening!"

Kait made a beeline back into the house and headed straight for the second floor. Michael followed close on her heels, his own feathers suddenly ruffled. "What do you mean 'now that we're about to part ways,' Kaitlyn? Who said anything about parting ways?"

Kait stopped abruptly, halfway up the stairs, and turned around so fast that Michael had to slam on the brakes to avoid knocking her down. "You did!" She jabbed a finger into his chest, carefully avoiding his bruised sternum, her eyes shooting sparks like a fireworks display.

"No, I didn't."

She planted her hands on the smooth, blue fabric that hugged her hips, and stood face to face with him, the stairs bringing her even with his height. "Yes, you did!"

Michael wanted to reach out and grab her, prevent her from running away again, but he controlled the urge and lowered his voice. "When?"

Kait heaved a sigh of frustration, "Yesterday, when you said we would go to the FBI, and I would be put into protective custody."

Michael choked back an angry response, realizing that her interpretation of his so called plan was correct. If the FBI put Kaitlyn into protective custody, there were no guarantees he would be allowed to stay with her. In fact the odds were against it because the FBI wouldn't want to put all their eggs in one basket. Whatever the case, he wasn't in any hurry to be forced away from her or held under lock and key by the FBI. "I was just trying to make you feel a little safer. You didn't seem very happy with the plan, and I didn't want you to worry."

"Not worry? My whole life is falling apart and I'm not supposed to worry?"

"That's not what I mean—"

"That's not even the point, Michael, and you know it." Kait cut him off when she realized they'd gotten off track.

"Then what *is* the point, Kaitlyn?" One minute he'd had everything under relative control, moving along smoothly according to plan. The next minute she had him playing defense, all tied up in knots, tripping on himself.

Her frustration was contagious.

"The point is, that you don't really trust me!" She punctuated her words with a triumphant nod and then turned to finish climbing the stairs.

It was his turn to be flummoxed, and Michael quickly grabbed her arm and pulled her back down to face him. "What the hell are you talking about, woman? I trust you almost as much as I trust my own Nana!"

Kait paused, taken aback by his words. The sudden image of him having a mischievous Nana somewhere in the world doused the fire in her gut and made her feel a little soft and steamy. She couldn't, however, afford to back down now that she was finally making some sort of progress.

"You have a funny way of showing it." Taking hold of her emotions, Kait cut to the chase. "You make plans and arrangements, without including me, you ask for every little detail of my life, but share nothing in return, and you flaunt your manly charms to get your way, then turn around and sucker punch me when I start to fall for it."

"The hell you say!" Michael yelled as he finally lost his cool. "I have damned good reasons for...*everything* you just said. Christ almighty, you were asleep when I made plans with Anton to sneak you across the border, and you *needed* the rest. I've asked you for details in order to figure out what the hell is really going on, and I've never even balked when you deliberately hold back information—which scares the hell out of me.

"And if you want to know more about me, all you have to do is ask. I'll tell you anything you want to know."

Kait's eyes grew predatory as a wicked smile cracked her lips. "Anything?"

Michael cringed at his mistake, but knew he would have to pay the piper to ensure her continued cooperation. "Anything—I have nothing to hide and I *trust* you completely."

Her features turned from predatory to precocious as an army of questions buzzed through her mind. Once she got started, he'd never get her to stop, and they didn't have all day to go tripping through the details of his past. When she opened her mouth to ask the first question, he quickly raised a silencing finger to her lips. "*After* I take care of a few important tasks. You can ask me a hundred questions after we've taken care of the basics."

Her left brow rose to an arch as she stared him down. "I suggest you move your finger before I bite it."

"I didn't realize you were that hungry, but food *is* one of those basics." He winked at her and lowered his finger, then realized he was using his so called "manly charms" to manipulate her just as she had claimed. *Shit!*

She lifted a hand to his cheek, and brushed her thumb over the light stubble with a sweet smile. "Don't think for one second that I didn't notice how well you just proved my point."

TWENTY TWO

Michael led Kaitlyn through the house, giving her what his dad had always called the "grand tour," and made a mental list of things they would need to make their stay comfortable. Thankfully he'd already made the two most important phone calls prior to their premature departure from his villa—the La Jolla house was *mostly* ready for their stay.

His first call had been to notify his home-security company of his pending arrival. He'd added a 24-hour patrolman to the perimeter—he'd sleep better knowing there was another set of eyes watching for trouble—and, he'd put them on high-alert about his girlfriend having a violent stalker. Ian would undoubtedly receive word of both his return and his requests, but that couldn't be helped.

Only a matter of time till big brother comes calling.

Speaking of which, he had yet to see any sign of the new patrolman. If someone didn't show up soon, he'd place another call and have a few words with the manager.

In the kitchen, Michael tested the water temperature at the faucet. His second call had been to make sure the natural gas would be turned on *before* their arrival—a man could live without electricity and running water when necessary, but after four days on the run, he was past ready for another long, hot shower and some savory, home-cooking. He couldn't help wondering if Kaitlyn enjoyed cooking, but it didn't matter since the kitchen had always been one of his favorite domains.

Upstairs, he ushered Kaitlyn into his bedroom and past his plush California-king bed as he pulled the dust-cover off. "This is the master bedroom." *Plenty of room to share since I'm not letting you out of my sight.* Then, pointing to the master bathroom containing a luxurious multi-head shower system he'd installed himself, he added, "You can wash the dye from your hair and the stain from your skin in there."

She didn't say a word, but hightailed it back to the hallway—*neutral territory.*

Following her out, he showed Kaitlyn the upstairs entertainment room where she could watch television while he went shopping, and his office-cum-library, which would almost certainly be explored in great detail during his absence. She wanted to know more about him and needed a distraction from her worries and fears—his bachelor house would be the perfect diversion. While she was busy analyzing his distant past, she wouldn't have time to wonder about his more recent history.

Directing her back toward the stairs, he caught her troubled expression. She'd been avoiding certain unavoidable topics since they'd landed in California, and he'd been letting her. "Are you ready to talk?"

She sighed and looked him in the eyes. "Why keep this beautiful house if you don't want to live here?"

Not the subject he'd been expecting her to breech—her unexpected and much too dangerous question slammed into him with the force of an arrow hitting a bull's eye. In two seconds flat, she'd blown right past any of the "easy" questions he'd been expecting, to one that he couldn't even answer for himself. And without trying, she'd neatly shifted the attention away from her own disquieting problems, back onto him. Her ability to zero-in on the exact things he didn't want to discuss was damned uncanny.

Feeling defensive, Michael had the brief notion that two could play that game. Then he thought better of it. They would get nowhere fast if they both kept pushing each other's buttons, and between the two of them, she really did have the better excuse for being reactive and defensive. Her life was in a state of massive upheaval, whereas he didn't really have a life left to upheave. Since he'd promised she could ask him anything, he gave her the most honest answer he could. "I don't know."

"Pshhh…I knew you wouldn't answer my questions." She tried to move past him in a huff and he snatched her arm to stop her.

"I'm not being evasive, Kaitlyn. Of all the questions you could have started with, you just happened to ask something to which I don't know the answer."

Wary determination settled across her face as she reclaimed the space in front of him, silently daring him to find out just what she would do if he continued to prevaricate. "Try."

Michael took a deep breath and thought about it. Then thought about it some more—thought so hard in fact, that he started to get pain in his chest and a headache. She was asking much more than a simple "get to know you" question. She was asking for something deep and intimate—*a sign of his trust*—without going straight for the million-dollar question that would most likely rip them apart. She was being *easy* on him, and while a part of him appreciated her continued patience, another part of him wanted to shake her for being such a pushover, for being so naïve and trusting given the extremes of her situation.

When she thought he wouldn't answer, she again headed for the stairs. He let her go this time, but the words forming somewhere deep down inside, finally slipped out. "This house is…*was*…a part of me. I guess I haven't been able to let it go yet."

Kait paused and gazed back at him with a small nod, acknowledging that he had finally shared something difficult, personal. "Some things are pretty hard to release. I'm sorry I started with such a difficult question. It wasn't fair, or intentional."

As she moved down the stairs, his uncertainty magnified exponentially. *You waited too long, tough guy. She's going to leave your secretive ass behind!*

Michael followed her, his heart lodging in his throat when she stopped just shy of the front door. She seemed calm, almost complacent, but he wasn't quite sure he was reading her right. He edged up behind her, poised to grab her if she bolted. There wasn't much he could do if she really decided to leave him, short of holding her hostage while he worked up the courage to bare his soul, but he would do just that, if he had to.

"Both of your homes are beautiful, Michael, but this amazing mural," her slender arms danced though the space with a flourish, "this takes the cake."

Surprise and relief kicked him in the gut at the sudden lightness in her voice and movements. She wasn't angry or dissatisfied with his nebulous answer. She had accepted it for the truth it contained, and moved on. Again, she was cutting him some slack, and he accepted her peace offering with gratitude. "You like the mural? My mom designed it a long time ago. It's one of her best pieces."

"Your *mother* made this?" Kait looked at him incredulously.

The tiniest flicker of hope, and something else, shown in her eyes. Clearly she hadn't given up on learning more about him, just changed her tactics. Michael took the opportunity to lighten the mood and share some of the more innocuous bits of his past. "She's a fish-hugger like you. I inherited a certain appreciation for the ocean from her and dad, but I haven't explored its depths like you have. I've always taken the ocean for granted."

He cast a sideways look through the house to the vast ocean beyond the deck. "It's always been there, and I enjoy it, but my real passion is boats." His eyebrows danced up and down playfully, though he wasn't feeling even the slightest bit playful.

"What kind of boats?" she asked, digging deeper.

"All kinds, I suppose, but I get the most out of restoring old classics, especially sailboats. They hold a certain kind of majesty for me. It's hard to explain."

Kaitlyn smiled, waiting expectantly for him to continue. Her genuine interest and curiosity made him concede that he really hadn't told her much about himself during their brief time together. In fact, he'd probably been just as secretive and evasive as she'd been—*not on purpose of course; more like habit.* His days as a recluse had seriously tarnished his social skills. She was hungry for information about the man she'd been trusting with her life. She would jump on every possible lead and try to connect the dots because she needed to know that her trust was well placed. It was a matter easily rectified. All he had to do was open up without letting the minefields slip out.

Yeah, real easy.

Michael led her back to the kitchen, adding a few small comforts to his shopping list as his imagination bounced back and forth between desire and necessity: plush terry cloth robes, sheepskin slippers, a few good bottles of wine to help them both relax—*scratch that; wine is too romantic*—a strong bottle of scotch whisky would be better to take the edge off. And now that his brain was working again, he added a small handgun, ammo, and pocketknife to the list for Kaitlyn. The handgun would be difficult, but not impossible to get ahold of quickly with the right connections.

She wandered back outside to enjoy the view from the deck, and he followed. He hadn't done this much talking in years, especially not about himself, but if it repaired the rift between them, he'd have to keep dredging. "I find it inspiring that something so small, and relatively helpless, can traverse something as colossal and powerful as the ocean without sinking. When you set aside all the laws of physics, forget about the engineering that makes the thing work, and just look at the bigger picture…well…it boggles the mind. It's amazing what humans create to get along in the world. Boats, airplanes, space craft—they're all fascinating."

"I know what you mean," said Kait with growing excitement. "I'll show you around the *Triton* sometime. She's the most amazing vessel I've ever crewed. She's massive, has all the latest technology, and yet when we get caught out on the ocean in the middle of a storm, I realize just how small and insignificant we are in the grand scheme. Like you said, it's a miracle any boat stays afloat."

"I'd like to see your research vessel. Do you have a large crew?"

"Well, she's not really *mine*…just on temporary loan for my project. She can berth a crew of twenty, but we've been operating on half that. Our captain has three people on hand to keep her running smooth, and they pitch in when we need them. My research team and I handle everything else."

Their brief conversation came to a standstill as they both stared out over the water, each lost in their own thoughts. Adele's blue dress hugged Kaitlyn's feminine curves, accentuating her small waist and round hips. Michael found it difficult to rectify the contrast between the soft, delicate woman in front of him with the image of her commanding a bunch of salty biologists and deck hands during a storm.

Kait shivered and changed the subject. "Is there a way down to that cove?"

Michael drew up close behind her, his hands instinctively rubbing up and down her arms slowly to warm her. She stiffened slightly, but remained otherwise motionless, accepting his touch. Bending lower, his mouth hovered just behind her ear. "The stairs are behind that paradise plant, but we can't go down. The tide is too high and the stairs aren't safe; they haven't been inspected in years."

A chill raced through her body, and she surprised him by settling against his warmth, her back pressing into his chest. Kaitlyn hadn't been particularly docile or cooperative since he'd met her—he liked her spunk even though it made her harder to contend with—so her tentative acceptance of his intrusion into her personal space made him feel like a prizefighter who'd *finally* won a round against the reigning champ. He absorbed her weight and kept the friction at a steady pace against her smooth arms.

This was a capable, outspoken woman, letting down her guard for just a moment. He'd observed her reluctance to let others do for her what she could do for herself, and for some reason that made him want to help her all the more. She was brave and tenacious—the spider incident and her fear of flying the only weaknesses he'd observed thus far—and her unorthodox tendencies drove him crazy, but they also made him smile, deep down in his soul. She'd proven her strength and courage ten-fold; she could fight to defend herself, swim through a sea of darkness all alone, and trek through the jungle injured and unprepared, but damn-it, she shouldn't have had to do any of it.

Holding her here, in one of his favorite places after all they'd been through, he felt a pang of want. *I could get used to this.*

And the want was quickly followed by the sharp sting of self-recrimination. *So you can let her down just like you did Maria? Never again.*

Staring across the horizon, Kait took a deep breath, savoring the salty ocean air and the cool wind. She turned slowly to face him, "It feels so good to be home." Her eyes locked with his for a moment, conveying deep gratitude. "Thank you for bringing me back. There were times I thought...I might not make it." Her face flushed with emotion and she turned quickly away, still ensconced in his arms, but once again facing the ocean.

One look, like he was the Sun and she a grateful flower dependent on his radiant light, and he was on the verge of spinning her back around to kiss her sweet, perfect lips, and much more. If he gave in, he would tell her how much he liked this soft, feminine side—*he'd been fantasizing about receiving such looks from her for days*—but that would lead to other words, other thoughts that he was not prepared to acknowledge.

She saved them both by quickly changing the subject.

"Do you know I can recognize certain beaches just by their scent? The guys at work put me to the test once. They blindfolded me and drove around town making me smell different beaches. I got four out of five correct and won twenty bucks." Kait laughed and inhaled the salty air again.

"This one smells like...kelp, wood, saltwater, a touch of sandstone from the cliffs, and...one of my absolute favorites," she took another deep breath, "honeysuckle. It's a unique combination; I'll never forget it now."

She looked beautiful standing here in his embrace, the dark ocean swelling beyond her, a stark contrast to her vibrant light. Disarmed and thoroughly derailed, Michael finally gave in to the urge that had hounded him for days—he shouldn't do it, but he couldn't stop himself this time. One hand drifted to the curve of her hip, the other scooped the dye-blackened hair away from the nape of her neck. Bending lower, he kissed her shoulder.

Another chill shimmied through her body, and she turned into his embrace again, wrapping her arms around his waist. To his surprise, she didn't duck and run. Tilting her head back, she licked her lips and rose up on her tiptoes until her mouth was millimeters from his. Their lips touched tentatively, once, twice, and tendrils of her hair tickled his chin in the breeze as she melted against him.

So damned sweet and sexy.

Fire licked at his loins as her belly pressed against his hips. Overwhelming need blossomed in his chest. He wanted her more than he wanted his next breath—wanted to lay claim to her affection, her body, her pliant lips, even her tantalizing female scent. If he let her walk out of his life without experiencing every part of her, he would be the biggest fool that ever lived. Or maybe he'd already won that title given the fact she still didn't know the truth about him. Once she knew his secrets she would walk away from him and never look back. And he would let her go, because that's all he was really capable of. He was a tainted man with nothing on which to build a new foundation.

Michael sighed, torn with conflict. Each soft press of her lips against his was a nail hammered into his coffin. Her body told him with simmering heat and softness that she wanted him—*whether he deserved her or not*—that she needed him in more ways than he could ever imagine. His inner demons whispered that what she didn't know about his past wouldn't hurt her, but he knew it wasn't true. *If he could give her now, did the past or the future really matter?* He'd already made the promise that mattered most; he would see her through this nightmare to the bitter end. He would protect her from Pablo, and from anyone else that tried to hurt her, but Heaven forgive him, he was no longer sure he had the strength to protect her from himself!

Kait relaxed into the moment, letting go of everything that had been holding her back, dismissing reason, logic, and prudence, and accepting the gift that the Universe had placed directly in front of her. She was grateful to be home, and alive, grateful that this amazing man had seen fit to make her problems his own. She was grateful that even though their time together was nearly over, he had finally opened up to her and shared a small part of himself to carry in her memory.

Michael's impassioned face set her body alight now, just as it had on several other occasions, but she no longer felt the need to resist. Overwhelmed by circumstances, she had run away each time he'd started to succumb to temptation—she'd caught glimpses of his inner battle, and had no desire to tempt a man who didn't want to be tempted—knowing she couldn't handle more trouble on her overflowing plate.

This time was different; she was no longer afraid of getting caught in his undertow. She had survived countless dangers, against impossible odds, and made it back home. Here, in her home town, she felt just a little bit stronger, a little more certain of her chances for a future. This time, when he gazed at her as if she was an irresistible siren calling him to his doom on the rocks, she gave-in willingly to their mutual fate. Doom, or dream-come-true, she yielded to the lust igniting deep at her core; she couldn't contain it or suppress it anymore. All her rules and imperatives raised their warning flags—*you're losing sight of much more important matters*—but sweet heaven, did it really matter in the end? Couldn't she cut loose just a little after all she had been through and take a little bit of pleasure to soften all the pain?

Yes, go for it!

No! Good criminy, what are you thinking?

She was supposed to be finding a way to salvage her project and save the whales; instead she was here in another romantic hideaway, kissing the man she'd been trying to steer clear of for days, about to start something she wasn't at all prepared for.

Her mind jumped briefly to Randy with a slight hint of guilt. He wasn't her boyfriend—*we only kissed once*—yet she felt like she was betraying him somehow, at least the idea of him. Before her life had crashed to pieces, there had been the possibility of something beyond friendship. They'd made no advances, no promises—they hadn't even talked about the kiss, and it had been so brief that she wasn't even sure she had enjoyed it.

With Michael, the fireworks were flying like the Fourth of July.

Answering the question in Michael's kiss, Kait wove her fingers through his hair, clasping two handfuls and pulling his head down for better access to his lips. She kissed him back like it was the end of the world, or at least the end of hers—*maybe it was.* If she didn't make it through the rest of this misadventure, at least she could arrive at the pearly gates with the happy knowledge that for once, she had walked the wild side and cut loose with a gorgeous man!

Michael met her kiss measure for measure, his heated body pressing against her in all the right places as he lifted her against him. She felt a strong urge to wrap her legs around his hips and hold on, but Adele's prim and proper dress kept her tightly ensconced. A frustrated moan slipped from between her lips as she wrapped her arms around his neck instead.

"Michael," she whispered softly in his ear.

He set her down, his hands settling on her hips, his forehead resting against hers as he fought to regain control. Withdrawing behind his impenetrable wall of self-recrimination and shame, he spoke softly, "Make no mistake Kaitlyn, I've wanted you from the first moment I saw you, but...I can't do this. I don't want to hurt you."

Kait tensed, lowered her gaze, but kept her arms wrapped firmly around him. "Why do you think you would hurt me after everything you've done to help me?"

If only he could find a way to explain the situation without dredging up his entire past. He didn't want to jeopardize her trust; he was her only ally, her only line of defense. He couldn't bring himself to tell her that he'd been responsible for his wife's death, or that he was to blame for Pablo's unrelenting wrath. If she rejected his help and ran away, she'd be left to fight Pablo alone, as helpless as a lamb to the slaughter.

"Kaitlyn, you're an amazing woman. You deserve someone who can love you with a whole heart, share a bright and happy future with you. I have no future...nothing to give you beyond this time right now, and my protection."

Kait nodded once, but didn't let go of him. "I wasn't asking for the future, Michael. I'm not sure I have one to share—"

Michael raised a finger to her lips, silencing any further response. "There are things you don't know...things I'll tell you when the time is right. I have no right to ask, but I need you to keep trusting me until then." He finally locked eyes with her as his hands drifted to his sides. "You're not out of danger, and I intend to keep my promise. I'll be here for as long as you need me."

Kait swallowed back the protest building in her throat. The black knight was back, his unseen ghosts nipping at his heels, tearing at his heart—she could see it plainly in his pain-filled eyes. What could she possibly say to his request? *No—after saving my life time and again, after risking your life countless times, I don't trust you anymore?* She might be a fool, but she couldn't be so cruel to the man she had come to rely on—and yes, trust. She had to accept what he was saying, and let it go.

The words of her childhood therapist came tumbling from the dustbin in the back of her mind. *"When someone you care about rejects you, Kaitlyn, never take it personally. It's their problems getting in the way, not you."* That sage advice had served her well over the years, but she had never quite gotten over the first rejection—the *worst* rejection—by her own father whom she had adored.

Michael held his breath, waiting.

Her lips moved, as if searching for a response, but words failed her. Hours passed in mere seconds until at last her arms fell away from him and she looked up with hurt and acceptance shining in her eyes. She wanted him—was willing to accept him with no questions, no strings, for however long fate granted—but she was letting him go.

Holy fuck! Fate was a fickle, hard-hearted bastard and Michael knew him all too well. Kaitlyn was more than a casual fling—she was the real deal, the one you took home to your family, married and started a life with. She was the kind of woman a man would be happy to spend his life pleasing in every way possible, and she was his for the taking. But he didn't deserve her. He never would.

Turning away from temptation, Michael walked into the house hoping she would eventually forgive him; he sure as hell wouldn't be able to forgive himself.

Time to get down to business and find a way to secure Kait's future. He had to stay in the here and now, stop wallowing in the past, forget his desire for the woman, and concentrate instead on her safety. If he didn't get his act together, he just might end up being responsible for her death as well.

Ruthlessly forcing their passionate encounter from of his mind, Michael grabbed a notepad and pen from a kitchen drawer and wrote down the pass code for the security system, the number for the security company, and the number of the cell phone he'd received with the car. Kait joined him inside after a few minutes and locked the sliding glass door behind her. She positioned herself silently on the other side of the tiled kitchen counter—*a safe distance from his reach*—and he realized she hadn't responded to his request for continued trust.

If I leave her alone, will she be here when I return? "I need you to stay here while I get food and supplies. Will you do that?"

She bristled, but remained calm. "I don't want to stay here alone."

"You won't really be alone. There'll be a security guard outside, and there's an alarm system connected to all the windows and doors. If the alarm is triggered, a whole team will show up. You'll be safe until I get back and I won't be gone long." He handed her the paper with the numbers. "Keep this with you and memorize the numbers."

"I'd feel safer with you, Michael."

She crossed her arms, hugging herself to control her emotions. He could see the fear slipping back into her eyes, the stiffness in her posture as she fought it. "We can't take the chance that someone will recognize you. It's safer if you wait here. When I get back, we'll plan our next steps, together, and tomorrow, after we get a good night's rest, we'll go on the offensive. We're going to bring Pablo down, and you're going to get your life back."

Kait nodded, conceding his point, and agreeing to his plan. "In that case, I'll need some fish tacos from Rubio's, some dark chocolate, and some practical clothes."

"Agreed," he responded, using her word from the night before.

TWENTY THREE

Kait held open the closed slats of the white wooden blinds in the living room and watched as Michael talked to the security guard before driving away in the Lexus. When the guard turned and waved at her, she let the blinds slide back together, wondering how he'd known she was there from 25-meters away. Leery of being watched, and loath to sit idly and wait, she retraced her steps through the entire house, much more slowly this time. If there were clues about her haunted host, she would find them.

What she had observed and pondered over the past several days had now been brought into the open and made abundantly clear; like so many people, Michael was emotionally unavailable and deeply troubled. He was a man with secrets, and had a past so foreboding that it clung to him like rotting seaweed, preventing him from moving forward in life. If she hadn't witnessed the pain and guilt pouring from him with her own eyes, she'd have thought he lived a charmed life. Clearly, money, mansions, and family did not guarantee happiness.

Standing in the master bedroom, she again peered out to see where the guard was and what he was doing. She didn't like the idea that he might be there to keep her inside just as much as he was there to keep others out. When he appeared again, making his way around the perimeter of the property, he turned his head and looked straight at her, though there was no way he could possibly see her through the closed draperies. He'd have to have X-ray vision to know she was there, yet he smiled and tilted his baseball cap at her—*a friendly warning that he was keeping a very close eye on things?*

Creeped-out by his extrasensory ability to locate her, Kait immediately backed away from the window. She would *not* go near them again.

Continuing her hunt for information, Kaitlyn returned to Michael's office. Sitting at Michael's desk, she removed the expensive diamond bracelet from her wrist, and was about to remove the matching earrings when she noticed a little black book—an old, and probably out-of-date address book with entries made by at least three different people—and a rolodex with a collection of business cards from people who had serviced the house over many years. These were the only personal effects she had found so far, which was very discouraging.

Reading through the entries on the B-page of the address book, Kait nearly jumped out of the seat when the doorbell chimed loudly through the air.

Good criminy! Who in the world would be ringing the doorbell? Kait froze where she sat and strained to listen across the distance. She wasn't going anywhere near that door until Michael came back!

When she didn't hear anything for several minutes, curiosity got the better of her, and Kait made her way back to the living room to peer through the blinds. As she neared the door, she heard voices arguing—at least two, both male, both verging on angry—and decided she had better find something to defend herself with in case the need arose. She thought briefly of grabbing the biggest knife she could find in the kitchen, but the blood-drenched images of the men on the fishing boat where she'd been held captive, and nearly raped, ran through her mind and made her sick. A knife could be taken away and used on her by an assailant—*not happening!*

Instead, she ran to the laundry room and grabbed a broom.

Dashing back to the living room, Kait peered out between the slats. The security guard stood facing the house, his back to the street, arguing with another man. His eyes flashed between the house and the intruder. The other man had his back to her, but it only took a moment to recognize him in his khaki shorts, striped polo shirt, penny loafers, and faded cotton ball cap—*Randy! What in the name of Poseidon is he doing here?*

As she debated the possibilities, the argument escalated. The guard shoved Randy to the ground and pounced on him, twisting one arm behind his back as he pressed a knee into Randy's back and held him down.

Blast it! Kait pulled the paper from her pocket and furiously tapped-in the code to disarm the security system so she could open the door. Running outside, she yelled at the guard, "What are you doing! Get off him! That's my co-worker you're attacking!"

The guard looked up at her and frowned. "Ma'am, you're not supposed to be out here. Get back inside and arm the system. Pronto!"

"Not until you let him up. I know this man. He's a good friend of mine!"

"Kait, is that you?" Randy squawked, his face being pressed into the grass as he struggled to free himself from the guard's grasp.

"Stop hurting him or you'll be in very big trouble when Michael gets back!"

"This man is an intruder, ma'am, and you're the one who will be in trouble if you don't get back in the house right now." The guard punctuated his words with an extra twist of Randy's arm, making Randy groan in pain.

"Stop it right now or I'll knock your block off!" Kait reared the broom menacingly several steps away from the mêlée. "I know you're just trying to do your job, mister, but I promise you, this man is not a threat!"

"Ma'am, my orders were crystal clear; nobody but Mr. Storm goes in or out of this house." He squinted at her in anger, a nonverbal warning that she had best not threaten him again if she knew what was good for her, then twisted Randy's arm even harder. In a cold voice, the guard made a deadly serious threat of his own, "Get yourself back in the house and arm the system or I'll break his arm. And if you hit me with that broom, I'll break a lot more than that."

"Do what he says," Randy huffed, using all his strength to resist the man's twisting action.

Kait backed off, unsure what she could do to defuse the situation. She had no idea what would happen to Randy if she went back in the house, but the guard clearly had the upper hand in this situation, and took his job incredibly seriously. "Look, mister, I'm not trying to cause trouble for you, and I certainly don't want anybody to get hurt here. If you let go of his arm, I'll go back inside. You can call for backup and Randy will go and sit in his car until the police arrive. Isn't that right, Randy?"

"Yeah, sure, whatever will get this gorilla off my back."

The guard eased up on the pressure ever so slightly. "Go inside first, then I'll let him up."

"Okay, that sounds fair." It wasn't fair at all, but she needed to appease the brut somehow. Kait backed into the house, broom still gripped firmly in-hand, then closed the door and reset the alarm. She opened the blinds and yelled through the window. "I've rearmed the system."

The guard released Randy's arm and it snapped to the ground like a rubber band. Stepping back, the beefy man drew his handgun from its holster, aiming it at Randy as he slowly got to his hands and knees. "That's far enough for now. Stay right where you are."

Randy looked up at Kait through the window, "Are you okay, Kait? Is it really you? The crew has been worried sick, and your roommate has half the San Diego police force looking for you—"

"Shut your mouth, and sit on your hands while I call for backup," said the guard.

One second, the guard was waving his gun in Randy's face and Kait was contemplating how to explain her altered appearance and disappearance—the next second, Randy was grabbing the guard by the arm and yanking him off balance. Randy's other arm arced like a bolt of lightning, his fist connecting with the guard's jaw in one knock-out blow. The guard collapsed on the grass, hidden conveniently from the street by a small flowering bush.

Randy swiped the gun from the ground as he rose to his feet and looked at her. "Who the heck is this guy, Kait? Tell me you're okay. If he hurt you, I'll kick his sorry ass!"

Kait remembered how fast and agile Randy had been at the park when she'd tried to steal his hat—remembered how confident he'd been on the *Triton*, and in the water when he dove into the frigid ocean to cut a swath of fishing net off of a struggling dolphin.

"I'm fine, Randy. Are you okay?" Kait gawked at him through the glass, incredulous that he'd disarmed the guard so easily. Randy was a powerhouse of energy and speed, but the guard was built like a boxer.

"Yeah...I'm all right. Can't believe this pansy got the drop on me." Randy approached the window near Kait. "You gonna let me in or what, boss?"

Kait swallowed back her instinctive response, remembering Michael's theory that someone she worked with might be smuggling drugs. Randy was the newest member of the team, the least experienced—*and the most enthusiastic*—a prime candidate for such nefarious business if she was honest with herself. "How did you know where to find me, Randy?"

"Pure dumb luck, boss. I just came in off the water for the day, was heading up to the offices to enter the data we collected, and I saw you go whizzing past me in that Lexus. Had to flip a U-turn right in the middle of the street to catch up. Almost took out a couple of other cars in the process, but I wasn't about to lose sight of you."

"But, I'm in disguise. You couldn't possibly recognize me from that distance," Kait challenged.

"Yeah, you do look pretty different in that getup. I almost didn't recognize you, but you turned your head, looked right at me with that worried frown I see sometimes, when you think nobody's looking. Different color skin, hair, and eyes—gotta admit that almost threw me—but I'd know that frown anywhere, and I always trust my gut.

"I followed the Lexus here, waited around the corner trying to figure out what to do, then I saw the Lexus leave again and you weren't in it, so I came over to check things out for myself. Pretty damned glad I did!"

Only slightly mollified, Kait turned her attention to her project. "You've been out collecting data this week?" She'd prayed countless times in the past ten days that the team had found a way to keep the population count going in her absence, but she hadn't really believed they would.

"You doubted me?" Randy put his hand over his heart dramatically and smiled that thousand-megawatt smile she'd seen only a handful of times since she'd known him. "That hurts, boss. I told you when you hired me, it would be the best thing you ever did."

Relieved and excited to hear more, Kait punched in the security code, opened the door, and practically leaped into his arms, hugging him fiercely as he walked through the door. "You have no idea how happy I am to see you, Randy!"

He lifted her off the ground and hugged her back, holding onto her for several long moments. "The feeling's mutual, boss. You had me really worried for a minute there."

When he set her down, he looked her over and gave a low whistle. "Looks like you've been swimming with a pack of sharks." He stepped inside and closed the door. "You really okay, Kait?"

"I'm a lot better now than I was a few days ago. You wouldn't believe what I've been through since the last time we talked."

Randy nodded and lifted her scarred hands to look at them. "I got your voicemail. Are we safe here? Maybe we should get out while the getting is good." He looked around with a shrewd eye, assessing their surroundings, "Preferably before the gorilla out there wakes up."

"I don't know, Randy. I'm beginning to wonder if any place is safe for me right now. I'm in a lot of trouble and you probably shouldn't be here or you're liable to get dragged into it with me." Kait sighed and turned to reset the alarm.

"Hold off a second, Kait. I don't like the idea of locking ourselves in here with that gorilla out there. Why don't we go for a drive and talk? You can tell me why you're all made up like Spanish diplomat Barbie, and I'll tell you what's been happening here. Between the two of us, I'm sure we can figure out what to do next."

Kait thought it through quickly and realized she really didn't want to stay here alone with the creepy x-ray vision gorilla, especially after she'd threatened him with physical violence. She didn't know how long Michael would be gone, but she didn't like the fact that he had given said gorilla instructions to detain her if she tried to leave.

"You're right." She grabbed her shoes and coat. "Let's get out of here until Michael comes back."

Safely tucked into Randy's sleek, black Chevy Camaro, around the corner from Michael's house, Kait let out a sigh of relief. She'd felt incredibly exposed just walking down the street, even with Randy by her side looking tall and lean, and ready for anything. As soon as he sat down in the car and locked the doors, the long pent-up questions that had tormented her began tumbling out. "Randy, please tell me everyone on the crew is safe...that nothing bad has happened while I've been gone."

He paused a little too long before responding, then turned the key in the ignition. The engine roared to life as her heart dropped in anticipation of bad news.

"The crew is safe, Kait." He reached across the gear shifter and took her hand to reassure her. "We managed to pull together a small fleet, mostly volunteers from the San Diego Yacht Club, to take the crew out and continue the count. We only lost two days coordinating everything; part of the crew is out there right now." He released her hand and shifted gears, pulling away from the curb. "We got a rotation going, one biologist per boat: six boats all together, three-on, three-off. We've been doing visual counts, line-of-sight, good old paper-and-pencil tallies."

Kait wasn't sure how effective the data would be, but it was a lot better than ten days of nothing. And it did her heart a lot of good to know the crew was so dedicated to their cause that they had banded together and devised a workable plan in the absence of their leader—not an easy thing to do without resources, funds, or support from the powers that be. "Didn't you get the gear off the *Triton* in time?"

"No, when I got there she'd already disembarked—and I got there pretty damned fast after you called." He looked at her pointedly, as if trying to convey that he regretted not being there when she'd needed him.

"Don't worry, Randy. I'm sure the gear and the data we left aboard the *Triton* are safe enough for now," she bluffed, reluctant to bring up the possibility of sabotage. It wasn't *his* fault they'd lost the *Triton*, and it wasn't *his* fault she'd been abducted—*it wasn't anyone's fault but her own.* Michael had been right to chastise her for boarding a strange yacht without backup.

She smiled at Randy to let him know everything would be okay, and saw reticence behind the half-hearted smile he returned. There was unpleasant news coming and she wasn't ready to hear it. "Sounds like you guys have really gone the extra mile these past few days. I'm so grateful for everything you did to keep things going! I couldn't have asked for a better crew," Kait swallowed back the emotions threatening to break free. Her eyes watered, her heart twisted, and she looked out the window seeking refuge and fortification as she took a deep breath.

Familiarity, home, friendship, work—these were things that could see her through whatever else was coming. Maybe her future wasn't so bleak after all, but she wasn't ready to bet her life on it. Steadier now, she mustered her authority, "The crew that took the *Triton* should be back tomorrow at the latest; William said they were only slated for a ten-day stint. We'll get our ship back and hit the water in no time."

Randy nodded and stopped at the next corner before turning right onto the main thoroughfare heading out of the small, exclusive La Jolla neighborhood. He looked at her, his face filled with apology. "I don't know an easy way to tell you, Kait, and I'm really sorry, but... Barney is dead."

Kait felt her heart crack like an ice sheet, the fractures spreading with each wrenching beat. Memories of their easy camaraderie over the years flashed through her mind: shared lunches at the pier with their feet dangling over the side, heart-felt hugs when she surprised him with small presents at the holidays, or just because. Sage advice she should have received from her father, if he'd cared enough to be part of her life, had been given instead by a saucy old seaman with a sparkling smile: a man who had married the Navy instead of a wife, and never had kids, or kin, or hearth—she'd never been able to figure out why.

A torrent of sobs clawed their way up her throat, several of them breaking free before she managed to cloak herself in buffeting, icy winds strong enough to refreeze the deadly fissures of heartbreak.

I knew it was him!

Barney didn't deserve to die in the line of duty at what was supposed to be a safe, benign job. He didn't deserve to die lonely and alone. Nobody deserves to die that way!

Had he still been alive when she tripped and fell? If she hadn't kept running, if she had stayed with him instead, would he be alive right now? Would she be dead instead of him?

The ice sheet cracked even deeper. A face flashed in her mind. Pablo El Diablo: murderer, drug lord, and relentless hunter that sought to destroy her—there was a man who lived up to his moniker. A killing chill rolled down her spine, splicing her back together, adding new thickness that would make the ice all but impenetrable. If anyone deserved to die that way it was Pablo, not Barney!

I should have hit him harder with the Bronco.

I should have killed him when I had the chance!

"Kait?" A worried voice broke into her vengeful, murderous thoughts, pulling her back to the moment.

Before she could respond to his simple, yet oh-so-complicated question, the squeal of brakes and burning rubber drew their mutual attention to a blur of metal directly behind them. A white Lexus had just passed, going the opposite direction, and then madly flipped a U-turn—*Michael!*

"We've got company," Randy announced as he floored the gas pedal of the Camaro and the car lurched forward.

Kait braced herself with both hands, grabbing the edges of the bucket seat beneath her, unsure what was happening. "It's only Michael. Pull over so I can let him know I'm okay."

"Are you crazy? That jackass was holding you hostage in his gilded cage, or have you already forgotten what his hired gorilla said?" He looked in the rearview mirror, mumbled something angry and indecipherable under his breath, and shifted gears again.

"No, I heard what the guard said, but I trust Michael. He saved my life several times in the past few days. You have no idea—" she stopped, unwilling to explain herself as confusion turned to anger. "Stop the car, Randy!"

The roads through La Jolla were crowded year-round. They wound around and over the slopes of Mount Soledad, an escarpment that rose from the ocean and peaked at only 822 feet above sea level, but served as a prominent landmark and vantage point for the surrounding area. Michael remembered the streets well—he was no stranger to the area, having spent most of his life in this small, sheltered corner of the world—and found his way quickly to his old haunts, efficiently gathering food and supplies. He needed to get back to Kaitlyn as quickly as possible for his own peace of mind.

He'd only been home twice since he'd met and married Maria; everything looked vastly different this time—foreign and completely disconnected from the life he'd been living in Mexico—yet somehow the same. Given his current circumstances, the perfectly manicured homes and the normal, happy families living in them took on a storybook quality, a feeling of surrealism and unreality. Nostalgic memories flashed through his mind as he drove through town, strengthening the budding desire to return to some semblance of life.

After picking up Kaitlyn's fish tacos in the neighboring town, Michael was heading back to the house with most of the supplies he'd wanted. He was only a few blocks away, about to turn into his cliff-side neighborhood when he saw her—still disguised as Adele, but with her hair flowing loose around her shoulders and a veil of hatred clouding her face—sitting in the front of a black sports car traveling the opposite direction. He'd only caught a glimpse of the driver: tall, white, sand-colored hair, and a determined look.

What the hell?

They hadn't seen him, but they must have heard his tires squeal when he'd reacted instantly and made a reckless U-turn to follow them without much thought about the consequences. Before he could even settle into a straight path in the confines of a single lane, the Camaro lurched forward with impressive speed. Michael pressed the gas pedal and raced after them, his mind spinning as fast as his tires, trying to figure out who Kaitlyn was with, how they had found her so quickly, and how he could have been so foolish as to leave her alone.

Then he remembered the hatred on her face. Had she somehow learned of his secret?

Maybe she called someone for help.

Maybe she decided to leave your ass behind!

His hands gripped the steering wheel a little harder as he accelerated, weaving deftly around slower moving traffic. He was nearly a block behind them and losing ground—the driver of the Camaro drove like a maniac, risking Kaitlyn's safety as well as the safety of those around them—he had to catch up quickly or risk losing them completely in the maze of surface streets that comprised Pacific Beach.

The Camaro veered left at a three-way intersection, leaving La Jolla Boulevard, perhaps to avoid the dense flow of cars, and Michael followed. Right—right—left, another right. With each turn, it moved even farther from view. Michael had only seconds after completing one turn to observe their next maneuver before they disappeared from sight. *Hell and damnation!*

They had turned onto Mission Boulevard, were heading back toward the ocean. He could risk getting caught at the light, or turn a block early and parallel them—try to cut them off—it was risky either way. Their escape options would decrease drastically if they made the mistake of continuing south into Mission Beach. The narrow strip of land between the Pacific Ocean and the man-made Mission Bay had only one narrow road; it slashed through a crammed network of postage-stamp houses and alley-sized roads, which were usually clogged with skaters, cyclists, pedestrians, and tourists, all vying for their own slice of sand-in-your-shoes paradise. If he could steer them into the fray, he might actually catch them.

Michael turned the steering wheel hard-left, executing a new plan as fast as it unfolded before him. He raced across the next intersection, strained to catch another glimpse of the black Camaro at the intersection a block away—the fates saw fit to reward him. They were there—still heading south, still moving recklessly fast. He paralleled them for several blocks until they arrived at the first of two major intersections. A left-hand turn at either juncture would lead them to the highway; all he had to do was anticipate the driver's next move. If the Camaro didn't turn left within the next four blocks, they would enter the beach strip with only one way out.

Michael waited and watched. They made the turn at the second intersection—Grand Avenue, a major road that would take them to Interstate 5, and anywhere in the world they wanted to go after that. Seeing only one opportunity to stop them, Michael sped into the intersection, directly in front of the Camaro and several other cars traveling the opposite direction, forcing them to turn right or hit the Lexus. The Camaro swerved mere feet from his front bumper and Michael got the only confirmation he needed to see the chase through; Kaitlyn was yelling at the angry driver, a frightened, incredulous look on her face.

She's not a willing passenger.

He didn't know if that made him feel better or worse—he only knew that he had to stop the Camaro and free Kaitlyn or he might never see her again.

When Randy refused to pull over, Kait took off her seatbelt, turned in her seat, and got up on her knees to watch Michael through the rear window of the Camaro. The Lexus grew smaller with increasing distance as Randy raced through town, apparently trying to steal her away from Michael. She was suddenly very confused. "Why are you doing this, Randy?"

"Sit down, Kait. Put on your seat belt." His voice was a calm command that held no menace, but demanded compliance. She was the boss, but he was in charge.

"Not until you tell me why you're doing this," she responded hotly.

Randy chose that moment to make a sharp turn at the last possible moment, cutting across a busy intersection like a sharp knife through soft butter, smooth and precise. Kait clung to the backrest of her seat, her knees digging into the seat bottom as the momentum almost threw her against the passenger door. Horns blasted behind them as he sped up the street, and she watched with dread as Michael cut across the intersection too, narrowly missing a collision with at least two other cars.

Kait looked at Randy with wary dismay. "Someone's going to get hurt if you don't stop this."

"It won't be you or me."

He didn't look at her, but made another sharp turn, this time to the right. Kait wasn't prepared for the sudden change in trajectory, and this time she fell right across Randy's lap, her right hand seeking something to brace against and finding purchase on his left thigh—*an incredibly hard, muscled thigh.* Embarrassment mixed with anger and fear as she looked into his cool blue eyes. His right arm reached over her, shifted gears, and then coiled around her waist to hold her steady.

"I missed you too, Kait, but you really should put your seatbelt on."

He handled the Camaro like an experienced racecar driver—cool, confident, and obviously enjoying the opportunity to burn a little extra fossil fuel and testosterone at the same time. She wanted to slap him, and almost did until she remembered they were in the middle of a high-speed chase through a small but busy beach town—*her home, her town*—running, not from rabid strangers that wanted to kill her, but from the man who had saved her life on numerous occasions, and was obviously trying to do so again.

Both men were strong and capable with sharp senses and fast reflexes; if they were speeding around a smooth racetrack, devoid of obstacles and innocent, less-capable drivers, she was reasonably sure they would all emerge unscathed. Unfortunately, this was not the Indy 500. The chance of a multiple-car-collision or other equally disastrous accident was extremely high, and not something she wanted to add to her list of experiences.

Kait pushed herself out of his lap, smoothed her coat, and settled quickly on her derrière, grabbing her seatbelt and pulling it tight. Her mind went to work on a solution to the problem: how to get Randy to stop the car long enough for her to get out. She looked in the side mirror hoping he hadn't yet managed to lose Michael.

Just before Randy made another hard turn, she saw the Lexus materialize a block away.

He's okay. I'm okay. Randy?

Definitely not okay.

She glared at Randy, her mind pulling together the only explanation she could find for his actions and feeling the first sting of betrayal. "So you're the one that brought danger to SIMR's doorstep? You're a drug runner?"

He took a moment to turn his concentration from the road to her, his eyes connecting with hers, asking unspoken questions, withholding vital answers. "I'm not sure how you jumped to *that* conclusion, Kait, but you're wrong."

"If I'm wrong, then prove it. Pull the car over and explain it to me—"

Randy cut her off, "Can't do that, boss."

"Can't, or won't?"

"They amount to the same thing at the moment. I'm sorry for everything you've been through, and I'm glad you're okay, but I have no intention of letting anything else happen to you. You *need* to trust me—I'm the good guy in all this."

Kait snorted with incredulity, her fingers gripping the edges of her seat as he made yet another hair-raising turn. "Ha! You're the good guy, and I'm supposed to believe you based on what exactly? The fact that you just kidnapped me? Maybe the fact that you have obviously been lying to me since the moment I met you? Or no, how about the fact that you are clearly *not* who you said you were?"

"Believe me based on your gut instincts." He looked in the rearview mirror and gave a slight nod of satisfaction that he had finally shaken Michael off his tail. "Throw everything else out the door and get down to basics, Kait. You know me better than you think you do. You trust me more than you want to because you know I am not here to hurt you.

You know you're safe with me because you know who I am and you've seen what I can do."

Kait swung her fist across the car and punched Randy in the upper arm, surprising him as much as herself. She'd never been a violent person, but she was so blasted angry right now that she wanted to hit something, and he was the most obvious target. "Cut the macho hero crap, Randy. I'm not buying it! I was safe with Michael. We've been through hell together in the past ten days, and he has proven himself over and over again. You on the other hand...I thought I knew you, at least a little bit."

"You know enough that you can hit me without fear of retaliation." He looked pointedly at her. "Next time keep your wrist straight, like a rod. You'll get more force behind the punch without hurting yourself."

Kait stopped massaging her wrist, unsure which irritated her more: the fact that she had indeed hurt herself without even fazing him, or the fact that he knew it. Before she could respond, Randy threw his right arm across her torso and yelled, "Hold on!"

The white Lexus shot across four lanes of traffic, placing itself directly into their path, forcing Randy to turn right. Tires screeched, horns blared, and rubber burned as the two cars suddenly raced side by side, trying not to hit the parked cars on either side of the narrow street.

Kait screamed, shutting her eyes and bracing herself as a cyclist crossed the street in front of them and both cars slammed on their brakes to avoid hitting the teenage boy. "You are both totally insane! Stop the frigging car, right now!"

With nerves of steel, Randy got the jump on Michael and accelerated again as soon as the kid was out of his path, but Michael was still hot on their tail, pushing the 306-horsepower engine of the Lexus to prove its reputation. The Lexus increased speed, pulling up on the left side of the Camaro, preventing him from making a left-hand turn toward the freeway. Randy realized Michael's strategy as he was forced to turn right toward the strip.

"Your new friend is persistent, Kait. I underestimated him." Focusing on the traffic light at the next corner, Randy smiled and floored the accelerator. As the light turned red, they careened around the corner into oncoming traffic, entering the narrow strip on Mission Boulevard. The new direction would carry them past the Belmont Roller Coaster, across one of several bridges that spanned the bay, and across the San Diego River, toward the harbor; exactly where he wanted to go.

TWENTY FOUR

Kait craned her neck in time to see Michael's car screech to a stop to avoid hitting the thick cross-traffic in the intersection—the steady stream of vehicles would block him from following them onto the strip until the light changed. He would never catch them now, and she was on her own against a whole new set of unknowns.

She eyed Randy without looking directly at him, and casually reached for her seatbelt. His hand shot out and grabbed her wrist. "Don't even think about it, Kait."

Yanking her hand away, she felt scorched by both his touch and his words. "Why are you doing this? Who the heck are you?"

Randy released a heavy sigh and looked at her, "A concerned friend."

Kait bristled at his unhelpful response. "Friends don't kidnap friends unless they are taking them to Denny's for breakfast in their pajamas!"

"Sorry, boss. I didn't have a choice."

"There's always a choice, Randy. And stop calling me boss like it means something. You are *so* fired!" Kait struggled to control her emotions but disappointment colored her every word. "Is that even your real name? Is anything you told me in the past few months true?"

Was I completely and utterly wrong about you?

Randy squeezed the steering wheel as they inched along in bumper-to-bumper traffic. He looked like a caged lion, menacing and calm at the same time, ready to start ripping things apart if they didn't get moving again soon. He kept a close eye on the cars and pedestrians behind them, and an even closer eye on her; she had to be really careful.

"The crew really has been counting blues while you were...away. I didn't lie about that, and I am not lying about being your friend, Kait. I need you to tell me exactly what happened the day you disappeared, everything that happened from then until now, and everything you know about this so-called hero of yours."

"Why would I tell you anything? You're probably a—" she wanted to call him a dirty, rotten, drug-dealing liar, but she couldn't afford to agitate him. "You're probably responsible for putting me through all of this hell in the first place! You should already know what happened, since I'm guessing you work for Pablo."

"I told you, I'm not a drug dealer, Kait. If you pay attention and start answering my questions, this will go a lot easier than you think."

The Camaro passed the road that led to the Mission Bay Yacht Club, and he knew Kait wondered about his childhood stories. He answered her question before she could even ask it. "Yes, I really did learn how to sail there. Most of what I told you about myself is completely true."

They finally came to the only road that led away from the strip and took a left, driving at a normal pace to blend in. Kait looked back hoping to see Michael, but he was nowhere in sight. The speed of traffic increased as they headed toward Sea World and historic Old Town. If Randy got on Interstate 8, there was no telling where they would end up: northern California, Arizona, Mexico? She had to be ready for anything; she needed a plan.

"Where are you taking me?"

"Somewhere safe," he answered without hesitation.

Kait frowned with increasing aggravation. He was a master of evasion, answering each of her questions without actually telling her anything useful. "Okay, how far away is this safe place? I have to pee." She didn't really, but if he actually stopped, she might find an opportunity to escape.

"Not far."

When he bypassed the interstate and headed toward the Sports Arena she got an idea.

As the Camaro rolled to a stop at a red light, directly across from the Kobe Swap Meet, she bent over in her seat. "These shoes are killing me."

Sliding the three-inch heels off, she made a show of massaging her feet for a second, then positioned the spiky heels so they would double as a weapon, and swung her left arm as fast as possible, aiming for Randy's face as she released her seatbelt with her right hand.

He blocked her shoe attack with his right arm, the heel of one shoe stopping just inches from his right eye. She threw the shoes at him then, as she opened the door, and managed to get one foot on the ground before he grabbed her arm and tried to pull her back inside. Throwing her full weight toward the door, she fell out and landed on the asphalt, his hand still gripping the sleeve of her coat, her arm twisting uncomfortably up and over her head.

"Kait!" He fought to hold onto her and get out of his own seatbelt while she struggled to free herself from the coat and his grip. "There's nowhere safe you can go."

She twisted free with a yelp, got to her feet, ignoring the new pain in her shoulder, and dashed between cars that were now moving with the flow of traffic. She heard Randy rev the 323-horsepower engine and blast his horn as he cut across traffic to pursue her, heard his tires squeal as he came to a sudden stop in the parking lot just outside the ticket booth, saw him slam the door as he left his car to chase her down on foot.

Kait snuck past the ticket taker while he was distracted by a large family with several raucous children, then inserted herself into the crowds of shoppers and vendors. She was unfamiliar with the layout of the swap meet but wound her way easily through the maze of booths that overflowed with everything from car parts and handmade jewelry, to iPod accessories and antique junk.

Walking in front of a man twice her size for additional cover, Kait dashed into a tarp-covered booth filled with every type of hat imaginable, and exited the other side wearing a floppy canvas hat she'd snagged to hide her hair. She felt bad not paying for the item, but had neither the money, nor the time to haggle.

Desperate situations call for desperate measures.

Next, she cut through a flower vender's patch of greenery and blossoms, and hid behind a clothing booth while she scanned the crowd for Randy. Seeing no sign of him, she snatched a black and gray, tie-dye sarong with white dolphins, and continued onward tying it around her torso like a strapless dress to hide Adele's much too easy to spot blue dress. Heading toward the farthest end of the swap meet, she hoped to find a taxi and catch a ride out of Dodge.

Randy made a phone call while he scanned the crowd, moving slowly with the herd. "Rendezvous at the Sports Arena, pronto. She's on the run."

The voice on the other end mocked him, "She got away from you? Damn, Skippy!"

"Just get your ass down here and use that hound-dog nose to find her before she gets too far."

Randy followed a woman with dark-brown hair wearing a Mexican poncho—right height and build, wrong gait—then turned down a different aisle, following his gut.

"I don't want her hurt, Perro. Got it?"

"No worries, Skippy."

Randy rankled at the nickname he hadn't been able to shake since they'd met almost two years ago. They'd hated each other instantly, had found every way possible to belittle each other's manhood and skill, eventually settling on Perro, Spanish for dog, and Skippy, which had more than one derogatory interpretation by Randy's count.

"One of these days, Perro, the pain will far outweigh the pleasure."

Kait eyed a booth filled with shoes, trying to figure out how to get her hands on a pair without getting caught. For about two seconds, she thought getting caught just might be the best solution to her predicament—they would call the police, she would be taken into custody, and presto, she'd be safe—then reality had set in. She didn't know how long it would take Lilly to find her, and she didn't know a damned thing about Randy or his connections. Maybe he'd be able to get to her in jail before Lilly even knew Kait was there; his last words had been to warn her there was nowhere safe she could go.

We'll see about that.

Emboldened by need, she took one last look around her then headed for the booth. She walked straight to a stack of white tennis shoes she had scoped out from a distance and started to pull out a box labeled size-8.5, then thought better of it. She didn't have time to try them on—this would have to be another snatch and run job—she pulled out the size-9 box instead, just in case the others were too small.

"Would you like to try those on?" The old, tattoo-covered man working the booth smiled at her as he cut off her would-be exit and looked down at the holes and snags in the ruined stockings on her feet.

Kait straightened with the box in hand and looked around nervously. "Umm...no. Thanks anyways," she started to set them back on top of the stack.

"Sure looks like you need 'em more 'n I do, young lady." He winked at her knowingly.

"I...uh...I don't have any money on me at the moment, sir." Kait smiled apologetically and looked around to make sure Randy hadn't spotted her.

The old man stared into her eyes as if he could see all the way into her soul. "You could pay for 'em when you come back...maybe one day when you're not in such a hurry." He smiled at her again, motioned for her to sit down and put them on, then tossed a pair of athletic ankle socks on top of the shoes and stepped in front of her to block her from the view of potential onlookers.

"Really? You'd do that—" Kait started to tear-up at the old man's generosity, then snapped back to attention and mentally bolstered herself. "I'm really grateful, sir. I *will* come back and pay for them as soon as I possibly can!" She hoped fate didn't make a liar of her.

With the shoes and socks on her feet, she stood up and hugged the old man, then spotting Randy several booths down, she squeaked and backed away. "I have to run! Take care!"

"You too," he said as he turned to see who she was running from.

Kait made a mad dash toward the exit, no longer interested in gathering supplies. She had all she really needed for now, and she would come back another day and pay back all three vendors for the things she had taken—if she lived long enough.

The smell of food got her attention as she left the complex—she hadn't eaten since breakfast at 0500 in Puerto Vallarta, and it had to be well after 1500 now. Unfortunately, with Randy in such close proximity, food and water would have to wait.

Outside the swap-meet, there wasn't a single taxi in sight—too bad, if she had them take her to work, she could get her keys, her car, and her emergency cash to pay the fare.

Abandoning that plan for the moment, she dashed across the street and around the nearest corner to get out of sight quickly. She would have to hoof it until another option presented itself, so she kept moving. Scanning the old buildings around her, the tops of the downtown skyline in the distance, and the landmark cliff nearby, she got her bearings and headed for Old Town—her next best chance of finding a taxi.

Randy reached the far end of the swap meet and stood out of site near the exit to watch for Kait, but his gut told him she was already gone. She'd left his car 22 minutes ago, and he hadn't caught a single glimpse of her since. On several occasions he'd felt a prickle of nerves along his spine; she'd been close, probably close enough to see him and hide. He waited only five minutes, then quickly made his way back to the Camaro and started cruising the surface streets immediately adjacent to the Sports Arena complex.

Where would she go? He cataloged the facts: she had no money, no shoes, and no phone. She was running scared, and would probably try to get back to Michael. She was smart enough to know that the La Jolla house was no longer safe, and she had no way to get there. If she went to the police, he would hear about it from his inside source, but she was paranoid enough now, that he didn't think she would go there either.

Logistically, the SIMR pier was only about five miles away, Harbor Island only three miles, but she would be greatly exposed if she tried to walk to either location; they were high traffic roads, not pedestrian-friendly.

She would choose something closer, something safer.

Following his instincts, he headed to historic Old Town State Park, less than a half-mile away, nestled just below Presidio Park on the eastern side of Interstate 5. It would be filled with tourists, hidey-holes, and mass transit options. He texted Perro to let him know where to meet, then pulled into a public parking lot in the southwest corner of the park, across from the train tracks and bus stop. If he didn't find her soon, he might never find her again—he'd gotten incredibly lucky the first time.

Kait bypassed the train station, and the two empty taxis waiting there, aware that she was running short on time. If Randy figured out which direction she'd gone, he would catch up with her any minute. The platform was too exposed, and who knew where the taxi drivers were, or if they would agree to give her a ride. She had to get out of the open and find a taxi that was actually ready and waiting. She jogged across the street and up the well maintained, crushed-gravel path into the complex of historic buildings, perfectly preserved and decorated with the rustic charm of the late 1800s.

Skipping the visitor center in the old Robinson-Rose house, which had once been home to the San Diego Herald, the Gila Railroad, and several other businesses across time,

Kait headed for Washington Square, the center of the park, with ample places to hide and rest while she recovered from her harrowing chase. Her shoulder ached from being wrenched backward, her mouth was parched with thirst, and her feet were aching from the combined abuse of wearing stiletto heels all morning, running for her life barefoot on a pebble-strewn blacktop, and then running on hard cement sidewalks. The tennis shoes had definitely saved her feet in the final stretch, but she wasn't any closer to home, and she desperately needed to drink some water and sit down.

Spotting the Barra Barra Saloon, a white adobe building with a red-tiled roof on the northernmost corner of the square, she walked into the courtyard, past a young hostess wearing a multicolored Mexican dancer's dress. The girl gave her a fake, I'm-sick-of-my-job-and-hate-all-tourists smile, then frowned at Kait's disheveled state.

Ignoring the girl and her equally unfortunate attire, Kait followed the signs to the restroom, and nearly jumped out of her skin when she opened the door and faced a stranger in the mirror. She'd forgotten about her darkened skin and hair, and had apparently grown accustomed to the brown-colored contacts on her eyes. She wanted desperately to wash her face, but couldn't risk looking like a patchy-skinned zombie, and didn't know how to remove the contacts Michael had worked so hard to put-in.

Isn't it bad enough I can't recognize my life anymore? Now, I can't even recognize my own face!

Unable to do much to fix her appearance, Kait twisted her long hair into a bun and tucked it into a knot. Next, she shifted and re-tied her sarong to cover more of the dress underneath. When she was finished, she made her way back to the dark-wood bar and asked for some water. "I'm waiting for the rest of my party," she explained when the bartender looked at her like a cheapskate.

"Would you like some chips and salsa while you wait?"

"Sure, that would be great!" Ah...food at last! The bartender set a tall glass of ice water in front of her; it was all she could do not to guzzle it down. "Thank you! I didn't realize how dehydrated I was!"

A waitress in another colorful, old-world, Mexican costume deposited a basket of chips and a small bowl of salsa in front of her and asked, "How many in your party, Miss?"

"Umm...three," she lied.

"Would you like to wait here at the bar? Or would you prefer to be seated at a table?"

Kait smiled as she eyed the front and back exits, "This is fine. It'll be easier for me to spot my friends when they arrive."

The waitress departed to serve a group of more promising customers, and Kait dug into her chips without further delay. The salty taste and loud crunching in her ears instantly reminding her of the last time she'd eaten tortilla chips—wrapped in nothing but a blanket in a motel room in Yelapa, with Michael—and her heart thudded.

He's probably beside himself with worry.

"Everything all right, Miss?" the scrawny, collegiate bartender asked, standing in front of her with a concerned frown."

"Yes, thanks. Can you tell me the best place to find a taxi around here?"

"That would be Hacienda de las Rosas, just around the corner by the parking lot. It's a wine-tasting room, so taxis wait there for the tourists that get too smashed to drive back to their hotels."

"Okay. Thank you." Kait glanced out the door and almost had a heart-attack when she saw Randy pass by on the pathway. She didn't bother to apologize or explain, but quietly hopped down from her barstool and walked very quickly out the back door. As soon as she was outside she edged the building, and dashed quickly behind a tree, then a low wooden fence, then another building. She searched the pathway to see where he'd gone, but couldn't spot him. He was lurking somewhere between her and where she needed to be.

Blast it!

Dashing across the path and behind the next building, Kait decided to skirt the long way around, behind the row of historic buildings; it was a lot safer bet than the short, direct route where she'd last seen Randy.

Her eyes scanned the grounds all around her as she moved, trying to look casual, like a tourist enamored with every historic detail. At the edge of the last building in the row, the first San Diego courthouse, she stepped out to walk behind a small group of senior citizens, her head angled down, and her wide-brimmed hat shielding her face. When she looked up, her eyes landed on a large familiar man moving in her direction, less than 100-meters away. His uniform made her heart skip another beat as she realized he was the security guard who had attacked Randy outside Michael's house. *What the—?*

He spotted her and their eyes connected for an instant, their roles becoming crystal clear: him predator, her prey. She turned to run back the way she had come, this time favoring speed over stealth. If she ran into Randy, she'd let him and the menacing guard duke it out, and take her opportunity to get away from both of them.

Sparing a glace behind her, she couldn't see the big man that was probably hot on her trail—*not good.*

Rounding the corner of another historic house at full speed, she collided with a human wall; the force of the impact knocked her backward. The security guard locked one beefy hand around her wrist, yanking her toward him as his thumb dug into a pressure point that shot pain up her arm. Before she could react, or even scream, his other hand tapped a second point on her forearm, increasing the pain exponentially, then tapped her neck with the edge of his hand, fast and light.

Kait's world went stark white.

Randy raced up to the guard as he hoisted Kait over his shoulder. "What the fuck did you do to her, Perro?"

"You said find her. I did." The security guard shrugged, "I figured fast and quiet was better than making a scene."

Randy remembered the excessive gusto Perro had used to take him down in their staged fight outside the La Jolla house. It still rankled, but he'd even the score later, when Kait's shapely ass wasn't on the line.

"Hand her over, jackass, and if you *ever* touch her like that again, you'll learn the real definition of pain."

TWENTY FIVE

Kait awoke with a start, the pungent odors of saltwater, seaweed, engine fuel, and rotting fish wafting through her nose as someone alternately pounded on her back, then rubbed it briskly and bellowed at her. Her whole body jerked in response to the last thing she remembered—the beefy security guard using some fancy martial arts moves that turned her world into white static in the blink of an eye.

Oh no—not again!

"You're okay, Kait. Keep breathing, slow and easy."

The fog between her ears began to lift when the pounding ceased and the bellowing receded to a quiet throng. Her assailant was very near, talking to someone, but his words were too muffled to comprehend.

Realization dawned; his forearm was strapped with too much familiarity across her chest like a seatbelt, his body wrapped around hers like a vise. Her elbow flew backward defensively, but struck with negligible force in the slight space between them. Her only thought—escape, evade!

"Simmer down, boss. You're safe now, the gorilla's gone."

Randy?

Kait lifted her head and opened her eyes trying to focus as the fog finally cleared and his words began to make sense. Her mouth was drier than baked sand, her muscles wound tighter than a mainsheet. Looking around she found herself perched like a rag doll in Randy's lap, his firm hold the only thing keeping her from plunging face-first to the deck inside the small hold of his sailboat.

"What's happening?" she squawked as she tried to wriggle free.

His other arm clamped around her in a bear hug to prevent her escape. "Calm down, Kait. I've got you. You're safe."

"Safe, my ass! Let me go this instant you back-stabbing, two-faced, slime bucket!"

"I'll let you go when you calm down. You're nowhere near ready to stand up after what that jackass did. You need to lie down and rest a bit until your head clears."

He loosened his hold, testing her ability to remain upright on her own, but he didn't let go. Kait swayed a moment then righted herself within the circle of his arms. "I'm fine…just give me some space, will you?"

Leaning sideways, she crawled out of his lap and flopped down prostrate on his bunk, dizzy with the effort.

"That's good, Kait. You're recovering quickly. You should feel a lot better in a couple more minutes." He reached across her and grabbed a thermos. "Here, drink some water."

Kait rolled over and scowled at him. "Where are we going? If you take me back to Pablo he'll kill me. You know that, right?"

"Nobody is going to harm one more hair on that crazy, stubborn head of yours, Kait. If you will just listen to me, and cooperate, I promise you'll be safe for the foreseeable future," he looked her in the eyes. "Right now, *this* is the safest place you could possibly be."

Kait snorted at the ridiculousness of his words. "Unless you're some sort of undercover super cop, which I seriously doubt, I can think of at least a dozen places I'd be safer right now than in *your* boat, if it really is *your* boat!"

Inexplicably exhausted, and frustrated to her core, she yielded to the soft mattress and pillow behind her, squeezing her eyes shut and draping her arms across her face. The irony of the situation was beyond reckoning; the insanity that had gotten her out of one frying pan, had tossed her squarely into another, but this time she didn't even have

Michael by her side! How could one person have such horrible luck?

Randy inhaled deeply then exhaled long and slow. "I'm *not* a cop, this *is* my boat, and I'm *not* taking you to Pablo. Whether or not you believe me, there is no place safer for you right now, than here, with me."

Kait uncrossed her arms and looked at him skeptically. "Why? If you can explain *why* you tricked me into leaving with you, *how* you got me away from the gorilla and his...white lightning, and *why* this is the safest place under the flipping sun, then I *might* cooperate."

As she spoke, her eyes casually scanned the interior of the boat, cataloguing and calculating ways to defend and free herself as soon as possible. The boat bobbed up-and-down on a swell, then bumped against something hard—*are we still at dock?*

Kait's senses jumped to attention and her gaze landed on the only portal that wasn't currently covered with a curtain. The top of a palm tree rustled in the breeze. In the distance, she heard a car horn blare at traffic. The smell of engine fuel suddenly made sense. They were still docked in the harbor! Randy hadn't had time to cast off yet because he'd been actively trying to revive her. That meant she'd only been unconscious a few minutes this time, and more importantly, she still had a chance to get away without having to swim for it!

Randy stood up and reached in his back pocket. "I don't have time to explain everything right now. I need to go topside and get us moving." He looked at her pointedly, "We've got work to do," then bent over her and slipped a metal cuff around her wrist, locking it to a metal ring bolted to the bulkhead, "and you *really* need to learn how to stop telegraphing your every thought."

Kait screeched in surprise and struggled to free herself. "You bastard!" she screamed as he left her below deck and closed the hatch.

After helplessly watching the black Camaro disappear, Michael pounded the interior of the car with his fists and cursed the world in general. Kaitlyn had slipped right through his fingers, like mist through air—had been kidnapped *again*, and this time from inside *his* house and on *his* watch! It was unbelievable, unforgiveable, and unacceptable!

To make matters worse, he had no idea where to begin looking for her. He knew where she worked, but not where she lived. He knew her roommate was a police officer named Lilly, but had no last name or contact information with which to track her down. Kaitlyn had mentioned a brother and a mother, who were likely worried sick about her, but he didn't even know their damned names! He had failed her completely by neglecting to gather such basic details about her life.

Crossing the Mission Bay bridges into the Midway District just north of downtown, Michael pulled into a parking lot to think. He needed a plan and he needed help, but he wasn't ready to open certain doors that he had intentionally slammed shut.

He had no idea who to trust with the knowledge that Kaitlyn was not only alive, but back on U.S. soil. He couldn't begin to guess which direction the man in the Camaro had taken her; they could cross back into Mexico in less than an hour or travel anywhere else in the cursed world if they hopped on a plane at San Diego International Airport.

Pressing the heels of his hands against his face, he could only pray that whoever had taken her, would stay in the region long enough for him to find her and steal her back.

Reaching deep into his own darkness, Michael pondered how Pablo had managed to get ahead of him again, and what Pablo would do if he was the one in this situation. Nobody was more wily or diabolical, and he'd been a step ahead of them from the very beginning. If Michael wanted to win this game he had to outthink his adversary, predict his next move and not only block it, but block all other possibilities too. He had to find a way to turn the tables and put Pablo on the run for a change, instead of letting him call all the shots.

Michael pulled the cell phone from his pocket and made the call he'd been trying to avoid. His brother answered after just two rings.

"Dr. Storm, here. How can I help you?"

His voice was as cool and confident as ever. Professional. Inquisitive. He didn't know the number displayed on his phone screen and probably assumed Michael was a potential client.

"Need your help, brother."

The drawn silence was fraught with unspoken questions: Where have you been, brother? When are you coming back? Are you whole? Can I come down and kill the bastard now? Everything was reduced to one simple word, "Mic?"

When Randy returned below deck 30 minutes later, Kait was steaming mad. While he'd been steering them out of the harbor into open ocean, effectively removing any chance she had at escape, she'd come to the shocking conclusion that Randy and the gorilla *must* have been working together. Since then she'd pulled and twisted, contorting herself until her skin was raw and her bones ached, trying to dislodge the handcuff, yet here she sat, like a helpless whelk stuck on a rock above the tidal swells, awaiting her doom. It was hopelessly depressing to go through so much, to come so close to freedom and justice, only to have it snatched away again by someone who was *supposed* to be a friend.

Randy took one look at her red, swollen hand and watery eyes and nearly punched a hole in the bulkhead. "Damn it, Kait. What's it gonna take to prove that you're safe with me?" He ripped open the tiny freezer in the galley and pulled out a bag of frozen, organic soy beans, then sat down beside her and set them on her hand. "What's it gonna take to break through that thick, stubborn skull and get you to trust me again?"

"Gee, Randy, I don't know. Maybe you should save yourself the trouble and take me back to Michael. Or hey, if you don't like that option, take me to the FBI. Heck, I'm not picky—why don't you prove that you're *not* affiliated with Pablo or any of his goons! Prove that you *haven't* been playing me for a complete idiot for the past six months."

Kait choked back a sob and fought hard to prevent her tears from falling. Her emotions were as raw as the skin on her hand, but she couldn't let him best her.

Randy closed his eyes and shook his head as he took a deep breath, visibly settling his temper. The man that looked at her then, was a man she had never seen before—no longer the playful, happy-go-lucky surfer dude with a brain and too much brawn for anyone's good. The man that looked at her now, was ice and steel, a stone-cold professional who could probably break her neck with his pinky if he so desired.

Gone was the mischievous twinkle in his eyes that had once lured her into temptation. Hidden was the small dimple that regularly puckered his cheek when he smiled; this man didn't know how to smile. If she'd ever thought this man was her friend, the next words out of his mouth proved her utterly wrong.

"How long have you been using SIMR as a cover to run drugs, Kait?"

What?

Kait recoiled from his accusation.

When she recovered from the verbal slap, she laughed it off. He was playing with her, changing his tactics in some bizarre new game. She was the innocent party here—not the criminal—and she was pretty sure he already knew that little fact because *he* almost certainly *wasn't* innocent.

She didn't know the rules of this new game, but she was more than ready to throw a few zingers of her own. "That's rich coming from you, pretty boy. How long have you been working for El Diablo? What are you, his North American bootlicker?"

Randy's eyes narrowed on her like laser beams at the mention of El Diablo. He hadn't used Pablo's nickname during their brief reunion, so she'd given herself away on that point.

Shoot! He doesn't miss anything!

"How did you get caught up in this business, Kait? Did you fall for the wrong man? Did Mr. Wonderful sashay into your life and throw his money around like King Midas until your mercenary little heart swooned?"

Her eyes blazed with fury as she braced herself for battle. "Right, because I'm suddenly a gold-digging hussy with nothing better to do than bust my ass trying to save a bunch of whales. What's the matter, Randy, have you been dipping into the candy you're supposed to be selling, frying your brain cells? Or have you just been telling so many lies that you can't remember the truth anymore?"

"Truth? You wouldn't know the truth if it reared its ugly head and bit you in the pert little ass. Which one of them does it for you, Kait? Did you sell your soul to the devil incarnate, or was it the Archangel with the golden halo?"

Kait's free hand slashed through the air like lightning but failed to strike its intended target; Randy blocked it just inches from his face—*again.* He'd insulted her so completely, and stopped her retaliation so effortlessly, that flames of pure hatred licked at her heart. "Like I'd sell my soul to any bastard that kidnapped me, drugged me, and handed me off to his minions to be raped and killed. What are you, a brain trust?

"I didn't see you there when Michael pulled my 'pert little ass' out of the black, flipping ocean after I drowned, and then yanked me back to life with his own two hands. I didn't see you there steering us to safety after we were run off the road and almost plunged over a 100-foot cliff. I darn well know I didn't see you there fighting at my side when men were coming at us from everywhere, hell bent on killing me! Gosh, Randy, maybe Michael really is an Archangel. Give the man a gold star, he actually got something right!"

Kait waited for his next volley, but it didn't come.

Instead, Randy released her wrist and stood up. His face was a mask of gray stone, expressionless and emotionless, until she caught a glimpse of the gunpowder burning in his eyes. *Score one for the plucky biologist that doesn't know when to quit.*

It occurred to her then, that she had just given him exactly what he wanted—information—and lots of it. He'd played her perfectly, accusing her of complicity in illicit affairs, riling her so completely that within seconds she had given him a nearly complete and oh so vivid snapshot of her missing days. She zipped her lips.

Not another word!

They stared at each other for several heartbeats, Kait defiant under his silent scrutiny, Randy still trying to rattle her with authoritative disapproval. He crouched and pulled something from a drawer, then whirled around so quickly that she flinched, afraid he was coming at her with a knife or a gun.

Instead, he held a manila folder, the edges worn with age and stained from extended use. He tossed the folder on the bunk beside her, "I'm willing to bet he's no angel, Kait. Care to take a look through my files and see if he's in there? Or do you even care? When you dance with the Devil, you're bound to sprout horns."

Kait stared at the folder as if it had fangs and claws—a monster ready to pounce on her and shred the last bits of hope in her miserable heart. "Who are you? Why are you doing this to me?"

He backed off, softened just a bit, "I know you've been through the wringer, Kait, and I'm sorry I wasn't there to prevent it. You dropped off the face of the Earth, and I couldn't break cover to come and find you. You have no idea how relieved I am that you're still alive. This is me doing my best to keep you that way."

Kait heard remorse in his voice—*it sounded sincere*—but this was the same man who had pulled the wool over her eyes for months. No way was she letting him off the hook that easy, and no way was she buying his story of being a good guy.

What a crock of whale poop!

She snatched up the folder, steeled herself against whatever she was about to see, and looked inside. The pictures were mostly mug shots and candid street shots of Latino men, probably gang-bangers and drug runners with gaping holes where they should have hearts, and darkness where they should have souls. Kait looked through them quickly, scanning for recognizable features so she would know if she ran into any of them. "I don't know what you were expecting. I don't recognize a single one of these men.

"Why do you have these if you're not a cop? For all I know this is a pile of junk you concocted, maybe a bunch of degenerates you pulled off the internet to trick me."

"You don't recognize *any* of them?"

Their eyes locked on each other in a silent dual. He knew she had been through far more than the proverbial wringer, but she appeared to be holding her own. He simply couldn't bring himself to bully her further. He would have to tell her the truth to win her trust back and then hope like hell she didn't burn him in the end. "Every one of those men is a hardcore criminal, Kait. The kind you don't ever want to meet. Most of them work for Castañeda. Some are missing and presumed dead."

"How do you know this?" she asked with continued defiance.

"Put it together, Kait. What am I *not* saying to you? Who would go undercover to investigate these types of men?" He placed a hand on her knee and waited for her reaction. When she didn't pull away or retaliate, he knew she was giving him the chance to prove himself.

"This man," Randy pointed to the photo of an older man, Latin, slim, gray hair and mustache, very clean-cut, "was the head of the largest drug cartel in Mexico. His name was Antonio Ortega. He was killed about three years ago by a younger, stronger, more ruthless man."

"El Diablo?"

"Yes. Pablo Castañeda."

"Who are the others?" Kait worked her way through the pictures a second time, this time looking much more closely.

"Various employees of Ortega and Castañeda."

She stopped at a particularly poignant street shot of a young man known to be missing, then moved on, asking "How does my crew figure into all of this? Why did you go undercover as part of *my* team? We're not criminals. We're scientists!"

"I'm fully aware of what you and your crew are, and what you are not. You and your team are in the clear if that's any consolation."

"Wait, so you *don't* think I'm a drug runner?" she asked with a small ray of hope in her eyes.

"What can you tell me about Michael?" he evaded, purposely keeping her off balance. It was underhanded, but he had to ease her down the proper path.

She was immediately defensive. "I'd never met him before all this, but he's a good man. He helped me without asking for anything in return, and he's *not* in your stupid stack of pictures."

She then returned fire with a volley of questions he wouldn't answer. "Who are you investigating if not my team? How did you *really* find me? And who's your pet gorilla?"

He'd known Michael wouldn't be in that folder; he'd used it as more of a scare-tactic, not wanting to give away too much at once. "His picture isn't there because he's a special case."

Walking back to the drawer, Randy pulled out another file that contained more pictures; black and white eight-by-ten-inch photographs he'd received from a cooperating CIA agent when he'd first been assigned to the case. "Take a look at these, but fair warning…they're pretty grizzly. I didn't want to show them to you, but you leave me no choice." He handed the pictures to Kait, "You need to know who you're dealing with."

For Randy, the horrific scene had been reason enough to doubt that Michael was only an innocent bystander who hadn't had a clue what his wife and brother-in-law were doing. There was no evidence against him, but if he wasn't the paragon of virtue he'd presented to Kait, if he *had* taken part in their nefarious activities, then Randy would take him down right alongside Castañeda.

Kait had to brace herself when she realized what she was looking at: a blood-bath, taking place amid the streets and people of a small Mexican village. Women and children were running for cover, many already lay dead on a dirt road and in their doorways. They hadn't made it to safety. Men with machine guns faced off against each other, hiding behind jeeps and trucks, and around the corners of ramshackle buildings.

"What *is* this?" Kait asked, her voice barely audible over the pounding of her own heart.

“That is one of several shoot-outs between Ortega’s and Castañeda’s armies of thugs—a cartel war of sorts—winner takes all: the territory, the holdings, the production plants, you name it. That particular battle took place about four years ago, when Castañeda first hit the scene.”

Kait kept looking through the small stack of pictures, then stopped cold when she came to a close up of a young Mexican woman, lying wounded in the arms of a man dressed in jungle camouflage fatigues—Michael.

Randy glanced at the picture that held her riveted. “That is...was...Castañeda’s sister. She married an American doctor who moved to the area under the guise of charity work. We aren’t sure if she was working directly with her brother, but she definitely ran a side business utilizing his resources. She was smuggling babies out of the barrios, selling them to American couples who were desperate to adopt. Infants are a real commodity in the adoption business. As far as I know, she was in the wrong place at the wrong time and got caught in the crossfire.

Kait looked up at Randy, icy dread chilling her bones. “Why was *he* there?”

Randy took the picture out of Kait’s hands and took a closer look at the man in the photo. Michael Storm had been a question mark throughout Randy’s investigation, a potential player who’d dropped into and out of the picture as fast as a lightning bolt, and left almost no evidence that he’d ever been involved. Either he was clean, or someone higher up the food chain was protecting him.

Randy knew it was the same man that had chased them across town just hours ago, but he wanted Kait to confirm it. “This is the man that rescued you and brought you home?”

Kait swallowed hard, choking on the answer, “Yes.”

Randy rifled through his files and pulled out another folder, handing it to her. “Michael Connor Storm; we never confirmed whether he was working with his wife or her brother. He got out alive and a team was assigned to watch him for about a year after his wife was killed, but they never linked him to anything. His name’s been associated with Castañeda ever since, and I’ve been keeping loose tabs on him and a few of his closest affiliates.

Kait was silent for a moment, shocked by the news that Michael had not only been married to a human trafficker, but that he was also the widowed brother-in-law of the man who was trying to kill her. She was struggling to piece together the puzzle from what Randy was and wasn't saying. "We went through customs at the airport—"

Randy answered her question before she could ask it. "Security was ordered to let Michael and Adele pass without detention. I needed to know why they had suddenly decided to come to the U.S. together after so long, and without her husband. I didn't dream I'd find *you* in disguise."

"We were followed?" She asked incredulously. No wonder she'd felt like a million eyes were on her. From the moment she and Michael had passed through customs, they'd been tracked.

"I've been searching for you the whole time, Kait. I knew you must have been nabbed. I got there eighteen minutes after your call but you, the mystery yacht, and the *Triton* were all gone. I didn't know what happened, or where you'd been taken...if you were even alive. When we found Barney—" Randy tamped down on the emotions creeping up his throat, "—the fact that you weren't with him gave me hope. Then I got the call—"

Kait cut him off, steeling herself against his emotional ploy. She would not fall for his lies again. "How long have you had the gorilla watching Michael's house?"

"We've been watching his assets for a while—long before I met you. When he called to beef up security at the house, I figured he was up to something."

"Wait a minute. You said you never linked Michael to any wrong doing!" Kait's voice ratcheted up a few decibels at the accusatory direction Randy was taking. She couldn't make herself believe that Michael was now, or ever had been involved in a baby smugging operation, or a drug cartel for that matter. He was as decent and humanitarian as the day was long. He was the type of man who helped perfect strangers with life or death situations, the type of man who ran into a burning building to save people instead of running out. If she was fitting him to a stereotype, he'd be stamped Hero through and through.

So why does he exude so much guilt and remorse?

He must have been deeply wounded by his wife's death, blamed himself for what had happened to her. He was probably suffering from PTSD, or what everyone who is left behind eventually feels—survivor's guilt. Or maybe it was just his type A personality that had to do everything perfectly the first time and couldn't tolerate even the slightest mistake without beating himself to an emotional pulp.

If he wasn't involved, what was he doing there?

Was he responsible for his wife's death?

Was the charitable clinic nothing more than a brilliant cover for his illegal dealings?

No way! Not possible!

Kait thought about the raw guilt shining in his eyes, his determination to keep her safe, his reluctance to be intimate. She drew a line in the sand, demarcating his wholesale innocence until proven otherwise, then reinforced it with another towering wall; the kind of wall that could only be toppled with incontrovertible proof; the kind of proof that reared up and smacked you down so hard that your world was left unrecognizable.

She was about to inform Randy that he was barking up the wrong tree when he stuck a giant lightning rod right into the middle of her newest wall.

"You tell me, Kait. If he's so innocent, why was he there, in the middle of a gun battle between two major drug lords? Why is he carrying an assault rifle and a combat knife?" He shook his head and stared her straight in the eyes. "Until I have proof otherwise, he stays at the top of my list of suspects. I'm grateful that he brought you home safe, but I have no loyalty to him."

Kait's mind raced trying to get ahead for once, instead of always fighting to catch up. "I don't know why he was there, but I know he was willing to put his life on the line to keep me safe. Keep him out of this and I'll do everything I can to help your investigation. I want to put Pablo and his goons away for good!"

"Don't put blind faith in a dark horse, Kait. You're bound to get trampled."

"What happened to innocent until proven guilty, Randy? If you're one of the good guys, then prove it. Stay neutral and protect *all* the innocent people that have been burned by Pablo, not just the ones who have a pert little ass."

"I think *impertinent* is the word you're looking for, Kait."

"You haven't seen impertinent, Ran...wait, what's your *real* name?"

He inhaled deeply—a man being pressed by innumerable, seemingly insurmountable problems—then he squared his shoulders and squinted at her like a school principle warning a wayward hooligan. "Donovan Randal, and unless you want to be killed, get me fired, or blow my investigation completely out of the water, you will do exactly *what* I tell you, *when* I tell you. Nothing more, nothing less. Got it?"

Kait bristled. *Here we go again with the badass He-Man bit.* "Loud and clear, *Donovan Randal*. Me, and my impertinent self are learning real darned fast."

She pointed to her handcuffed wrist still dangling from the wall. "You can remove this now."

He crossed his arms and stood there, nonplussed.

"What? Do you think I'm an idiot? I promise, I won't try to hurt you...or escape."

"As if you could," his lips twitched as he reached to uncuff her. He placed the cuffs back in his pocket and then bent over and got right in her face. "Don't make the mistake of thinking for one second, that you have a clue who or what you're dealing with, Kait. You're in over your head and have been from the start. If you try to pull *any* shenanigans, I'll throw your ass into protective custody and leave you there however long it takes to finish what I started, and you can kiss your project goodbye."

Kait swallowed back a smartass retort. That was two men who'd had the gall to tell her she was in over her head. It didn't matter how right they might, or might not be; pride and honor demanded that she do whatever it took to prove them both wrong.

"So, who are your primary suspects at SIMR? And how are we going to keep my project going and get my life back?"

TWENTY SIX

Dr. Russell drifted into his office and sank into his chair like a lifeless mass of flotsam after a shipwreck. He'd managed to fish Frankie out of the water and save both his leg and his life thanks to years of first-responder training and a well-stocked medicine chest on the *Triton*. He'd certainly never had to treat a gunshot wound in all his years at sea, but there'd been other injuries that required compression of a puncture wound, debridement, and sutures to stop the bleeding. Frankie had been incredibly lucky that the bullet had not hit a major artery or bone, and had left only a relatively small entrance and exit wound on the lateral surface of his thigh.

Unable to report the incident to authorities, or seek proper medical attention for Frankie, the onus had been on Dr. Russell to not only pull him from the chilling water as Pablo's yacht pulled away, but stop the bleeding, treat the wound, get the ship back underway, and keep a close eye on the kid for the two hours it took to steer the ship home without help from his only assistant. Somehow he'd managed to dock the ship at the SIMR pier by 1700 hours on Sunday evening, deposit his and Frankie's gear back on the *Neptune II*, deliver Frankie to his dark, musty apartment in Pacific Beach with a supply of pain-killers and antibiotics, and drive to the main office to upload the data they had collected on the trip.

Russell leaned back in his chair, thinking about what he had done, what he still had to do, then heaved a heavy sigh, and closed his eyes. *Been one hell of a week—one hell of a year!*

"You got a minute, Russell?" A weary, pensive voice penetrated the silence.

Russell sat forward startled, his eyes flying open as he made himself ready for anything. His eyes landed on the tall, wafer-thin man standing in the doorway to his office. His pale skin gave away his tech-driven existence, his thick glasses confirming the fact that he was always neck-deep in the books and computers, running complex calculations on strings of tiny numbers that amounted to big bucks.

Millions of dollars ran through the SIMR accounts every month, and Casper, as everyone called him, was the magic man that made sure every dollar and every cent was accounted for. "This isn't a good time, Casper. I'm only here for a few minutes."

Casper stepped further into the office and closed the door furtively behind him. "I think you'll want to make time once you hear what I have to say."

Russell motioned for his long-time coworker to have a seat in the chair on the opposite side of the desk. He sat just a little straighter, bracing for whatever was coming; he'd seen this particularly troubled look in Casper's eyes only once before, and that day had started his long, and arduous fall from grace. "What's this about?" he asked, wishing he could just walk out the door and head home, without having to clean up any more messes.

"I think you already know why I'm here." Casper looked pointedly at the man he had once called friend. "What I can't figure out, is how you thought you'd get away with it."

Unsure how much the accountant had uncovered, or what exactly he thought he knew, Russell played it cool, "Is this about the engine repairs I requested for the *Neptune II*? I assure you, I did everything I could to fix her myself, but she's beyond my abilities."

"I wish that's what this was about, but you know it's not. The request was approved and the repairs are already underway. She'll be up and running in time for your next run...*if* you make it."

The slight edge in his voice could be construed as a subtle threat, or a question. Russell chose the second option with his response. "The buoy maintenance contract doesn't end until next summer, and I'm fairly certain they will renew at that point."

"Cut the crap, Russell." Casper's voice wavered with anger and betrayal. "I want to know exactly what you did with the money, how you plan to put it back, and when, or this time next month, you won't be working at SIMR anymore."

Russell thought about his next words carefully before responding to the threat. Casper was giving him an out—time he may not actually have, to set things right—but it was quite possible there was no real out at this point. If life was a ship, then Russell's had run aground and was taking on water faster than he could bilge-pump it out.

There might still be a chance to salvage things.

"How did you do it?" Russell asked with true curiosity and a little admiration.

"It's not hard to spot when $60K suddenly disappears from the books—"

"That's not what I mean." Russell cut him off, ignoring the arrogant response. "How did you recover when the housing bubble burst in 2007 and the stock market crashed in 2008?"

Casper was taken aback for a moment but quickly redirected his energy. "I didn't mortgage my inherited home to the hilt; I didn't buy a second house in order to flip it or rent it out at a profit; and I didn't sink the majority of my retirement into the stock market. If you recall, I warned you about all three actions. I explained the risks to you each time you came to me with your latest plan to get rich or recover your losses, and I told you in no uncertain terms that your income did not support taking such risks—risks that in *your* case would likely outweigh the potential for reward. Am I to understand that you did not heed any of my advice?"

Russell's face reddened with a cocktail of shame, regret, anger, and perhaps a tinge of jealousy. He had indeed inherited his mother's home on Mount Soledad when she'd passed in 2003, and it would have been free and clear of a mortgage if she hadn't been forced to get an equity loan to pay off thousands of dollars in medical treatments that in the end had only given her a few extra months of misery.

He'd been living paycheck to paycheck, helping her pay the mortgage, which she couldn't afford on her fixed income. When he'd inherited the house and discovered that its value had doubled, twice, and it was suddenly worth six hundred grand, he'd thought the god of mice and men had finally seen fit to reward his efforts.

Like all the other homes in the highly desirable area, the value of his home had continued to skyrocket, reaching more than a million at its peak, right before the housing bubble burst. And, like so many other American hopefuls, he'd jumped in and tried to ride the wave of financial success all the way to easy street, never knowing that a devastating tsunami was hot on his heels. If he had known, he would have listened to Casper's advice. He would never have taken out another equity loan to purchase a second house; he wouldn't have succumbed to his mid-life crisis and bought a damned hotrod; he wouldn't have lost hundreds of thousands of dollars!

It was enough to drive a man insane, as evidenced by the countless suicides that occurred the year the housing bubble burst. Then, as if that wasn't bad enough, he had tried to make up his losses by moving a large portion of his 401K from low-risk, low-gain mutual funds and bonds to high-risk, but highly profitable stocks. Within a year, the stock market had crashed and he had lost hundreds of thousands more.

In a period of only six years, Russell, like many other middle-class Americans with simple tastes and minimal expenses, had become an overnight millionaire with two properties, elevated tastes, and significantly increased expenses, only to be smacked down hard into poverty, bankruptcy, repossession, and foreclosure on the second home, which he'd never managed to sell. He would have been made homeless just last year when the one asset he'd managed to keep, his mother's house, hit a new low and became top-heavy with a mortgage greater than the value of the house. If not for his steady income at a job he loved, and the birth of a creative, if less than perfect solution to his personal financial nightmare, he might have elected to join the ranks of the dearly departed, and blown his own brains out.

"What's it going to take, Casper?" He asked with a stubborn set to his jaw.

Casper hesitated, not wanting to ruin his one-time best friend. "If you put the full amount back, $60K, before the audit next month, and promise never to do something so asinine again...I can cover you. Nobody will ever have to know it was gone."

"Why would you do that for me? We've barely spoken to each other since—" he didn't finish his sentence since they both knew exactly when and why they had stopped talking.

"Old times, I guess."

Casper's eyes were like a nostalgic tractor beam, pulling Russell back to the past: to shared bottles of Irish whiskey and bonfires at the beach, to evenings at Hennessey's Tavern hitting on hot young blonds as each other's wingman, to burning the midnight oil while plotting ways to be modern day eco-warriors and stick it to *The Man* or more often, the corporations that controlled *The Man* like a puppet on a string.

"I really wish I could, Casper. It's not that simple."

TWENTY SEVEN

After a hellish weekend trying to track down any leads on Kait and her mysterious voicemail, Lilly approached her apartment feeling dead-tired, deflated, and disgusted with the world. Noting that the door stood slightly ajar, she went instantly into stealth mode, adrenaline quickly nullifying her need for caffeine.

So much for getting some much needed sleep!

Pulling her custom-made 1911 handgun from its shoulder holster—its smooth black and cherry finish instilling a polished and professional look to its handler—she removed the safety, pushed the door open wider, and stepped quietly inside. Allowing her eyes to adjust to the dim light, Lilly surveyed the living room and strained to listen for the slightest sound. Silence permeated every inch of space in the apartment, as if a black hole sucked away even the hushed wisps of her own breath while she stared at the ravaged remains of the room.

Belatedly she realized she'd stopped breathing; Kait's beloved blue leather sofa had been slashed savagely and her pampered plants dumped from their pots. Lilly's oak bookcase and all its contents had been knocked to the floor and her old cathode-ray television lay shattered. Whoever had done this wasn't just looking for something or someone; they were sending a vengeful message that nothing was safe or sacred.

Where in the name of all that is Holy are you, Kait?

Lilly took a moment to cloak her heart in impenetrable armor, a coping mechanism she'd had to learn in order to deal with the violence and fear she faced almost daily at her job. Kait was okay—she *had* to be. All implications to the contrary, this was a good sign; it showed that the perpetrator was royally pissed off, frustrated, and on edge. That had to mean that Kait was winning somehow in whatever war she was fighting.

Yeah, but how many battles has she lost?

Continuing forward to inspect the kitchen and the second level, Lilly braced herself against the psychic onslaught of being the victim in her own crime scene. Heart racing, she tried to observe everything with professional detachment. She'd be useless if she allowed herself to ponder whatever unknown horrors Kait might be facing, or dwell on the personal violation she felt knowing that violent, possibly psychopathic strangers had invaded their home and destroyed their things.

You're a police detective for chrissake; man-up!

Things can be replaced. Kait can't.

In the kitchen she found the refrigerator hanging agape, food jars and dishes shattered and scattered on the counters and floors, condiments splattered like blood on the cabinets, and an ominous message written on the white erase board stuck to the freezer door: "*You're both dead.*"

Thank Jesus I took Sheba to the vet.

Lilly had been pulling double duty ever since she'd figured out Kait was missing—had known she wouldn't have the time or energy to take care of the white, fuzz-ball princess in the manner to which she was accustomed, so she'd deposited her in safer, saner hands. She refused to contemplate the horrible things they might have done to Kait's precious cat if she'd been in the apartment. On the upside, the vague threat told Lilly two essential things that fed her hope: Kait was probably still alive, and they, whoever the bastards were, did not currently have her in their evil clutches.

Picking her way back across the obstructed floor, she headed upstairs, her nerves perched on the razor's edge, ready for anything. More destruction awaited her in the bedrooms and shared bathroom: pictures smashed, bedding and mattresses slashed by something long and sharp—*a sword or machete? Very weird in either case*—clothes dumped on the floor, and the distinct odor of piss emanating from them. *Big mistake, asshole!* The perp or perps were long gone, but according to the article she'd read recently in a forensics journal, urine could be used to make a DNA-based identification. *Your ass is grass!*

Lilly headed back toward the stairs in disgust, but a distant footfall stopped her cold. Someone else was in the apartment now, creeping around downstairs. Scrunching her face, she cursed herself for the rookie mistake; she should have radioed for backup before entering the premises, but she'd only come home for a quick change of clothes and some food. She hadn't expected to find total annihilation.

Her portable radio was in the car collecting dust—it was a handy backup when other technology failed, but she rarely used it—and her cell phone was plugged-in charging, right next to the radio. *Effing brilliant, Z! What if the perps came back?*

Not likely; nothing left to destroy.

Unless they were waiting for you.

Lilly shook off the ominous thought.

It could be a neighbor, maybe even Kait!

Yeah, or it could be Santy Claus here to replace your stuff!

A soft male voice made her jump when it called her name from the base of the stairs. "Lillian Zamora—"

Her skin prickled with edgy awareness.

"—best friend of Kaitlyn O'Donnell. I need to talk to you. I know you're here. I arrived just in time to watch you enter."

Shit! How the fuck was she going to get downstairs to see who was talking without getting shot in the leg on the way down? She picked up the cordless phone from the floor beside the overturned console between her bedroom and Kait's, and pressed talk. The line was dead. She followed the cord from its base to the wall and found that it had been torn out. *Double shit!*

Raising her voice, she issued a firm command, "Raise your hands in the air and step outside where I can see you. Don't come back inside until I tell you."

"I'm not here to harm you. I need your help. *Kaitlyn* needs your help."

"Mister, you could be the Dalai Lama and I wouldn't trust you. Step outside or I'm going to start shooting and save the questions for later."

"All right, I'm going."

Lilly slipped quickly to the right side of Kait's bedroom window to get the drop on him before he could turn around and get the drop on her. This was only moderately better than walking down the stairs with her lower body exposed—there were plenty of bullets powerful enough to penetrate the exterior of a wood and panel building—but at least this way he was out of her apartment where she could lay eyes on the bastard.

A tall man with dark brown hair emerged from under the awning, his empty hands raised near his head. Dressed in khaki cargo pants that fit his muscular legs to perfection, and a black, long-sleeved shirt that emphasized his broad shoulders and carved biceps, he looked the part of a predator in sheep's clothing. About three meters from the apartment building he turned around and looked up at the window where she was crouched, watching him. The telltale form of a handgun shaped his right front pocket. Her first thought—*what an amateur*—was followed quickly by another—*looks can be deceiving*—which left her wondering if he was purposely trying to look disarming, or if he really was a novice.

Even amateurs can be deadly.

Lilly reached up and unlocked the window, sliding it open a couple of centimeters. "Walk down to the street, and when you come back, step inside the living room, nice and slow."

He nodded, lowered his arms, turned and started walking in long, purposeful strides. When he was about 15-meters away she turned and raced down the stairs, confident that she could get downstairs and position herself for the best advantage before he returned. In less than a minute he was back, crossing the threshold, his hands in the air again. He'd taken his time, given her what she wanted.

"That's close enough," she said when he was three feet inside her apartment. "Now reach into your pocket, pull out that pea shooter, and slide it toward me."

He pulled a handsome, flat-gray and mahogany Sig Sauer P229 from his pocket and set it on the floor, nudging it away with his foot—*not a pea shooter by any means.* "Give the man a merit badge for knowing how to follow instructions."

Both the man and his gun were clean-cut, good looking, and much larger than expected; Lilly kept her 1911 trained on him from the dining room, ready to take him down quickly if she had to. "Okay, let's hear what you have to say."

"My name is Michael Storm. I've been helping Kaitlyn for the past few days; she was kidnapped from the SIMR pier about ten days ago and taken south to Mexico. That's where her path crossed with mine, and I've been helping her ever since."

"Yeah? So where is she now, Boy Scout?" Lilly asked sarcastically.

"We arrived in town this morning, but while I was out getting supplies, she was…taken. I don't know who grabbed her, but I'll recognize him when I see him. I think he's someone she trusted."

As if on cue, another man filled the doorway, aiming a mean looking HK P30 Smith and Wesson at the back of Michael's head. "With good reason, Storm. I'm a much better bet than you are."

Lilly's heart hammered in her chest and Michael reacted faster than anyone expected, lifting a knife to the man's throat as quickly as he had whipped around to face him. "You son of a bitch! Where did you take her?"

"Are you seriously bringing a knife to this gunfight?" The second man lifted a cocky eyebrow at Michael, daring him to give it his best try.

"Have you ever *seen* what a knife can do?" Michael warned. "It's not pretty."

Lilly adjusted her aim slightly, targeting the handsome guy Kait had hired this summer to work on her crew. She didn't know what in unholy hell was going on here, but she was damned sure going to find out. "Randy? As in the hottie that kissed Kait a couple weeks ago?"

"In the flesh," he replied, staking his prior claim.

"I *knew* there was something off about you," Lilly scoffed.

Michael and Randy stared each other down, neither one budging from his position. Michael was trapped, nowhere to go except forward through Randy, or backward through her. Fortunately, she was an excellent marksman; she could incapacitate whichever one pissed her off most without injuring the other.

"Sorry to break it to you, but the pissing contest is over boys." Lilly cocked the hammer of her pistol and kept her sights trained on Randy, watching him for the most miniscule of movements. By her estimation, he was the greater threat.

"I can take you both down in two seconds flat, so I win. Boy Scout Michael is going to drop his knife and step back and to his left, three paces; Lover Boy Randy is going to lower his gun and slide it toward me."

Randy spoke first, "If you want to see your roommate, I suggest you reconsider that decision, Lillian. She sent me to collect you."

Michael's shoulders bunched with tension, "If you've hurt Kaitlyn, I swear to God, I'll kill you."

"Now, I ask you, Lillian," Randy shifted his gaze to her without yielding a millimeter, "do those sound like the words of a Boy Scout?"

Maybe, she thought quickly, *if the Boy Scout is in love, or desperate to cast suspicion off himself.*

"No, Randy. They don't." Lilly took a steadying breath, mustering her bravado. What she wouldn't give right now for some quality backup. Even Barbie-Boy Bryson would do, and that was saying something! "Then again, that hot rod in your hand doesn't look like something a member of Kait's crew should be carrying either. Care to enlighten me?"

"Not until the Boy Scout backs off," Randy replied coolly.

Lilly was baffled; the guy with the gun, whoever he really was—not a surfer dreaming of becoming a biologist as he'd told Kait, and definitely not an amateur—was as cocky and confident as any government agent she'd ever met.

FBI? DEA? DHS? *Probably* not *CIA based on his attitude and attire.*

The details of Kait's stories about his athleticism and agility heightened Lilly's suspicions, but if he was an undercover agent with the feds, he wasn't going to just whip out his badge for show and tell. Michael, on the other hand, was a total wild card. He'd come out of nowhere claiming to know a *hellofalot* more about Kait's situation than she did at the moment, and she couldn't afford to discount him, or any credible information he might have.

"What's it gonna be, curly-locks? We gonna do this easy or hard?" Randy didn't wait for her response before training his aim on her instead of Michael. "Kait is waiting."

Michael held his position and kept the knife poised at Randy's jugular. "Don't shoot him, Lilly. He's got Kaitlyn stashed somewhere. We've got to find her before Pablo does."

This turn of events was both confounding and enlightening. Odds were good that Lover Boy really was some sort of government agent who knew that Boy Scout wasn't much of a threat, otherwise he wouldn't have shifted his aim and left himself open to an uncomfortably close shave. Odds were also good that Boy Scout wasn't in a hurry to inflict harm on the man who supposedly had Kait tucked away somewhere, or he'd have done so at the first opportunity—*Randy calculated that one correctly.* But her biggest question of the day had to be, *Who the hell is Pablo, and why is he after Kait?*

Lilly found herself back at square one, in a quandary about her next move. "If Kait really sent you, then you have something you want to say to me."

"Yeah," Randy's eyes bored into hers like laser beams. "Don't go to the market unless you're bringing home fish food."

Well, *that* sealed the deal. If Kait had shared their secret SOS code with Randy, then she was definitely cooperating with him, or at least had been at some point during her disappearing act. Lilly didn't have nearly enough information to make her comfortable with the idea of parting company with Michael before he'd shared every detail of his tale, nor the idea of going willingly with Randy into what could easily be a trap, but he wasn't giving her many options.

She shifted her aim from Randy to Michael. "Put the knife down and back off like I said, Boy Scout. We're gonna do this easy."

Michael shifted his weight as he sifted through his options. He couldn't decipher her intent without turning to face her, but he couldn't turn his back on Randy and leave himself exposed. He was SOL and they *all* knew it, but that didn't make Lilly feel any better about what she had to do.

As Michael stepped back and turned to see both her and Randy at once—his knife still poised to defend himself—the spark of hope burning in his eyes just moments earlier was smothered by the ash of betrayal. Boy Scout had read her like a score board—knew she really was choosing his rival as the better asset—and he wasn't going to take it lying down.

"You're making a big mistake, Lilly," said Michael as he increased his distance from Randy.

"Be that as it may, I'm going to need you to put away your knife and step into this coat closet so nobody gets hurt." Lilly pointed at a short, narrow door directly in front of her, directing Michael into the closet under the stairs.

He was steaming mad—*rightly so if he's telling the truth*—but she had him over a barrel. If he truly cared about Kait, he couldn't do anything to hurt her best friend; if he was only pretending, then she'd shoot him in the leg and deal with the consequences later.

For lack of a better plan, she would get all the information she needed from Randy, then rescue Kait on her own, because when push came to shove, she didn't trust...well, anyone!

With both guns aimed at Michael—and his own gun on the floor near her feet—he wisely acquiesced. Lilly felt immediately relieved, and yet somehow just a little bit disappointed too—*if this guy was so fired up to save Kait, he should have fought harder on her behalf!*

Yeah, but then you would've had to shoot him. He wouldn't be much good to her then, would he?

Grudgingly, Lilly conceding the wisdom of his choice, hoping he really was on Kait's side. There was something about him that she couldn't pinpoint, and she'd like another opportunity to question him. Right now, her instincts, or maybe the lump of dread sitting like a stone in her stomach, told her time was of the essence and Randy was holding all the aces. If she played it real careful, she'd be seeing Kait much sooner than expected, and that was the only thing that really mattered.

As Michael stepped toward the coat closet, Randy and Lilly both shifted their aim back onto each other. Randy closed the distance behind Michael like a confident bully who knew he ruled the playground.

Lilly couldn't help but wonder as she watched them, if she had mistakenly reversed their roles in her first assessment. *Was Michael actually the Lover Boy in this scenario, and Randy the Boy Scout? Or,* and this was her biggest fear, *had she seriously overestimated both of them?*

She'd find out soon enough in either case.

What if something happens to one of them before you find her?

Another shot of adrenaline pumped hard through Lilly's system, raising a flurry of goose bumps on her skin, and a chill wind to fan her hot temper. She would be royally pissed if her budding rescue attempt got preempted by an attack of stupidity.

Stay focused—find Kait!

Lilly closed the closet door on a very dark, outraged Michael, and looked squarely at smug Randy. Pointing at her fallen bookshelf, she told Randy, "You can do the honors, tough guy."

"Only got one hand available, Lillian. If you want a barricade you're going to have to help."

Lilly bristled at the casual tone of his voice. There was nothing *casual* about the situation or the man, though he wore the lazy, beach boy exterior like he was born to it. She didn't like the way he said her name, either; like a father-figure chastising a willful girl, it played at too much familiarity and male dominance.

"What? A big strong man like you can't lift that itty-bitty bookcase all by himself?"

Randy shrugged his shoulders and smiled at her accusation, refusing to holster his weapon and move the bookcase. He didn't trust her and wasn't buying her cooperative act—the man was two hairs shy of rousing her ire to an unreasonable state!

"Fine," she smiled back, then bent over to lift one side with her left hand, while casually and *unintentionally* aiming her weapon at his chest with the other.

His smug smile disappeared and he lifted the other end of the bookcase with one hand as well. Together they wedged it into the hallway, flat on the ground, the shelves facing upward. Lilly walked across the shelves, warning Michael through the door, "Stay outta trouble till I get back, Boy Scout," then followed Randy out the door.

Michael waited until he heard the door of the apartment close behind Lilly and Randy, than bent and felt through the darkness for the toolbox he'd noticed on his way into the closet. Once he had it opened, he rummaged through the various tools, feeling each one to determine which would be his most effective means of escape. He had to act fast if he had a prayer of catching them.

With hammer in hand, he started pounding a hole in the sheetrock wall adjacent to the lowest section of the stairs. Within seconds he could see daylight, wooden studs, and a cross brace. In less than a minute he'd made a hole large enough to crawl through. When he was out, he spared only a few seconds to look for his gun, then ran out the door when he didn't find it.

On the street he found only his borrowed car, the front tire slashed, and the same empty cars that had been parked on the street when he'd arrived. Randy had taken Lilly as easily as he had taken Kaitlyn because Michael had been too damned soft to stop him.

He looked up at the sky, ready to curse God, Fate, Karma—whoever might be listening. "Is this what you want?" He pulled his cell phone from his pocket and punched in Ian's number. "You want me to fight? To *take* life instead of giving it, you callous bastard?" he yelled, shaking his fists at the clouds.

"You want me to call down the thunder and be one with the lightning?" he raged, finally letting loose all the anger and resentment he'd been trying to bury for four long years. "Well you've got it!"

Standing in the middle of the street, his heart blazing like a man on fire, he pressed send and waited for his brother's voice.

Ian skipped over the niceties when he answered, "What do you need?"

"The TEAM," Michael replied with newly forged determination.

Ian paused then asked, "As a client or as a member?"

Michael could hear the hope in his brother's voice. This had always been his gig, his way to buck a broken system and do something that delivered real results for people who were in real need. He'd all but begged Michael to stay with the TEAM after Maria had been killed, had put his own neck on the line to ensure that Michael could do what no one else had ever done before—walk away without consequence.

"As a brother in arms who's finally ready to kick some bastard ass."

"No going back this time, little brother. They won't give you another pass."

"Deal me in, big brother. I'm playing the baddest game of my life, and I'm in it to win."

Another pause on Ian's side told Michael that Ian was not alone. A cacophony of deep male voices shouted "Hoorah," and another familiar voice called out, "Glad to have you back, Stitch!"

Ian came back on the line, "We'll be there in two hours."

TWENTY EIGHT

Kait alternately stared out the large picture window overlooking Sweetwater Reservoir, or paced back and forth from one side of the waterfront safe house to the other, keeping a close eye on the three agents Donovan Randal had placed her with for protection. One agent kept watch over the front perimeter, one was stationed inside the ultramodern house with her, and the third patrolled the waterfront—they had the house guarded from every angle except the sky, but with their numerous high-powered weapons, even that was an unlikely point of attack.

Donovan had assured her before leaving that he'd personally vetted all three agents who would guard her in his absence: *"They're all reliable, highly trained, and loyal to me. There's no way Pablo or his men will find you here."* She knew she ought to feel safe, but she didn't; not without Michael at her side.

Don't think about him. He's safer without you.

Donovan insisted that she couldn't trust Michael because he was suspected of complicity in his wife's human trafficking business and her brother's drug operations. Could she actually trust Donovan? She wasn't sure of anything anymore, least of all her current champion. During their latest skirmish, Kait had balked at his use of the term *human trafficking* in an attempt to defend Michael and his dead wife. Donovan had quickly set her straight on that point; any illegal buying and selling of babies, no matter the supposed reason, or their purported placement with loving families, was still trading in human flesh. It was untenable in any form, and on that point, Kait had quickly agreed.

Had Michael known?

How could he not?

Was there any way to put a positive spin on baby smuggling?

Definitely not.

The inside guard, Agent Meyers, entered the dining room after one of his nearly constant sweeps of the entire house, and spoke to her for the first time since he'd arrived. "You've been staring out that window a long time, ma'am."

Kait looked at him, her body language projecting, *what's it to ya?*

"I'm going to have to ask you to stay away from the windows at all times."

Kait's jaw dropped. "Why? Looking at the water is the only thing that gives me peace."

He stepped up closer and pointed out the window. "You see those houses across the water?" Kait nodded and he continued. "There could be a sniper on the other side of any one of those windows, lining up a shot right now. When you stand still too long, you make a better target."

A chill raced up Kait's spine as she backed away from the window. "They're so far away—" she swallowed, unable to finish the sentence.

The agent cocked one eyebrow and tilted his head as if to ask if she was really that dumb. "With a high-powered scope, they can count the teeth in your mouth at that distance."

Kait squared her shoulders as she walked away, "Then it's a good thing they don't know where to find us." Renewed anxiety and disbelief threatened to swamp her tenuous sense of control; if she let go of the reins now, she'd release a wave of emotions greater than Noah's flood.

The drive to Spring Valley was the longest, most tense ride Lilly had experienced since her first call to the scene of an active gang shootout as a rookie. She'd learned a hellofalot since then, rising quickly through the ranks and kicking some major sleazeball ass in order to make detective. When Randy lowered his weapon and laid it across his lap to appease her, she *didn't* reciprocate; she had no doubt that he would retrieve his weapon in a flash if she let down her guard or made a move against him. He was unnaturally fast, according to Kait, and Lilly wasn't ready to test him just yet—*not until I have eyes on my best friend and an escape route in mind.*

After an hour of circuitous double-backs and misdirects, he finally pulled into the driveway of a modern, gray, lakeside house, nearly identical to all the other houses on the block—*perfectly nondescript in true government style.* Lilly's senses ratcheted up to high alert when Randy looked at her with supreme confidence, his body simultaneously relaxed and calm, but ready for anything, "Wait here until I give you the all clear."

Lilly nodded her agreement realizing they were not alone. She couldn't see his backup, so she had no idea how many there were, but the goose bumps on her skin told her with certainty that they were there. He stepped out of the car and walked to the left of the garage, to a small stand of shrubs and trees, purposely planted for just such occasions—when cover was needed for armed guards to stand watch outside what *had* to be a federal safe house—providing more evidence in support of her hypothesis.

When he came back, he was still alone. *Either he's bluffing, or these guys are that paranoid.* Determined not to be outfoxed, she had to assume there was at least one armed guard keeping watch over the outside of the house, and possibly more.

Randy waved her out of the car and headed for the front door. Looking at the pristine, quiet neighborhood, Lilly lowered her weapon and held it ready at her right thigh to obscure it from view, then followed him.

Stepping through the doorway, her eyes quickly scanned the living room, the staircase, and the hallways leading to other areas. A large man who looked more akin to an attack dog with his canines on full display than a government agent, stepped out of the hallway on her left, an assault rifle held at the ready by two beefy hands and a pair of bulging biceps that were clearly visible beneath his starched, white shirt.

Boy do these guys have the goods!

Within seconds, Kait came racing around him like he was nothing more than an overgrown puppy, and another shot of adrenaline flooded Lilly's system making her ready for fight or flight.

"Lilly! Thank gods, you're actually here!"

Lilly started to raise her weapon toward the large man, but Kait flew into her arms and hugged her so tightly that she could do nothing but stand there with her weapon pointed haphazardly at nothing.

"I was so worried that something else would happen before I got to see you again," Kait exclaimed breathlessly. Still holding Lilly tightly, Kait lowered her voice, "I'm so glad you're okay. You have no idea how much I've missed you! Before anything else happens I have to tell you..."

"Kait!" Knowing at least part of what Kait had to say, Lilly unceremoniously cut off her sisterly love ballad and broke her bear hug, determined not to give the men any more information than necessary about the strength of their bond. If these men knew that Lilly and Kait cared for each other like sisters, they wouldn't hesitate to use it against them. They'd be able to coerce them into just about anything to protect each other. "Are you okay?"

Stepping back just far enough to take a good hard look at Kait, Lilly plastered a neutral mask across her face and kept both hands on Kait's shoulders, her 1911 still firmly in her grip. Kait was clearly stressed—pale, slightly gaunt, her eyes watery from unshed tears—Lilly had to dig deep into her anti-emotion tool bag to steady her voice and refrain from pounding someone into the ground. "Have these goons been hurting you?"

Lilly turned to Randy, while Kait just stared at her with a mixture of confusion and relief, "Have you been starving her to death or something? What the fuck?"

Randy lifted an eyebrow at her, "She has only been in my care since yesterday. The damage you're seeing is all from the *other* goons that had her."

She turned her attention back to Kait. "Is that true? Cuz if these guys have mistreated you in *any* way, I'll kick their pansy asses." Lilly winked at Kait to reassure her, and Kait smiled back mischievously.

Kait turned to Randy, sisterly pride beaming from her shimmery eyes as a single tear finally cascaded down her cheek, "I don't believe you've been formally introduced to my roommate. Donovan Randal, meet Lillian Zamora, ass-kicker extraordinaire."

For the next several hours Kait updated Lilly on everything that had happened, answered Donovan and Lilly's endless questions to the best of her ability, which unfortunately was abysmally poor. They feasted on home-cooked, traditional Italian spaghetti and meatballs: a recipe that had been passed down through generations of Zamoras, and was Lilly's one and only specialty in the kitchen. Kait mediated between Donovan and Lilly each time they butted heads, which was frequently since they pushed each other's boundaries relentlessly, both vying for dominance and asserting their power.

Though Donovan continued to reassure Kait that he was on her side and would keep her safe, he refused to reveal who his suspects were at SIMR until the "right moment." He insisted that he was close to bringing Pablo down, and that he was conducting a bust that would, in theory, solve *most* of her problems, but he remained evasive about the details and timeline of said bust, and just what would be expected of her once that happened. Everything "depended" on the way things panned out.

Amid the angst-filled probing, the my-gun-is-bigger-than-your-gun strutting, and the frequent exchange of scorpionesque barbs, Kait noticed that Donovan was keeping a close eye on the time. When next she caught him peeking at his wristwatch, she called him out. "Do you have some place you need to be, Randal? Or are we boring you?"

Lilly shot him a suspicious glare and chimed in. "Yeah, you been eyeballing that Rolex wannabe like it's a snake coiling up your arm."

Donovan squinted his displeasure at both of them as his cell phone rang, then he rose from the dining table and turned his back. "It's about damn time you showed up. Yeah? Well just bring him in already and let's get this bonfire started." He clicked his phone off and turned to face them. "Wait here, ladies. My partner has someone that's going to answer a lot of your questions."

Lilly grimaced, "Smooth as a porcupine, that one. You sure know how to pick 'em, Kait."

Kait shrugged unapologetically since she hadn't really picked him, but rather been picked to play the dimwitted dupe in his master plan. Not following Donovan's instructions, both women rose from the dining table and walked into the next room just in time to see two men enter through the front door of the safe house.

Kait's eyes landed first on William Russell, her long-time supervisor, mentor, and friend, being pushed through the doorway with his hands behind his back and a large red welt staining his left cheek. Behind him was the gorilla who had attacked her in Old Town and rendered her unconscious in two seconds flat with his ancient oriental hoodoo. She tried instinctively to back away from him, but Lilly was directly behind her and the pair collided.

Kait stood dumbfounded and stared at the three men, trying to make sense of the scene. Randy—no, *Donovan*; when would she get that through her thick skull?—was indeed working with the gorilla—*his partner*—who had attacked her. That meant the gorilla was probably a government agent too. Thankfully he was ignoring her at the moment; instead he was manhandling William as if *he* was a criminal. William—*are those handcuffs around his wrists?*—looked implacable, obstinate, and outraged to be treated thus by the ruffian. The implications of what she was seeing were too vast and horrible to consider!

Seeing the fear and confusion on Kait's face, Lilly stepped quickly forward and inserted herself protectively in front of her. "What gives, Donovan? You trying to imply that Kait's boss is somehow wrapped up in all this insanity?"

"I'm not trying to imply anything, Lillian. The facts speak for themselves well enough."

At Donovan's nod, the gorilla pushed William further into the room and William's eyes locked onto Kait, first with surprise, then with a mixture of relief and concern. "You're here? You're safe? What a relief..." William paused, his face and voice shifting an instant later to incredulous accusation, "...Kait, what have you done?"

Her entire body constricted as his tone and words lanced through her like a harpoon. "What have I—" she choked. *No! This is* not *happening!*

Chills raced through her core, cooling the fire even as the questions hurtling through her mind stoked it to a fury. She was a dichotomy: at once a frozen inferno and seething stillness, fractured and made whole again by this new twist in reality. She was in a single moment undone and reborn, years of admiration and respect dismantled and reconstructed into scorn and distrust.

"William, did you take the *Triton* away from me...to run *drugs* for El Diablo?" she asked with disbelief, putting things together much too quickly for her own peace of mind. "Are *you* the one responsible for jeopardizing not only the whales, but the lives of myself and my entire crew?"

"I don't know what you're talking about, O'Donnell." He backtracked to his original story. "An international research crew took the *Triton*, and I guarantee they were *not* running drugs! Who is this El Diablo and why have I been forcibly abducted and brought here?"

Kait blinked, her attention drawn to every nuance of his expression and manner. Had she jumped to the wrong conclusion about his sudden presence at the safe house? Maybe he'd only been brought here to corroborate her innocence. Or maybe he'd been brought in as a bargaining chip to use against her—*as if they need another when they already have Lilly.* After watching her all these months, Donovan had to know how significant William was in her life.

The gorilla jabbed the back of William's left knee with his foot, forcing him to fall into a kneeling position. He then aimed a menacing gun at his temple, "Stop lying, asshole. I watched you bring the *Triton* back to the dock yesterday. I have confirmation from the Coast Guard that you were aboard the *Triton* off the Coast of Eureka five days ago."

Kait gasped and Donovan angrily silenced his partner, "Not here, Rodríguez."

Kait looked at Donovan for confirmation and saw the roiling anger in his features turn to sympathy and apology. *Could she believe him? Could she afford not to?* Events on the morning of her abduction came together in her mind like a whirlwind; William's call hadn't made sense at the time, but she'd never gotten an opportunity to do anything about it. If he was the one who'd taken the *Triton*, then there was no international crew of usurpers, the board had never known there was a problem, and her crew had never been placed on mandatory shore leave. The whole thing had been a ruse to take her ship without a fight.

Her gaze returned unwaveringly to William, praying she was wrong, begging him to address the accusations lodged against him and explain it all away.

William stared back at her, trying hard to present a neutral mask while he struggled to catch up with what was happening and calculate a way out; that was his specialty. He reigned supreme when it came to keeping calm and navigating a smooth path through troubled waters. But Kait knew better than anyone that there was no way out of *this* disaster. All she could do was continue clawing her way forward, garnering as much support and protection as possible and collecting whatever fragments of her life were left, so that she might have something with which to start rebuilding if she ever managed to reach the end of the nightmare. But this nightmare *never* ended—in fact, it grew darker and more nefarious by the day—twisting her heart and ripping it from its foundation like a kelp forest ripped from the seafloor in a storm.

William made no reply, and in one crystallizing moment, she understood—*it was* all *his fault!*

Kait moved slowly toward William, her body resisting every step. If she turned around and walked away, could she forget this devastating new insight into her own destruction? Could she somehow change the outcome? Stopping three feet in front of him, holding herself together with an iron grip, the only word she could shape was, "Why?"

She watched him consider his options, weighing and measuring the possibilities before he answered. He'd always been a genius, especially at twisting untenable circumstances into something useful. When hard times fell, he was always the first one to find the silver lining, and he'd been instructive in helping her find it too!

Not this time.

It was on the tip of his tongue to feign innocence—she could see it in the desperate gleam in his eyes—but Donovan stepped between them and grabbed his shirt with two fists, pulling him back to his feet. "Before you answer her, consider that you've been under investigation by the U.S. Drug Enforcement Agency for months. We have your bank records, your ship's log, your GPS records, everything we need to put you away for a *very* long time; there's no escape for you at this point."

"Circumstantial," he replied, rising to the challenge. "My log and GPS records show that I followed the same route I've been following for years, per my contract," William jutted his chin adamantly.

"Maybe," Rodríguez grunted, "but we've also got your accomplice tucked away getting the medical care he needs for that gunshot wound. He'll be well again just in time to testify against you and save his own ass."

William bristled and paled, then finally sighed with resignation and met her questioning, wounded gaze. "I never meant for you or anyone else to get hurt, Kaitlyn. I...got into some financial trouble. I thought I could get out of it on my own, but...it's like a damned rip current; it just keeps sucking me further and further from shore. I had no choice but to go where it took me."

Betrayal—it stung her for the third time in two days: first, Donovan Randal with his devious trickery and half-truths, then Michael Storm with his deadly omissions, and now William Russell with his blatant lies and treachery. The three men she had allowed herself to trust—*had let into her life*—had all stung her with their various forms of betrayal. She'd known its sharp blade as a child and been helpless against it back then, but as a grown woman with the advantage of age and experience, she was surprised to find that it cut nearly as deep!

There was no silver lining for betrayal; it rocked your world, shook your foundations until they crumbled, then left you breathless and broken, trying to piece everything back together with nothing to fill the gaping holes that had been pulverized into dust. But she was still standing, and with this betrayal—*the most devastating of the three*—she suddenly found herself more determined than ever to right the wrongs she had endured, to level the playing field if she could, and pay the Devil his due.

"You threw away my project, my career, my *life*, with your decisions, William!" She slapped him across the face, only a small tribute to the rage she felt welling inside. "I hope you got what you needed out of the deal, because now you're going to settle the debt by telling Donovan everything they need to know to destroy Pablo."

She whirled on Donovan as he approached her. "And *you* are going to stop withholding information. No more secrets, no more lies, no more omissions." She stood tall—her right hand pointing at him with authority—the captain of her own life, back at the helm.

Determination radiated from her like an avenging angel. "My life is in ruins because of *both* of you! I want justice, for myself and for the whales."

"Now, Kait," Donovan started, not backing down from her hellfire, "I was only doing my job, protecting you—"

"Stow the placations, Donovan. You could have told me you were with the DEA as soon as you came to Michael's house yesterday, and saved us both a lot of grief. I thought you were my friend, but you used me to get to William. Now, you're going to make up for it by turning the *Triton* into my safe house while you go after Pablo. Give me your cell phone."

"Just what do you think you're going to do with it?" Donovan asked warily.

"I'm calling Bowie and Reese and the rest of the crew back to base. They can ready the ship while we wrap things up here, then hit the water ASAP."

Turning back to William she added, "I hope you left the *Triton* shipshape, because every day that we miss counting those whales is another nail in *your* coffin."

Donovan massaged his jaw with one hand, calculating his options while Kait waited impatiently, hands on her hips, unrepentant and unyielding in her new found ferocity. His face went rigid as he started to shake his head. "It won't work, Kait. There's another storm rolling up the coast and Pablo is all set to conclude another big handoff tomorrow. I can't have you out on the water, or anywhere near the bust, in case something goes wrong."

He turned to Rodríguez, "Take William to the basement. We're wasting precious time."

Kait stepped in front of Donovan when he turned to follow his partner and his prisoner. "The *Triton* is safer out on the water than at dock during a storm, and you know it. The crew can make ready in a matter of hours, and we've dealt with storms before. Please, Donovan? We'll stay far away from your bust. Lilly can come with me and you can put as many guards with me as you see fit—"

"No, Kait. I need every available agent to pull off this bust. It's the biggest operation we've ever planned, and if that tropical depression keeps gathering more steam and turns into another hurricane, the bust will be ten times more dangerous. I can't risk years of undercover work just so you can get the project back online in a few hours instead of a few days. Maybe a day or two *after* the bust, when I know Pablo and his ringleaders are behind bars—when there's nobody left to hunt you."

She started to follow him, but Lilly grabbed Kait's arm and pulled her the opposite direction. "He's right, Kait. You won't be safe until after his bust, and I'm not even remotely interested in being out on the ocean in the middle of a storm. It's supposed to hit So-Cal really hard: record setting swells, high winds and driving rain! Besides, you won't be able to see anything, much less count whales in those kinds of conditions. It's better to just wait and take the time we need to build a solid plan."

Kait whirled on her in frustration, yanking her arm away. "Are you seriously taking his side right now?"

"I'm not taking sides; I'm trying to keep us safe." Lilly's hackles rose defensively. "We'll work something out when we have a more complete picture."

Kait faced off against Lilly, returning dagger for dagger with her eyes. They didn't fight often, but when they did they could blow the roof off the house, each trying to force the other to see her point. Lilly was a power house, a force to be reckoned with, but Kait had learned to stand up to her over the years, and this time, she was the one being wronged. An entire conversation was conducted without a single word uttered aloud, and the men watched them with fascination, as if they'd never seen a cat fight before and couldn't tear their eyes away.

Lilly wanted to talk to Kait alone, wanted her to calm down and give her some time to figure out a safe plan, but Kait was sick to death of waiting and hiding and running for her life. She wanted to go on the offensive and kick some serious bad-guy butt, even though she had no real idea how to do so. Lilly promised to help her figure it out, promised to stay by her side, right through the worst of it, and even offered to help her figure out what to do about Michael. At last, Kait threw up her hands with a howl of defeat, "Fine!" and stomped from the room ignoring the stares of the startled men.

She'd been tossed into a sea of stinging jellyfish, but the more they stung her, the more immune she was becoming! Donovan looked like the biggest, baddest jellyfish of the three, but he was harmless enough; she hadn't let him into her heart yet, so he couldn't really hurt her more than he already had. William had stung her to her very core; she wouldn't recover quickly from his numerous barbs. Michael—*what to do about him?* She hadn't a clue—was a rare species she had never encountered. She didn't yet know if his barbs would be benign or deadly.

It didn't matter; if anyone thought she was down for the count, they were going to learn otherwise real fast.

TWENTY NINE

After an arduous night of questioning, during which Kait and Lilly eavesdropped at the top of the stairs, the early hours of Tuesday morning arrived with blended tones of steady resolve and heady anticipation. Donovan and Rodríguez had gotten right to the business of prodding William, who had agreed rather swiftly, to testify against Pablo for the crimes he'd witnessed. He'd then proceeded to identify all the drop points he'd hit along the California coast while working as an "unwilling" mule. He described the men and boats he'd encountered, including their armaments, and he estimated the quantities of drugs and money he'd transported.

In the end, he'd claimed to know nothing about Pablo's operations, beyond his own role, and had confirmed that he was slated to continue making the same run once each month for as long as Pablo saw fit—on pain of death or dismemberment.

As the night progressed, Kait found herself feeling somehow victorious at finally receiving so much information, and confirmation of the wrongs committed. It was only a small victory of course—*what could possibly make up for everything she had been through?*—but she'd take it, and gladly! She suspected, based on the stillness below and the disquiet in his voice, that Donovan's satisfaction with the results were a bit more dubious.

What more could he possibly need to take Pablo down?

More than once she'd heard William insist that he'd only intended to make the run twice, "to pay off his debts," but Pablo had had other ideas. That small detail held little sway for her since his involvement with drugs at *any* level had jeopardized the safety of countless SIMR employees, including herself, and would tarnish the entire SIMR reputation when it came out in the news.

Yet another *reason it's imperative to forge a success out of the whale count!* If the data collected by her teams did, in fact, sway the Commission to reject the proposal to reinstate hunting on blue whales, it would be quite a feather in SIMR's cap.

But will it be enough to erase the scourge of drugs?

Donovan's voice called upstairs from the basement, startling Kait from her thoughts. "Ladies, if you're tired of crouching in the shadows, you're welcome to join us now."

Lilly looked at her pointedly, her brow lifting in a sarcastic arch, and spoke in an intentionally loud voice. "I tell you, Kait. This guy is a real smart ass! I don't know what you ever saw in him."

"Well," Kait replied with a fake smile as she rose from the floor and stretched, "I never saw the ass, only the smart."

As they descended the stairs, Lilly ended the brief conversation with a parting barb for their obnoxious male audience, "I'll admit that both aspects of a man are essential on their own, but put them together wrong and it's enough to spoil the whole package."

Kait snickered and shushed Lilly as they entered the basement. "Stop harassing my ticket out of this mess," she whispered.

Donovan stared at Lilly, the twinkle in his eyes not quite reaching the rest of his stony face until he blinked, visibly relaxed his shoulders, and slowly released the rakish smile that had been trying to escape. "Glad to know you've got your priorities in order, Lillian."

Rodríguez pushed William past them and up the stairs to be guarded by one of the other agents, then came back to the basement for the next part of the agenda: The Plan. In the wee hours of the morning, Donovan revealed that he would meet a special ops team at sunup to bust Pablo's San

Diego contingent, then replace their boat crew with his own and head to the designated drop point, at a currently unknown, offshore latitude and longitude, for the big take-down. The Coast Guard would provide support and was ready to move as soon as he had the coordinates. In the meantime, Kait and Lilly would remain at the safe house with their assigned guards, and Rodríguez would guard William, and take him to headquarters for processing; they didn't want too many eggs in one basket.

At 0300 hours, Kait left the three arguing about the plan and went upstairs to the room in which she'd slept the night before—*if you could call it sleeping*—and found Lilly's cell phone. She debated the merits of calling Michael to let him know she was alive and well and safe. He was an unknown risk now, but after everything he'd done for her, she felt she owed him at least that much. Unless she was completely wrong about her black knight, which was entirely possible given her track record thus far, he was probably beside himself with worry, agonizing over his inability to find her and berating himself for having failed to keep her safe.

If she did call him, it would *not* be because she missed his reassuring presence, his warmth, or his offbeat humor. And it certainly wouldn't be because she missed the way he deviled her with his manly charms.

Yeah, right. Keep telling yourself that story, Chicken of the Sea. He really was better off not getting dragged further through the unnatural disaster that was her life now; and she was better off not finding out that he really was guilty of human trafficking and drug smuggling.

Can't argue with that, said the little inner demon that usually tried to prod her into all kinds of mischief. But, it might be interesting to know how he got involved with a family as devious as Pablo's in the first place.

Interesting, or utterly depressing.

Michael had been honorable and generous during her time with him; it made no sense for him to save her life and risk his own to defy his evil brother-in-law if Michael was involved with Pablo's ring. A part of Kait wanted desperately to talk to him about it, to give him a chance to explain his innocence and start their friendship anew, with all his dirty little secrets out in the open. But another part of her couldn't ignore Donovan's insistence that hiding out in Mexico for the past four years only proved Michael's guilt.

A sudden presence behind her sent goose bumps racing along Kait's spine. She quickly stashed the phone in the waist of her pants, under her shirt.

"Whatcha doing up here *alone*, boss?" Donovan eyed her suspiciously and looked about the room as he stepped closer, blocking her exit. "We agreed you were *never* to be out of sight of your bodyguards—for your own safety."

Kait raised her hand in the air, deflecting another lecture about her safety. "I didn't think it would be a problem to slip away for a couple minutes of peace. The house is well guarded, the windows are covered, and I haven't had a moment to myself for days." She backed away, trying to put some distance between them, but he followed, backing her up to the edge of her bed. He then settled both of his hands on her shoulders, holding her there forcibly.

Kait set her chin at a glacial angle and met his questioning gaze, eye to eye. "I told you not to call me boss anymore. I fired you, remember?"

"I remember—that and a few other things." His gaze softened and his left thumb began sweeping back and forth softly along her skin. "I'll do everything I can to make the *Triton* your new safe house after the bust." He squeezed her arms gently to punctuate his next words, "But Kait, I can't keep you safe if you don't obey my rules."

"Rest assured, Donovan Randal, or whoever you *really* are, that I have no intention of doing anything to jeopardize my safety or that of my crew." *Including anything as stupid as falling for a handsome liar like you!* Her eyes blazed as she tried to shuck out of his grasp, and failed.

"You're still angry with me," he stated flatly.

"Damn right, I'm angry. I don't appreciate being used as a patsy—"

"I wasn't using you," he cut her off. "When I joined your crew I didn't *know* you, or any of the rest, except on paper. I figured out pretty quickly that *you* were as clean as freshly fallen snow, but I still had to figure out who was working with Pablo."

"Why did you target me and my crew?" she asked once more, in a hurt tone. "There are countless other crews at

SIMR that you could have infiltrated, and they work in international waters!"

"The other crews operate too far from Castañeda's territory. He only runs the Mexico and California coastline and hasn't tried to expand beyond that yet." He pulled her infinitesimally closer, his eyes projecting his apology better than any words could. "Your team was the most logical target because you operate strictly within his territory. Being on your crew gave me the access I needed to offices, files, computers—everything." He sighed, released her shoulders and took a step back, giving her the space she wanted.

"And?"

"And what?" he asked intractably.

"Don't stop now, Randal. You owe me a lot more than that."

He squinted again, as he was apt to do when he was displeased. "And, when I started to suspect William, I realized you were too close to him to get through unscathed, so I hung around. I got worried that something would happen to you, and before I knew it, you were gone," he frowned and fisted his hands.

"That's your apology?" Kait asked irately, placing her hands on her hips so she wouldn't wrap them around his throat. She scrunched her face and lowered her voice to imitate him, "I'm sorry I thought you were a criminal and wormed my way into your life under false pretenses, Kait. I'm sorry you were too stupid and inept to keep yourself out of trouble in my absence, Kait. I'm sorry that I have to keep you under lock and key while I clean up this mess, Kait," she scoffed.

The muscles in his jaw worked as he clamped his mouth shut to hold back a nasty retort. She'd finally managed to tug the strings of his temper and loose the tiger raging under his skin, which may or may not have been wise, but within seconds he had it back under control.

She wasn't quite sure why she was pushing him so hard, except that words would *never* be enough to undo everything that had been done to her. He had abused her trust, endangered her life and her project to further his own goals, and done his best to squash her faith in the man she might have been foolish enough to fall in love with if things had gone a different direction. Yes, maybe it was all for a good cause in the end—drug smuggling was right down there with the worst of humanity's crimes—but damn it, how was she supposed to forgive him for all of that?

"You're right, Kait. I failed you when it really counted, but I won't make that mistake again." He stuck his hand out, palm up, "Give me Lillian's cell, and stay with your guards until this is through, or I'll take you to headquarters."

Kait bristled under his continued scrutiny wondering how in the world he had known about the phone. She wanted to fight him, rally against his tyranny and set him straight on a few more points, but his stance and visage brooked no argument, and she wasn't ready to poke the tiger further. Instead she slapped the phone into his waiting hand and turned her back on him.

As quickly as he had materialized within her space, he dematerialized, leaving his tense vibration hanging in the air like a heavy mist. Kait heaved a sigh of relief. Donovan Randal, whoever and whatever he really was, was easily the most physically and psychically intense man she'd ever known: not the happy-go-lucky man he had presented during their days out at sea, and not a dark brooder with the weight of the world on his shoulders like Michael. She'd caught occasional glimpses of Donovan's intensity during the times they had worked together, but had never felt the weight of it directed at her until the past 48-hours. It was a distinctly disquieting experience that she hoped never to repeat.

I really do know how to pick them, she thought sarcastically. Stepping into the hallway to follow him, she nearly jumped out of her skin, finding him waiting, arms crossed with restraint, just outside her door.

"Holy buckets!" Kait punched his arm reflexively. "Don't scare me like that," she hissed as she slipped past him to find Lilly.

"I'm not kidding, Kait. Twenty-four, seven," he insisted, hot on her trail.

"All right! I'll stick to them like stink on fish! Get off my case!"

"You haven't seen me *on* your case," he huffed as she descended the stairs to the main level of the house.

Reaching the bottom, Kait found Lilly and Meyers approaching from the kitchen. "Can you get this monkey off my back?" she asked mockingly.

"Happy to," Lilly replied stepping between Kait and Donovan. "I see you're looking to spar again; why don't you try it with someone a little more your speed?"

Donovan tilted his head to look down at the pint-sized police officer, her wild, black curls pulled back into a pony tail. Her wiry muscles, sculpted by shadows and light, were emphasized by her bright white tank top and the black straps of the shoulder holster that held her 1911 within easy reach and plain sight.

"You think you're up to the task, short-stuff?"

"I know I am," she replied confidently, giving Kait a wink.

"I can't take this anymore; I need some sleep!" Kait grabbed Agent Meyers, "You're with me," she said as she left Donovan and Lilly to their sparring.

A short time later, Donovan and Rodríguez departed, each to their own tasks, leaving the three agents with Kait and Lilly. The statewide sting was officially underway, and if everything went according to plan, Pablo and his henchmen up and down the California coast would be captured and arrested, their shipments seized simultaneously at multiple locations, and their destructive activities brought to a grinding halt.

Donovan had been a key player in setting up the entire operation, but he wasn't ready to celebrate just yet—not with dark clouds and heavy wind rolling over the southern coast like an ominous blanket. He'd learned through other challenges, that things always got worse, sometimes a lot worse, right before they got better. This damned storm was about to prove his theory, but did it really have to hit on the same day at the same frigging hour of his bust?

He pulled into the parking lot of the Point Loma Yacht Club at 0555 hours, five minutes ahead of schedule, and began gearing up: bulletproof vest, HK P30 hand gun with ten-round magazine, three extra magazines loaded and ready in the pockets of his black tactical vest, .38 special tucked in his ankle holster, KA-BAR combat knife strapped to his right thigh, and a Remington AR-15 assault rifle slung across his chest on a combat sling. This was what he'd been striving for since the beginning of his career, busting his ass for, living the minimalist life for, never laying down roots or getting entangled in relationships for. It was the culmination of ten years of hard living—the last three being the worst by far—that would either make or break his career, and would set the course of his life for the next ten years, give or take a few.

The teams were en route, armored SUVs, helicopters, and/or high-powered watercraft, carrying field operatives to fifteen confirmed strike points: three warehouses, five boats, six houses, and one sun-tanning boutique operating as a front. Once in place, they would storm the premises, mow down anyone that resisted arrest, and bag and tag all necessary evidence for the prosecution. Donovan wanted to be everywhere at once, to make sure nothing was missed and no one significant got away—no matter how much they had planned and prepared, he knew something, somewhere, was amiss—but in the end he had settled for staying in close proximity to his primary witnesses and the grand finale of the day.

Thankfully, six of the sting locations had matched the general vicinity of the drop points identified by William Russell; with any luck they would still be well stocked and prime for a bust. The extra confirmation was a welcome reassurance, but Donovan needed this Op to be over and done, needed to feel like he'd finally accomplished something worthwhile with all his efforts. Three years was an awfully long time to wait for one hard-earned reward, but the time was upon him at last. Nothing would ever bring his little brother back from the overdose of tainted cocaine he'd tried at a high school dance, but this bust was a damned good tally on his road to vindication.

Donovan heard the whirr of the approaching helicopter seconds before he saw the lights of the approaching vehicles. A gust of wind buffeted his car, and his radio buzzed with confirmations as the water-, air-, and land-based tactical teams got into position, right on queue. He closed the trunk of his car and headed toward the dock as a light rain began to fall and gunfire broke out in a halo of light from the hovering chopper.

Into the fray, little brother; this one's for you!

Kait lay restless and awake beside Lilly on the queen-sized bed in their now shared safe room. "How do you tolerate the stress, the waiting...the not knowing?" she asked in a hushed voice.

"We know the plan, know how much work went into developing it," replied Lilly equally hushed. "There are a lot of good men and women out there right now, getting ready to put it all on the line for this. You just gotta have faith."

Kait sat up and started to roll out of bed but Lilly stopped her, "Shhh—be still." They listened through the dark stillness, the last hour before sunrise. "I haven't heard Meyers pass our door for at least ten minutes. He's overdue for his sweep."

A door closed in the distance, then the stairs creaked as someone ascended to the second floor. Kait released a heavy sigh of relief, "There he is now. Don't scare me like that, Z." When she started to get up again, Lilly stilled her again.

"He's moving much slower than normal. Get down beside the bed," Lilly moved swiftly into the corner behind the door, gun drawn, and safety off.

Kait gulped back the feeling of panic that swept through her. He *was* moving slower, as if stalking something. *Had someone snuck in past the outer guard?*

The floor creaked just outside their door, then all was silent again except for the quiet scrape of metal against the strike plate as the latch of the door knob slid open. With a burst of energy, the door swung open, slamming into Lilly, knocking her gun from her hand. Lilly grunted and flew into action as the dark figure turned to attack. Kait watched shadowy fists fly, heard blows connect with body parts, and knew she had to help take down the dark figure that looked nearly twice Lilly's size.

Rising off the floor, Kait lifted the tall bedside lamp and yanked its cord from the wall. In two steps she was behind him, swinging the lamp like a Double-A batter. It connected with his shoulder and sent him stumbling into the wall, which gave her just enough time to snatch Lilly's hand and run.

Together they flew out the door, down the hallway toward the stairs, their attacker thundering behind them. Halfway down the stairs, the guard from the waterfront appeared, gun raised, eye's locked on his target, and yelled for them to duck. Several shots were fired over their heads from both directions, then Lilly yipped in pain and stumbled, tipping too far off-balance to catch herself as she fell.

Still holding Lilly's hand, Kait tried to brace herself, to stop Lilly's fall; her weight and momentum pulled Kait hard, and the railing slid from her other hand like a wet bar of soap. Both women tumbled down the last few steps and landed with a thud on top of the agent who lay dead at the bottom, a pool of blood seeping out from under his body.

Kait tried to get up, slid in the bloody tangle, then realized Lilly wasn't moving. "No!" she screamed, turning Lilly over to find whatever wound had incapacitated her.

Before she could pinpoint the problem, the attacker grasped a handful of her hair and yanked her from the jumble. Her arms and legs smeared blood across the otherwise pristine wooden floor as she struggled to erect herself and alleviate the pain in her scalp. Desperate to escape, her eyes zeroed in on the gun in the dead agent's hand and she reached for it.

The assailant jerked her back and stomped his foot down hard on the gun, blocking her grasp. "You won't need that where we're going."

Kait recognized his voice immediately and gasped from the fear and pain. Rodríguez, the awful gorilla who was supposed to be Donovan's partner, was back, attacking her mercilessly for the second time in two days. Her mind reeled as her gaze landed on Agent Meyers, the man who'd been guarding her from inside the house. His throat was dripping with blood, his eyes staring lifelessly at the opposite wall. Rodríguez had killed him, had killed all *three* of the agents Donovan had left to protect her.

The gorilla murdered his own agents!

"Let me go!" Kait screamed, trying to get back to Lilly before she became another casualty. "I've got to stop her bleeding!"

His hand, still fisted in her hair, began to pull her up, and she locked both hands around his wrist to relieve the pressure on her scalp as she came to her feet.

"Leave her," he commanded. "We have places to go and people to meet." He smiled wickedly as he pulled Kait out the front door.

THIRTY

Michael felt the raw power of the surging ocean beneath the smooth hull of the Hann 40 Peacemaker, and gave thanks as she slid effortlessly over the slate blue water. The *Slippery Squid* was Ian's latest acquisition: a 40-foot, militarized, fast patrol boat (FPB) designed for all-weather, medium-range, quick-strike missions in deep or shallow water.

A favorite anti-piracy boat along the coasts of Africa, and other hijacking hot spots around the globe, Peacemakers were built to protect crew and cargo while maintaining maneuverability and speed in diverse conditions. The *Slippery Squid* had a few well-planned extras: large-caliber, deck-mounted, automatic machine guns on her bow and stern, electronic surveillance and night vision equipment in the wheelhouse, and bullet-proof windows.

As a critical component of their mission to track, and if necessary, disable the *Spanish Maiden* without being seen, the Peacemaker had been loaded with gear from the San Francisco TEAM headquarters and brought south by Char, a former Army Ranger nicknamed for the ferryman of Hades because he could navigate anything, anywhere, and in any conditions. Char had raced through the night to rendezvous with the rest of the team and deliver the majority of their equipment to the assembly point in Long Beach well before dawn.

Like homing pigeons, the rest of the team had materialized, ready for action: seven highly trained specialists—two in a chopper and six on the FPB—plus Michael. Their mission: to provide anonymous support to the DEA and Coast Guard teams that would go after Pablo during phase two—the grand finale of the statewide cleanup.

The Tactical Extraction and Assault Mob (TEAM), in which Michael was now thoroughly enmeshed for the *second* time in his life, was his best hope of preventing Pablo from slipping through the cracks and continuing his assault on Kaitlyn.

The stakes were high, but the risks were even higher now that the TEAM had agreed to run an Op not officially sanctioned by the government. They would be considered a rogue team of mercenaries if detected—*possibly hostile and definitely expendable*—so they planned to stay well below the radar to avoid any repercussions. Thankfully, the benefits of the sting far outweighed the risks in their collective opinion: they could guarantee the elimination of one of the biggest kingpins on the Pacific coast, reinstate their best all-around fix-it man—*and save his woman,* according to Hono, the most chivalrous of the bunch—all while conducting a genuine test of their brand new FPB in storm conditions.

These were people used to operating in the shadows. They knew no fear and had a long history of prevailing in impossible situations.

Michael was grateful to have such a supportive and talented team at his back and a top-tier boat at his disposal, regardless of the personal cost he would pay in coming years. But he was too worried about Kaitlyn, too preoccupied with the rapidly approaching assault on his nemesis, to be demonstrative about that gratitude, and it wasn't needed anyway.

While the rest of the team ogled the high-tech features of their new million-dollar baby, Kaitlyn remained the only female on his mind; he'd been thinking about her nonstop since he'd lost her, or perhaps even before. He knew only one thing with utter certainty; he had to find her and bring her back under his significantly improved protection before it was too late.

Having once sworn that nothing could lure him back to the dark underbelly of the TEAM, and that nothing could tempt him to take another life, no matter the evil being done by the perpetrator—*all souls were precious*—he'd finally had to admit to himself, his brother, and his team, that he'd been wrong. He finally understood Ian's truest calling—which had once seemed to conflict utterly with the physician's code to *first, do no harm*—to thwart the monsters that thrived in the darkness by extinguishing the light of others.

Kaitlyn was a light in the darkness, and this time, Michael would extinguish the monster to insure that her light continued to shine.

Behind the transom, a powerful jet stream of water shot 15-feet into the air, testament to the furious whirling of the twin-diesel, 500-HP propellers carrying them at a sustained 40-knots toward their target—the *Spanish Maiden*—currently 30-miles offshore of Newport Beach, cruising south at 30-knots toward San Diego and the encroaching storm. They knew the yacht's exact location because Eagle Eye, their resident computer whiz and former CIA agent, had hacked all the harbor masters' computer systems in the state and located her occasional berth at a marina in Long Beach. Frog, the aquatic combat diver of the team, and a former Navy SEAL, had then planted an underwater tracking device on the outer hull of the yacht, below the waterline.

What they didn't know with any certainty, was the yacht's next stopping point or final destination. Were they running for the border with their spoils? Would they stop in San Diego and make another attempt to capture or kill Kaitlyn? Would they head full-steam into the heart of the storm to avoid pursuit, or push further offshore to skirt around the worst of it? Michael stood beside Ian at the wheel and watched the green blip on the surveillance screen, the *Slippery Squid,* move slowly closer to the red blip, their target, as they moved to intercept. He was too restless to sit in the racks with Eagle Eye and Frog, too intent on watching the screen to go out to the gunner's stations with Char and Hach.

The sun was set to rise at 0700—an eternity unfolding in endless milliseconds, the last two minutes before daybreak—but the thickening clouds overhead guaranteed heavy rain and a sustained cover of semi-darkness. The blue and gray aquatic camouflage on the topside of the Peacemaker would blend perfectly with sea and sky in these conditions, making her difficult to spot until she was right on top of her target. The TEAM had the tactical advantage on several counts, but Michael suspected they would need every advantage they could get.

Today, they would all be tested, individually and as a unit; he, on his mettle and his merit as a member of the team, and as a worthy protector of the woman he loved; they, on the wisdom of welcoming him back with open arms, and then embarking on an unpaid, unsanctioned, Hail Mary operation. There'd been no time for the usual in-depth attention to detail that usually made their operations a seamless success. And yes, he could admit it now, to himself, if not to others; he loved Kaitlyn O'Donnell—danger magnet, fish-hugger, button-pusher, adventurer, warrior, and independent woman extraordinaire.

Michael thought about the shining examples of love he'd witnessed throughout his life: the happy, unified love of his parents and of his friends Anton and Adele, the luminous, universal love of his Nana, Consuela, and Maria. That brought him to his patient and loyal brother, a confirmed bachelor, dedicated to the art of love in numerous ways—healer, humanitarian, protector—but as yet unwilling to take the plunge with a lifelong partner, perhaps because of the damage he'd witnessed when Michael had taken the plunge with Maria.

Love was a funny thing: an elixir that had a different effect on each man that dared drink from its fountain, and a different effect each time he dared drink. The want of it made wise men fools and fools, gods. The winning of it tested each man's fortitude against the ensuing chaos that frequently accompanied the blending of two souls, two lives, two hearts and minds into one. Love made hard hearts soften, and soft hearts harden, drove some men to drink, and others to sobriety. The loss of it challenged the strong and the weak alike, pushing some right up to the precipice where they gained enough strength to move forward in life, and pushing others right over the edge to a bottomless pit of despair and ruination.

As his thoughts returned full-circle to Kaitlyn, the woman who'd not only found the broken pieces of his heart, but put them back together and forced it to beat again, a clipped female voice with a European accent came through on the radio.

"*Ink Spot* to *Slippery Squid*. I have a new fishing report, over."

It was Bast, their occasional associate and airborne contingent from the International Criminal Court (ICC), checking in from her bird's-eye reconnaissance of the safe house, where an inside source had assured them that Kaitlyn, and her roommate, were safely tucked away with two undercover DEA agents and a team of bodyguards. The fact that she was breaking radio silence with their pre-designated code did not bode well.

Ian grabbed the handset and squeezed the talk button, "*Slippery Squid* to *Ink Spot*. How are the salmon faring this season? Over."

"They've left the shady banks of the reservoir and headed out to see King Triton. One hen, two cocks. Can't tell if there's blood in the water, but I don't see any sharks in pursuit. Do you copy?"

"We copy. Keep your shadow out of the water so they don't spook, but stay on their tail. I'll see what I can find out."

Michael and Ian turned to Eagle Eye in unison, but Michael was the first to say what they were both thinking. "Use the Sat phone to call your DEA contact again. We need to know why they left the safe house and went to the *Triton*."

Ian turned to Michael with one possible explanation, and one of many big questions. "If the DEA decided to move Kaitlyn, then the safe house must have been compromised. But why separate the ladies?"

"And why take Kaitlyn to her research vessel with this storm breaking?" Michael asked, unwilling to give voice to the numerous, nefarious answers that came to mind.

"How do we know it's actually Kaitlyn and the DEA agents?" asked Frog from a passenger seat.

Leave it to a SEAL *to cut right to the chase.*

Ian got back on the radio, "*Slippery Squid* to *Ink Spot*. We need visuals to confirm the species, over."

Eagle Eye chimed in, still holding his cell phone snug against his ear listening, "Source says, phase one of the sting is still underway at several locations; it was a rousing success at several other locations. The ladies should be safe under lock and key—no known deviations from the plan." He shook his head, disappointed by the lack of current information. "Intel is spotty, coming in surges from different locations."

While Eagle Eye updated his source on the situation and raised an alert on the safe house, Bast came back online, her voice ice cold and pissed off.

"*Ink Spot* to *Slippery Squid*. King Triton is disembarking the SIMR pier. Had to drop eyes in the drink to get visuals without casting a shadow, over."

Ian answered the question on Michael's puzzled brow, "Hono went into the water to get closer to the *Triton* without being spotted. He'll get onboard if he can, and mitigate any issues that might crop up, but we won't have comms until he's back with Bast."

Michael smacked the back of the captain's chair in frustration, "Maybe we should change course and intercept the *Triton*."

"And lose our window with Castañeda? No," Ian responded decisively. "We need confirmation of Kaitlyn's location and status before we deviate from the plan. Hono is one of our best; give him some time to work it out."

Michael frowned grimly at his brother. "Kaitlyn may not have any time to give."

A single ray of light entered an east-facing window of the safe house and inched its way across the room until it shone like a laser beam on a pair of closed and blood streaked eyelids. After a few seconds the light ray disappeared behind swift moving clouds spreading darkness across the land.

Lilly scrunched her face and opened her eyes, the high, pitched ceiling of the living room looming overhead at a dizzying height. The house was silent, her heartbeat the only noise thrumming in her ears, her head throbbing with each beat. The ground was hard beneath her back and her left shoulder burned like she'd been skewered by the Devil's poker. Lifting her right hand to massage her head, she saw that it was covered with drying blood.

Holy shit!

Searing pain shot through her shoulder, neck, and head when she tried to sit up, stopping her in her tracks. Instead, she rolled her head to the left, her eyes landing first on the bloody bodyguard lying beside her on the ground, Andretti, then on the other guard, propped against the wall like a rag doll, Meyers, his throat cut from ear to ear. The memory of two men shooting at each other while she and Kait tried to descend the stairs roared into her mind.

Sweet Jesus! "Kait?"

Lilly forced herself to sit up, not allowing the pain to stop her, and scanned the room. Kait was nowhere to be seen. Sitting on the cold, wet tile of the foyer, she swooned with dizziness and began to palpate her head. She found an inch-long laceration right smack in the middle of her forehead where she'd apparently done a face-plant when she fell.

At least I didn't break my nose.

Next, she tried to assess the damage to her left shoulder. She couldn't quite lay eyes on the bullet's entry point, couldn't tilt her head far enough without triggering shards of lightning, but it felt like it had hit high and passed clean through. *Lucky!* Blood still oozed down her chest, staining her white tank top a dark crimson.

Gotta stop the bleeding ASAP.

A loud, intermittent buzzing began somewhere in the vicinity of the two dead guards, and she couldn't help but jump, her skin instantly prickling with chills. She was in fight or flight mode, hyper aware of everything, and yet not quite in control of her responses.

When she realized it was a cell phone, Lilly leaned over and began searching Andretti's pockets. Not finding it in his coat or front pockets, she tugged him onto his side and pulled it from his rear pants pocket just as it stopped vibrating. Swiping the touch screen with her bloody finger, a security screen popped up, asking for a pin before allowing access to the phone. "Damn it!"

Two seconds later, another cell phone began vibrating farther away. She looked straight at the other dead guard and scrambled over to him in a hurry to find it. The buzzing came from Meyers' front coat pocket this time, and she pulled it out, wiped her hands on her jeans, and swiped the screen triumphantly, panting with pain and exertion. "Zamora."

"Lillian? What the heck is going on over there?" Donovan yelled. "Why are you answering Meyers' phone?"

"He's dead. Somebody took out *all* of your so-called bodyguards and grabbed Kait!"

Was that hysteria creeping into her voice?

Oh, hell no. Get a grip, Z!

"Lillian, are you hurt?"

Donovan's voice was strained; the bastard was worried, and with good reason. If he didn't bring Kait back to her in one happy, healthy piece, she was going to flay him alive! "I'm still breathing, lover boy. Bastard shot me in the shoulder, but I'm stopping the bleeding right now with compression," she lied, looking around for something absorbent and soft to press against her wound.

Not finding anything useful, Lilly crawled to the banister, pulled herself upright, and headed for the kitchen. In the periphery of her mind, she could hear Donovan talking to her, but she'd stopped paying attention to him when she'd realized she was losing too much blood.

He was yelling now, his voice drifting through the air to her ears even though the phone was clutched in her left hand, tucked tight and low against her stomach so she could press on the bullet hole in her shoulder with her right hand. "Yeah, yeah...almost there...gimme a minute will ya!" she said to the air hoping he could hear her.

In the kitchen, she found the hand towel and pot holders she'd used while cooking dinner the night before. They weren't exactly sterile, but they were a whole lot better than nothing. She pressed one potholder to each side of her shoulder, awkwardly leaning against the refrigerator for assistance, trying to hold them both in place with only one hand. She couldn't do it.

Lifting the phone a few inches higher, she pressed the speaker-phone button on the smart screen with her elbow. "Um...I think I need help, lover boy." She swooned and caught herself on the counter. "Any idea where I can find some duct tape? It's a girl's second best friend you know."

"Lillian, how much blood have you lost?"

He sounded real calm now—past worried and into the territory of scared shitless. "I don't know what's mine and what's from your waterfront guy," she admitted, feeling a touch scared herself.

"Okay, short-stuff. An air ambulance is already on the way. I need you to get to the kitchen and look under the sink. There should be some tape there, and you should find a med kit under the bathroom sink if you can get to it. Tell me when you find it."

"Already there," Lilly bent over to look under the kitchen sink and fell; the phone, her good hand, and both knees slapped hard against the cold, hard tile. "Ouch! Shit—hope you're still there."

She dropped to her butt and opened the cabinet, her eyes landing instantly on a big stack of shiny silver tape stacked next to a red tool box. "Found it! Hold on while I—"

"I'm still here. Good job, Lil. Can you roll the kitchen towel into a ball and use it to get better compression?" he asked, his voice wavering in and out of her ears like a zephyr.

"Workin' on it..." she whispered, fighting the pull of unconsciousness.

"Lillian, can you tell me who shot you? Who killed my men and took Kait?"

Yup, lover boy had a voice just like a gentle breeze. It cooled the burning in her shoulder and eased the ache in her head, and that was just plain funny. Tough little Z had a new soft spot, and it only took a bullet and a near-death experience to admit it to herself. Ha!

"Sorry, Donny...couldn't see him in the dark. He got in without a sound; must have taken out Meyers...without much of a fight. Got Andretti last." She could hear herself panting now, feel herself fading.

Gotta give him more clues, Z! "Best guess, they knew him...doubt he could creep...on all three."

"Okay, Lil. Can you remember anything else? Did you hear his voice?"

"He was real big and dense. Hit me like a brick house...kinda reminded me of..." Lilly was silent a moment while she finished winding the tape around her shoulder to lock the pads in place on both sides. When she finished, she strained to remember the name of Donovan's partner, but her head hurt and her shoulder was a blazing inferno. "I'm cold," she said as she began to shiver.

"Lillian, stay with me," Donovan ordered in a stern voice.

Lilly smiled as her mind caught a familiar word that would tell him what he needed to know. "What happened to the gentle breeze, lover boy? Gorilla got your..." Her hand slipped to the floor as her back sank against the cabinet.

"Lillian, can you hear me? You better fight. Medevac is on its way! Stay awake, short-stuff, do you hear me?"

When she didn't answer him, a string of expletives wafted through the air from the cell phone. "Damn it, Lillian Zamora. You stay alive until I get there or I'll kill you myself!"

Donovan made his way to the support chopper assigned to the Pt. Loma raid, and climbed inside without preamble. "I need you to take me to the Sweetwater safe house, pronto." He handed the pilot the coordinates on a piece of paper and dialed the number for headquarters, swearing another blue streak when he was put on hold.

When the pilot didn't immediately comply with his orders, Donovan barked at him, in no mood to deal with red tape or chain of command. "We've got three agents and a witness either dead or missing, and an officer of the SDPD down at that location. Get me to those frigging coordinates, now!"

The holding tank for persons of interest at DEA headquarters took him off hold. "Agent Randal, here. I need to know what time Agent Rodríguez checked in with William Russell, and I need to know right now!"

The agent asked him to please hold again as the chopper engine roared to life and the blades began to rotate overhead.

"You'll have to put on your seat belt," the pilot warned.

Donovan strapped himself into the seat, and the agent on the phone came back. "They have not checked in yet, sir."

Donovan looked at his watch with consternation: 0710. "They should have been there thirty minutes ago. I need you to call me at this number the minute they arrive. In the meantime, issue an Agency-wide alert for Agent Rodríguez. I want him detained, wherever the fuck he is found, until I talk to him. Got it?"

"Yes sir, but why detain one of our own agents?"

"If he doesn't hand over our key witness in the next ten minutes, he's either a turncoat, or an infiltrator. Either way, three of our agents are dead. Consider him armed and dangerous; he doesn't get a pass, under any circumstances, until *I* have cleared it!"

THIRTY ONE

Kait struggled to calm herself in the dark, uncomfortable confines of the car trunk in which she'd been abruptly dumped by the gorilla known as Agent Rodríguez. Throughout the interminable ride to wherever he was taking her, she used both hands to feel what she could not see all around her: the felt-lined walls of the compartment, the metal door above her, the door latch locked in place, and the ends of an ominous black tarp spread out beneath her. She'd hoped to find an emergency latch release button, or a crowbar she could use to pry the door open. Unfortunately, anything useful had been removed from the trunk before its conversion into a human crate.

As for the large mass hidden beneath the tarp, she carefully avoided contact with any part of it, which wasn't easy since it filled at least half of the trunk space, and jabbed at her back and hips. Her mind had registered both the tarp and the bulge with alarm, when she'd been dumped into the small space, and she was loath to explore either one.

In the darkness, Kait's senses were heightened. She felt the pull of momentum each time the car turned, stopped, or accelerated, felt the changing intensity of friction between the tires and the road. At the start of the journey, she had tried to memorize the direction of each turn, the time between turns, and the approximate speed at which they might be traveling, so she could try to predict where Rodríguez was taking her. She'd quickly realized that she'd never been told where the safe house was located, so she didn't have a starting point from which to construct the map in her mind. She had no idea which direction they were traveling and couldn't even be certain that she was still in her home state. Instead, she strained to listen for telltale sounds through the irregular hum of road noise.

Remembering that most car trunks have a false bottom with storage for a spare tire and the requisite tire-changing tools, she shimmied, pushed, and rolled to her side, reluctantly using her own body to shove whatever was concealed under the black tarp deeper into the back of the trunk. If she could find the hidden compartment and get her hands on a jack or a wrench, she could come out fighting whenever the traitor finally stopped and opened the door.

Kait ran her fingers over the front of the compartment cover at least ten times before finding the small finger latch recessed into the cover flap. When she tried to pull it open, her own weight prevented even a millimeter of access. Unable to repress her fear a moment longer, she pounded on the small recess several times with her fist, her feet kicking the wall of the trunk.

"Let me out of here!" she screamed.

Apparently she'd made herself heard because the driver suddenly floored the accelerator, then stomped on the brakes, causing her body roll face-first into the locked metal door where it curved down, then back toward the bulky mass under the tarp. Unable to brace herself in time, she smashed into both objects with a yelp of pain. A car horn blared just outside the trunk and the road noise increased and changed from a dry hum to the wet sizzle of water drops being pressed, torn, and sprayed apart by the force of the tires as they hydroplaned at high speed along an otherwise nondescript roadway.

Kait revised her first assessment, unsure if he had intentionally retaliated against her noisy rebellion, or narrowly avoided an accident. In either case, she would not repeat her tantrum.

Forcing herself to exhaust all options, Kait turned her attention reluctantly toward the black tarp. It had been a sinister sight, looming out at her, larger than life when Rodríguez had opened the trunk and tossed her inside. Was it a foreboding herald of unpleasantness still to come, or the specter of misdeeds already concluded? Perhaps it concealed weapons that she could use to escape, rather than the hard and soft parts of a body that had been conjured by her imagination.

The gorilla had supposedly taken William away from the safe house to put him in protective custody at DEA headquarters, but he hadn't been gone very long before returning to kill everyone and snatch her from her safe haven. She hadn't seen William with Rodríguez during the attack, or sitting in the passenger seat of the car when she'd been abducted.

Was he dead under the tarp?

Could she handle it if he was?

Despite the horrifying revelation that William was the root cause of each and every disaster she'd been forced to endure for the past eleven days—the catalyst that had started the unending explosion of her life—she didn't want him to be dead. The thought of her mentor dethroned from his esteemed station at SIMR was much more tolerable than the thought of another friend having been reduced to a corpse.

Then again, she would never forgive him if Rodríguez had killed Lilly—*definitely can't handle that right now.*

To protect the last shreds of her sanity, Kait convinced herself that Lilly was alive and William couldn't possibly be under the black tarp because he and the gorilla were on the same side, both working for Pablo the Devil.

It's not even a body, she promised herself. *Just a conglomeration of gear the gorilla stores in his car.* Bravely, she turned herself over and searched for the edge of the tarp. She couldn't see what lay beneath it so she would have to use her hands to feel it.

Please don't let it be William.

Kait's fingers landed on a soft nest of short hair crowning a hard, round, human skull. A primal scream began to claw at her throat, but she choked it back and clamped her left hand over her mouth. Her mind reeled as she forced her right hand to move lower, past a rigid face, devoid of warmth, whose nose brushed the outer edge of her hand and made her skin crawl.

Suddenly the car came to a jolting stop, transporting her instantaneously from one nightmare back into another. The momentum rolled her toward the black tarp again and she quickly braced her hand against the telling layers of cloth, skin, ribs, and sternum, stifling another scream before it could escape.

The car shifted, a door opened and slammed closed, followed by another door, then a key began grinding in the latch and the trunk began opening above her.

Gloomy light, salty wind, and heavy raindrops streamed in to arouse her already magnified senses. The gorilla and another man loomed over her, and a cold body lay stiff beside her. As the gorilla reached to pull her out, she grasped the black tarp and yanked it down to see who it was.

Not William.

Her brain stopped for a millisecond, frozen in confusion. A youthful, freckled face, sculpted by terror and surrounded by fiery red hair gaped at her from the darkness and she gasped with recognition when her mind started working again.

Frankie Nestor—William's intern!

The scream finally escaped her throat like a wild thing fighting for its life. Rough hands pulled her from the trunk and her arms and legs shot out in a frenzy, resisting further entrapment even as she fought to extricate herself from Frankie's coffin.

Rodríguez forced her to stand, then slapped her face, ending her hysterics and shifting her attention back to him and their immediate surroundings. Kait knew this place well, even through the gusting wind and rain. She'd come full circle, back to the starting point where everything had gone so drastically wrong: the SIMR pier, facing off against *two* traitorous bastards, one glaring at her with venom in his eyes, and the other standing impotently beside him, his hands cuffed behind his back.

Kait stared dumbfounded, her emotions a stormy brew of feral hate, staggering fear, and bewildering relief that William was still alive.

William's eyes shifted from her to Frankie, the dawn of recognition twisting his helpless resignation into raw, paternal anguish. A fire leapt to life in his veins, and William shouted accusingly at Rodríguez, "You said you'd taken him into custody! That he was going to tell you everything!" The emotional blow wracked him harder than any physical blow, as he stared at his very young, very dead assistant: the troubled kid who'd filled his head with bad ideas and false hope in the first place, when all along he should have been man enough, wise enough, to fill the kid's head with solid solutions and real hope.

"Why'd you kill him?"

Rodríguez grimaced in disgust, "Don't cry, you spineless wonder! I thought you were supposed to be some kind of genius, but you don't get it yet, do you?"

Kait watched William's mind race to find an explanation for his confusion, but he refused to believe what was right in front of him. Taking pity, she spelled it out for him in a single word, "Traitor." The word applied to both men equally, and she knew by the devastated, humbled look in William's eyes the moment he figured it out.

At that, Rodríguez returned his attention to her, "Not a traitor, you stupid bitch. A patriot to the true kings of Mexico! A strategist and warrior with his fingers wrapped around the seedy underbelly of American society, poised to make a killing for my country—my people—and take my rightful place at the head of the table!"

Finally understanding that Rodríguez was a psychopath, and that he was taking them both to Pablo instead of offering them DEA protection, William rammed him with his shoulder as hard as he could and yelled, "Run!"

His action caught Kait off guard, but she tried to make good on the opportunity. Rodríguez immediately knocked William to the ground and clamped a strong hand around her arm like a vise. Pulling her to his chest, he aimed his gun at her temple to demonstrate the futility of the situation. "You can both die here and now, or we can save it for later. It doesn't matter to me; I will be richly rewarded for taking you both to Pablo in either condition."

Kait shook her head slightly at William, hoping he would cooperate and buy them both some much needed time to figure out a solution instead of fighting an obviously losing battle here in the parking lot.

When William did nothing, Rodríguez took it for the crushing defeat it was. "Good, it will be a much better surprise if I present you both alive and let him kill you himself."

To William he said, "Lead the way to the magnificent *Triton*. You'll be taking us for the ride of a lifetime!"

Aboard the *Triton*, the trio made their way through the windy downpour to the helm room on the second deck, where Rodríguez handcuffed William to the wheel. "Make ready while I situate the bitch and cast off. And don't get any genius ideas while I'm away or I'll slit your wrist and let you bleed out slowly while I have some fun with her and the kid."

Kait raced through several possible scenarios in her mind, looking for their best chance of escape. This was her turf—she knew every inch of this ship, from bow to stern—but Rodríguez was far more ruthless and dangerous than she'd ever guessed from their previous encounters. He spoke like a man who'd taken a dive off the deep end, and she didn't want to be anywhere near him when he hit bottom. This time she was *definitely* in over her head.

If she found a way to escape but left William behind, he'd be a dead man for sure. She certainly didn't want *his* blood on her hands, but how was she supposed to free herself from a highly trained agent, free William, and then make a break for it? Rodríguez was a heartless predator with skills she couldn't begin to fathom. He'd outwitted Donovan and everyone else in the DEA, killed three trained agents without breaking a sweat, and was apparently Pablo's biggest fan!

Leaving the helm room, Rodríguez led her back outside and down the ladder to the main deck, past the external equipment lockers, into the water lab. Below deck were the crew's quarters, the galley and two heads, the engine room and other high tech areas accessed only by the captain and his crew. At the door of the water lab he pushed her inside and went directly to the nearest locker, startling her with his knowledge of the ship. He'd been here before and knew exactly where to stow her so she couldn't escape.

So much for my home field advantage!

Kait made a break for the door hoping to reach the rails and jump overboard. The memory of her previous escape flashed in her mind: the black water, the glowing moon, and the jagged rocks. Conditions were vastly different this time—she knew her location, and was still reasonably close to shore—but the benefit of daylight would not be enough to offset the effects of the turbulent storm stirring the ocean to a frenzy. If she did manage to get away, her chances of making it to safety and sending help for William were miniscule.

Still better than being locked up and escorted blindly to the firing squad!

As she ran toward the starboard rail, Rodríguez swiped the air to catch her, anticipating her move. Kait countered by twisting her torso just out of reach, her center of gravity low and resilient. Like lightning, his foot swept the ground and hooked the tip of her shoe. She stumbled, but caught herself with her other leg and kept moving.

Her next steps carried her past the winches, toward the stern where the giant A-frame loomed overhead, but an unexpected pressure on the back of her knee made it buckle. She couldn't bring her other leg forward fast enough, and fell to the deck, panting and crawling to get away. Rodríguez lifted her by the hips, swiftly turning her to face him, then tossed her over his shoulder in a fireman's carry.

"Put me down!" She screamed, pounding his back with both of her hands. She couldn't kick him with his arm locked around her legs. As he passed into the wet lab again, Kait reached out and latched onto both sides of the door frame, bracing herself against his pull.

"Let go of the doorway, bitch," Rodríguez growled. "You're only making things worse for yourself."

Kait writhed, trying to free her legs, but he gripped them harder and pulled. She was about to lose her grip when he backed up, set her down, and rammed her against a bulkhead. The shockwave slammed through her, jarring her bones to the marrow.

"Stop fighting me, or I'll start breaking bones."

He hoisted her onto his shoulder again and stepped through the doorway, unimpeded this time, while Kait struggled to regain both her breath and her focus. *Would he simply lock her in a storage room, or did he have worse things in mind?*

In desperation, she reached for anything with which she could fight him. The counters in the lab were clear, all equipment stowed in the lockers and cabinets, out of sight and out of reach. Finding nothing, Kait reached behind her, trying to pull his hair or claw his face. He blocked her hand, set her on her feet again, and slammed her against another bulkhead with brute force. The wind left her lungs in a rush, and her legs collapsed under her, unable to withstand the beating. She strained to maintain consciousness as he backed out of the locker cursing, then slammed the door shut and bolted it from the outside, leaving her in an abyss of darkness.

Kait lay there for what seemed an eternity, an amorphous puddle of worn out nerves, unable to regain her equilibrium. Slowly her breathing eased and her headache subsided to manageable proportions. Despite the darkness, she knew exactly where she was, where to find William if she got out, where to hide if she got the chance, and where to find the handgun the captain kept hidden in his quarters for emergencies, if it was still there.

Unsure how much time had passed, she finally sat up and groped through the blackness, orienting herself in time and space. It probably hadn't been very long, but she could feel the *Triton* moving, heading out of the harbor. She had to move fast while she was still a swimmable distance to shore.

Using the wall of shelves, Kait got to her feet in the storage locker and moved quickly to the light switch by the door. Blinding light illuminated the 8- by 12-foot room, at once lending comfort and renewing her strength.

Looking around, she saw the box of GPS fin tags ready and waiting to be paired with new subjects, the rack of wetsuits and life preservers kept on hand for water rescues, and testing kits used to collect on-the-spot water quality data out in the dinghy. She was safe enough for the moment, barricaded in her own small shelter with all this equipment, but she saw nothing that would help her escape or ensure her continued safety.

Kait pounded the door, rammed it with her hip and shoulder testing its strength against her resolve. Unless she turned into the incredible hulk, she couldn't hope to knock it open without assistance. She looked for something with which to pry it open and found only the lightweight telescoping rods used to look under water without getting wet. The air tanks would make a nice battering ram, but each one weighed at least fifty pounds. She gave it a try and managed a few weak blows against the door before her arms gave out from fatigue and her back protested from the strain.

Sitting down on a pile of fishing net Donovan and Matt had cut away from an entangled whale, she wracked her brain for a solution. As the minutes ticked by, the *Triton* began to roll and pitch much more intensely; either the storm outside was picking up strength, or they were already out of the harbor and heading into open water.

If both are true, you're totally screwed!

Rodríguez was en route to meet with Pablo. He would hand her over to her most deadly foe and she would be utterly at his mercy. With no idea how much time she had left, Kait knew her only chance of survival was to somehow get out of this locker in the wet lab and take control of the *Triton*. It was a tall order, but she'd rather go down fighting than succumb to her miserable fate; she might die trying, but the alternative was a guaranteed lights-out.

There has to be a way out of here!

Out in the lab she could hear glassware clanging against each other as the *Triton* rocked and rolled with each ocean swell. Waves smashed against the hull and the *Triton* creaked and moaned under the pressure; Kait had never seen her tossed so wildly. She was a solid and capable vessel and had been put to the test in many a squall, but never without a full crew to keep watch. William was an excellent seaman, but even the best captain could make a wrong move and capsize, or even sink them in weather this rough.

Donovan arrived at the safe house in his purloined support chopper at the same time that two police cars rolled up the street and parked in his only clear landing zone. The medevac coming for Lillian had been delayed by complications at another emergency, and all other medevacs within a sixty mile radius of the safe house were already on route to other locations to rescue agents wounded during the bust.

The pilot cast him a sideways glare, "What do you want me to do?"

"Land on top of them if you have to; just get me down there!" Donovan shouted, motioning downward with his thumb.

The chopper hovered over the police cars for only a moment before beginning a painfully slow descent. It didn't take long for the cops to realize they were about to be crushed if they didn't move; they quickly scattered, clearing just enough space to land. When Donovan stepped down from the chopper, the cops drew their weapons and aimed at him, steaming mad and ready for anything.

Steadfast, he approached them without drawing his own weapon and flashed his DEA badge, "Agent Randal, DEA. I need you men to cordon off the area and keep everyone but the paramedics out while I investigate the scene. I have agents down and witnesses missing." He intentionally skipped the part about a wounded police officer on scene hoping to keep Lillian's cohorts out of his hair long enough for him to get to her and scan the scene for evidence.

"Dispatch says we have a wounded detective inside," said the boldest of the three, offering a challenge to his authority. "That falls under *our* jurisdiction."

"She's a Federal witness, and you're wasting precious time, officer. Get out of my way and start helping, or get suspended."

Donovan pushed past the officers and ran straight into the house, not stopping to check on the agent who was supposed to be stationed out front; he would return and give him his due after he took care of Lillian.

Pulling on a pair of latex gloves as he scanned the bloody scene in the foyer, he tried to avoid disturbing any evidence by leaping onto the stairs, then over the railing. Within seconds he was in the kitchen, by her side, feeling for a pulse with one hand, checking her wound with the other.

"'Bout time you got here, Randal," she said weakly, straining to open her eyes.

Relief trickled through his nerves like a silent spring. "Never thought I'd say this, but you just keep talking, short-stuff. Your little barbs are music to my ears."

She smiled and managed three more words he could barely decipher, "Real smooth, Donny."

A second chopper approached from the north, the swarming buzz filling the air as his ride lifted-off to yield the only landing space to the medevac. In under a minute the paramedics were beside him, taking over. One immediately set to work fitting her for a blood transfusion, while the other checked her body for additional wounds.

While he stood there watching, his heart heavy as a stone in his stomach, Donovan's cell phone rang, jolting him back into the big picture. "Donovan here," he announced smoothly to his supervisor, the Chief of Intelligence, as he stared at Lillian's blood on his free hand.

In a voice strained by the stress of another unending day in a long string of unending days, the chief spoke. "I just got word about our crew out at the safe house. What can you tell me, Randal?"

"I'm with the wounded SDPD officer and the paramedics right now. They're getting ready to put Officer Zamora on the medevac chopper." He headed for the front door, bypassing the two agents that were dead in the foyer, and stepped outside to check on the agent in the bushes. Rounding the hedge, he found the agent lying flat on his back, eyes closed, mouth agape, and continued his report. "The witnesses, O'Donnell and Russell, are both MIA," he bent over the agent and felt for a pulse, surprised when he found one. "Hold on, Chief—"

An ambulance pulled up to the curb and he hollered to the paramedics, "We've got a live agent over here. No obvious injury but he's unconscious. I need help, right away!" He stayed with the agent and began searching for the source of his injury as he continued reporting to his chief. "—Erikson is alive; Andretti and Meyers are dead."

Erikson's hand shot up and grabbed a fistful of Randal's shirt as his eyes flew open. "Rodríguez! He came out of nowhere like a fucking wraith and kicked me in the solar plexus. Did you get him?"

Randal shook his head no, then held the man down when he tried to get up. "Take it easy, Erikson. Paramedics need to check you out."

"Did I hear what I think I just heard?" the chief yelled through the phone at Randal.

The paramedics from the ambulance started checking Erikson, which freed Randal to return to the crime scene and make sure the deceased agents were not being disturbed in the rising flurry of activity. "You heard right, Chief. Rodríguez was supposed to deliver Dr. Russell to headquarters this morning, but he never showed. Erikson just confirmed: looks like Rodríguez doubled-back during the sting and killed the other agents to get to Miss O'Donnell."

A flurry of curses and shouted orders came through the line aimed at those in closest proximity of the Chief at his location. Donovan held the phone away from his ear until the tirade was over. When he'd calmed, the chief came back on the line, his voice the personification of cool authority.

"Castañeda's rendezvous coordinates were confirmed about ten minutes ago: Latitude 32.729, Longitude -118.252, but we've got another problem."

Donovan waited for the other shoe to drop, watching the medics finish loading Lillian on the medevac chopper. "We just got an anonymous tip that Castañeda was warned off the rendezvous, and is instead heading southeast at full throttle, toward the storm and international waters. If that's not bad enough, the *Triton* has been spotted heading out of the harbor in the same direction with three known occupants: one woman and two men."

Donovan held back a curse, "That has to be Rodríguez with Russell and O'Donnell!"

"My thoughts exactly," said the chief. "We need a new plan PDQ!"

THIRTY TWO

Kait's spirits ebbed with each crashing wave. She was on her way to her doom, never to see Lilly, her brother Nick, or Michael again. She'd never know if Lilly was alive and safe, never learn the rest of Michael's story, never be able to give proper thanks for all he and Donovan had done to help her. She would never finish her project and present the data to the Commission, never get a chance to vindicate Buck.

On a more basic level, she would never discover why her father had really abandoned her when she was a child, or why her mother resented her so much. There would be no time to explore romance, marriage, or children, no time left to read the new articles and exposés her globetrotting brother would write about his endless adventures and intrigues.

Michael, who'd tried so hard to save her, who'd risked life and limb countless times to protect her, would never know how she'd met her final demise. From what she'd learned about him in their brief time together, it seemed likely that he would blame himself for her loss, dive even deeper into his inner torment, and maybe never break free. It was a cruel twist of fate that had presented her with the singular man that gave her hope in the notion of love and happily-ever-after, only to end it all with such a violent and unjust string of events.

A tear slid down Kait's cheek as her lips trembled. She would give anything to see Michael one more time and tell him that no matter what horrors haunted his past, he was still a good man that deserved to be happy. And while she was making wishes, she hoped Nick would win a Pulitzer, Lilly would find love true enough to soften her protective shell, and her mother would finally figure out that she didn't need a man to take care of her because she could do just fine on her own if she tried.

Why am I sitting here giving up?

"Because I can't win. I've tried so hard, but everything just keeps getting worse!"

That's not the real reason.

Another answer floated to the surface of her mind and made her cringe with self-loathing. *Because I'm just like her! I want someone else to show up and save me, because I don't know how to save myself!*

Her spine stiffened, her skin suddenly hot, constrictive. "That's a bunch of bull honky," she protested aloud, sitting up straighter, rejecting the ploys of her inner demons. She hadn't heard this particular brand of insult in five or six years—not since her last big fight with her mother, over who had the greater need to stay at Nick's condo for a few weeks: Kait, between seasonal field contracts, and nursing several injuries from being hit by a car, or Margaret, between sugar-daddies, and nursing six months of hangovers.

Haven't I conquered this yet?

Apparently not.

Preparing for an inner battle to end all inner battles, Kait took a deep breath and centered herself. "I'm going to get up off this floor and do something! I'm not going to feel sorry for myself, and I'm not going to give up, period, no matter how hopeless it seems!"

The instantaneous response from somewhere primitive and deep slipped into her mind like a runner stealing home-base. She felt it trying to assert itself in the vicinity of the shallowest neurons of her mind, not deep in her heart, which had grown accustomed to commanding the day, and not in her gut.

You don't have what it takes, baby. You pretend real well—got everyone else convinced you're the great KO punch—but I know the truth. I know what you really are.

"I'm human. I'm fallible," she conceded to the storage locker and the things it contained as if they were living, breathing spectators. "I know I'm just one tiny, little spec in the Universe, but if I don't try to make a difference, then I never will. Buck taught me that."

You're dreamin', baby. Been dreamin' your life away, hoping for things you can't have and don't deserve. This was said with the high-pitched trill of her mother's voice, a new twist on an old theme.

"You must have me confused with somebody else," she said, brushing the brittle, old demons away like flecks of dust. "I've worked damn hard for everything I have, and if I lose it all because of this tragic comedy, then I'll pick myself up and start over, and I'll work hard to create something new, because that's what I do."

Kait braced herself and took another deep breath, shaky in both conviction and stamina. She needed a lot more than bravado and a pep talk to win this fight, but fight she would, until her last breath—if for no other reason than to prove herself worthy of the help she'd received thus far. And so that nobody could say that Buck, Barney, or her DEA bodyguards had died in vain.

What about Lilly? her demon asked, in one last effort to topple the mighty KO.

She's not dead! She's too ornery to die.

"And she'd kill me for giving up! Ergo, she's alive and well."

Right! And what if you actually survive this endless disaster?

"I'll never bust her chops again for being so overprotective. And I'll give William heck for getting me into this mess. And I'll give Donovan heck for lying to me. And I'll track down Michael and tell him..." she struggled here, not sure she was ready to admit what she'd been trying so hard to hide from the very beginning, "...that he's the most confounding and intriguing man I've ever known, and I want a chance to know more!"

As an afterthought, she added to her list of To-Dos, "And I'll take a vacation—right after I finish my project and present my findings to the commission."

Okay then! Kait stood up again, bound and determined to break out of her prison. She looked at all the equipment with fresh eyes, hoping to find something she'd missed before, something that would tilt the odds in her favor. Her eyes landed once again on the dive tanks in the corner. Hadn't she seen some show where they'd used a gas-filled tank to break through a brick wall? What was it?

Myth Busters—yes, that's it!

Kait set right to work pulling two tanks from their spot beneath the shelf and laid them side by side on the floor. Next, she tucked wetsuits on both sides of the tanks to keep them from rolling around in the turbulent conditions; the dive tanks were filled with pressurized gas, so if she knocked their valves off quickly, the gas would rush out and propel them into the door, knocking it off its hinges.

In theory, it should work, but she was no expert, and her luck these days was beyond abysmal. All she could do was try—*and hope the tanks don't explode in my face.*

Standing above the tanks on the floor, Kait hoisting a third tank up into her arms, wishing she had a hammer instead. She placed her feet as far away from her makeshift battering rams as possible, then slammed the end down on the valve of the nearest tank. The valve held fast. Lifting the metal tank again, she slammed it down once more with all her might; it was loose now—almost ready to give—and she could hear a slight hiss as the gas began to seep out. One more time, she lifted the tank and slammed it down, then jumped back when the pressurized gas shot out at the back wall, releasing a miniature tornado, punching the tank through the bottom of the door with a blast.

It didn't knock the door down, but it did leave a gaping hole. If she could punch the second tank through the door in just the right place, she could double the size of the hole; then she might be able to squeeze through.

Sweat broke out on Kait's brow as she prepared to blast the second tank. Her strength was flagging, but she muscled her way through with grim determination, hitting the valve stem five times before it finally let go and punched a second hole in the door. As Lilly would say in her humorous determination to unite the two branches of her Spanish-Italian heritage, ¡ahí está! voilà! *There it is, voila!*

Quickly, she lay down on the ground and stuck her head through the opening, testing its size and pliability. What remained of the door was as rigid as ever; she couldn't break pieces off to make the hole larger, and she still couldn't knock it down. It was going to be a very tight squeeze. *Shoulders and hips,* she thought, for the first time in her life wishing she was wispy instead of curvy. *Those are the limiting factor.*

Pulling her head from the hole and pushing one arm through, Kait shimmied forward until her head emerged on the other side. Pushing the opposite shoulder down as far as possible, she expelled her breath, sucked in her ribs, and pushed against the shelves with her feet. The edges of the hole dug in, biting her ribs and shoulder as she inched forward until she was stuck.

Buck, if you're watching this, please *don't let Rodríguez walk in while I'm down here!*

After several shallow pants, she pushed again until her second shoulder slid through. Now the breasts—her mother's voice scurried through her mind: *"Take your vitamins, dear. Boys prefer girls with soft, pillowy breasts, and you've got a ways to go in* that *department."*

This is so not the time, mom!

Again, she sucked in her ribs and pushed with her feet, snaking her way through despite the pain and pressure on her chest. With the same sluicing rush that happened when the widest part of a baby dolphin passed through the birth canal into its new watery world, her breasts were suddenly free and she could breathe again. Relief trickled down Kait's spine. Pushing on the outside of the door with her free hand, she soon pulled the other arm to freedom and continued forward until her hips filled every fraction of the opening. No longer able to bend her legs and push, she then had to rely only on her upper body to finish the job.

The *Triton* tossed and dipped more violently with each passing minute as Kait pushed, writhed, and strained, at last winning her freedom.

On her feet now, and certain she was racing against time, Kait ran to the refrigerator across the lab and found the specialized concoction of drugs used to sedate whales and other sea mammals during stressful disentanglements and rescues. She quickly estimated the amount needed to incapacitate a 250-pound man and filled two syringes—*probably more than needed, but better safe than sorry*—then loaded them into two 8-foot poles used to deliver the drugs across a distance. She would have to get much closer to Rodríguez than desirable using this method of attack, and he was significantly more dangerous than her usual targets, but it was the only non-lethal way she could think of to put him out of commission.

Hoping for some slightly more deadly backup, Kait made her way below to Captain Hallor's quarters and opened the chest where he kept his handgun. She riffled through the clothes and other personal effects that he'd left aboard, but did not find the weapon.

Of course not! That would have been far too advantageous!

Shaking off another defeat, she headed back topside to do what she had to do. *This is it,* she thought, approaching the bulkhead door. *If you miss, you're dead.* The outcome would be the same no matter who pulled the trigger. *Game over and you lose...everything!*

With a silent prayer and a steadying breath, Kait stepped out into the blustering rain. Within seconds she was drenched by the wind-whipped barrage of rain and saltwater spraying every direction as waves crashed against the hull and spilled over the deck. Crouching, she worked her way to the aft ladder and climbed to the second deck. Bypassing the computer room, she dashed across the open passageway to the forward corner of the helm room and stopped just past the port door.

Thirty miles offshore of Chula Vista, and only one mile from her prey, the *Slippery Squid* reduced speed to match the *Spanish Maiden*, and went dark. The USCGC *Boutwell* operating out of San Diego Harbor was twenty miles north, closing fast, but not fast enough. A team of DEA agents aboard the commandeered drug-smuggling yacht, *High Life*, and an SDPD patrol boat were also on approach, only ten miles away, racing to intercept the *Spanish Maiden* which had indeed abandoned plans to pass off another shipment of cargo, and appeared to be making a run for international waters.

Less than two miles away, the *Triton* was plowing through 12-foot swells, also bearing down hard on the *Spanish Maiden*. In the air, *Ink Spot* was flying a five-mile perimeter around the *Triton*, fighting to stay aloft in sustained 25-mph winds, 40-mph gale-force gusts, horizontal rain, and rapidly decreasing visibility. Half of the *Slippery Squid*'s crew would hold back, maintain cover, and support the mission from a parallel position while the DEA, SDPD, and Coast Guard intercepted Pablo's yacht. The other half of the crew would enter the water with scuba gear and diver propulsion devices (DPDs) and get close enough to intervene instantly, and anonymously if, or rather when, the need arose.

Michael pulled a black neoprene dive hood over his head, the picture of determination and focus as he checked his dive computer, centered the double-hose regulator in his mouth, and rolled backward into the roiling ocean, right behind Frog and Char. The weight of his scuba gear pulled him down toward Earth's gravitational center even as his buoyant wetsuit lifted him toward the surface, making him tumble briefly, looking for the horizon.

Char and Frog were already situated in the driver's recesses of two, 2.5-meter, torpedo-shaped submersibles; Michael latched onto the nearest DPD, positioned himself slightly above and behind Char, and signaled thumbs-up. Both vehicles lurched into motion, quickly accelerating to five knots, and Michael held fast with both hands to prevent the ocean from pulling him off his aquatic steed.

Hach, torn between the desire to test his long-distance marksmanship using his new favorite assault-rifle, and his more shark-like desire to dive into the center of the meat-ball and start biting, perched on the bow of the *Slippery Squid* and watched the divers disappear.

Eagle Eye, monitoring communications between the three converging teams without announcing their TEAM presence, confirmed what DC—their team leader, Ian—already knew from watching the radar screen: the cavalry would arrive too late to save Kaitlyn O'Donnell from her clandestine date with the Devil.

DC grumbled about the rapidly developing cluster-fuck and watched the two DPD blips carrying Char, Frog, and his little brother, whom he still couldn't quite believe was back, converge with their target, far in advance of the other three vessels. This was exactly why they had come—to prevent the worst case scenario from becoming a reality.

While Char controlled the speed and direction of their two-man submersible, Michael kept watch over their immediate surroundings and maintained a firm grasp on both the DPD and several weapons. The chill of the ocean seeped slowly into the few small centimeters of his skin that remained exposed; the majority of his body was covered by 7-mm thick, black tactical wetsuit designed to keep heat in and cold out, while still allowing relatively unrestricted movement. But the chill of the ocean was nothing compared to the ice already running through his veins at the thought that, already, he might be too late to save Kaitlyn from a fate worse than death. She'd been out of his reach for almost 48-hours, enduring unknown tortures, at the mercy of men who had more interest in their next paycheck than in her life.

He knew without confirmation from Bast and Hono that Kaitlyn was aboard the *Triton*, barreling toward his greatest nemesis—and hers—perhaps helpless or injured, maybe even incapacitated. Through the inexplicable connection he'd felt since the moment he'd met her, he could feel her fear tugging at him, her perseverance and bravery rolling over him like waves in the face of her latest challenges. Despite his renewed pledge to the TEAM, and his inevitable acceptance that he could no longer stow away in his villa and play the recluse, he could think of nothing but his brief time with Kaitlyn and how easily she had brought him back to life with her innate courage, strength, and innocence.

Without hesitation, he would move mountains and part oceans to get her back unharmed, dedicate the rest of his life to fighting evil with his brother and the TEAM to see her once more, vibrant and alive. And if it came right down to it, he would gladly die today, or any other day, if it meant she could go home safe and continue her life unencumbered by soulless bullies, thugs, and murderers like Pablo and his men. She was the light in his sea of darkness, and Michael finally understood what he'd once resisted—*when darkness waged war against the light, that darkness had to be obliterated.*

THIRTY THREE

The *Triton* slowed in the thrashing ocean, the whir of the engine quieting as Kait peeked through the window into the helm room to locate the traitors, William and Rodríguez. Directly in front of her, William stood handcuffed at the wheel. Beyond him, just outside the starboard door in the wind and the rain, Rodríguez waved at two approaching halos of light. The ship rose on a massive swell, revealing the yacht she'd last seen eleven days ago at the SIMR pier—when her world had still been reasonably ordered and somewhat recognizable.

Kait recoiled, instantly heart-sick. They weren't slowing for the storm or turning back to shore as she had hoped; they had reached the rendezvous point! Pablo and his thugs were only a heartbeat away, and unless she took immediate and drastic action, Kait, her ship, and William, would all fall prey to the most dastardly men she'd ever encountered.

Not without a fight!

Two lousy pole syringes were no match for a bunch of men with bullets.

No, but they'll do just fine against one!

The lights from the other vessel loomed overhead one second, then sank below the horizon in the next, both vessels bobbing like corks on the rolling swells. Like two giant magnets, the vessels drifted closer to each other, attracted by their sheer mass and proximity, and yet repulsed by the likelihood of a devastating collision. The *Spanish Maiden* was only a few meters away, getting ready to throw a line across the distance and tether the two vessels together for some sort of exchange.

Kait forced herself to make her move. Keeping low, she crept along the narrow walkway around the helm room, just below the windows, stopping at the front, right corner. Rodríguez stood at the top of the forward stairwell, his attention focused on the yacht off the starboard rail. She leveled her aim and jabbed the pole, sinking the syringe to the hilt in his left gluteus muscle. He jerked and whirled on her in surprise, then ripped the pole from her hand and stared at it.

"What the fuck did you do?" He didn't wait for her explanation when he saw the empty syringe at the end of the pole, just lifted his arm and pulled the trigger, firing a series of bullets into the white, non-slip deck in rapid succession. Each bullet moved steadily closer to her position, carving a line of deep pockmarks, like a trail of cookie crumbs, right to her feet. His strength ebbed within seconds, his aim changing trajectory just before it found its mark, and his arm began to fall, followed quickly by the rest of him.

Kait felt herself lifted unexpectedly from behind, a pair of neoprene-clad hands the size of boxer's gloves wrapped firmly around her waist as her world spun with confusion. Just as quickly, her feet landed on the deck again and she turned in time to see a large shadow drag Rodríguez down the stairs and around the corner, toward the stern.

What was that?

Kait gripped the second syringe pole like her life depended on it, and doubled back to deal with William, rather than stand and wait for whatever had just carted Rodríguez away like a sack of potatoes. Across the churning water, Pablo's men shouted at her and each other, then lowered an inflatable boat into the water to make the crossing.

Stepping through the starboard door, into the helm room, she shouted at William, "Get us out of here! We can't let them board!"

"Where's Rodríguez?" he asked shifting quickly from resigned obedience to enthusiastic rebellion.

"Don't worry about him; I stuck him with a sedative. Just get us away from that yacht!"

William's eyes flashed on the second syringe pole in her right hand as he pushed the throttle and nodded his agreement. Suddenly, a volley of bullets sprayed the starboard windows of the helm room, cutting through the safety glass like rocks through water. His body jerked and his free hand rose to his chest as his cuffed hand clutched the wheel.

Kait screamed at the blood splattered across the control panel, "No!"

"Take the wheel, Kait," he urged as his legs gave out.

"William!" Kate dashed to his side and crouched beside him, immediately pressing her hand against the blood pumping rapidly from his chest. "Hold on." Replacing her own hand with his, she opened a nearby cabinet and pulled out the captain's first-aid kit. She ripped it open and stared at the bandages, scissors, splints, disinfectants—none of it would save him! She tore open several packages of gauze and pressed them over his wound, wishing she could lay him flat and elevate his feet, but the handcuff around his wrist prevented it.

"Kait...forget about me," he moaned. "Take command!" He coughed, and blood covered his lips.

Gunfire rent the air again, but she dare not look to see where it was coming from. Instead she kept her head down, reached up to the control panel and pushed the throttle. The *Triton* rose up high and listed heavily starboard as a giant wave hit her port side; William slid helplessly into Kait and caught her with his free arm—releasing the pressure he'd been applying over his wound—jerking in pain when the cuff prevented them both from sliding across the floor.

"Turn the wheel hard-a-port, Kait! Bring the ship perpendicular to the waves or she'll capsize."

Kait placed his hand back over his wound and regained her feet, turning the wheel hard left. Behind her the port bulkhead door burst open. A tall man clad in black combat scuba gear from head to toe stepped inside, dropped his fins on the deck, and fired several shots at the other vessel, which was now behind them. As he slammed the door shut and turned toward her, Kait dove for the second syringe pole, which had rolled away from her in all the tumult, then hoisted it like a spear, aimed at the invader.

"Stay back! This contains a deadly toxin, and I won't hesitate to use it!"

The diver raised his hands and handgun in the air, signaling his cooperation, and William coughed up more blood, then began convulsing at her feet.

Oh my gods, what now?

Overwhelmed and unsure what to do, Kait glanced at the radar screen to make sure there was no imminent danger of collision with the other vessel trailing so close behind. To her surprise two more blips had appeared on-screen.

Is help on the way, or am I heading into a trap?

"It's all right, Kaitlyn. Let me help him."

When she looked up again, puzzled over the invaders words, he pulled off his dive mask.

"Stay where you are!" she yelled, still threatening him with the syringe pole. Next, he pulled off his hood, and the weight of the world lifted off her chest, as if Atlas himself had walked in and taken it from her. "Michael?" *Is that really you?*

Their eyes connected across the room, both relieved to see the other alive, both hungry to reconnect, and somewhat leery of what might happen next.

"Kaitlyn," he stepped forward tentatively, waiting for her to lower her weapon. "I'm here to help."

She followed his concerned gaze down to her blood-soaked hands and the spatter across her shirt; her heart flip-flopped painfully, and her vision blurred in a crimson cloud. *Is that Lilly's blood, or William's?* She dropped the pole, her arm suddenly limp as a noodle. "I'm f-fine, but he's..." she choked on the words "bleeding out," too confused and unhinged to finish responding.

Michael stepped forward without further delay and shot the links in the handcuff holding William to the control panel, then laid him flat and began treating him. Kait did a double-take, noticing the accumulation of gear that made him look much larger than she remembered: front-mounted breathing apparatus, a scary looking rifle draped across his broad back, a short, double-edged knife strapped to his bulging left bicep, and a second, much larger blade strapped to his left calf along with a flashlight.

Why does he look like a Navy SEAL?

Never mind that. Where did he come from?

Good question!

The radio crackled as Kait steered the *Triton* perpendicular to another rogue wave and gave the engines a little more throttle. The force of the water reverberated through the prow and the hull of the ship like a shockwave. One of the approaching ships identified itself as the USDEA aboard the *High Life*, accompanied by the San Diego Police, then demanded that both the *Triton* and the *Spanish Maiden* cut engines and prepare to be boarded.

Kait, eager to gain some much needed assistance, lifted her radio to respond. "U-S-D-E-A *High Life*, this is S-I-M-R *Triton*. We are in extreme distress—unable to cut engines until help arrives—over."

Another round of bullets fired in the distance and Kait heard a high-pitched scream as Michael pulled her down, gave her a small shake, then removed a water-tight medical kit from his dive-vest and tore open William's shirt.

Was that me screaming?

The storming ocean, rapid gunfire, and radio chatter split her attention in too many directions at once. Kait watched Michael work with complete focus on William: unruffled by the chaos around them, he pulled off his neoprene gloves, opened a sterile XStat syringe filled with tiny round sponges, and injected them into the bullet hole, effectively plugging it and stopping the bleeding within fifteen seconds. It was miraculous, incredible—*Who is this commando, and what did he do with Michael?*

No longer playing the role of the reticent, emotionally-scarred black knight who'd shut himself away from the world, and had emerged only to rescue her, this man exuded confidence, competence, and composure under pressure. He filled a syringe with morphine and injected it into William's shoulder for the pain, then returned his attention to her.

Their eye's met across mere inches this time, and Kait read the questions gleaming in his soulful brown eyes more easily than any book: *Did they hurt you? Do you still trust me? Will you hear me out and give me another chance?*

Pain seized her heart and she had to look away. The radar screen provided a perfect out; the blips approaching from the west had been joined by another blip, dead ahead. All five vessels, including hers, were set to collide violently if they didn't change course.

Kait straightened her legs and peeked out the windshield to confirm the proximity and size of the blips on the screen in the real world: the USCGC *Boutwell*, a 378-foot, high-endurance cutter, which dwarfed the 85-foot *Spanish Maiden* on her tail, and her own 125-foot *Triton*, was steaming toward her from the north at about 15-knots. Still at least a half-mile away, she could see its white hull shining in contrast to the slate ocean, its twin black radio towers outlined high above the water line, its lights shining brightly through the wind and rain.

Wow, help really is on the way!

Off the starboard rail, the other two vessels were suddenly much closer than expected. Bright lights blinded her as rapid fire and several explosions reverberated through the air and the ship. Kait tucked her head into her arms, once again screaming, terrified that this was the end. William would die and the *Triton* would explode into a fiery inferno before the Coast Guard arrived; she and Michael would sink to the bottom of the ocean without having resolved anything.

Strong, ice-cold hands shifted her attention, lifting her face gently from its shelter, "Stay with William while I get us out of this mess. Keep him talking."

Kait nodded, wanting only to leap into Michael's arms and seek shelter; instead she moved closer to William, cradled his head in her lap and soothed his worried brow with her fingertips. "You're going to be okay, William. Michael is an amazing doctor."

William opened his eyes and strained to speak, "Sorry, KO. Never meant...for any of this...to happen. Never thought...you'd get caught in the crossfire."

A tear slipped down Kait's cheek at his use of her nickname from college, the name Buck had teased her with way back when—*"I've been KOed...knocked out by Kaitlyn*

O'Donnell, in both the literal and the figurative sense."—she hadn't been called that name in years.

"Don't talk right now, William. Just listen." She took his hand and squeezed it, "You're a good man who made a terrible mistake and...got caught up in something more horrible than you could ever have imagined."

Kait flashed a quick glance at Michael, hoping he too was listening, since her words applied to both men in different ways. He turned the wheel hard-a-port to steer them out of the path of each of the approaching vessels and maintained a trajectory perpendicular to most of the swells; he was far more skilled in the operation of a large vessel than he'd once suggested. *Skilled with weapons too, and diving, and field medicine.*

Kait watched Michael in awe. *What else don't I know about you, aside from everything?*

Still stroking his forehead, she returned her full attention to William. "Pablo Castañeda is diabolical to the core. You and I are going to make sure he gets the punishment he deserves. You're going to live through this, William."

He coughed up more blood as if to contradict her words, and the floor suddenly tilted under them, forcing Kait to wrap herself around him and hold on as they slid across the floor. Trying to avoid a collision with the bulkhead, she jutted her legs out and pushed-off, but their combined weight and momentum slammed her against the door.

On the opposite side of the room, the other door opened and in washed Rodríguez with a wave of water.

Michael released the wheel and immediately stepped between them, blocking Rodríguez's path to Kait and William as the *Triton* surged over another swell and leveled out again. "Kait, take the wheel!"

Water sloshed across the floor as she rose to her feet and lunged for the unmanned wheel, abandoning William to his own defenses. She worried that he would somehow manage to drown in just a few inches of water, but she had no choice—if she didn't take command of the ship again, they would all drown.

"It was you?" Michael asked incredulously when he recognized the security guard who'd been sent to patrol his house and provide extra protection for Kait.

"He's DEA, Michael," Kait shouted, clarifying the situation while she steered the ship, "but I think he's on Pablo's payroll too!"

In the blink of an eye, Michael and Rodríguez collided with each other like giant wrecking balls bent on destruction, both armed and dangerous, both furious with deadly intent.

Seconds later another man, a giant Samoan with long hair, a baby face, and a crazed look in his eyes, burst through the port door, clad in aquatic camouflage clothes and combat gear. Kait recognized him as the shadow that had hoisted her out of the way and tackled Rodríguez outside.

The Samoan saluted her, "Ma'am," then turned his attention to Michael and Rodríguez fighting.

"Time to go, Stitch," he said calmly, as if there was no urgency or danger remaining. He made a sour face when Michael took a hard blow across his jaw. "Castañeda's crew is all wrapped up. The fire's out on the *High Life,* and the cavalry's almost here."

Unsure why the Samoan wasn't stepping in to help Michael, Kait looked at the radar screen and noted that the *Spanish Maiden* had fallen behind and was now flanked by the *High Life* and the SDPD harbor patrol. The Coast Guard cutter was directly ahead, cutting off her path, forcing her to turn hard-a-starboard to avoid a collision; the cavalry was indeed here, circling the wagons, or ships in this case, preventing any further escalation of the situation.

She breathed a sigh of relief, and turned back to Michael just as Rodríguez pulled a gun from his boot and fired two shots. The first shot hit the Samoan in the arm, but barely fazed the big man, who responded by stamping his foot and charging like a bull toward Michael and Rodríguez.

Michael grabbed Rodríguez's gun arm as the Samoan wrapped himself like a shield around the grappling men and shoved them all out the starboard door, away from Kait. The second shot fired into the cluster of men as they wrestled for control. Before Kait could react, all three men fell over the railing in a frenzy of arms and legs, hit the water, and disappeared.

The world slowed to a blur, each heartbeat an eternity of panic and strife. Kait held the wheel, praying that Michael was okay; if she left the helm, there'd be nobody left to steer the ship. If she left the ship, there'd be nobody left to watch over William. Staring between William and the door, she powered down the throttle and turned off the engines. Michael had done what he could for William—his life was no longer in her hands—but who would help Michael?

Grabbing the syringe pole and Michael's medical kit from the floor, she knelt beside William, "Take these; I'll be back as soon as I can!" He nodded weakly and she ran out the starboard door, ripped the nearest floatation ring from the bulkhead and scrambled down the ladder to the rail on the main deck, searching the surface of the water for any sign of the men.

"Michael!" she called through the howling wind, her heart hammering slow and hard as grief flooded her veins. Heavy rain pummeled her eyes and blurred her vision as she ran to the stern searching for them; there was still no sign. "Michael," she screamed as the police patrol boat came into view about 25-meters away.

Clutching the floatation ring, she jumped overboard and began bobbing her head underwater to search for him. Releasing the floatation ring, she dove deeper, turning her body 360-degrees, but still she could find no sign of them. When she came up for air, Donovan was beside her in the water, grabbing her, preventing her from diving under again. "Let me go," she screamed, fighting him as he wrapped an arm around her.

"What are you doing, Kait? Did someone fall overboard?" he yelled, trying to understand her frantic behavior.

"It's Michael! He was here...with the gorilla, and another man!" Water kept filling her mouth as she tried to explain. "They all fell into the water...and...I can't find them!"

Donovan looked around at the storming ocean and the boatloads of people whose lives were in jeopardy every moment they stayed out here, exposed. "We need to get back to safety, Kait. We'll freeze or drown in this water."

"Not without Michael," she shouted, pushing him away.

Donovan wrapped an arm around her neck and shoulder, pulling her into rescue position, and started swimming to the nearest boat.

"No! No! Let me go," she struggled against him, forcing him to stop and reposition.

"Kait, listen to me!" he yelled, wrapping his legs around hers to prevent her from kicking him, and blocking her fists as she tried to hit him. "Lilly needs you to get out of the water with me! There's nobody here...just you and me. Lilly's at the hospital and she needs you, Kait."

Kait stopped fighting then and burst into tears, so heartsick with loss that she didn't think she would ever be able to stop crying. "He was here!" she wailed, allowing Donovan tow her to the boat. "I don't know how or why, but he was here and he helped me command the ship."

The SDPD harbor patrol boat threw a net over the side, and Donovan pulled her toward it and grabbed on. "Climb the net, Kait. Can you do that for me? Lilly is waiting for us."

Kait wailed even louder, "I can't leave him to drown! We have to find him...we have to save Michael!"

"He's not here, Kait." Donovan lifted his head and shouted at the men above him, "Tell her you've searched and there's nobody else in the water. Tell her, before we both frigging drown!"

The line of police officers hovering above them in the torrential wind and rain, all nodded vehemently in agreement. "Everyone has been accounted for on all vessels. There's nobody lost in the water, ma'am."

"You're wrong," she wailed, attempting to get away again. "I saw him! I touched him!" she screamed hitting Donovan again when he tried to hold her. "He saved William!"

At that, Donovan wrapped himself around her once more and jammed his feet and hands into the holes in the net. "Lift us out, now!" he yelled to the police officers above, and they immediately began to hoist the net out of the water. "I've got you, Kait. I'm taking you to Lilly and everything's going to be okay."

THIRTY FOUR

Randy's face crunched into a deep frown as he turned the key in the doorknob and let himself into Lilly's apartment for the tenth time in two weeks, preparing for the next round in what was quickly devolving from a daily check-in, to a daily joust. Lilly was recovering quickly from her shoulder injury and becoming more difficult to manage by the day: prickly, combative, and territorial about all things Kait. She was just plain ornery for such a small package, but he had to admit that she was sharp as a whip and twice as fast.

And relentless when she has a bone to pick.

"Don't shoot" he announced before ascending the stairs, "it's just your friendly neighborhood watchdog." At 0800, he was fairly certain she would still be in bed, groggy from another sleepless night, pain-killers, and her inability to adjust to the time change; she was clearly *not* a morning person.

"Go away, unless you brought Kait with you," Lilly groaned, flipping onto her stomach, and pulling the pillow over her head to block out the morning sun that was now prying her eyelids open an hour ahead of schedule. Her hand searched automatically for the gun under her other pillow, just to prove to her unreasonably fearful subconscious that it was still right where she had left it before falling asleep in the early morning hours.

"You know I can't bring her out of protective custody until we confirm that Rodríguez is dead and resolve the unanswered questions about Michael and the mystery man she claims to have seen fall overboard."

Donovan walked over to Lilly's window and opened the curtains, then doubled back to her bedside, "I brought you an organic, pumpkin-spiced latté to jumpstart your day. You really should eat some breakfast to give your body the nutrients it needs to heal."

Lilly lifted the edge of the pillow and glared at him with one eye, then tossed the pillow off the edge of the bed and took the piping hot paper cup from his hand. "This is the third foofoo drink you've brought me. If you're not careful, I might start to question your manhood." She took a sip, made a sour face, set the drink on her nightstand, and rolled out the opposite side of her bed, away from her tormentor.

Lifting the pillow off the ground, Donovan brushed it off and set it on the foot of her bed while he started straightening the comforter. "You could just tell me your preference instead of trying to force me to guess. A little cooperation is always welcome."

Lilly stopped rifling in her closet, as if contemplating the idea of cooperation, then stared at him in mock horror, "Are you making my bed? Seriously, you're such a priss!"

She pulled an old, red, paint-stained sweatshirt off a wire hanger and gingerly lifted her arm to put it on over her tank top, then opened her dresser and pulled out a pair of blue SDPD sweat pants. The cut-away neck of her sweatshirt revealed the bandage covering her shoulder, front and back; she caught him staring at it again and cringed at the worried look in his eyes. "Stop making my bed, and get out of my room."

"How's your shoulder today?" he asked snapping back to attention.

"It still hurts like a son-of-a-bitch," she pushed him toward her door, inexplicably irritated by the fact that he always focused on her injury instead of the rest of her. "Ever heard of a little thing called privacy?"

He turned before she got him to the door, "I didn't think you cared about such trivial matters. You're always running around in your skimpy little tank tops and boxer shorts. Are you really going to wear those grungy sweats to the memorial?"

So he had *noticed the rest of her*—a chill shot down Lilly's spine made of equal parts satisfaction and dissatisfaction. A woman liked to know she was desirable, but in her line of work, she didn't like to draw unwanted male attention to herself—*his attention is definitely unwanted*—because it was usually negative.

Most of the younger men, and even a few of the older ones that she worked with, were fully indoctrinated with the idea that women could, and should, work in law-enforcement, but there were still plenty of cavemen around who'd been inoculated against the idea of women's liberation—certain members of her own family chief among them. And while Donovan seemed to accept her independent, kick-ass-and-take-names-later attitude, he was always trying to sand-down her edges, which just plain irritated.

Great gobs of goose grease! Who cares?

Sloughing it off, like she did whenever anyone dared to try to change her, she corrected him, "That's not till next week." Then, reaching automatically to pull her hair into a ponytail, she winced and dropped her arm, unable to complete the simple task.

"No—it's today from 1200 to 1300 at the SIMR pier, aboard the *Neptune II*. They have family members and coworkers set to speak on behalf of all three fatalities." He hesitated, studying her through those sharp blue lenses that didn't miss much. "Do you need your bandage changed, or maybe some help with your hair?"

"No, no, and hell no!" Her temper shot straight past irritation to fury, "They are *not* 'fatalities' you ignoramus! Barney was a sweet old man, and Kait's friend. William, despite his idiotic mistakes and apparently criminal proclivities, was her boss for several years, and one of her closest allies. And Frankie, well he was a stupid kid with a propensity for trouble, but he was her coworker too—she's inexorably linked to all three people!

"You're not seriously going to keep her from attending their memorial after all she's been through? She needs closure, especially with Michael missing." Lilly scowled at him, anger flashing in her green eyes, coloring her cheeks.

"I don't have a choice in the matter. She's not safe until Rodríguez, Michael, and the mystery man have been found and Pablo has been prosecuted and convicted. We need her testimony more than ever with William gone—she's the only reliable witness we have left to testify against El Diablo. She's professional, has no criminal record, and until recently had no history of mental illness—I can't risk her life on sentimentality."

"Don't give me that crazy crap! Just because you didn't see what happened, and can't explain it, doesn't mean Kait has gone mental. She told me about the sponges in William's wound; that alone proves someone else was there. Plus there's the matter of the handcuffs being shot apart to free him—"

"Those clues don't prove anything," Donovan interrupted. "The lawyers will argue that she broke the cuffs and treated him herself, and just doesn't remember."

"With what," Lilly snapped, "her teeth? She told me she never found the captain's handgun, and the first-aid kits aboard the *Triton* don't stock XStat."

Trying to keep his usually unwavering calm, Donovan responded in a logical, reasonable tone, "So, despite the fact that there were more than fifty people present between the Coast Guard, the SDPD, and the DEA, and not one of them witnessed two divers disappear into the water with Rodríguez, or saw any evidence of any other vessel in the surrounding area, either with radar or binoculars, I'm just supposed to *believe* her hysterical ranting, and drop everything to find these supposedly missing men?"

"She wasn't *hysterical*; she was scared to death because you were leaving three men to drown in the raging sea," Lilly sneered, disgusted with his choice of words. "I'd say that's a pretty damned good reason for her to be upset."

"You weren't there, Lillian. You only know what you've been told. You have no idea how bad it really was: the chaos of the storm, the dangerous proximity of the boats, the rampant gunfire. Kait wouldn't get out of the frigging-damned water to save her own life. I had to forcibly hold onto her, kicking and screaming, while the officers hauled us both out."

Lilly and Donovan stared at each other, each immovable on this point, each keenly aware of how effortlessly she was learning to get under his skin and challenge his heretofore implacable resolve and self-assurance. "Yeah, well maybe she's not in the habit of leaving people behind or letting them die if there's something she can do about it."

Unflinching, Donovan ignored her pointed implication that maybe *he* was in the habit of leaving people behind to die. Those were fighting words—she was lashing out, trying to rile him in her aggressive, battle-maiden way. She was feeling vulnerable in her injured state, out-of-control and helpless to rescue her best friend from an uncertain and unhappy future. She might even be feeling guilty for failing to protect Kait in the first place—*definitely not the time to battle the little hellfire princess.*

"Look, *her* safety is my *primary* concern—"

Lilly cut him off again, pouncing on his placations, "Bullshit! Her *testimony* is your *only* concern, but you don't even believe her story. By your own account, she's an unstable, unreliable witness at best, yet you're willing to ruin the rest of her life by forcing her to testify against a deadly psychotic, to pave your own career-path in gold."

"Nobody is forcing her to testify, her life will not be ruined, and hell yes, I'll do whatever it takes to make sure that mass-murdering, drug-smuggling deviant is put behind bars for the rest of his life."

"Are you seriously that ignorant? You're willing to take away everyone and everything Kait cares about—her family, her career, her project, her entire identity. You're willing to move her away from her home and subject her to years of witness protection and relocation to seal the deal on the biggest collar of your life, but you don't think that will ruin her life?"

"We've gathered a lot of evidence to support our case; it should only take a year or so—"

"Yeah, right. More like two to ten!

"No—it'll be over in less than two years and then she can get everything back she had to give up. It's only temporary."

"Right! No harm done, no foul—except several years alone on the run with a bunch of strangers. If you believe that crock of shit, then you must be living on *Fantasy Island*. It's a complete sham! She'll be irreparably changed and she won't get a damned thing back. Somewhere deep down in that thick skull of yours, you know the truth, but you're choosing to ignore it!"

"Lillian, her project is being completed by the remaining team-members, even as we speak, and I have it on good authority that her job will be waiting for her when this is all over and done."

Lilly grimaced in visible pain from the absurdity of the situation, and then exploded, "Fuck her project, fuck SIMR, and fuck *you* for not admitting the truth. I don't give two shits about those whales, except for the fact that *she does*, and her employers don't care about *her* any more than you do. They only care about what she can do for them, but just like everyone else in this shitty dog-eat-dog world, they think she's replaceable. Only she's *not* replaceable, Donovan Randal! She's a one-of-a-kind original who's already been put through more hell than she ever deserved! And this is the rest of her fucking life we're talking about, not just a couple of years."

"How do you figure, Zamora? If you think the criminal system is so inept and corrupt that putting her under federal protection long enough to convict an international criminal mastermind will ruin the rest of her life, then why are you a cop? Why put your own time and energy into a system that is bound to fail her so completely?"

"I'm a cop, because I get off on sweeping scum off the streets and putting it where it belongs. I'm a cop, because there are just too many fucking people in this world who think they're above the law, who are so greedy and selfish that they don't care who they hurt to get what they want. I'm a cop, Donovan, because I want to be part of the solution, instead of part of the problem."

"Well Halle-frigging-lujah! Something we can finally agree on! I'm doing my damnedest to be part of the solution too, Lillian, which is why I have sacrificed the last three years of my personal life to bring this evil bastard and all of his minions to a halt. And don't think for one second that I didn't warn Kait how hard it would be if she agreed to testify. I told her all the gritty details: the risks, the schedule, and the rules. Heck, I practically talked her out of it, because I agree that she is a unique woman with a lot to give this world, and I wouldn't wish what she is about to go through on anyone."

"Then how exactly, do you propose to keep her alive after he has been convicted? Do you really think he will magically just stop coming after her once he has been incarcerated? Do you think he won't have the motivation or the means to have her killed while he is behind bars, just for the pleasure of getting a little revenge? And for that matter, how do you propose to keep the people closest to her alive after you've gotten your big conviction? Do you seriously think he won't send people to kill her brother, her mother, and maybe even me, just for the added pleasure of hurting her a little more before he kills her?"

Heart pounding with adrenaline, lungs panting from remembered fear, Kait screamed herself awake from another nightmare, sweating and shaking. She couldn't stand to watch William die again—couldn't dive into the black ocean to save Michael, only to find no trace of him. The haunting specters came several times a night, had been coming for more than a month now, bringing different variations on the same unresolved theme. No matter what she did with the rest of her life, William and Buck would still be dead and Michael would still be missing. She couldn't decide which would be worse: having some stranger approach her one day to tell her that Michael had died from a gunshot wound, or never knowing his final fate.

Kait swiped away the tears, pressed her palms over her eyes, and took a deep breath trying to calm the storm raging inside. It was still dark outside—any second her bodyguards from the U.S. Marshals Service would come charging into the room, guns raised, ready to protect her from another false alarm. No matter how many times she cried wolf, rousing them to battle with her nightmare screams, they kept responding with the cold certainty drilled into them by years of training. Each time, they performed their perfunctory routine; the younger man faded into the background, his face as blank as uncarved stone, while the older man sat at the edge of her bed and dutifully offered a strong and comforting shoulder for her to cry on. Would that always be the case? Or would there finally come a day when the wolf really did show up to rip out the last vestiges of her heart, and her guardians failed to respond because they had finally learned to discount her night terrors?

Kait hated letting them see her at her weakest, detested seeing the pity that inevitably filled their eyes, but there was simply no way to avoid it. If she slept, she dreamed. If she dreamed, it always became a bone-chilling nightmare. She hadn't yet figured out how to stop needing sleep, or how to get warm in this freezing city to which she'd been brought in order to give testimony to the IWC. The longer she went without a decent night of sleep, the colder she felt at her core.

Here in the frigid city of London, England, where the icy winter nights felt interminably longer than the short, gloomy days, and the sun hid behind the thickest marine layer she'd ever seen, she thought even the most basic needs of warmth and sleep were lost to her forever.

Did the sun ever shine in England? Did the summer rains penetrate people's bones as deeply as the winter rains? Would she ever feel the warmth of the sunshine on her skin again?

Despite everything Kait had survived, she hadn't yet figured out how to stop being afraid, not for herself, but for the people she loved. And without even the small comfort of knowing she would see them again soon, she was learning to live in a constant state of shivering stillness.

Lying in bed, Kait suddenly realized that at least a minute had passed since she'd awoken with a start but nobody had come running to her aid.

Maybe I didn't scream aloud this time.

Writing-off the anomaly as progress on her part—easily the most optimistic thought she'd had in days—Kait uncovered her eyes and reached for the glass of water beside her bed. A shadow loomed over her, so large in the inky blackness of the room that she could barely discern it, and so close, that she had no time to react. He was on her before she could react, his hand covering her mouth to suppress her scream, his arms and chest trapping her where she lay.

"It's me, Kaitlyn. Don't scream. I'm not here to hurt you," he whispered.

Michael's hushed voice penetrated her frenzied thoughts and she stilled instantly.

Is he really here, alive?

"You *must* be silent. Nod if you understand."

Kait nodded and a small flashlight clicked on in his hand, illuminating his face like the light at the end of a very long, very dark tunnel.

"I had to see you...talk to you. Will you be quiet if I release you?"

Kait nodded again, unable to do more under his restraining weight as she stared up at his beautiful face. Her Archangel was alive and well! *Thank Poseidon, Neptune, Njord, Lir, and any other god of the sea that had spared him from Davy Jones!*

He removed his hand from her mouth and released her, a wary, worried look etched in his features. She sat up quickly and wrapped her arms around him in a fierce embrace. "I was so scared, Michael," she whispered near his ear, a rush of relief flooding her body. "I didn't know what happened to you, if you'd been shot or drowned. That man acted like he was helping you and then ripped you away from me and..." she squeezed him harder, trying to prevent another onslaught of tears.

Michael wrapped his arms around her and held her tightly, "I'm here, Kaitlyn."

She held on for several seconds—not nearly enough to sooth her tormented soul—then pulled just far enough away to see his face again without letting go. "Are you okay? Where have you been?"

"I'm fine, now. I'm sorry I couldn't get to you sooner. It took a little while to recover and work things out, but I knew you were safe."

Recover?

He's really here—and had indeed been wounded.

It's a miracle he's alive!

The brevity of his words belied the truth—there was much more to be said, but time was of the essence. A slew of questions burned in his eyes and apologies bit his tongue as he stared at her. Among the questions, Kait saw layers of fear: danger, rejection, and loss. In the weeks they'd been apart, he had judged, convicted, and hanged himself a hundred times for everything that had happened. He had failed to protect her, had kept dangerous, deadly secrets from her, and had rejected her affection when she had offered it. He was teetering on unstable ground, unsure how she felt about him in this new paradigm, and still hiding behind the business of keeping her safe.

Her black knight was back but she knew his secrets now—*at least some of them*—and he knew it. He was exposed and vulnerable, unsure if she would trust him again or call for help from her new protectors. Would she give him a second chance and hear what he had to say? Would she see the underlying truth in his actions? Or had she been poisoned against him by the knowledge of his secrets?

When she opened her mouth to respond, he prevented her from doing so with a fingertip across her lips. "I saw what you did yesterday at the first legislative session of the IWC. You really knocked their socks off," he said with a note of pride. "Congratulations."

Kait smiled like the automaton she'd forced herself to be in order to get through the pain, misery, and work of the past month. Her world had exploded at the most inopportune time in her career, and when the tsunami of information about her kidnapping, William's involvement with drug runners using SIMR ships, and his subsequent death had rolled through the organization, the impact had been felt at every level. There'd been a massive battle to keep the *Neptune II* and the *Triton* from being put into dry-dock as evidence by the "Powers" within the DEA who'd been building a case against Pablo and his crew for several years.

Kait had been swept into the Witness Security Program, commonly known as WITSEC, as the only living witness willing to testify against Pablo for all he had done. Her project had been handed off to other biologists to finish in her absence. The outcome of the trial against Pablo, and the decisions made by the IWC would determine whether her position at SIMR would be waiting for her in the end, but after everything that had happened, she wasn't altogether sure she would still care about such matters when she reached the end of the road.

"Don't congratulate me just yet; I'm only here because the majority of the data presented was collected under my supervision and the IWC insisted on getting my direct statement. We're leaving in two days and they won't make a decision about hunting blue whales for several months at least—they need time for their panel of experts to review the report."

Michael nodded, about to speak again, but she continued rattling on about her problems, hoping he wasn't here to say goodbye forever. "In the meantime, the Japanese are so upset by the claims we made, that they are threatening to drop out of the commission, and the DEA and U.S. Marshals are so pissed about having to jeopardize the safety of their only witness for the sake of a bunch of "useless" whales, that they've made life more difficult than I could have ever imagined."

Kait rested her head against his shoulder, absorbing his warmth, "Donovan tries to advocate on my behalf, with both the DEA and SIMR, but he isn't in charge."

I can't do this alone!

Michael kept nodding throughout her litany of troubles, his face as dark and stormy as she had ever seen it. She wanted to grab hold of him and beg him not to leave her again, to tell her everything that had happened after he had fallen in the water, to explain how he had had come to be there in the first place, and why it had taken so long for him to come back to her. She wanted to rail at him for the position he'd placed her in when he'd appeared and then disappeared, without explanation, in the midst of the biggest drug-bust the California coast had ever seen, but this was neither the time nor the place. And seeing him alive and well was enough to patch her together for now.

As difficult, unspoken questions assailed her, Michael watched frantic emotions race across Kaitlyn's face like a runaway train. He wanted to hold her tight and answer every question, wanted to reassure her that she didn't have to go through this alone, that he was here for her and wouldn't leave her again unless she wanted him to. Instead, he did what he had come to do. "You're not safe, Kaitlyn. Pablo ordered a hit on you from inside prison, and these idiot marshals can't keep you safe," he said with disgust. "You have some very important decisions to make."

Kait's mind stilled as she absorbed his words. Everything she'd been feeling faded to the background as her focus zeroed-in on him and the awareness that her life once again hung in the balance of whatever he was about to say.

"Are you determined to stay with WITSEC and testify against Pablo?" he asked in a guardedly neutral voice.

"I don't have a choice, Michael. There's no one else left. Somebody has to stop him from ruining more people's lives—bring him to justice for all the people that are dead!"

"There's always a choice, Kaitlyn. If you don't want to remain in witness protection with your life on proverbial hold and in constant danger, I can take you away from here right now. I know people that can keep you much safer than this." He squeezed both of her shoulders gently. "Or..." he hesitated, looking for the right words, hoping she wouldn't think him a monster, "those same people can eliminate the threat entirely with a single phone call."

He watched her absorb his words, tumble them around looking for their exact meaning, and saw the moment that the finality of his solution hit her like a rogue wave.

Michael had given it a great deal of thought over the past few weeks, looked for every alternative, but had always come back to the same conclusion. She would never be safe as long as Pablo was alive. He hated admitting to her that he knew people both capable and willing to kill Pablo at his request, hated admitting that he would make that request in a heartbeat, if she agreed. But given all that he knew, he couldn't escape the fact that, in this case, the ends justified the means. She would be free and safe to move on with her life; no more devious drug runners hunting her, no more worrying that her family or her crew would be Pablo's next targets, no more worrying that others would be killed trying to protect her from his former brother-in-law.

Kait studied the man sitting before her in the dark, in the fourth "safe house" in a seemingly endless lineup in which she would be sequestered from society so that she could spend the next several years of her life under house-arrest, being totally controlled by strangers, just so she could live long enough to testify against a madman.

Eventually she would be assigned a new identity and settled, if she was lucky, in some anonymous location far from everyone she loved and everything she knew. She'd only seen Donovan twice since the big shakedown, and he'd promised he was doing everything he could for her, and that he would see her again soon, but she knew his hands were full. Worse, she hadn't been allowed to see or talk to Lilly in three weeks, despite her credentials with SDPD. Everyone was being kept away from her "for their own good," and despite the two sets of agents who'd been assigned to her in 12-hour shifts, to provide 24-hour protection, she felt just as alone now, as she ever had when she'd been on the run.

Now, the one person she had grown to depend on, the one she wasn't sure she could survive without, was back, offering her a way out of the long, arduous road ahead. And it didn't take a genius to know that his solution, while expedient and in some regards much more palatable, went against every philosophical and moral bone in his body. He was a life preserver, a care-taker and humanitarian. He was a pacifist who had suffered great losses and never retaliated in the Biblical sense, even though his foe was rabid for it.

Kait had never given more than a cursory thought to the issue of an eye for an eye, or capital punishment, and had never expected to have to. She'd always straddled the fence on the issue, unsure what was right in the face of extreme injustices like multiple homicide and repeat rape offenders. Part of her wished all such criminals would be removed from the world in the most permanent way possible, if only so they could never commit such heinous crimes again, and yet the other part of her believed, or needed to believe, that everyone was redeemable under the right circumstances.

Now, she was being put to the test—asked to play God and decide the life or death fate of the man she most feared and hated.

"You don't have to decide about that right now, Kaitlyn, but I need to know if...no," he shook his head in frustration, searching for the right words. "I *want* you to come with me. Will you trust me and give me another chance to keep you safe?"

The fire in his eyes was urgent, almost desperate. Yes, she was in danger again, but didn't she have the full protection of the American government and its justice system behind her this time? Was she really so lost without him, that she would once again accept his protection and put his life in jeopardy?

"Will you tell me everything? Will you promise not to keep any more secrets from me, no matter how bad they seem?"

He set his jaw determinedly, as she'd seen him do each time he prepared himself to argue and withdraw. "Yes, I'll tell you everything that is mine to tell—but you won't like most of what you hear. If you come with me, I guarantee that you and your family will be protected, but there'll be no turning back. You'll be required to make certain promises and keep secrets to protect the identities of the people who will help us."

Kait's lip quivered as a chill crept up her spine. "Who are these people?"

"They're protectors of the innocent and the powerless."

It was a non-committal answer, just the sort he'd been so masterful at giving throughout their time together, but she suddenly realized that it was the most honest answer he could give. He was a man trapped on a thin wire between dichotomous worlds, a doctor who wanted nothing more than to help people who had been dragged into a nefarious world of malicious evil-doers, and an idealist who'd been thrown into the hell fires of a reality he had never been willing to accept.

Forty days ago, she would not have understood his position, or its perilous and paralyzing nature. She'd been living her life in the light, keeping the darkness at bay by refusing to acknowledge its ability to touch her. Now that it had not only touched her, but catalyzed a series of reactions that had changed her on a fundamental level, she could no longer ignore it. More importantly, she found it much easier to forgive the mistakes of others whose fabric had been irretrievably altered by the darkness.

Judge not, lest ye be judged.

"Yes, Michael. I'll come with you."

EPILOGUE

Lilly walked out of her police precinct plagued by the perils of paper-pushing after only one day of light-duty. Her first day back had been spent filing reports, answering calls, interviewing recruits, and pandering to city officials on a witch-hunt. She couldn't wait to get home, shed the uniform blues and go for a run on the beach to work out the kinks in her back and shoulder. She might even break open a bottle of wine Kait had purchased, and commiserate with her best friend across time and space, pretending, not for the first time, that she was already home safe.

She had just about reached her car when a black Camaro pulled up behind her and revved its engine. She turned and glared at Donovan; she'd been hoping she wouldn't have to see him again for a few days now that she was off disability and back in action. He'd been driving her crazy for weeks, evading her questions about Kait, but sticking his nose where it didn't belong, trying to change Lilly's eating habits and asking questions about her family. The man was a regular nuisance!

"What do you want, Randal? I'm too tired and cranky to deal with you right now."

Donovan cocked his head, restraining one of his not so witty comebacks. "Get in, Lillian."

The look on his face was serious—*seriously worried*—so she got in his car without argument. "What's wrong?"

"Kait has disappeared right out from under WITSEC's best noses."

"What?" The air between them vibrated with palpable tension. "I knew she wouldn't be safe with them! I just knew it!" She slammed her fist against the car door, wishing for all the world that Pablo's neck was bared in front of her so she could choke the life out of him with her bare hands. Or at least punch his lights out!

"They've never lost a witness before, Lillian—she should've been safe. There were no signs of a struggle. She disappeared sometime in the middle of the night. One of her guards went into her room to check on her, and found her bed empty, the window open, and a note on the mirror."

"What did the note say?"

"I'll bring home the phish-food when the party's over."

Lilly's heart leapt in her chest at the private message meant to reassure her that Kait was okay and would be home when she was able.

A sheen of tears popped out, coating her eyes, and she quickly looked away from Donovan to hide them. Taking several deep breaths and swiping away the salty evidence of her soft side, she turned to face him, "We gotta find Michael Storm."

"My thoughts exactly."

Keep reading for an excerpt from

STORM RISING

Book Two of the Storm Series

PROLOGUE

The blood seeping from the bullet hole in his side was just one of his many problems at the moment. The massive swells of the raging ocean, the potential for shark attack, the departure of the ship on which he had arrived at this particularly shitty location, and the possibility that the human steamroller who'd tackled him might decide to come back and finish the job, were also high on his list of shit to fix.

One by one, the lights of the 125-foot *Triton*, the 378-foot, high-endurance cutter USCGC *Boutwell*, and the 85-foot *Spanish Maiden*, all dimmed in the distance, leaving him floating without aid in a veritable washing machine of epic proportions. No matter, he needed them all to depart so he could call in a favor and proceed with the rest of his plan, unencumbered by law enforcement. If everyone thought he was dead, they would never see him coming.

As the last light disappeared behind a 25-foot swell, he pulled the GPS beacon from his pocket and switched it on. Timing would be everything. Next, he pulled off his shirt and belt, wadding the shirt over his wound and fastening it as tightly as he could with the belt. His gut burned with the hellfires of Hades, but not just because of the bullet hole. These hellfires had been burning for years, raging like the storm around him for vengeance, recompense, and the recognition that he deserved.

To stay warm in the chilling ocean, he focused on those hellfires, on the fruition of his long thought out and meticulously planned rise to power. He'd been denied his birthright for far too long. He'd played the dutiful minion not once but twice in his lifetime, and the taste of it still soured everything.

Never again. The time was now to make his move.

Knife in hand, ready to bite back if any sharks decided to snack on the day's buffet, he floated on his back, using as little energy as possible to stay afloat. He needed every ounce of strength to keep his dense body above water until help arrived.

Shards of rain pelted his face as white-capped swells lifted and tossed him like flotsam left behind by a shipwreck. The dark sky and even darker water threatened his end with each passing minute, one seeking to tow him under, and the other seeking to freeze him to the core with icy wind and hail.

Stiff with cold and weak from blood loss, his waterlogged eyes squinted against the continuous assault for what felt like hours, until finally a beam of light cut through him like a laser and held him like a tractor beam. Help had finally arrived, and just in time.

A diver dropped feet-first into the water beside him and swam over with a rescue basket. Overhead a large, repurposed rescue chopper hovered, fighting the gusts and gales that threatened to smack it down out of the angry sky. Few people would be crazy enough, or skilled enough, to attempt this rescue, but he had the ultimate ace up his sleeve, the foremost backer a man could ask for in this treacherous world.

Aboard the chopper, he stepped out of the basket and allowed a woman from the rescue party to wrap him in a thermal blanket, while a skilled EMT began surveying his wound. He snatched the headphones and microphone from the woman's head and looked at the pilot, who was already heading for safety and dry land.

"Take me to Cerberus."

The pilot shook his head no. "Namea wants to meet you.

Made in the USA
Charleston, SC
02 October 2016